"Rannulf may have let you in, but I guarantee he's just outside the door listening.

He's listening for you to sound the alarm, for furniture to fly. I am...infamous."

"That's ridiculous. Rannulf's probably back in his own quarters by now. Why would I raise such a ruckus?"

Matthias's hand tightened on hers. "Care to test me?"

Carrie figured he'd meant his notion about the eavesdropping knight, but for some reason the way he'd said it, voice all deep and gravelly, she conjured up intriguing images of her testing him. All of him.

The stone walls were thick. You had to be right by the door to hear raised voices within. She could sing "Free Bird" at the top of her lungs and probably nobody would hear to come ask what the racket was.

"If I kissed you...would you scream?" he whispered.

"Of course I wouldn't." Oh, she hadn't meant to sound as if she welcomed another kiss. Which she just might..."I mean, kissing you isn't exactly frightening. Right now, you're paranoid and drunk, but you're not a beast. I'm not afraid of you, and nobody thinks you're going to hurt me. I certainly don't."

He pressed her palm to his lips for a warm kiss and then placed her hand just above his heart. Butterflies danced in her stomach at the sensation of his skin beneath hers. His chest rose and fell on deep breaths. He stroked his knuckles along the sensitive skin of her inner arm, outstretched toward him. Awareness spurred the blood in her veins to quicken under his motion.

Wish for the Moon

Circle of Destiny, Book One

by

Sandra Jones

Wish For The Moon: Circle of Destiny, Book One

Cover Art by *Nicola Martinez*

The Wild Rose Press
PO Box 708
Adams Basin, NY 14410-0706
Visit us at www.thewildrosepress.com

Publishing History
First English Tea Rose Edition, 2009
Print ISBN .1-60154-554-1

Published in the United States of America

Dedication

For Jennifer, a strong heroine herself.
I would like to give thanks to God,
to my family for encouraging me,
and to the best critique partners in the world:
Tina, Christyne, and Pam.

Prologue

1273 A.D., Wales

The crack of Isabelle's hand against Matthias's flesh echoed across the bedchamber. His head snapped back from the blow, and his cheek kindled with flame. When he opened his eyes, the bed blurred through unshed tears—though not from the strike. 'Twould take more than a woman's scorn to bring him real pain. 'Twas his own doing. His crime and shame.

"Brother! Isabelle!" Matthias clambered off the bed, still groggy from sleep. His long legs tangled in the covers in his haste to distance himself from Isabelle. He struggled for equilibrium and raised his voice beseechingly, "Please, Giles...I do not understand—"

"Scoundrel. Devil. Defiler!" Giles shouted at him above the din of his wife's sobs.

The room spun, and his stomach roiled with nausea from too much wine the night before in the castle's great hall.

Blinking to clear his vision, his gaze focused on Giles. The robed earl stood in the open door with a guard and a servant at his back, both striving to avert their eyes from the tragedy.

Silver wings of hair at Giles's temples fanned out in wild disarray, and his lips pulled back from his teeth in a mocking sneer, full of hate and disgust.

"*You* do not understand? Math, by God, I should kill you. Bastard!"

1

In one drunken night, he'd achieved more condemning monikers than he had in the past three years of wars. The slaughter of Saracens had never seemed an honorable enterprise to him before, but now with the knowledge of his own true evil nature, the service he rendered for Prince Edward in Acre seemed saintly in comparison. As a boy of five and ten years of age, he'd rushed off to battle with God and king in mind. He returned to Wales as a man, but he was the mere shell of his former self, tainted with arrogance and madness left over from the Crusades. Had three years changed him so completely, transforming him from a chivalric young knight to a man who would lie with his own brother's wife?

"This cannot be happening!" His hoarse words rang hollow.

What had he done to Lady Isabelle? His heart raced and blood roared in his ears.

He feared he knew the answer.

Steadying himself against a bedpost, he risked another look at her. The blonde beauty had enthralled him as well as Giles. The innocent woman, whose body occupied much of his waking thoughts in wicked, sinful fantasy, drew back from him. She huddled at the far side of her bed and trembled under the cover from their sinners' nest as she hid her nakedness. Her eyes, pale blue and wide, regarded him in horror.

Matthias dropped his forehead against the bedpost, fingers biting into the wood. He clamped his eyes shut. *Remember, damn it. You must remember what happened.*

But he remembered naught.

****

The thundering of the horse's hooves failed to drown out the memory of Giles's final curse and edict. *"Banished from Wyldnell forevermore!"*

Matthias's shoulders hunched as he rode, fleeing from guilt. Warm wind beat against his face, and his unbound hair tangled in the thick branches of the oak trees as he raced past. Despite the tree limbs and bramble tearing at his flesh, physical pain seemed somehow trivial after all he had been through earlier that day, so he pushed onward. True ache gnawed at his heart.

His own brother.

How could he commit such treachery against his own flesh and blood?

Nothing could repair the damage of last night.

Better off dead.

If the trees of the Marchlands ripped him asunder, it would be a mercy for his soul. Tonight, however, his horse Zengi demonstrated his unequaled ability. The warhorse was more familiar with dodging blades and soldiers, but with the same adept skill, the ebony animal navigated through the ancient trees, guided by the glow of the moon alone.

The day was Beltane, he vaguely recalled, and the Druid moon had never shone brighter as far as he could remember. A ripple of apprehension ran down his spine.

He leaned closer to the animal and urged it to go faster. Welsh villeins still celebrated the pagan holiday in secret in these parts, despite Giles's strict orders that they should abstain.

Digging his spurs into the horse's flanks, Matthias drove the animal into a sprint. He crossed the field leading up to the rocky hillside that overlooked the Wye River. The standing stones of ancient man came into view where Druids had once held court high atop the cliff. Now the stones were silent reminders, worn from time and the elements.

Zengi whinnied beneath him, though still far from overexertion. Matthias slowed the animal, baffled by its sudden skittishness. Then as he drew closer to the stones, his own flesh made goosebumps. Someone was on the hill with him.

He scanned the crop of stones. There were eighteen lichen-encrusted rocks left standing and two fallen. All tinted a vibrant blue-green color by the moonlight. Then he saw it. A flash of white dashed between the wide pillars.

"You, there! Why do you hide?" he called across the darkness, halting his horse inside the stone circle.

No answer returned. It was probably a monk. The Cistercians often crossed the land along the Monks' Trod on their way to Castle Wyldnell from their encampment in the north. Still, it didn't explain why the traveler wouldn't respond to him.

Or, was the figure a solitary worshiper of the ancient religion? A Druid?

Matthias refused to waste time thinking about it. He had to leave Wales and be quick about it lest he find his head on a spiked post.

"Onward, horse," he commanded and checked his back to make sure his stolen possessions were still there. The blanket containing his father's sword and a small satchel of coins remained securely strapped against his shoulder blades. He had left behind his loathsome hauberk, shield, and battle blade, abandoning the persona of a knight as easily as he wished he could abandon his own soul.

The animal suddenly shuddered beneath him and fell still again, ears set forward.

"Come on, now. Move!"

Zengi reared with a wild, unearthly squeal. Taken by surprise, Matthias fell backward, slamming into the ground. The alarmed horse fled, hooves casting a shower of dirt over him as he pushed himself into a sitting position.

"Jesu," he spat. Did he still have an audience? If the watcher was a sentry from his brother's castle, his humiliation would be complete.

He braced himself with a hand on the ground as he got up, only to find fresh, loose soil beneath his bare palm. The entire area inside the ring of stones had recently been turned. A perfect row of leafy vegetation grew in the exact middle of the circle.

A strange place to put a garden. Tiny yellow flowers, drawn into buds, dotted the strange plants. Drawn by curiosity, Matthias grabbed the one nearest him and broke off a handful of the leaves. Grinding them between his fingers, he lifted them to his nose and smelled their tangy odor. Herbs, the scent unfamiliar, he couldn't say for certain what name they bore. Probably the work of the local healer. He threw the remains in the dirt and wiped his hands on his tunic before beginning to look for his horse.

Looking up past the stones, he saw a mist rolling in. Cool and moist, the late spring air wrapped around him in a cocooning blanket. Thicker than the dragon's bane of the bardic tales from his childhood days, it poured in to fill the stone ring. Matthias waved his hands about, trying to clear his view, but it did little good.

Where is that bloody horse? Gone without a trace. A moment of envy for the beast shadowed his heart. *Would that Fate favor me and allow me to vanish as easily.*

Matthias stepped between the stones of the Druid ring to search the mist for Zengi and suddenly walked right off the face of the earth.

Chapter One

Present day, Cardiff, Wales

"What the devil?" a voice boomed.

His presence filled the office before he did, and Carrie found herself looking at a broad chest as he came through the door, not expecting a man of any greater height than most. This man loomed head and shoulders above her. Tilting her gaze up, she looked into the face of fury. Professor Matthias Thorne?

He was young, for a historian—if indeed it was him. Not at all the grizzled scholar she'd pictured when reading his letter. Tall, dark, but not exactly handsome.

The hair on her neck prickled as she stared, but for the life of her, she didn't know why. Perhaps his irritation discomforted her. After all, she'd been waiting in his office without an invitation, like a lurking pest.

Dark brown hair swept back off his brow, shiny and a little long. His face was strong, just like his build, and his cheekbones rose in angles, wolf-like and daunting. Beneath the clean-shaven jaw of the striking face, her appreciative gaze crossed a long narrow crescent of white skin. The ghastly scar puckered across his wide tan neck where someone had most likely taken a knife to him.

Carrie had never seen the aftermath of violence before, but violence had to be its cause. No competent surgeon would leave such a scar. The contrast of his dreadful wound upon his splendid physique shocked her so thoroughly she took a step back, temporarily speechless.

She had enjoyed her solitary anger, venting her sorrows on him. But seeing this testament of a traumatic past, her stomach gave a flitter of sympathy.

"Pardon me. I was under the assumption that this was my office. My *private* office," his voice intoned in a dry august manner. He surveyed the room behind her, probably looking for missing items.

Sparse, expensive furniture decorated the room. Overall, the place was stark with the exception of the few medieval reproductions mounted on the wall behind the professor's desk. A shiny sword, a few ancient coins, and a pair of knight's spurs. The only books on the historian's shelves were ones he'd written himself. And on the desk—instead of the mounds of unfinished work she'd expected the overworked professor to have—sat a Rubik's cube, of all things.

One of Thorne's black eyebrows arched, and his unsettling gaze fixed on her. His eyes were the color of icy, gray fathomless seas.

"Oh, I'm so sorry. I was just looking for you." She took another step backward, giving the professor room to enter his office, but he remained where he was, a thunderous frown on his brow.

She swallowed a lump in her throat, suddenly knowing how a bug must feel as it looked into the face of the person about to squash it.

When his menacing look mercifully left her, Carrie reached to see if her hat was still in place and found that it was. Her awkward appearance in the presence of one so darkly attractive made her feel even more like an unwanted insect.

Ok, Carrie. Let's see you charm this one.

"You must be Professor Thorne," Carrie began, forcing Southern sunshine into her voice. She extended her hand. "There wasn't anyone at your assistant's desk outside. Your door was open. I took the liberty of waiting in your office until you returned."

"I see. Are you just visiting the university or are you a student?" The professor didn't seem interested in waiting to hear her answer. If he even noticed Carrie's proffered hand, he ignored it.

As he brushed past her, en route to his desk, Carrie felt the caress of his white dress shirt's sleeve against her arm. She let her gaze follow his slow, determined approach to his desk. He labored in the minor movement with stiffness, though he couldn't be more than thirty years old. Too young for arthritis. Her eyes traveled the length of him, down his muscular, long legs clad in black dress pants. He walked with a slight limp.

Before he could catch her staring, she jerked her gaze upward. Hopefully he'd missed her lack of manners. His face betrayed nothing as he settled into his chair behind the massive desk and regarded her.

Cool, collected, and reserved.

Professor Thorne might dress like a buttoned-down snob, but the business clothes failed to disguise the jagged nature just beneath the polished veneer. He reminded her of a half-breed wolf—tame in domestic captivity but ferocious underneath.

Carrie moved to take a seat since she doubted the man would offer her one.

"I'm Carrie. Caroline Greer. I came from the States to see you. I've written you a few times."

Vexation flashed across his face before he schooled it. "You've traveled all this way? From South Carolina, wasn't it? I believe I've answered your question. Did you not get my letter?"

"I—I did, but—"

"What did you not understand? I told you, you're

wasting your time. *My* blasted time." The professor's voice, in its perfect Welsh accent was barely audible, but there was no denying the threat behind it.

Carrie glanced at the door. She never should have entered his office. Somehow being alone with the professor made her feel as nervous as a cat. She hugged her purse against her chest. The crisp paper in the outer pocket crinkled. His letter had probably been written on the very same desk. The memory of his frosty answer strengthened her resolve.

On the long airplane trip to England, she'd read and reread the elegant, bold script, fueling her anger for the professor and supporting the necessity of her visit.

Madam:

This letter is written in response to the unwelcome correspondence which you have been sending me. This is also to inform you that your inquiry is not met with indifference; however, it is met with concern for your misplaced efforts in seeking the information you desire. As you must know by now, Professor Hagee, who was in charge of the field research at the university's Llysdinam Field Centre as well as the research and care of the plant found on my property has recently passed away. No other bioscientist here at Cardiff University chose to carry on his work in this matter. Professor Hagee was unable to successfully transplant a living specimen to the conservatoire. If the herb still survives, I highly doubt it. The climate in our country today is very different from what it was in the Middle Ages. Regretfully, I must advise you to cease your attempts to reach me, as I am a very busy man, and I recommend you to look for medical care in the United States.

Sincerely,
M. Thorne, Prof. of Medieval Studies
Cardiff University

"'Look for medical care in the States.' Gee, I hadn't thought of that!" She remembered telling her mother caustically. She'd steamed with indignation. "What an arrogant man!"

For twenty-six years, her entire life, she'd undergone treatment for epilepsy. The side-effects from her last medication were numerous. Nausea, headaches, red splotches, and—two weeks after her doctor had taken her off the offensive prescription—hair loss. Her affliction with its unpredictable nature often caused unease in those around her. She had seizures frequently, sometimes violently. Thankfully, her family, her assistant, and one short-term boyfriend were the only people who had witnessed her in the grip of a grand mal seizure.

Her single alternative to prescription drugs was neurosurgery. Risky at best. Not an option, as far as she was concerned. In her dismal future, she could look forward to seizures, side-effects, or lobotomy.

And then came hope...

Two months ago in her doctor's waiting room, she read an article in an old *National Geographic* that seemed like providence to an herbalist such as herself. The dormant seeds of a medieval herb rumored to treat seizures had been unearthed in an archeological dig in Wales. A natural cure documented by thirteenth century monks.

Would it work? She had nothing to lose if it didn't.

If only the plant had been discovered on someone else's property.

But it hadn't. The property, along with the ruins of a Cistercian monastery and a seven hundred year-old castle tower, belonged to the professor.

She cleared her voice.

"What I need won't take more than a minute." Carrie's glance swept the empty desktop pointedly, and she twisted her lips into an ironic grin. "Then you can get back to more...important things. After all, you're a 'busy man.'"

The professor didn't share her smile.

She felt more at ease with people who possessed a sense of humor, even a crude one. The professor's face would probably shatter if it ever cracked a smile.

His cold stare met hers. "Miss Greer, most people wisely choose not to anger me."

Carrie's grin melted. "I hope I haven't made you angry by coming here. All I need is the address for your property, and I'll search for the plants myself. I told you I know herbs. It's the specialty of my natural health store back home. If I find a sample, I—"

"The herbs are dead," Thorne cut her off flatly. His jaw tightened. "After your last inquiry, I called my caretaker at Wyldnell. He checked the grounds for me. All the plants at the excavation site died during the last winter. They never propagated. You've wasted your time."

"So, you haven't seen for yourself?"

Thorne's intelligent gaze slid over her in casual assessment and then back to her face. Instead of remorse or the familiar sympathy, there was only hardness in his expression. Profound detachment.

In return, Carrie's impression of him solidified. Before, she felt like a plain-Jane in his dark, sexy company with her baseball cap and her pale blotchy skin. Now all self-pity evaporated. Her blood boiled with anger.

He picked up the puzzle cube and began to twist it between his big, deft hands. "Why should I? I'm in the middle of writing another book, and I have too many obligations here at the university to drive all the way to Wyldnell. The plants simply aren't there. Really, Miss Greer, you should see a physician for your illness. Your parents or perhaps your boyfriend would agree with me, I'm sure."

Thorne dropped the cube on the desk and rose dismissively.

"No, they wouldn't!" Carrie retaliated in mounting annoyance.

She stood. What did he know about what she should or shouldn't do? He seemed healthy, other than his limp, and in control over his own destiny, while she was under the restraint of an incapacitating disability. Hot righteous anger pressed against her lungs. She could take no more of his aloofness.

"Look, this is really important to me, Professor Thorne. I live alone with my mother, and she trusts my judgment, regardless of how idiotic the idea might seem to her. I don't have a boyfriend. As for my physician, he is the one who is doing this to me!" She wagged a rigid index finger at her covered head. "I'm out of options. I need to find that herb. For others as well as me. You have no idea what it feels like to be so dependent."

Thorne stood arms akimbo. Color suffused his neck, running from the starched shirt collar past the pale tissue of his scar. Her outburst seemed to have caught him off-guard because his condescending brows lowered. His lips parted as if to say something.

She waited. He might change his mind.

Then, almost as an afterthought, he turned away.

"I have a lecture to prepare for. Since you found your way in, you can see yourself out. Perhaps you could take a tour of Cardiff or something so your trip won't be a total loss."

With that, he strode around her and blew out the door.

After a few deep breaths to calm her anger and allow plenty of time for the awful professor to vacate the hall, Carrie left the room.

Her head pounded. As she walked to the street to catch a taxi, she created excuses for the man. The professor was probably tired or stressed-out from some encounter with a smart-mouthed student. Tomorrow, after he'd forgotten her little visit to his office, he might feel differently. *Yeah, right.*

Doubtful. No one was capable of changing that stubborn man's mind.

****

Matthias circled around the building and ended up back in his office. Leaning against the closed door, he sighed. It was no use trying to work today. Tomorrow was Beltane again, and that thought alone consumed him. He would ask his assistant to cancel the rest of his lectures and go home for the day to prepare for another visit to his estate.

Now he had this pesky woman bothering him. Jesu, she was a troublesome thing. Flying from America to see him! Had he not brushed her off the best way he knew how?

He rubbed his thumbs in circles over his temples. Their brief conversation reverberated in his skull. He hadn't a shred of chivalry left in his body. Wasn't it obvious?

He'd told her the herbs were gone. Why did she not believe him? *Could she see through the lie?*

Women usually reacted to him in one of two ways. Either they were repulsed by his gruesome scar and boorish behavior, or they were attracted to him. In each case, he always found ways of deflecting them. Miss Greer was no different. He classified her as the "repulsed" sort. Too meek and timid to meddle with the likes of him.

However, she had stood up to him in a way that was most surprising for such a delicate looking woman.

Maybe his lie had done the trick. Maybe he'd

finally gotten rid of her. The last thing he needed was someone nosing around Wyldnell again. She would probably find that the herb didn't work anyway. She was better off at home, not chasing some miracle that didn't exist.

Alas, in his experience, miracles were unfortunately real. He'd certainly gotten his wish several years ago when he'd asked to be far away from his past.

Would it have hurt to promise to bring the plant back for the woman?

Matthias shook the guilty thought from his mind. If he brought her the rare plant from his estate, it would only bring further inquiries. Word would spread, again. People would ask about Wyldnell and then inevitably about the ancient henge. And then...

No, the plant should be left forgotten, as well as the wisp of a woman who had flown across the ocean for it.

****

Carrie awoke the next morning in a pool of red-gold sunlight. The view from her hotel room, the night before, included a lighted Gothic cathedral nearby. And she left the curtains open to view the beautiful scene. She rose from bed, tired from jetlag, but the BBC report on TV called for a clear day in Cardiff. Just right for sightseeing. She told herself she wasn't taking the professor's advice. Touring Cardiff was something she'd planned on doing anyway and had already purchased a Wales travel guide at the airport in London.

After scanning the contents of her room, she procrastinated packing. Nothing could be more depressing than that. She wasn't ready to admit defeat just yet. The beginnings of another scheme had evolved in her mind the night before.

She called the university, intending to apologize

to Professor Thorne for barging into his office. But she was told the man was taking the day off.

Perfect. Relieved, she smiled to herself. One less obstacle.

Her epilepsy prevented her from getting a rental car and driving. Bicycling probably wasn't the wisest thing to do either, but it was legal. In the U.S., at least. In Britain, who knew? After a phone call to the hotel desk, she arranged for a touring bike to be delivered for her.

Encouraged, Carrie showered and dressed in khaki shorts and a top in her favorite color, periwinkle. As she glanced at her image in the vanity mirror, her confidence boosted. Her skin was clearing! Perhaps she would even go without a hat. The Welsh climate had given her hair more wave and volume.

She gave her golden brown locks a few twists of her curling iron, brushed them out, and marveled at how much closer she was to being her old self. Feeling almost normal, she added a touch of powder and lip-gloss.

She rode her bicycle straight to the university. The professor's wing of the humanities building was empty. No assistant, no students, no faculty. Everyone gone to lunch.

In the archeology department, she found exactly what she'd been looking for—a fourth-year student who knew Wyldnell Castle and claimed he'd been present for the excavations.

When he realized she was a "Yank," the amiable young man slipped into a long conversation with her, frequently commenting on her accent.

To the English, she was a "Yank," but at home no one would dream of saying such after hearing her soft Southern drawl. She had the same elegantly slow speech as her grandmother. As the Charlestonian matriarch aptly described her own euphonious voice, it was that of a woman whose greatest trouble in life was deciding which china teapot to use when the preacher's wife came to visit.

The archeology student, Claude, excitedly answered all her questions about the excavations, and she was able to coax the property's whereabouts out of him.

As he walked her out of the building, Claude gestured toward the travel guide sticking out of her purse. "You should use that little book of yours to visit all the tourist stops—eat the traditional rarebit, hear a choir, and visit a pub—but don't miss the museum. You'll love all the historical figures of Wales in glowing white marble. Women always say Llywelyn the Last is quite a charmer."

Carrie faked enthusiasm. She couldn't care less about long-dead princes and fallen heroes. *Nor about ruined castles belonging to Professor Tall-Dark-and-Hostile.* The day was so beautiful. How could she wander the city streets, wasting her time, when she should be out scanning the countryside for herbs?

She had to be patient. The professor said he kept a caretaker. The trip to the estate would have to wait until dark.

After an early meal that evening, Carrie caught the train at Cathays Station, near the university. She brought her bike along for the short journey north to the Welsh March lands and gleaned information from her travel guide as she rode in a passenger car.

She occasionally glanced up from her book at the passing scenery. Deeper in the Welsh country, the English road signs included Welsh translations. Apparently, the ancient Celtic language hadn't been extinguished this far north. Some of the town names were unpronounceable to her, compounding the foreignness of her new locale. But her first sight of the sun setting in the pastoral hill country took her breath away.

With her forehead pressed against the passenger window, Carrie fell in love with Wales. Raw and rugged, the rocky hills pushed upward from the elegant patchwork of gentle fields like the brawn of granite muscles in a demonstration of the power of nature. Sheep dotted the landscape of rolling pastures. More bucolic than anything the best English artists could conceivably harness in simple oil paint and canvas, the beautiful countryside was unlike any she'd ever seen.

Why shouldn't she expect miracles in such a land?

Professor Thorne was wrong and she would prove it.

The day was May Eve, a fellow passenger rambled on beside her, and by Celtic calendar the night before the first day of summer, or Beltane, when the ancient Druids had built their bonfires in long forgotten rituals.

Carrie bobbed her head attentively and smiled. *Not much longer now.*

Dusk settled over the station where Carrie disembarked with her bicycle. Following the student's directions, she rode down a lane beside an Edwardian inn. She passed a small brick farmhouse and then endless miles of pastures, illuminated only by the fading light of dusk. The pastures flattened, sprawling over the darkening horizon, as if the hills had reclined as a sleeping giant. When she spotted a sign reading St. Mary's Church, est. 1898, she pulled the bike off the road.

Carrie squinted, trying to make out landmarks in the shadows. Other than the church sign and the road, the only marks of modern man were the wooden fence posts strung with barbed wire alongside the weedy shoulder.

No driveway. She opened her purse and fished

for the little flashlight she'd purchased at a gift shop.

Turning it on, she could make out the slight indentation of a dirt footpath running across the field on the other side of the fence. Claude had told her the whole place was part of a neglected farm for at least a hundred years before the professor bought it.

Carrie ignored the trepidation in her gut as she leaned her bike against a post.

She eyed the darkness beyond the fence. The trail disappeared into nowhere. The road back to Cardiff behind her, she squared her shoulders and grasped the rusty barbed wire. Bending low she swung one leg through the parted wires and then the other, catching her shirt on the barbs in the process.

"Ohhhh! Drat."

She attempted to extricate the fabric of her top from the fence without creating further damage. It took several minutes. As soon as she freed herself, she glanced up to find she wasn't alone. A second flashlight beam caught her from across the field.

Chapter Two

After walking the cloud-capped hills, woods, and pastures from dawn until dusk, Matthias made the torturous climb up the steep grassy slope of the old motte to where one ruined tower of Wyldnell Castle remained. The centuries had seen the removal of the outer curtain walls and the destruction of the other towers, but not his own. While men had coveted the aging stones and masonry, hauling them off to raise stately country manors, his tower had been left untouched. Like him, rejected.

He burst into the renovated dwelling, nearly staggering as he pushed the door shut. Sweat poured off him in streams. Of the many things he'd acquired over the past few years, he was most thankful for the introduction of plumbing and electricity to his solar.

He collapsed into his armchair before the cold stone hearth and closed his eyes as he allowed the ceiling fans high above to revive him. Later he would shower and let the warm water ease the ache of his muscles. Once again, the walk failed to send him back, but he hadn't really expected anything to change on this particular evening, no different from all the rest. The effort was worth a try just in case a ghost might still be lingering in the tower's stone walls, judging him and everything he did.

Nothing much of the old Wyldnell estate remained, but what was there belonged to him. A piece of paper declared it so, and no one in this century would ever dispute it.

The irony of it made Matthias's lips form a

bitter smile. If only he could see Giles one last time to tell his brother what had become of him and what he had achieved. Who would have ever thought the wastrel second son of a thirteenth century baron would be capable of accomplishing anything during his time on earth without a king's war to fight or a wealthy brother to give it to him? Certainly not Giles. For that matter, he could hardly believe it of himself. He'd built himself up from nothing to become a respected intellectual in these new times.

An intellectual? Ha! Giles would find that laughable. His entire new career was built on the mere common knowledge of his youth. There, he'd had virtually no education, and here, he was a bloody genius.

Matthias scanned the room. His gaze rose to the timbered ceiling he'd put there two years ago. Was Giles watching down over him, and did he approve of his brother's changes?

And had he forgiven him?

The ormolu clock on the mantel clicked in the otherwise silent room, reminding him of its emptiness. Warm yellow light bulbs overhead now replaced the hot illumination of tallow candles and burning sconces. No more did the flames dance on the walls with the bustling of servants and the merry stir of guests in the castle. No one came to Wyldnell now, except himself and Nigel, the caretaker.

As long as he lived, he would keep it that way.

Opening the grounds to the university's archeology department had been a mistake he wouldn't repeat again. The risk was too great. How could he bear the guilt if another unlucky soul fell into the abyss? He didn't wish to imagine what would happen if he wasn't there to prevent someone from accidentally finding the doorway between two worlds. Or, a worse scenario, if someone stole his only chance to return to the century where he truly belonged.

Violet eyes flashed in his thoughts. Large, hopeful, and then accusatory, Caroline Greer's eyes were seared into his brain today.

He'd done her a favor. If she only knew...

He stretched his legs in front of him and scowled at the surge of pain that ripped through his calf muscle. He'd injured his ankle when he was still a lad running about the curtained wall, trying in vain to impress his father. The leg hadn't grown as it should have and as a result, he would always be slightly lame.

Perhaps he'd pushed himself too far that day, just as he did every Beltane now, to no other outcome but his own physical expenditure and a wasted workday from the university.

Without fail, he'd visited the stone circle on the Druid hill, month after month. At first, he came frequently as a trespasser. He slipped onto the property at midnight, recreating that fateful night time and again. Nothing ever changed. A few years ago, he bought the property but after that his ritual visits became more sporadic. He immersed himself in his work. Now he only came on the nights of the pagan holidays.

Round and round, he paced the circle in the moonlight. Try as he might, the stones wouldn't take him back. Sometimes he felt damn glad of it.

As he repeated every semester to his students in Cardiff, the Middle Ages were hell on Earth, and he thanked his lucky stars he wasn't there.

Yet, his guilty soul would not give him peace. The past kept creeping back into his thoughts. He'd left as a coward and a traitor to his brother. If he didn't return, he couldn't rectify his actions. The sins would linger, making him feel forever as if he still lived in hell.

****

"Sorry 'bout all this, Miss."

They walked across the lawn behind the wide yellow beams from the flashlights, wrapped in silence until now. Just like a criminal, she'd been caught red-handed, climbing over the fence on Thorne's private property only a few dozen feet from the caretaker's gatehouse. She hated the fact that Professor Thorne would have to be dealt with, as well, since he'd come to Wyldnell today, too. *Drat.*

"It's not much farther now," the deep male voice of the caretaker said beside her. The cluster of keys on his belt jangled against his hip as he walked.

Tears threatened at the sheer embarrassment of it all, but she wouldn't allow herself to cry. Instead, she held her hands at her sides, digging her stubby fingernails into her palms. Had she done anything so rotten as to deserve this humiliation?

Why had she come to Wales? Why hadn't she just stayed home?

At least Dr. Ferguson had *attempted* to take care of her. He'd changed her prescription, and the intolerable side-effects seemed to be wearing off. She should've stayed at home and saved the expense of the trip to Wales.

The worst part lay ahead of her, however, outweighing all her other regrets. Repulsion and dread knotted her stomach, and she prayed she'd taken enough medicine on the way to Wyldnell to allay any onset of seizure her panic might cause. The thought of facing that awful professor again...

"Are you all right, Miss?" The caretaker turned his flashlight on her face. "You've gone pale."

"I'm fine," she lied.

"The professor should be up here unless he's gone out scouting the property again," the caretaker told her as casually as if she'd been invited over for tea.

So, he never visits his own property, huh? If he lied about that, maybe Thorne lied about the moon plants. A new rush of hope and anger spurred Carrie on.

The guard pointed the flashlight high above them. She wrapped her arms around herself bracing as the lighted stone tower and the crumbling remains of a castle curtain came into view. Truly, the structure had once been magnificent. The hill alone impressed her with its great height.

"I'm afraid it's black books you'll be in tonight," the caretaker said. "Sorry, but if I send you away without asking the professor's permission first, he'll have me on toast."

Carrie expected to hear a chuckle from the stocky man following his dry remark, but there wasn't one. Taking a glimpse at the man's wide face beside her, she saw only a bleak expression, which brought her senses hurtling back to reality.

Clambering up the grassy slope in the dark, they came to the tower entrance. Not needing the flashlights anymore, they flicked them off, and the caretaker took hers, sliding it under his belt.

Ground lights along the skirt of the outer wall colored the castle keep pale green, and she could hear the mournful sounds of music coming from a stereo inside. The moody melodrama of Berlioz spilled out as the caretaker pushed open a heavy, carved door. No one inside would hear a knock if he'd tried it. The loud, whirling lamentations of the orchestra only served to heighten her fear as they stepped into the living quarters.

"Professor Thorne, I'm sorry to disturb you," the guard raised his voice above the stereo to the lone figure across the room.

Silhouetted by lamplight, Matthias Thorne stood with his back to them, bracing his hands on the stone mantel of the hearth. His dark hair fell in waves to his shoulders. Beneath the tight white fabric of a damp dress shirt, the muscles of his broad back were plainly visible. As if a dark sorcerer contemplating the fate of the world, he stared into the black pit.

Finally, he spoke, "What is it, Nigel?"

The caretaker turned the stereo volume down.

A lump formed in Carrie's throat.

"I found this lady on the grounds, sir. She says she knows you."

Thorne glanced sharply over his shoulder. His eyes glinted. "What the hell are you doing here?"

The room echoed under the weight of his barked demand. He rounded on them, his mercurial glare passing over Carrie.

The gatekeeper answered, "I found her near the gatehouse. Her bicycle is parked by the road, sir. She says all she wants is to see the grounds. I can show her around and let her straight out, if you like..."

Thorne waved a dismissive hand in the air, silencing poor Nigel. The man could do more communicating without talking than anyone she'd ever met.

He strode toward them, a gothic nightmare. Light and shadow fell across his face as he drew near, and his eyes gleamed with outrage. He obviously wasn't used to people challenging his orders.

Her gaze took in the way he was dressed. His shirt, unbuttoned to the waist of his black pants, revealed taut, damp musculature, as if he'd only just come inside to relax. At the moment, however, he looked far from relaxed. A vein in his neck began to throb beneath his scar.

Thorne stopped in front of them. "That's exactly what Miss Greer came for, Nigel. I'd rather not give her the satisfaction," he replied smoothly.

Carrie felt a chill creep up her forearms.

Somehow, there seemed no other place on earth better suited for the man than this remote ancient dwelling.

"You seem to think I have a sense of humor—which I don't. Did you think I'd just allow anyone to wander around my property without my permission and against my wishes?"

Carrie swallowed. "No, I knew you wouldn't. But I have to admit, I never expected the grounds to be patrolled at night." Making herself meet his hard eyes, she forced a smile. "The plan was weak. I should've done my homework."

Thorne slapped a hand to his forehead in exaggeration. "Are you completely gormless? Of all the stupid ideas," he bellowed. "You've already squandered your money to come here, chasing a cure-all, a miracle elixir that doesn't exist. Cor, lady, I told you the herbs were dead. Did you find them? Well, *did you?*"

No one had ever yelled at her like that in all her life. Carrie flinched and looked at Nigel. Her captor averted his eyes. No help there. Did everyone carry his tail between his legs like a dog when the professor spoke?

Carrie turned back to her accuser. His hands planted on his waist, a scowl deep on his brow. How could she defend herself from his attack on her character when she felt so impossibly stupid herself?

She gathered her courage as best as she could and stared back. But looking at the professor made it hard for her to think. His eyes were fascinating, gray and turbulent like stormy Welsh seas, rimmed with dark eyelashes. Distracting. Intimidating.

Aside from his temperament, maybe vanity was another of his failings. No man could be so gorgeous and not know it.

If he was vain, she could use it against him somehow. It always helped boost sales in her health food store when she knew what the customer's vanities were. Claude had told her the ruined castle was his "special project..."

"No, I haven't seen the herbs." Carrie shrugged. "There's not much here but fallen masonry, is there? Certainly nothing to be so protective of. I can't believe you keep a caretaker. As if anyone cared about this place. Why, I doubt even the National Trust would want to spend their time on Wyldnell. It's such a waste."

Thorne blinked. "You would say so because you're an American. Your people don't have a sense of history like we do in the British Isles." He looked down his nose at her. "Wyldnell was once an important strategic stronghold to the monarchs of England."

Had she found which buttons to push?

Carrie pressed on, hiding her sudden hope. "You've made a very stereotypical assessment of my countrymen, Professor Thorne. As it happens, the house I live in with my mother is on the historical register. It's antebellum. There are rigid building codes in place to protect the architecture's integrity. Many of the houses in my neighborhood were carefully restored or preserved by their owners, which is more than I can say for this worthless heap."

Carrie scanned the uneven stones of the gloomy chamber's walls and intentionally made her words scathing, "No wonder the university ended their excavations. There's nothing at all here. It's a joke. I'll bet the weeds of the monastery were their biggest discovery, not your castle."

The professor didn't contradict her, but worked his jaw angrily. Instead, he curtly amended, "They found nothing at the monastery. It's far north of here. The construction was timber-frame, leaving nothing but the foundation and the monks' refuse.

The herbs were on the hill overlooking the river and in the bailey nearby, not in the excavations of the monastery, as Ms. Spencer wrote in her article. That was a misquote. I would be surprised if it was the only one in that ridiculous article."

"The herbs were found in two places?" Carrie registered. She wheeled around to consult Nigel. "Did you check both places to make sure all the plants died?"

Nigel frowned. His face clouded in confusion. He looked over her head at Thorne.

Stunned, Carrie whirled back to the professor.

"You didn't have the caretaker check them, did you? You lied. Why, Professor? Why don't you want anyone to see them?" Unable to conceal her rage, she cried, "What a hateful thing to do. There are researchers who want to study them. Scientists. Doctors. People who need them. Why keep them to yourself? They're just plants. God put them here for everyone, not just you!"

A tear slipped down her cheek from fatigue and frustration. Had she traveled this far only to be lied to? She rubbed the offensive moisture away with the back of her hand. The professor's face had gone tight, and she knew she was right. He didn't know or care if the moon plants had survived. She pushed past the slack-jawed caretaker.

"Where are you going?" Thorne demanded at her back.

"To look for the moon plants," Carrie sniffed.

"No, you're not!" He growled and moved between her and the door, standing too close.

She looked from side to side, instinct urging her to move away from him, but she remained where she was. The slight, musky scent of sandalwood clung to him and teased her senses. His presence would crowd her across a hundred acre field.

He put a dark hand on the door. "This is my

27

property, worthless or not. You may not go out there, Miss Greer. It's not safe on these grounds at night. You'll stay inside while I call the constable." His Adam's apple bobbed, and Carrie briefly considered he might be afraid of something.

Impossible. That alteration of his character conflicted with all she'd witnessed from him so far. He wasn't capable of fear—or apparently compassion on her part.

She crossed her arms over her chest and sighed. Thorne left the door, heading in the direction of a phone lying on a cherry end table.

The grounds not safe? As if wild beasts roamed the woods. She wasn't a fool. There was nothing but sheep for miles around.

"You're insufferable." Carrie blew out a frustrated breath.

"What you did is called *trespassing*, Miss Greer. First my office and now here. What else should I do?"

"Well, if I'm going to jail, then I'll go knowing whether or not those herbs are alive."With her exit now unhindered, Carrie sprang for the door, swinging her purse over her shoulder.

She bolted out to freedom into the thick night air and sprinted down the hill, her legs pumping through the slick grass. She found the slope more precarious when descending quickly. Gravity grappled with her. To keep from losing balance, she leaned with the hill, toes feeling for solid places to step.

From the tower, Thorne called after her. She heard several blasphemies hurled at her back. His shouts followed as he pursued her. She ran without direction, the castle's lights fading behind her. What would she do if he caught her? What would *he* do, for that matter?

She wouldn't allow that to happen. Not yet.

She didn't know where she was going. The clear sky clouded with mist. Precipitation hung like sequined curtains in the moonlit air. She had no flashlight guiding her, so only her outstretched hands kept her from plowing into trees as she entered a wooded area far below the castle ruins.

She discovered a worn trail through the bramble and ran along it. Briars pricked at her clothes. She ignored the painful scratches on her bare calves and ankles. The farther she ran, the farther away she noticed Thorne's voice became. Since the professor was lame, if he tried to keep up with her in his condition, he may have tripped and fallen by now.

All of a sudden, she felt a pang of unwanted guilt.

But then she reminded herself how incredibly mean he'd been. If he could spare no understanding for her situation, then she would spare no feeling for him.

The plant would be on a hill overlooking the river, Carrie recalled him saying. Unfortunately, she didn't know where the river was. She jogged to a stop. Winded, she braced a hand on the rough trunk of an ancient tree and tried to catch her breath. Vision was nearly impossible with the moonlight disappearing behind intermittent clouds, but she didn't feel defeated. She felt glorious. Thank heaven she'd been using a treadmill at the gym, because without it she'd never have made it this far.

As she rested, she held her breath and listened.

Yes, there it was.

The River Wye. Flowing water not too far away.

Carrie pressed on, no longer running but walking briskly. She emerged from the forest to a clearing several minutes later. She stood in a pasture. The bleats of sheep in the distance confirmed her location. Ahead on a rise, she saw strange shadows silhouetted against the lapis sky.

The black forms looked like human figures, but they were much larger.

"Get back here!" Thorne's enraged tone, sounded somewhere behind her.

How could he still be following her? She must've rested too long. Carrie felt a swell of shame over her behavior. She was being inconsiderate, making the man chase after her in his shape. Why didn't he just send his caretaker?

Perhaps he was only worried about her safety. She glanced back. He closed the distance between them. Agony etched his features and fury, too, that even the blue-black cloak of night couldn't hide.

"You must come back. You're too near the cliff," he panted when he caught up with her. "There beyond the henge."

Well, that danger explained his unreasonable reaction of alarm to her trespassing. He was afraid she would fall off the cliff.

Calmly, she replied, "I'll come right back. I'm only looking for the plants. You'll soon be rid of me."

"Don't go in there, Miss Greer."

Carrie entered the circle of towering stone spires. She'd read something in her travel guide about henges. This was the kind of place where Iron Age men worshiped at sacred altars, not where herb gardens grew. Maybe he was mistaken about the herbs being here. And why wasn't this particular henge on the guide map? The whole place reeked of esotericism that New Age enthusiasts seemed to flock to and enjoy.

The mist chilled her, and she trembled as she picked her way between the rocks.

"Get out now! You don't belong there!"

Carrie turned at the sound of the professor's ragged voice.

"Jesu!"

He looked as if he'd seen an apparition, staring

at her from outside the circle. A heavier mist had begun to rise between them, quickly concealing him from her sight in a hazy barrier. She looked down, surprised at the fresh dampness of the ground sucking at her shoes—and then she caught her breath.

There, at her feet were a dozen or more little shrubs, flourishing. Tiny yellow blossoms opened for the night, but these were herbs even *she* couldn't identify. Recalling the magazine article's description, they had to be her moon plants. Her heart leapt.

"They're here. I knew it!" Carrie crouched to examine them closer.

"Nay!" a primal roar ripped from Thorne, and before she could look up, she found herself caught up in his arms in a full-body tackle. The impact was stunning. Bones meeting bones, shoulder against shoulder, limbs tangling. She fell along with Thorne into the thick, shrouding mist.

The fall knocked the wind from her chest, and life crushed out of her. Her senses went numb, pain vanished, and the world went silent. She was undeniably dead.

Chapter Three

The tiniest tickling sensation on Carrie's arm awakened her. As she lifted her head, feeling oddly stiff that morning, her eyes focused on what had disturbed her peace. A butterfly. She smiled as the fog in her brain lifted. Pale yellow, the creature landed on her arm and took flight again, its margarine-colored wings fluttering softly in the warm summer air. *Warm air?*

Carrie pushed herself up. Squinting in the sunshine, she realized she was outside. Why had she fallen asleep outside? And on the bare ground?

Rubbing her eyes, she tried to remember where she'd last been. Did she have another seizure? She didn't think so. A peculiar warmth rushed across her bare thigh. Her body trembled at the sensation. Glancing down, her heart lurched as she recognized the prone body of the livid man who had chased her the night before. Matthias Thorne.

He lay unmoving on the ground, one brawny arm draped heavily across her legs. The side of his face pressed to the earth. He was alive, because his deep breaths trailed rhythmically across her bare skin below her shorts.

Lying there so innocent in his slumber, he looked almost carefree. No frown lines marred his smooth, tan brow. A sheen of sable hair fell over his forehead in a wild tousle. The slight shadow of a beard darkened his jaw and contrasted against the collar of his loosened white shirt.

A sensuous wave of desire washed over her. She changed her original opinion of him. Minus the murderous frown, Thorne could be dangerously handsome.

Had they really slept there together all night? Or was she dreaming?

"Professor Thorne?" Carrie nudged his shoulder with her palm and determined it wasn't a dream. The professor was made of flesh and bone and was lying perfectly still.

No sound came from the clearing around them except the gentle gurgle of the nearby river and the whisper of a bird's wings.

"Professor? Uh, M-Matthias? Are you all right?"

She became worried when she raised her voice and he still didn't answer. Carefully, she shifted his weight. Jostling him slightly, a dark tendril of hair slipped aside, exposing a red rivulet staining his forehead and a deep crimson mark on his hairline.

Carrie tried to swallow the cry of alarm in her throat. "Oh, God!"

He must've hit his head on one of the fallen stones. Was he hurt badly? Taking hold of his big shoulders, she maneuvered his head onto her lap. Her fingers shook as she plucked away bits of grass and dirt from his wound. She scanned the ground for her purse, finding it within reach.

She dug out the handkerchief her grandmother had embroidered and insisted she carry with her. Also, in her purse, she discovered a half-empty, pocket-sized bottle of hand sanitizer, which she applied to the handkerchief and touched to the man's bleeding temple. Mostly, the blood was dried and crusty. Thank God, there seemed to be no chance of him bleeding to death.

Matthias's eyes flew open on a sharp intake of breath. He winced, knocking away her hand. "Jesu, what are you doing?"

Carrie smiled down at him, relief pouring through her. "Taking care of you. You're a mess."

Where did he get that strange expression of his, anyway? He'd used the same word the night before.

His shoulders relaxed. "Aye. It hurts, though. Are you sure you know what you're doing?"

"Yes. I think we had an accident, Professor. You've hurt your head, so I'll have to get help."

"Okay," he sighed. A slight smile curved on his lips as his misty gray eyes fluttered closed again.

He'd be madder than a wet hornet when he got his senses back, and she dreaded what would happen then.

A nervous giggle bubbled within her. "You're much nicer with a concussion. I should've hit you over the head myself."

Her fingers sifted through his thick hair, combing away a few blades of grass.

"Did we make it?" His head leaned into her touch.

She guessed he meant to confirm that they were really alive. She tried not to laugh. "Yes, we're still alive. We haven't left the stone circle."

"Nay. Did we make it through to my time? What year is it?"

His words were odd, but he was clearly dazed from the blow to his head. Maybe his injury was more serious than she'd thought.

"I don't want to make you sit up or stand. I wonder if I could leave you alone here."

His hand lifted to hers on his forehead where his fingers touched hers tentatively. He tried to open his eyes. "You must stay here...might be sentries. Got to have my name...protection. Don't speak or they'll know." The words slurred together on his lips.

Carrie shook her head and murmured, "You're not making any sense, Professor. Wait here. Promise me you'll stay still. I'll be back. Promise me...."

"Still." The word echoed, and his eyes closed again.

Carrie had no time to waste. She gently slid out from under Thorne and eased him back down. Leaving the handkerchief at his temple, she rose on wobbly legs and headed back in the direction she thought they'd come from.

Although she felt achy, she had tons of energy. Her memory nagged at her as she walked. Why hadn't the caretaker come after them? Surely, he should've come looking for them by now. Thorne had been yelling loud enough to wake the dead last night. Why hadn't Nigel followed his employer's voice?

She didn't recall the forest being quite so dense. All shades of green winked at her in the sun from the canopy of the summer trees overhead. Then she finally came to the clearing. Startled birds flew ahead of her from the brambles.

"You, there!" A voice thundered at her in an odd accent. Carrie squinted as she looked into the bright sunlight for the man who'd addressed her. "What is your business in my lord's forest?"

A man on horseback rode to meet her at the edge of the woods. The rider was dressed in a shiny, hooded costume of mail. He held a round helmet and visor in his lap. A green surcoat emblazoned with a tree finished his outfit.

"You're a strange wench, aren't you?" He eyed her clothing with a curiosity that must've reflected her own stare at his odd attire. "What do you mean by disturbing our watch?" His huge gray horse paced, nervous at the sound of its rider's impatient voice.

Carrie blinked rapidly, feeling out of sorts herself. His speech, the costume—did Thorne use his land for historical reenactments?

"Sorry. Look I'm not in your history-thing." She dared to touch the horse's flank in a stilling gesture, emboldened by the pressing need to help her companion. "There's been an accident. Professor Thorne was hurt. I've got to get to the telephone at Wyldnell. We may need an ambulance. He's hit his head, and I think he's got a concussion."

"Wyldnell?" The man scowled at her. He wore his auburn hair in a short, blunt cut, and his nose was riddled with blackheads, his cheeks marred by boils. He couldn't have been more than eighteen years old. "Why do you make these lies, wench? Lord Wyldnell rests in the castle. You speak strange, too. Are you...are you Rhiannon?" His eyes widened with wonder.

"Rhiannon?" Carrie shook her head. Wasn't that a Fleetwood Mac song? Then she remembered the mention of the Welsh goddess and her accompanying birds from the Mabinogion tales in her travel guide. Oh, for Pete's sake! "Hey, I don't have time to play along right now. Seriously, Thorne needs help. Get a cell phone or go call a doctor, send him to the henge, and I'll meet him there."

The young man scratched his grimy head thoughtfully. "God's teeth! Methinks the earl will want to hear of this. These are foreign words you speak. Whose kingdom are you from? You're not Welsh, for certes, and that being so, you'll be of some interest to Lord Wyldnell."

He shoved his helmet on his head.

Who was this moron? She was ready to throttle him. "Well, can you at least take me to the castle? Take me to Thorne's castle."

The man reached down and hauled her up in a rough grip onto the horse in front of him. He leaned over her shoulder, gaping openly at her bare legs. He looked at her as if he'd never seen a woman's legs before. Weird. Carrie's stomach rolled with disgust, and for the second time in the past twenty-four hours, she wished she'd worn jeans instead.

"This is an emergency. Let's hurry up, damn it!"

She rubbed at the pain of his offensive grip on her arm.

His vile breath rolled out as he spoke in her ear. "Wench, hold your tongue, or I'll cut it off after my lord speaks to you. Aye, I think I will. Then I'll plow you till I get my fill, since you won't be able to speak anymore."

Carrie saw only naked honesty in the flashing brown eyes leering markedly at her breasts. He meant to do just as he said. She started to climb off the horse, but the man caught her with a steel grip. Shocked, she struggled to free her arm, but he wouldn't release her.

"Whoa, you're not getting down. You asked to be taken to the castle, so you shall." He withdrew a leather strap from a bag on his saddle, wound it around Carrie's captured hand, and bound it behind her to his own belt.

Carrie screamed for help, her heart pounding. But who could hear her? The professor? Not likely, too far away and too addled. She had nothing to retaliate with, no pistol or even a can of mace. The purse dangling from her shoulder wouldn't swat flies, let alone harm a deranged young man. She strained to wrench her wrist free from its binding.

Hoof beats announced the arrival of others. Two more armored men circled the woods astride large black beasts. Thank God!

"Hey! This guy's nuts! He tied me up," she cried, half hysterical.

The men joining them were older, but they were no doubt part of the same troupe, carrying swords and shields but no helmets. One had fair hair and the other had black, matted to their heads with what looked like weeks of grime.

"Who have you got there, Ian? A wench who runs about in her shift?" The blond laughed. "You always find the daft ones."

37

The other two men laughed, and tears burned her eyes. What kind of reenactment was this?

Or am I about to be gang-raped?

Her bottom lip quivered. If it weren't for the pain of her tight binding and the stench of the men, she would have thought she was deep in a nightmare.

"Let's be on, Ian," the black-haired man said. "The earl was awake when I left him. If we're lucky he'll still be that way."

****

Matthias eased himself into a sitting position as slowly as he could. His skull was killing him. Damn, where was that bloody woman?

Caroline Greer. Or Carrie, as the woman called herself. She was the reason his head felt this way. Matthias vaguely recalled her hovering over him. Was that real? His thoughts were scattered. He remembered her smile. He remembered her light fingers stroking his head. A woman hadn't touched him with such tenderness in a long time.

She'd asked him to stay still. There was a handkerchief.

Matthias picked up the soiled cloth from the grass. It was real. She'd been there.

But *where* were they? Or *when*? And where was she now?

Casting his wary gaze over his surroundings, Matthias had a sinking feeling. The rising dread conflicted with a sense of excitement. Were they no longer in the twenty-first century? He sniffed the air, gauging for a difference. Could it be possible he was finally back home?

Pressing fisted hands against his aching temples, he rose. The movement caused throbbing pain, and he closed his eyelids.

Then he heard the faint approaching sound of horses and metal.

****

The trio rode on the skirts of the wooded area, keeping the horses at a brisk pace. Carrie gasped as the castle came into view. It wasn't the professor's Wyldnell. It was different, but somehow it was comparable. Only on a grander scale. A much newer edifice than the professor's solitary, derelict tower.

The stone curtain loomed high above the motte, beginning from a dry crevice far below. They rode toward a stone gatehouse that could've come straight out of a fairy tale, approaching it across the deep, dry ditch on a suspended bridge. Costumed guards moved on the top of the curtain wall between the crenellations.

"Where are we? Where is this?" she demanded, her heartbeat thundering in time with the horse's hoofs.

The castle was enormous. As they slowed, people moved about inside the walls, people everywhere. All the men wore either chain mail or tunics. The children wore costumes as well. Chickens and goats meandered about. Oh, the smell of it. The air stunk worse than the organic fertilizer she used on her little vegetable garden.

It was an amusement park. Of course! An amazing amusement park. How had Thorne kept this a secret? Maybe the place was invitation-only, like some exclusive club for wealthy history-buffs.

The men dismounted in the bailey, and the man who held her, Ian, untied her and pulled her from the horse. Gripping her wrist in one gloved hand, he led her into one of the castle's four towers. Inside they plunged into darkness. She blinked hard as her eyes adjusted from the change of lighting, or lack of it. Surely, the place had electricity?

She tried to wrench herself free, thinking she might lose him in the dark, but he wouldn't let go. He forced her up steep, winding stairs toward a light as the others followed. The spurs on his shoes, much like the ones she'd seen on display in Thorne's office, chimed against the steps.

Stopping at the top of the stairwell, he proclaimed loudly, "My lord! My lord, I've brought someone for you to see."

They stood outside a closed door. "Who's in there?" Carrie inquired of her captor. She pictured the manager of the park at a desk, plotting out scenes for his guests. Or maybe it was yet another re-enactor, ready to impress her with his costume and Middle Ages-talk. She rooted herself on the threshold. "I told you Professor Thorne is on the cliff. He was hurt. Look, I've got to get back to Wyldnell."

"Well, come in and see me," a male voice shouted impatiently from inside the room. Ian pushed the door open, pulling Carrie in behind him.

The room showcased a luxurious canopied bed. A man sat, propped up by several velvet-encased pillows in the center. Curiosity thrust her forward despite Ian's forceful hold on her wrist. The man wore a scarlet tunic, and as she drew near, she realized what might have caused the confusion in her escorts. Professor Matthias Thorne had a mirror image.

"My God, you look almost exactly like him."

They had to be related, though he was older. His hair was thick, wavy, and gray. Not merely gray, but the truest silver of precious metal. His eyes were the same as Matthias's. The same wolfish face, too, though his jaw bore a trimmed beard of silver whiskers. There the similarities ended.

The man wasn't well. His skin hung on bones, grossly withered. The hollow planes of his face made him seem almost skeletal, and the dark purple crescents beneath his eyes made her illness seem paltry in comparison. Violet veins crisscrossed on his ghastly pale skin like a roadmap of his suffering.

"I look like whom?" he asked in almost the same haughty manner as Thorne.

The contrast of the professor's health and vigor against this wretched shell of a man shook her.

"Professor Thorne."

Carrie's captor released her reluctantly, leaving her to rub her aching wrists.

"You do know Professor Thorne, don't you?" Her voice sounded desperate to her own ears. She edged a step toward the bed.

"Nay, who are you?" He looked to the man behind Carrie for an answer.

Ian explained how he'd found her and how strangely he thought she dressed. He repeated his belief that she was Rhiannon, appearing from the woods with her magical birds.

"But now I think she's from Brecon. She has a Norman look to her." The leering brown eyes passed over her again, making her fingers ball in two fists, ready to sock him.

She'd had enough of their ridiculous conversation.

"Hey, I've explained to you that I'm not in your medieval production. There was an accident at the stones on the hill. I was there with Matthias Thorne. He was hurt. I need to use a phone."

"'Matthias?'" The man on the bed sat straight up. "Did you say Matthias?"

"Yes!" Thank God, now she was getting somewhere.

The man in the bed began to cough. At first, the cough rattled dryly in his thin chest, and then wet matter rose with his hacking until he leaned over the side of his bed and emptied his stomach. The air of the chamber became instantly putrid.

"My lord—" Her captor moved to his side as Carrie staggered back two steps. "Shall I fetch some wine?"

41

"Nay, nay!" He waved the man away. "I need a healer. Get the physick. Or better yet, get Maud."

"The witch?"

"Aye. Mayhaps, she'll kill me and put a final end to this interminable death."

Oh, lord. Her heart went out to him, but this sickly man wouldn't be any help.

Doubts niggled at her brain. What in the hell was going on in this place? She wished she *had* been taken to the manager. She'd like to give him an earful.

"Matthias—. The phone?" Carrie reminded them.

"*Phone?*" Ian, her captor, echoed her last word as if he'd never heard of a phone. This act was getting really old. He didn't know when to quit.

"What year is it?" The professor had asked.

The silver-haired man regarded her quietly, deep in thought. He rubbed a trembling hand across his mouth.

Ian said to him, "She's using his name to provoke you. Matthias has been gone so long I know he must be dead."

"But...she knew we looked alike."

Ian made a sketch of a sympathetic smile. "Bards tell the story in the villages. Maud spins a yarn about him disappearing in the mist. His memory is well preserved in tales."

The older man stared at her. His eyes were the same gray as the professor's. It was so bizarre. Then dropping his head to his pillow, he flicked his hand at them. "Take her away, Ian. She's yours."

Carrie ducked the young man's grasp as he reached for her with a nasty grin.

"I must be dreaming. You're all crazy!"

Ian chuckled as he caught hold of her shirt. "Aye, I'll make you think you're dreaming, wench. The earl of Wyldnell said you were to be mine."

"Nay. He's wrong. She's mine."

Carrie recognized that dangerous voice. She pulled free from the Ian's hold, ripping the hem of her top in the process. As she looked toward the door for escape, the room began to fill with men. More costumes. Tunics of various shades. Armor, some tarnished and some polished. Amidst the men, she found the one who'd spoken, utterly out of place among the costumes in his slacks and modern dress shirt.

"Matthias," the older man rasped from the bed. "You're alive?"

"Aye, Giles. I've come back."

One of the new arrivals spoke to the sick man. "The hunters found Sir Matthias on the hill and escorted him through the gates. I hope we were not amiss, my lord."

"Nay," he croaked.

"I see you have found my bride, as well," the professor added curtly.

His bride? What was he thinking? Had he totally lost his mind from the bump to his head?

"Brother, I did not know. I mean her no harm. Is it really you?"

"Aye."

Carrie watched as Matthias's eyes took in the condition of the older man, as if seeing him for the first time. Then his gaze found her. He extended an open hand.

"Come," he ordered.

In her present company and situation, Carrie didn't hesitate for a moment to follow his command. She recognized the seriousness in his steel gray eyes and quickly moved to his side. This time she was glad to see him and was thankful to feel his larger hand enveloping her own.

His chest rose and fell in deep breaths. How he'd managed to find her so soon, she couldn't fathom.

She searched his face at close range and was relieved to see he looked better than he had back at the stones. His eyes gave her no sign of compassion, however—just a dark emotion. Somehing she was sure she didn't want to know. That look was the only thing keeping her from throwing her grateful arms around him.

Did he think she'd abandoned him on the hill? She'd better explain.

"Professor, I left you to get help. You were rambling nonsense. Then these people," Carrie sent a heated glare at the strange men, "no one here seems to want to listen to me."

Matthias raised a silencing finger. "I told you, don't speak. I know these people." He leveled a dark look over her head at the older man, who coughed with new violence. Half to himself, Matthias mumbled, "Giles is my brother."

"Matthias, by the rood," the invalid choked, "I have much to talk to you about. It's been nearly ten years. You must stay here tonight. I cannot-cannot talk now."

Whatever rift lay between the two brothers, she could see lines of concern on her companion's face.

"The tower is still yours," Giles sputtered, face constricted.

The curious onlookers parted, allowing them an exit. Carrie clung to Matthias's hand as if it were a lifeline while he led her out. Although she tried to avoid looking at Ian, she saw the malicious glare he shot her as they passed.

The castle was so authentic, from its earthy odors to its burning torches in the walls and the dirty rushes on the floor. With her gaze still trained on the floor, she caught the movement of a small brown creature darting over the straw in their path. A *rat*?

Downstairs, Matthias paused to talk in hushed

tones to a woman who seemed to know him. He asked for another woman by the name "Edwina" to be sent to his tower.

Outside in the bailey, Carrie found it hard to keep up with the professor. He was practically pulling her arm out of its socket in his haste. His limp noticeable but not slowing him down. He seemed fueled by anger, channeling strength into his limbs. His dark hair fluttered behind him, mouth set in a stern line.

Carrie asked, "Where are we going?"

"To my tower. I'll explain everything to you there."

"Good. These people are all crazy. Your brother, everyone. I think they were really going to hurt me. These guys take their jobs just a little too seriously here."

A shudder racked her body.

"You should've listened to me."

His calmness chilled her. Why didn't he seem ruffled by this turn of events?

Carrie halted, taking in the looks of the castle again. Something was terribly wrong. So many people with such bad hygiene—

Terror climbed in her throat. *What year is it?*

It couldn't be possible.

Wherever Thorne was taking her, it definitely wasn't to the tower she'd been in the night before. Was he lying again? Or...

No!

It was too much...too much. Maybe he was just as crazy as the guys in the costumes.

She pulled free from him. "Look, I think I've suffered long enough. I'm sorry I trespassed on your property. You're going to be all right, so I'll go home now."

Hot tears pricked her eyes.

"Miss Greer. Caroline," he said more softly. "You

cannot."

"Like hell I can't!" She was going to be sick.

His somber demeanor frightened her more than anything else that day. She backed away from him and dashed for the gate.

No one attempted to stop her as she dodged gawking men, women, and animals. Tears dripped down her cheeks as she ran through the gatehouse and out the open portcullis. She had no idea which way the road was and where she parked her bicycle, but she had to put distance between her and the madness behind.

Chapter Four

Matthias dismounted the horse, a restless black destrier he'd taken without preamble from his brother's stables, and walked the several yards distance between him and Carrie. She finally stopped running in a meadow. She must've run in circles in her panic, and he allowed her that time. He'd done the same thing when he'd first passed through the stones.

The woman lay curled up in a small huddle among the tall wildflowers. Matching her blouse, the columbines nearly camouflaged her, but her golden hair was a bright beacon giving away her hiding place. A warm shade of honey, her hair was different than he recalled from the day they'd met. Maybe he hadn't really noticed. He was glad to see she hadn't brought that foul hat along to cover it up.

Stopping above her, Matthias could hear her weeping softly, her face buried in her knees. His stomach squeezed at the sound.

Damn! He'd known it would come to this. He could only hope she was a stronger girl than she looked. Alas, he had little faith in that. Her whole constitution was fragile. Her illness and her body's inability to endure medication added up to her being weak. How long would she survive the Middle Ages? Weeks? Days?

Matthias conceded to himself that Carrie was bright, because she'd tricked him into revealing the whereabouts of the moon plants. And she'd actually located them in the dark. He hated he'd been unable to keep her from the Druid ring. He knew the danger, and he failed miserably at protecting its secret.

After all these years, the stupid stones finally worked. He'd always had mixed feelings about returning, but Carrie Greer took care of all his indecision when she dragged him back with her.

If only he'd promised to retrieve the herbs for her, this whole situation could've been avoided.

When he first clamped eyes on her in his brother's solar, relief flooded him. It was a mighty weight off his conscience to see her alive and unharmed. Damnable woman! 'Twas a vexing problem he faced now. He ought to strangle her for all the trouble she'd created, but he vowed long ago to never raise a hand to a woman again.

"Carrie," he said sternly over her sobs. "I'm taking you to my home now."

She sniffled and looked up at him through sorrowful violet blue eyes. She tried to speak with trembling lips, but nothing came out.

"Are you hurt?"

She shook her head. With an outstretched arm, she pointed to nothing in particular. She finally rasped, "I parked a bicycle there. By a fence. By the *road*!"

Matthias squatted down beside her. The field was empty now.

"I know, Carrie." He hadn't called a woman by her first name in a number of years, but somehow uttering her nickname seemed to ease the tension within him. Carrie, spelled C-a-r-r-i-e, reminded him of the Welsh name of a different spelling.

"It was there, the road. I'm certain. We're not in the twenty-first century, are we?" Her haunted eyes drifted toward the castle.

He shook his head, reading the unspoken thought on her mind. Neither of them wanted to return to Wyldnell. "We have to stay there. There's no other safe place nearby. I've given you my name. That should protect you for now, but I'll try not to leave you unnecessarily until we can go back."

"When will that be?" Hope brightened her eyes.

Matthias stood to get the horse. "We can try tonight, but I believe it may take longer than that."

When he went back to her, he saw she'd made no move to get up. He needed to get her to his quarters and away from the prying eyes of the castle's residents. She needed rest, and they both needed new clothes. There were more dangers for her than Ian, he feared. At least she would have his help. He'd had no one to help him when he'd gone ahead in time. Carrie would have to learn to heed his orders and stay quiet. Jesu, what a trial he faced now.

Matthias wrapped his arms around her and carried her to his horse where he placed her sidesaddle. She made no protest as he mounted behind her, and she clung to him like a child.

Inside the castle's walls, she was able to walk when he set her on her feet. He tossed the horse's reins to a stableman and guided her to his tower.

As soon as he closed the door of his solar, Carrie sank on the canopied bed. Her eyes were glazed and listless. He knew she was considering all that had happened. All she had lost. But she did not yet know the worst of it.

Watching her forced an uneasy feeling in his gut so Matthias distracted himself, surveying his quarters. He hadn't expected to be welcomed by his brother—unless it was at the end of a blade to his heart. Finding he still had a room was both a surprise and relief. Sans the twenty-first century luxuries, the room was as he remembered it, except for the walls, which bore a new coat of whitewash. A desultory check up the stairs revealed his loft and view of the bailey were much the same, also.

Blessed be. Even his possessions remained—his best broadsword from the wars, his dagger, his surcoats, some tunics, braies, and his mail. With each item he laid hands on, a memory washed over him. More important, they were all possessions he may need in the coming days, months, or years.

Opening a coffer at the foot of his bed, he discovered the remnants of his favorite hobby. Pieces of wood, in different sizes and grains, cut in rectangular blocks, awaited his consideration. The familiar forest scent still lingered on the blocks, wafting up to him as he took a deep breath. As a young man, his talent had once been to look at a piece of wood, see a form to be made within, and to use his skill with a knife blade to make it so. The mantel above his hearth bore half a dozen of his wooden sculptures. The coffer contained one he had left unfinished.

The new century had given him other interests, so he'd quit carving. His new life kept him too busy for hobbies. Well, actually, work and the renovation of Wyldnell were his life. There wasn't room for anything else, and he preferred it that way. Matthias's gaze was drawn back to Carrie.

Her purse was clutched in her hands in a white-knuckle grip. It was her only link to her world, along with whatever meager possessions it contained. He knew exactly how she felt. He'd been unable to part with any of the articles he'd come through the portal with. They adorned the walls of his office and flat in Cardiff, always reminding him of the man he'd once been.

A knock sounded at the door, causing Carrie to jump. Matthias waved a reassuring hand at her and opened the door. A serving woman cowered in the hall. Eyes on the floor, she handed him a jug of wine and two goblets before disappearing down the hall. Matthias poured one glass and set the other on the table along with the jug.

****

Carrie cleared her throat.

Her hands trembled as she rubbed her face. "I'm the only person here who doesn't know what's going on, aren't I?"

The professor's back was to her. His broad shoulders made a good target for the rush of anxious thoughts. She babbled, "I think I've either gone mad or...we've just traveled through time. That fact doesn't seem to surprise you at all, so I'm beginning to think you've done this before. Have you?"

Turning, he didn't answer. His stare centered on the drink in his hand as he casually sloshed the liquid in a circle.

"Oh, for Pete's sake, why would I ask *you*? So far since I've met you, you've only lied to me." Despair engulfed her.

"I did what I thought was necessary. Drink this, and I'll tell you everything you want to know."

He thrust the drink at her.

Carrie frowned. How could she drink anything here? Nothing seemed real, and everything seemed threatening. The horsemen. His brother. Vermin. Strange beverages. Him. What could she trust when she couldn't trust her own eyes?

"It's harmless as long as you drink it in moderation. It's not the purest, but it's not contaminated, either. You're going to want it when I tell you what you need to know."

His eyes watched her steadily. Of everything else he'd told her, Carrie could see he believed this was the gospel truth.

She preferred not to drink. The possibility of a seizure always loomed. Now, stranded in this situation with Matthias, she didn't want him to witness one of her attacks. If he saw the spectacle she made of herself, he wouldn't want anything else to do with her. She couldn't afford losing his help now and from her experience with men, he would abandon her lickety-split during a grand mal. Her stomach churned.

But his expression brooked no protests. He still held the wine in his extended hand. She didn't know how to refuse without explaining why. It was hopeless.

At least she'd been taking her meds regularly. Maybe, just this once, it would be okay. Lifting her shaking arms in a monumental effort, Carrie took the cup from him. She preferred avoiding his hostility, not wanting another confrontation. Not now. She raised the drink to her dry lips.

"Wait!" Matthias stilled her arm with his hand. "I must warn you; this isn't the stuff you're used to. It comes from Bordeaux. The grapes are distilled for higher alcohol content, and then the sediment is...well, it isn't pleasant. Try to drink it quickly. I recommend tossing it back."

Carrie slid him a dry look. "Can I toss it *at you?*"

"I'd rather you drank it."

She sniffed the drink. It smelled sweet and spicy. If aroma accounted for anything, she just might like it. She took a tentative sip and rolled her tongue in the liquid.

"Paw!" The wine spewed out of her mouth and across the fresh rushes of the floor. "Ugh. Where did you say this came from?" She swiped the back of her hand across her mouth, trying to wipe every trace of the offensive brew away. "I usually don't consume alcohol because of my doctor's orders, but a lot of my customers make their own beer and wine. I've tasted some of them, and some are awful. But this isn't suitable for consumption."

Matthias's lips twitched before he visibly checked his humor. "Trust me, Miss Greer, *this* won't hurt you. I grew up on this wine as a lad. It's highly flammable, so don't drink it near a flame, but it's fine to drink. Try again and this time, swallow."

She took another quick sip of the rancid wine and then another.

Matthias eyed the bed and then, frowning, sat on a bench at the nearby table. Bracing his elbows on his bent knees, he began the explanations he'd promised her.

"I've never shared with anyone what I'm about to tell you." He shifted uncomfortably on the bench. "I've been through everything you're going through now."

As she listened, his voice softened, a comforting sound like a shallow brook over pebbles. "We made a trip through a very unpredictable portal. I know. I was born here, in the year 1254. I left this life in my nineteenth year, which was nine years ago. The year I entered the stone circle and discovered the abyss was 1273. After going through the henge, I wandered the property for days. I thought every stranger I met that next day had gone mad. No one knew my name or my family—and we were well known in the kingdom." He made a sweeping gesture toward the window, encompassing the land and everything else outside his family would've claimed. "I'd never before been treated with such insolence as I received that day. Then I wandered out on the A469 and nearly got my stupid ass run over by an automobile. Thereafter, I thought I was the one who'd gone mad."

"The 'abyss,'" Carrie broke in. Her heart began to drum as her recollection of the night before became clearer. "I remember that. I remember you grabbing me and falling. It felt as if we'd fallen down a long well. There were roots and moisture...echoes, but no light at all. I don't remember seeing a well before the fall."

Matthias flexed his hands, staring at them

thoughtfully. "That's because it wasn't there. We didn't fall down. We fell back. This morning when I awoke, the moon plants were gone. Do you remember seeing them in the daylight?"

Carrie gasped. They *were* gone. She hadn't noticed before, but they hadn't been inside the ring that morning.

"I fear if we return tonight, we'll find not one trace of the abyss. The portal opens only briefly and then closes."

"No, that can't be. It's still there, surely." She took a deep drink of her wine.

"Carrie," Matthias's gray eyes locked on hers, "I've been trying to get back all these years. I've tried too many times to count."

Carrie dropped her stare to her shoes, reminded of the archeology student's words when he'd told her how important Wyldnell was to Professor Thorne. She also recalled the professor's possessiveness when she'd asked to visit the property.

If it took him nine years for the portal to open, how long would she have to wait to go back? She caught herself biting her lip nervously.

She was aware of him standing over her, pouring more wine into her goblet.

He continued, "I don't know the answer to the portal. It's a mystery to me. I may never know why I came to your time."

He explained to her about falling off his horse on May Eve and about picking the strange plant in the moonlight. Taking the pitcher away, he paced as he spoke. "I've wanted to ask other people in the Marches if anyone else had heard of strange happenings at the henge. There could be others like me who've passed through—Druids, drovers, hunters, shepherds, hikers, but how could I trust anyone with what I'd experienced? It was preposterous. Madmen in my century are treated horrendously, and I didn't want to make the mistake of being branded one in your century, either."

He stilled long enough to give her a serious look.

Between sips, Carrie said, "I don't understand how you functioned in our time. How come no one realized you were in the wrong century? You must've stood out like a sore thumb."

His lips twisted mockingly. "I'm sure I did. Enough so that I was picked up by a constable in Gwent. I had no ID and could tell the authorities nothing that made any sense, so they assumed I had amnesia and promptly had me placed in a facility."

He stared at his feet, but his gaze was a million miles away. She looked at him, feeling as though she had never really seen him at all before now. The scar, the limp, his surliness—what would they have thought about this man found wandering alone? They might've surmised he was the victim of a mugging or some other worse crime. That he lost his memory in his struggle—and lost his mind, also. Hadn't she assumed the same?

She touched her neck, staring up at his marking. "I take it that wasn't from a switchblade?" She sucked in a breath. "I'm sorry. That was rude."

He shrugged. "War wound. I was in Acre with Prince Edward. The Crusades. Your modern doctors weren't sure what to make of me. I'll wager I was one of the strangest cases they'd ever seen."

Carrie's stomach wrenched with empathy. Words rushed out of her mouth before she could stop them, "How-how on earth did you cope? How on earth did you turn out so well?"

Matthias blinked, and Carrie felt a flush from the wine in her cheeks.

"You mean, how did I get released from the mental hospital and become a college professor?" His chin lifted slightly as he made the distinction.

Carrie forced a smile and nodded.

"I've been told that I am an excellent liar."

At least he was honest about that.

His voice sounded detached. "After two years in the facility, I realized my best hope of freedom was to use what knowledge I possessed. I'd been found carrying several antiquities, so I told my doctors I must be a student of medieval history. After many interviews and no success at finding my true identity, they had to believe me. I was released to find my own way in your society, which I did."

"It must've been awfully lonely for you to have been stuck there, so far from home," Carrie searched his face for emotion.

Matthias stared down at her. His gaze churned, darkening into stormy accusation. "No, not 'stuck' there. Until you disobeyed me, I was very happy and safe living in modern Cardiff. I had a bloody good life!"

Obviously, he'd convinced himself that was true, and he was laying all blame at her feet. Guilt rubbed her raw inside, but her face went hot with pure anger. It wasn't as if she was having a blast being seven hundred years from home.

She'd left behind a loving mother and grandmother, but what had Matthias left? Maybe he'd experienced a loss, too. Had there been a woman?

Whatever he found so great about the twenty-first century, it apparently meant more to him than his brother and his home.

So, why had he even bothered to try to come back? He scowled down at her with such fierceness that she chose not to pursue the answer. Instead, she crossed her arms over her chest, shielding herself.

"Look, I never knew this would happen. It was an accident. I want to go back just as much as you do."

"Good." He ground the word out.

"This all could've been avoided if you'd just been honest. You could've warned me before I went through the circle." She regretted the words as soon as she said them.

His dark brows arched dubiously.

How could he have told her? There was no way she would've believed it.

Why couldn't she have a more compassionate person to come here with, though?

"We're in this together now," she leveled at him, "and I need you to be civil and honest with me. We can't lie to each other. We may be here until next Beltane, for Pete's sake. That's a whole year."

She tried to stand, rubbing her blurring eyes. The room was spinning gently.

Her anger at him disintegrated under a rising wave of fearful thoughts. She mumbled, "A whole year. Oh, my mother is going to find out I didn't check out of my hotel. She'll think I've been abducted. My family will go nuts with worry. And— I'll run out of medicine soon. I never even got the moon plants. Oh, God!"

She dropped back to the bed, covering her face so Matthias wouldn't see more of her tears and pain. The wine burned in her belly, but it hadn't yet dulled her worries and sorrow.

Carrie's mind spun to other hopeless scenarios of her new plight. People of the Middle Ages sometimes thought seizures were the work of the Devil, didn't they? Surely, he realized that, too. Could she be burned at the stake? Her head swam with dire visions of chanting villagers with pitchforks.

The ropes beneath the bed sagged under his weight as he sat beside her.

"'Tis my penance, of course. Only I could bring with me the worst possible woman for the Middle

Ages."

Carrie looked at him from between her fingers. Was he serious?

Matthias wasn't looking at her but playing with a block of wood he'd picked up. A slight smile curved on his lips, making him almost boyish beneath the shadow of his chin stubble.

"You're laughing at me?" she asked, incredulous.

"Nay. 'Tis true. You're nothing but trouble."

His voice was gruff, but she detected a change in his manner. "No more lies, you said, and remember, I have no sense of humor." With that, he took the goblet from her hand and stood. "Now let me show you our garderobe, so you can see just how lucky you've been to have a modern lavatory all your life."

Carrie allowed him to help her up and went with him, thankful for his attempt at truce.

****

A knock on the door woke Carrie from her nap. Sitting up, she realized she'd fallen asleep on Matthias's canopied bed. She wasn't in the habit of taking naps during the day, but she supposed the wine she'd drunk made her drowsy.

Matthias rose from where he sat at the table. He'd changed clothes, she noted. Now a white tunic and a deep blue surcoat adorned his sensual body. He looked as though he'd just stepped right out of an illustrated story of *King Arthur and the Knights of the Round Table.* But no artists' renderings of Lancelot had anything on the real deal. Large and powerful, thick-shouldered and lean, Matthias filled out the clothing like a Celtic warrior, not a dreamy poetic character from literature.

As he walked, she admired his muscular legs, wrapped in tight, slate-colored leggings, exposing the strong curves of his calves. Her lips pursed in appreciation, but it wasn't right to feed her attraction to him. She jerked her gaze up primly.

How long would they have to share a room, and where would they change clothes when they were both awake? Her face grew hot.

Matthias opened the door to another serving woman.

"Milord?" her deep voice asked skeptically.

"Edwina." Throwing the door wide open, he opened his arms and embraced her round form in a hug. "My God, I cannot believe you could bear my brother's company this long."

Carrie watched the older woman's eyes widen and a smile broaden on her face. The white wimple she wore made her face look a little like a ripe apple. Her fingers squeezed up and down his shoulders as if she were judging fruit at market.

"Math? My Math? 'Tis you!" She began to sniffle, so Matthias set her back from his embrace.

He held her at arm's length, as they both looked each other over. "Did I hurt you, Wina?"

"Oh, no. It's just so good to see you again, my lord. We all thought you'd died. When you sent Mary to fetch me, she told me 'twas you who sent her. I fear I slapped the poor girl."

She put a hand on her own rosy cheek, looking remorseful.

"I could hardly believe...and now you're a grown man. When your brother first sent you away, I thought you'd be back in a few months or mayhap a year." Her gaze swept him again with a new seriousness. "Your brother sent men out to look for you on your land in the north. Then to England and Scotland. They even went to the king, but he didn't know where you were. Oh, Math, how we missed you."

Her voice trailed away. The professor rubbed the back of his neck, seemingly silenced by the emotions of his visitor.

Her voice softened, "Giles has been ill for

months now. It's been such a terrible time without you."

He touched her shoulder. "I should've taken you with me, Edwina, but Giles would've had my head."

"Look at you," she grinned up at him. "You're taller than your brother and broader, too. Have you been wielding a sword where you have been?"

"Some in practice, but not against anyone as good as our men. I'll need to train anew to get back in fighting shape. I vow I'm strong enough to rescue you, though, Wina."

Edwina chuckled affectionately and punched his arm. "Well, Math, I hear you have taken a bride."

Matthias grabbed a large sack Edwina had left in the hall and deposited it near the bed. Carrie stood and greeted her, allowing the older woman time to look her fill.

The deception sickened her. How could she pretend to be Matthias's bride in his own household? But she remembered what he'd said: it was the only way to keep her safe. Being alone and single in the Middle Ages didn't sound safe to her especially with men like Ian around.

"What's your lady's name?" Edwina asked Matthias as she frowned over Carrie's modern clothing.

"Carrie Greer," she told her.

"My lady," she nodded in return. "Where are you from?"

"South—"

"Coast," Matthias interrupted. "The south coast of England. Very far away."

Edwina frowned. "Greer—the name is Welsh. Her sire was Welsh?"

Matthias made a slight grunt in answer.

"My lord will not like that, Math, and you know it. Neither will King Edward, if he does not know already."

Carrie had researched her father's surname once and learned that it was a corruption of Gregor, a Scottish name, probably changed by some careless bookkeeper on a ship of immigrants bound for America, but there was no way to explain any of that to a woman who'd never heard of America.

Carrie recalled that the Welsh and English had been at war in medieval times. She wondered what state the country was in politically. Apparently, Matthias and his brother were allied with King Edward I of England.

"Nay, I haven't told the king I'm back yet either. Leave my business to me, Wina. Now did you bring what I asked for?"

"Aye. Some clothing for your lady-wife and a sack. Food is on its way. Tomorrow night Lord Wyldnell says there will be a grand feast to welcome you and your lady-wife home."

"Fine." Matthias looked at Carrie and told her firmly, "I want you to dress in the clothes Edwina brought and give your old clothes to her. Then I want you to empty your purse of anything you need to keep and put it along with your old clothes in the sack and let Edwina burn them. Do not leave this room, Carrie. Is that understood?"

Nodding, she squelched the remorse she felt at losing her only good clothes, but she knew she'd be thought a witch if they examined her modern clothing with its elastic and zipper.

"Where are you going?" Carrie stopped him as he opened the door.

A shot of fear ran through her.

For a moment, Carrie thought he looked as though he'd rather not tell her. Finally, he said, "To speak with an old friend—if he still considers me as such—and inquire after Giles and the garrison."

When he left, Carrie wished she'd asked him when he'd be back. Ironically, she found herself

61

dependent upon a man who made her feel completely ill at ease.

Edwina set about pulling clothing from the bag she'd brought. The things women wore here were very different from what she was familiar with in her own time. The gowns chosen had belonged to the earl's late wife, Isabelle, according to Edwina, who told her she was about the same size. Edwina apologized for the age of the gowns, promising that better fabrics would be found and purchased, befitting a noblewoman such as herself. Carrie flushed with shame.

"These will be fine, but I hope the earl won't mind me using them. I, uh, didn't have time to pack my own things," she lied.

"No matter. My lord's estate is large. Since Giles has taken no new wife these past nine years and he has no heir, I'm very pleased Math has brought a lady to the house."

"I don't mean to be a burden."

"Nay! These hands of mine will be relieved to have some help with the sewing, my lady." She chuckled happily.

"Oh, dear. I'm sorry. I'm afraid I won't be much help with that, Edwina. I haven't learned to sew yet, but I'd be willing to try."

"You cannot sew?" Edwina dropped the gown she was holding and gaped at Carrie. "'Tis a shame they don't teach ladies to sew in Southern England. I'll wager you can sing like an angel to entertain us, as they do in King Edward's court, though."

Carrie slowly shook her head. Her singing voice earned nothing but scowls on Sunday morning in church.

"Play an instrument?"

"Sorry. I can't do that either." She had learned to play "Michael Row the Boat Ashore" on an electric keyboard once, but there was no point in trying to claim that talent now.

"Oh." The older woman sighed, and the corners of her lips drooped. "No matter, my lady." Edwina waved a hand and turned her attention to the task of straightening the bed.

To be on the receiving end of such disappointment cut Carrie to the quick. She'd been a people-pleaser all her life. Running the health food store, cooking and gardening for her mother and grandmother and their friends, volunteering at one of Charleston's homeless shelters—as she thought about it, there were lots of constructive things she did back home. None of which would be useful here. She hated to disappoint Edwina, and honestly, she hated to disappoint Matthias, as well.

He'd already shown his disapproval of her. Apparently, he expected her to cower in the bedchamber while they were stranded there. She longed to prove her independence. To prove the professor wrong.

"Wait. I can cook. Yes, I could help out in the kitchen. I'm sure I'd be useful there." Carrie smiled with relief.

"Oh no, milady. Not the kitchens. Cook wouldn't allow it, and I'm certain Matthias wouldn't either. That's no place for a lady." She clucked her tongue and helped Carrie off with her old dress.

"I don't mind. Really. I'm great with herbs. Didn't I see a garden outside?" Carrie stepped out of her dress.

"By the kitchen, milady, with all manner of vegetables, flowers, and a grand fish pond," she said, eying Carrie's strange undergarments. Thankfully, she said nothing about them. "Cook wouldn't expect you to labor there. Don't trouble yourself. We'll begin work on your sewing tomorrow."

Disheartened, Carrie removed the remnants of her old clothes and put on the new. Her breasts tingled against the fabric; made sensitive from the bra she'd worn all day and night. That was one modern contraption she wouldn't miss.

Presently, her stomach started to growl and no matter how strange the food would likely be she'd be glad to eat. Edwina excused herself, taking the things to be burned, and melted away to the kitchen.

Carrie scanned the room, trying to decide what exactly to do with her time with no TV, no books, and no Internet. A knock came from outside. She smelled it before she even opened the door. Food.

Chapter Five

Matthias made his way through the familiar rooms of Wyldnell. Not much had changed in nine years. The only thing that surprised him in coming home was how he felt upon seeing the place where he'd grown up. His heart raced as he turned each corner, knowing exactly what furnishings he would see: handmade tapestries, fine-crafted chairs, and bristling fires in the spit.

Truly, the keep flourished with life, and the kitchen was no exception. Children played in a mock sword fight and dodged Cook as he chased after a fleeing squire who'd just stolen a fruit pie. How many treats had he stolen while away squiring at Chepstow Castle? Following in the footsteps of the knights always worked up an appetite for a youth.

He breathed deeply the aroma of the roasting bird in the spit and hoped it was his dinner. By God, he was almost weak with hunger.

The spit boys regarded him with curiosity. The men of the kitchen were too new to know him. Probably Welsh, as were most of Giles's servants. Then, spying the laundress, a woman he recognized and nearer his own age, he received a contemptuous frown. Scorn. The usual greeting from all who remembered him thus far.

All except his devoted wet-nurse Edwina and...oddly enough—Giles.

The rest of the castle's residents who remembered the earl's deposed brother clearly shunned him, like a demon in their midst.

The dark shadow he'd cast on Wyldnell

stretched through the years. His throat tightened. Would the chilly reception carry over to his "bride?"

Outside, Matthias set off in the direction of the lists and was very nearly barreled over by a towering guard.

"Matthias! Do my eyes deceive me? Or has the dragon that ate you spat you back to us?" Mouth spreading in a grin, the redheaded man grabbed his arm and slapped him on the back.

"Aye, Rannulf Fitz George, dragons never had a taste for me."

The big, ruddy captain of the guard threw back his head and laughed until tears formed at the corners of his eyes. Matthias had hoped his best friend wouldn't have forgotten him. Nor condemned him. And thank God, he appeared to have not. His friend's warm smile eased the tightness in his chest.

"Jesu! Bless my eyes. I heard the lads say you were back, but I ne'er believed it. Where have you been?"

"Worlds away from here."

"And you're back to stay?" He raised two arching, copper eyebrows.

"No." Matthias had no honest answer for that question. "I'm not sure how long I'll be here. You know how Giles and I parted."

Rannulf's smile fell. "I'll warn you, Math, no one here is allowed to speak of that night. The earl has forbidden it."

His chest tightened anew. He had no intention of reliving the hell of that long-ago night either.

"Walk with me," Rannulf glanced over his shoulder for those who might overhear.

"I know I tread on ice by coming here, Rannulf."

He shook his head. "There's more to consider now than when you left. Your brother is dying, Math."

The captain's words hit him like a physical blow,

66

yet he knew it was true.

"Ian thinks Maud is killing Giles with her spells. I do not know. The illness is sporadic and slow. It's not the ague. There's no fever. Just sickness and weakness."

"My being here won't make it any easier on him," Matthias muttered, half to himself.

"Don't bend your mind to that, Math. I know your brother wants to reconcile with you. Have you spoken with him?"

"No more than a few words."

The captain watched him too closely, making him uncomfortable.

"You should resolve matters with him, Math. Lady Isabelle passed away with a fever not long after you left. Your brother has changed since his wife's death in many ways."

Matthias felt sympathy for his brother and relief for himself. He wouldn't have to worry about running into Isabelle somewhere in the castle. That would simply be unbearable. But he wouldn't have wished her dead. Ever. Feeling wretched and ashamed, bile rose in his throat at his selfish thoughts.

A stableman passed, leading two horses, and they fell into an uncomfortable silence until he was out of hearing range.

"I'm not alone. There's a woman."

"A wench? You've brought a wench under your brother's roof?" Rannulf's grin returned, and he lowered his voice conspiratorially, "Are you trying to kill your poor brother? You know how he disapproves of cavorting, and the abbot is always underfoot, visiting him."

"Nay. It's not like that this time. I've brought a bride. I'm only staying here until we can settle somewhere else."

Matthias relished in his own quick-thinking

that morning. His deception had saved both he and Carrie from being thrown out by Giles.

"A bride! That's a relief, Math. So...where are you hiding the poor luckless creature?"

"My tower for now. Carrie experienced a rough welcome from your loutish son, Ian."

"God's wounds!" Rannulf hung his head wearily. "It's Ursula's doing. My wife should've let me send him away to earn his spurs elsewhere. Chepstow, maybe. He's had too much idleness here."

Matthias remembered the boy years ago, trailing after his father. His copper hair cropped too close, it stuck out all over his head like a young orangutan. Ian tried his best to be more helpful than the squires, but at seven or eight, he was in the way more oft than not.

"I trow it's my fault, too." Rannulf sighed. "I'm sure you remember how I doted on him after Ursula died. He's had his run of Wyldnell, and your brother only encourages his behavior. Giles has taken him under his wing, and now my boy thinks *he* is commander of the garrison, not his father."

"I'm sorry, Rannulf."

His eyes grew large. "Pray tell me, Ian didn't hurt your lady. If he did—"

Matthias shook his head. "I arrived in time to stop him, but you would do well to stamp that behavior, Rannulf. As for Carrie, she's unaccustomed to our ways here in the Marches. She was a little shaken, so I left her to rest awhile."

"A foreigner? God bless her. Come, you have my permission to give Ian a lesson in chivalry."

Rannulf turned, intending to draw him to the lists, but Matthias stood stock-still.

"We both know I should not be the one to give that lesson."

The captain dropped his gaze.

Heavy-hearted, Matthias promised to speak

with Rannulf again later, then left to join his "bride" for a meal he no longer had an appetite for.

****

Carrie sat, impatient, by the table. Her family had always held with the traditions of Southern hospitality—no one ate until everyone was seated for dinner. Drat, if she had to wait on Matthias any longer...

Dishes of delicious smelling meat, onions, and leeks set before her, tempting her patience to the max. The rude man probably wouldn't have waited for her. A saint wouldn't have waited as long as she had. Now the food was lukewarm; she knew because she'd stuck the tip of her finger tentatively into one meat pie at least fifteen minutes earlier. The other main dish appeared to be a single roasted fowl of some sort.

She poured them each a cup of the nasty wine she'd had earlier and chose the roasted bird for herself. Company or not, she was here and Matthias was late. His choice of food was therefore null and void. Her stomach's complaints couldn't be ignored anymore. After dipping her fingers in a bowl of water provided for that purpose, she stabbed the bird with her knife and dropped it on her plate.

The sound of footsteps outside stopped her before she could take a bite. The door opened this time without the benefit of a warning.

Her first thought upon seeing Matthias was to greet him with a jibe about being late. She'd rehearsed a teasing response about keeping his wife waiting, but the words died on her tongue before she could get them out. His expression sent a chill through her.

Had his meeting been a bad one? He'd said he was going to find out about his brother. The news must not have been good, judging by his demeanor. Rather than press him, she would wait until he was ready to talk.

Face grim, he settled on the bench across the table from her. He made no move to eat or drink, gray eyes staring vacantly at the meal.

Carrie offered him the wine she'd poured.

"Nay," he grunted.

He took the cup from her and poured his wine into her half-full cup. He poured himself a cup of water from the pitcher instead.

The cloudy well water didn't look appealing to Carrie. She wrinkled her nose.

"I see how you are, Matthias. The wine is all right for me, but you don't drink it yourself, do you?" she chided.

He narrowed his eyes at her. "I drink but rarely. One of us should keep our wits about us."

He drained his water quickly and stared at the food anew.

"It's not that bad, really," Carrie said between bites of bird. "Except it's very bland. I guess I shouldn't expect a port wine marinade here, though. Try the meat pie. Tell me how it tastes."

Matthias lifted his spoon to the pie and tapped at its edges.

"Cook's pies were always too spicy."

Carrie sighed. There was no pleasing the man. "You know, you should be starving. I am. We both need to rebuild our strength."

She bit into a piece of bread and spit it back out in her napkin. Ewww. Forget table etiquette. The grit made her teeth hurt. Matthias hadn't seemed to notice her reaction.

She studied the professor's face. His dark hair fell over his forehead, hiding the wound from the fall.

"How's your head, Matthias?"

"'Tis only a scratch and a bruise." His ancient Welsh accent had already begun to deepen, she noticed, surrounded by so many people speaking the language from his own time.

"You could've fooled me. It was a bad injury, and you were knocked senseless from it." She tried to peer into his eyes from where she sat, but the angle of his head prevented it. Her fingers tightened on her drink, disturbed by the thought of his head being rattled. "If you've lost your appetite, it could be nausea caused by a concussion. Have you had any vision problems or vomiting since we've been in the castle? Maybe we could ask the cook for some broth instead. Fluids would probably be better to keep down..."

"Shut your mouth. I'll eat, dammit!" He grabbed a leg off the bird in her plate and unceremoniously took a bite of it. "And I wasn't senseless."

Carrie smiled inwardly as he grumbled. It was an improvement over his silence. Since they were both famished, she let him finish eating with only a little pestering.

When most of the food was reduced to crumbs, Matthias went still again, staring moodily at the remains of the dinner.

"Well," Carrie decided to test the waters of conversation again, "I wish I'd brought a camera in my purse. I can hardly believe this is the same tower you renovated in the twenty-first century. I take back what I said about Wyldnell, you know. Your home is a magnificent place. I can understand you wanting to keep it to yourself."

The professor closed his eyes and lifted a hand to rub his brow. "Yes. All to myself. I live alone. It's quieter that way."

"I'm bothering you, aren't I?" Carrie sat back and crossed her arms, loving her small sadistic triumph over him. Annoying him seemed to sate her need for revenge after the long wait for supper. "If I'm bothering you, just tell me so."

They were going to drive each other crazy, so why bother being nice to the man?

"I have a headache, if you must know," he sighed beneath his hand. "And before you say it, I'm sure it has nothing to do with a concussion."

Of course not. At least his bad attitude wasn't her fault this time. But she didn't want to see anyone in pain. Headaches were within her realm of expertise. Perhaps she could steer him towards benevolence with a friendly gesture.

"There are two things we could do that'll make your headache go away."

This time, it was his turn to look at her from between his fingers. His suggestive glance made her toes curl in their medieval slippers. She laughed, "Not that, pervert!"

"Bloody hell, tell me you brought some ibuprofen in that purse of yours!" He straightened.

"Sorry, no. But I can make a really great painkiller with feverfew leaf and valerian. It works wonders on migraines. My customers ask for the recipe all the time."

"And the other option?"

"Not quite as long-lasting but it's effective, too."

Carrie moved the dishes and drinks aside, scooting her chair around the corner of the table, closer to Matthias. Bracing her elbows on the table, she took his hand from his forehead to hold it between her own. His lips parted in surprise, but he quickly schooled his features into an expressionless mask.

Her admiring gaze examined his fingers as she straightened them. Long and elegantly tapered, but roughened from years of exertion and training. Slowly turning his hand over, she stroked her fingertips in a swirling circle in the middle of his outstretched palm. Matthias watched her intently, making her feel more self-conscious than she'd ever felt before in doing the simple familiar procedure.

After several minutes, she began to gently massage his hand, kneading the muscled pads of his palm and thumb. Their heads nearly touched as she worked. His nearness distracted her in a most unwelcome way. She allowed her curious gaze to slowly lift from his hand to his whiskered jaw and across his lips, so near she need only lean forward a fraction to press her mouth to his. The unbidden thought jarred her. She lifted her eyes and found him watching her face now as well. She hoped her thoughts weren't transparent. She dropped her perusal and fixed her gaze firmly on her work.

The massage would work better if he was lying down, relaxed, but she couldn't ask him to do that in the intimate confines of his bedchamber. Instead, she kept rubbing his hand, the friction kindling heat on his skin, like her cheeks.

She thought she heard his breath catch.

"It doesn't work."

He withdrew his hand from hers abruptly with a scowl.

"You haven't given it enough time. It'll work. I..."

"No, it's not helping at all." Matthias pushed away from the table and stood. "Come. Let's go to the henge. We can ask Cook for your herbs later if we're still stuck here together."

Carrie tried to bury the sting of Matthias's words deep as she hurried to follow him out of the castle and down the path to the Druid ring. Rejection spread its familiar ache, and she fought back angry tears as she trailed him.

The stones looked different in the evening light. The colors of sunset painted them an odd greenish blue against the orange sky. They didn't seem at all magical without the swirling mist. With no bizarre cluster of yellow flowers in their midst, the stones seemed almost ordinary.

Just old and weary, as if they'd been left to languish on the land long after their better days. Days when the Druids gathered and performed arcane rituals between the weathered rocks. They'd no doubt seen times when noble kings were crowned in monolith circles and wars were waged on stone tables. Now nothing arcane or noble remained about the henge, but she hoped she was mistaken.

Matthias threw one frustrated glare at her as she stood unmoving within the ring, and then he trudged off on his own, walking inside the perimeter of circle. He moved clockwise, she noted and wondered why it mattered. When they'd gone through before, there'd been no pattern in their paths whatsoever. They'd simply entered the ring and vanished.

She didn't suppose it would do any good to point that out to him. He was clearly in no mood for common sense.

Her offer to help had been simply that, an offer—nothing for him to get upset about. It had taken all her nerve to hold his hand and draw so near him, with the attraction she felt for Matthias growing stronger. Obviously, he had no such idea. He couldn't wait to get back and be rid of her. But why? Was she so intolerable? Repulsive even to his touch? Had he any idea what kind of company *he* was? Did he even care? Just when she'd thought they were about to get along, he seemed to want nothing more than to be away from her.

His wasn't a personality that attracted friends. They were alike in that respect. She had trouble keeping friends and men who could tolerate her condition. When her girlfriends wanted to go out barhopping, what good was she? She couldn't drink. She couldn't drive, either, so she couldn't even be their designated driver. So, poor ol' Carrie sat at home with her Mom and her cat, Elvis.

She stared at Matthias's broad back as he briskly passed her. He hadn't told anyone about his experiences before her. So much to keep to one's self. No one to talk with about the good and the bad of his life. Matthias reacted with impatience to her humor. How very sad life would be without people to laugh with. Was she cursed now, like him, to live without friends, laughter, and love?

She would be glad to be back in her own time, in the company of people who weren't quarrelsome and rude. Making deliberate progress of her own within the inner circle of the stones, she tried to concentrate on what she'd left back in Charleston: her family, her cat, her store, and her garden. Her mother would soon be calling Scotland Yard demanding to know who was looking for her daughter and what efforts were being made in the search. Her assistant, Allison, was capable of handling the customers and ordering vitamins, tofu, gingko, green tea, and everything else indefinitely, but she doubted Allison would be very pleased about having to manage the inventory count next month without her help.

Yet, Carrie's thoughts kept returning to the irritating, stubborn medieval man doing doughnuts in the dirt and weeds just a few feet ahead as if he was being pursued by a she-devil. Everything he ought to care about was here—his own home and his brother. What was wrong with him? Moron!

And why had he lied? Her hand-massages *always* got rid of headaches.

Chapter Six

Matthias watched the sun rise over the river valley from his perch at the window. The serenity of the view lightened his mood and gave him a rare moment's peace. Despite its presence in the keep, Giles hadn't added glazed glass in the tower bedchambers, and Matthias was pleased his view was unobstructed. The sky began to brighten in the early morning dawn. A warm curtain of gleaming rays slowly filled the room, making its way toward the bed and the woman sleeping there.

Last night, they'd waited in the stone circle until late in the evening. Just as he'd expected—no ethereal mist, no mysteriously appearing yellow flowers in the moonlight, and no open portal. The past nine years seemed as unreal as a dream now, or would be if not for the troublesome woman he'd brought home with him.

Neither had spoken a word last night. Matthias spread a blanket and slept on the floor, leaving Carrie the bed.

He didn't know how long he'd been awake watching her sleep. Perhaps hours. Time that he should have used to think and figure what he needed to do.

Yes, every five minutes he was distracted by some movement of hers on the bed or some small sound she made in her sleep. The blasted woman looked content, sleeping like a cat curled in the sun. Her golden brown hair shone bright on her pillow, soaking up the rays of sunshine with her face turned away from the intense daylight. Was she warm enough, too warm? Should he make sure?

Jesu. He turned his head away in self-disgust. 'Twould be yet another excuse to get his hands on her. Ever since she'd caressed him with her soft touch, he'd been unable to divert his attention to anything else. What was he, a dog that needed petting? What did he care about her comfort? *He* was the one who'd slept on the floor.

"Morning."

He glanced back to see her watching him through squinted eyes. She smiled sleepily.

He grunted in return. His loins tightened at the sight of her body stretching under the cover.

"You look as though you're sorry you gave me the bed." She covered a yawn with her hand.

Matthias shrugged. "It couldn't be helped. If I'd asked for another room or another mattress, the household would've gossiped. My brother would've asked questions. If I were truly married, I'd be sleeping with my bride."

"I guess you're right. I'm still sorry."

Her eyelashes swept down over her cheeks where a shade of pink rose. Then she looked up, a smile on her lips.

"I guess we could take turns with the bed. I don't mind sleeping on the floor. It'll be like being eight years old again at a sleepover. Only, you probably won't want your hair braided, and we don't have any popcorn," she laughed in a pleasing, dulcet sound in the too-quiet room. "I can't just leave you on the floor all the time."

He rubbed a hand over his whisker-stubbled face.

Not even he would stoop so low as to allow a woman to sleep on the floor while he snoozed contentedly in bed. "The sleeping arrangements will stay the same," he announced flatly to end the discussion.

Sandra Jones

To this, Carrie merely sighed and stared at him with her lips pressed tightly together. By next Beltane, he would probably be hunched, decrepit, and broken, but her lovely body wouldn't have to suffer.

"Matthias." His name sounded tentative on her lips. "I've been wondering...what are you going to tell your brother about where you've been all this time?"

He groaned inwardly. This was the conversation he most dreaded having with Carrie.

He knew he ought to tell her why he left, and how things were between Giles and him, but he found he couldn't. It might make her fear him and that would only make their situation worse. He would tell her about his gruesome history later, when she'd grown to trust him.

Rubbing the back of his neck, he prepared to tell her what he felt necessary to end her questions, "The last time I saw my brother, we had an argument. He cursed me and told me to make my home elsewhere. I was leaving Wyldnell when I disappeared through the portal, so now I can hardly believe he's allowed us to stay here."

She angled her head slightly, watching him like a hawk. Her lips curved slightly as if she mocked him—or as if she saw something he couldn't.

"Blood is thicker than water," she commented solemnly.

He shook his head. "Not with us. It's out of his character to condone me. He was always unforgiving. Impatient with me. Our father died when I was eleven, and Giles has felt the need to press his dominion over me ever since. Our blood is our only bond, you see, so I dare not try his patience with tales of Druid magic and passages to faraway places."

She pushed up on her elbows. "If I had a brother or sister, I would've shared everything with them.

78

I've always regretted that I didn't have a sibling. Even someone to fight with. Didn't you miss him at all?"

"Our fights involved more than borrowed clothes and rankled nerves."

She shared a soft smile. "But you've had the most phenomenal experience in the world. I can't believe you don't feel the need to share it with him."

"So he can toss me out on my ear and curse me for listening to too many bardic tales? He'll not listen to a word I say. There's no point." He clenched his jaw against the tension invading his head.

"Surely your family feud can't be so bad after all these years. Maybe now that you've had time apart, the two of you can work things out."

"No, we *cannot* work things out!" he snapped.

Hot pressure surfaced in his chest. Hadn't he wanted to talk to Giles all these years? But now that it was possible, he wanted to run far away from his brother and this place. Centuries away wasn't far enough. The guilt would follow as it had before. He squeezed his hands into hard fists and watched the color drain from them.

"Matthias, he looks really, really sick. He might want to talk about the past. I can't help but think we might've come through time for a reason—both you and me. Maybe Fate wants you to make a truce. If he's dying—"

"You know nothing about it!" his voice echoed off the rafters.

Immediately, he wished he could take back the tone he'd used. Carrie turned her back to him. Before their conversation had turned to Giles, she'd looked so adorable with her sleep-tousled hair and perky attitude. Mute, he stared at her, searching his wits for the right thing to say to change the subject.

He could just say he was sorry for being an ass.

But the topic must be dropped, and he knew no

Sandra Jones

other way to thwart her than with his temper.

Leaving Wyldnell had been the best thing he could've done for his brother all those years ago. Now here he was again, underfoot, stirring up old ghosts, opening old wounds. He didn't want to see Giles. He didn't want to talk to him. What would he say? What would ever take back what he'd done that awful night?

After a tedious length of silence, he stood, defeated and unable to make the atmosphere of the room better. He dropped his arms at his sides.

"So much for being civil," she muttered.

He regarded her frame, taking in her small, rigid figure. She'd slept in the clothes she'd worn the day before, and it was his fault, because he hadn't given her any privacy. He would make up for it.

"You'll want to get dressed. I'm going to the lists to see if I can still wield a broadsword against real opponents. I'll send Edwina to keep you company."

"You mean I have to stay here?" Carrie faced him again, drawing the cover up under her chin. The corners of her pert mouth turned down in disappointment.

"I think that would be best, since the household hasn't been introduced to you yet. Speaking of that, when I come back for you this evening, we'll have to attend Giles's bloody feast."

"You make it sound like a form of torture."

"After jousting and tourneys, it's our greatest entertainment."

Her lips curved into a new smile. "A real medieval feast. If I don't mess up, I think it'll be fun, Matthias. I only wish your brother was well enough to enjoy it."

"Aye. So do I."

He left, wishing he could share her innocent enthusiasm. She thought a feast would be *fun?* Could anything here be enjoyable again? Carrie had

80

lost so much and might never return home. Yet, unlike him, she didn't seem to dwell on it. How could anyone be so optimistic? He most definitely wasn't. Life had taught him cynicism.

Alhough he didn't want to tell Carrie, he knew why his brother wanted him home. Giles was dying and had no heir. The castle would soon have no Marcher lord to govern the stronghold. The king would then replace Giles with whomever he favored.

Having been squired away at Chepstow at age thirteen, Matthias had spent little of his upbringing within Wyldnell's walls. After the Crusades and then with his absence for the past nine years, he'd never been formally trained on how to marshal a keep and protect England's border. However, he earned his spurs and paid his dues in the Middle East. Giles would have considered Matthias's past service to King Edward. The thought of his brother's calculation made his blood run cold.

He hadn't forgiven him—he only wanted an heir.

****

After dressing, Carrie took a tattered cloth from Matthias's large oak chest, determined to make the best of her surroundings. The bedchamber wasn't in bad shape, for a medieval dwelling, she guessed. Yet it was a far cry from the cleanliness she was used to.

Climbing on top of the chair, she began whisking away dust from the white walls near the hearth. The room seemed stark, gloomy—very similar to its owner. Aside from the marvelous canopied bed, the only decorations in the room were the curious wooden sculptures on the mantel. She enjoyed picking up each one as she dusted them, admiring their artistry. There was a rearing horse, a prancing unicorn, a fish, and a griffin. What they were doing in Matthias's care, she had no earthly idea.

There was a soft knock on the door, and Edwina poked her wimpled head in.

"Good morning, milady. Oh! You shouldn't be doing that. Poor Gweneth will feel ever so bad. She'll be coming to clean later, you know." Stopping to stand just below Carrie's chair, Edwina planted her hands on her hips and smiled up at her. "I see you've found the lad's creatures."

Carrie smiled, feeling foolish now. She put down the griffin she'd been admiring and stepped off the chair.

"These can't belong to Matthias." Weapons or trophies, she could understand, but not the quaint little sculptures.

"Oh, aye. Math has a great eye for wood. I think it's the Welsh in him, you know. His mother was the same. She loved trees. The orchard was her doing."

"There's an orchard? I can't wait to see it."

Edwina's eyes went round. "Oh, I almost forgot."

She went back out the chamber door and then returned carrying two heavy-laden baskets of greenery with purplish-blue flowers.

"Lavender!"

"Yes. For your rushes, if you like. It was Math who chose the lavender. He hoped the fragrance would suit you."

Carrie took a basket from Edwina and breathed the flowers' fragrance deeply. The scent was her favorite. Lavender grew along the sidewalk of her backyard where anyone brushing against it could smell it. Tears misted her eyes as she remembered the sweet fragrance of home. She kept lavender throughout her mother's house in sachets, potpourri, and in brews for the bath.

"They'll be perfect. If I could, I'd like to keep some back to use in my bathwater." Carrie bit her lip after she'd spoken. They took baths in this century, didn't they?

"Of course, milady. I wager you'll be wanting one today, too. When the earl bathes, he washes in his bedchamber, but the rest of us take our baths outside. Math said we were to bring you a tub directly to your room."

Men and women bathing outside? Where *anyone* might see them? For the first time that day, Carrie was thankful for her confinement.

And Matthias.

"I really appreciate that. Thank you, Edwina."

The older lady winked and took Carrie's cleaning cloth away. "But first, a sewing lesson. Let's learn to *mend* Matthias's tunics, not turn them into rags."

Carrie passed the day away easily in the company of Edwina. Although her attempts with sewing were ultimately humiliating, she enjoyed their conversation. As she sucked on her needle-pricked fingers, she learned a few things about the importance of the Marcher baron and Wyldnell itself.

Giles was distantly related to King Edward through his mother, who'd died in childbirth. Matthias had a different mother who was a direct descendant of the Welsh prince, Rhys ap Gruffydd, but that made him no more than a bastard in the eyes of the English. Edwina told her that Welsh princes were once "more common than rabbits" in Wales. Matthias's mother also died in childbirth, and Edwina had been his wet nurse. Her own baby had been stillborn.

A widespread belief among the local villeins was that pregnancies were best when undertaken with the guidance of old Maud, a "witch." That was why, Edwina claimed, the Welsh babes were so much hardier than the English. If a woman chose to ignore Maud's advice, she would be unlikely to bear a healthy child, or she might lose her own life in the process. For all local medicine, there were only two respected sources—either Maud or the Cistercian monks. And as for the earl, he chose to use both resources, as well as his own physick, just in case.

Servants came and drifted throughout the day, and Carrie began to get the distinct impression that their presence wasn't truly necessary. Edwina shooed them away when they became too obvious. Curious about the newcomer, they came unbidden, hovering around the tower chamber while the women sewed, always listening and watching. She wondered if they thought her strange—a woman who couldn't sew in a straight line. Or, if they thought she said or did the wrong things for a medieval woman. Or perhaps they simply thought her American accent odd.

Carrie took a long bath in the wooden tub the servants brought. Its round shape forced her to draw her legs into a pretzel just to sit in it. Cumbersome at best, the vessel had been lined with cloths, but the water was deep. The scent of the lavender in the steam rising from the tub eased her troubles. The hot water soothed the sore muscles in her neck where she'd bent too long over her botched stitches. She gratefully scrubbed away the dirt from her travels and the dust of the bedchamber with a cake of soap infused with soapwort. After drying, she air-dried her hair and dressed herself for the evening. Edwina had brought in a new gown for the occasion.

The dress was amazing. Fashioned of deep blue damask and gold piping, it clung to her body as if tailored for her alone. Her arms were encased in snug-fitting sleeves that flowed in a bell shape from her wrists. Edwina helped her fasten a low-riding girdle of gold links around her waist.

Standing in the new garment, Carrie felt like a fairy tale princess.

"It was made for Matthias's mother. She died

before she ever wore it. I hope you don't mind its age, milady."

"Oh, not at all," Carrie said in all honesty.

"Your hair is lovely with this dress." Edwina's soft eyes ran over her. "And your skin is just the shade of fresh peaches from your bath."

Carrie's hands flew to her cheeks. Her skin! She hadn't seen herself in a mirror for two days. Her face felt smoother. She smiled with relief.

"Matthias will think he's won the competition."

"What competition?"

Edwina laughed, a warm, rich sound. "The boys have been competing with each other all their lives. Each one trying to achieve greater things than the other. Tourneys, weapons, the king's favor, and women. Take Matthias's carving, for example. Poor Giles tries, but he's never been able to make anything as complicated as Matthias has."

"This competition—is it something they enjoy doing with each other? Or is it a bitter rivalry?" She tucked a few loose strands of hair behind her ears.

Edwina ran the back of her hand across her brow, thinking. "Why, you would think it was a celebration when one of them bested the other. I've seen them come close to blows, but they're just men. It does not mean anything. The next minute they are planning another competition."

Carrie couldn't keep the grin off her face. "I knew it. Matthias denied they had anything in common, but there it is." They shared a common goal—to upset each other.

"I suppose so. In tourneys, Math was better with a sword, and Giles was better with a lance but that didn't stop them from trying to best each other. As for women, the lads were always trying to see who could win the favor of the prettiest girl." Edwina paused to straighten Carrie's girdle. "We long thought Giles had won with Lady Isabelle. She was

very beautiful. All the men vied for her. Then when
Math came home from Acre, he had more female
admirers in Wyldnell than ever before. Such a
charming and gallant knight."

Trying to picture Matthias as a youth, Carrie
wondered if Edwina might be slightly blinded by
bias. Matthias *charming?* She swallowed a laugh.

"The king gave him a barony and some land
north of here. I expected the king to offer him a bride
very soon after, but Giles was in no hurry to let him
leave. And then after..." Edwina broke off with a
frown, and then flashed a cheery smile at her, "if
he'd stayed here, he would not have met you and
won the competition."

Won? With *her*?

"Oh! Surely you can't mean me. You're not
comparing me to the earl's wife, are you? I'm not
beautiful and there certainly aren't men vying for
my attention." Carrie laughed in earnest.

Edwina frowned. "I'm not making a jest, milady.
Make no mistake. The competition is still on, and it's
very serious."

"For Pete's sake, Edwina. They've probably
outgrown that. It's been years, and now the earl is
ill. Trust me, Matthias didn't marry me to try to
upset his brother." Carrie slid her feet into the
slippers at the foot of the bed.

The lie of their marriage forced a lump in her
throat. She was dying to be honest. How could they
go on deceiving his family and friends? They weren't
really married, and the longer they led this
deception, the worse it would be when they finally
had to admit the truth.

"Think what you will, milady, but Math chose
the dress you're wearing and bade me bring it for
you to wear tonight. None would argue, it's the
finest dress to be had in Wyldnell."

Backing toward the door, Edwina gave Carrie a

wry smile before turning to go.

The door opened nearly as soon as it closed behind the older woman. A teasing reprimand for Edwina died on Carrie's tongue as she looked up to see her dinner date.

"Good, you're dressed."

His gaze danced over Carrie's body from head to toe, assessing the transformation. He circled her, causing her momentary worry in his quiet study. His expression was unreadable. Tonight would be important to him, competition or not, and she didn't want to cause him any embarrassment.

If theirs had been a blind date, she believed he would've been the one feeling cheated tonight—a mismatched couple if ever there'd been one. As a knight, he was dead sexy. She—a toad.

Carrie rubbed her arms in an effort to rid them of the sudden tingling of anticipation he caused as he passed behind her.

"What's the matter?" A line creased his brow, as he seemed to sense her unease.

He was resplendent, wearing a surcoat of a blue color matching her gown with a red dragon emblazoned on his broad chest. His jaw was clean-shaven, and his dark hair thick and glossy. Perhaps he'd bathed outside that afternoon. In two steps, he was near enough for her to smell the fresh, clean spice of soapwort plants, proving her assumption correct. The warmth of his body invaded her senses. She shivered.

His gray eyes peered down at her. "Are you well?"

"Fine. I'm fine."

Actually, thinking on Edwina's parting suggestion, she did feel a little anxious.

She smiled faintly and shook her head. "No, not really. I'm nervous, Matthias. What if I do something or say something wrong tonight?"

She expected him to grumble at her again or berate her, as she was becoming accustomed to, but surprisingly, he did neither.

"They'll be well into their cups after about two or three hours. Then after that, you can tell them all about the Beatles, television, and the Internet, if you like."

"Was that a joke? From you?" She laughed and couldn't help feeling better. "I think I'll still be on my guard, even so, Matthias. There'll be a lot of people there, won't there? I've never been crazy about being the stranger at a party."

"Did you take your medicine?"

She nodded.

"Good. That's all you really need worry about. I'll handle everything tonight."

She hoped so. Tamping down her fears, she sighed and followed him to the Great Hall.

Chapter Seven

Carrie's hope of slipping unnoticed in Matthias's shadow shattered upon their arrival in the crowded Great Hall. Elevated to the second story, the hall could only be accessed by its wide staircase. They were late, making them the focal point of attention. Dozens of people lined the stone steps, spilling out from the hall, craning their necks to see around each other to get the best view of the errant Wyldnell son's return.

Instead of welcome in their faces, Carrie caught snarls of disdain from both the men and the few women of the castle. It was almost as if they despised Matthias. She could feel the heat of their glares, and her chest constricted at the unfamiliarity of such condemnation. She resisted the urge to clutch his hand as Matthias strode ahead.

A hush fell over the gathering like a wet blanket on a fire. Their footsteps on the stone floor were the only sounds in the expansive hall. As they passed the onlookers, a few souls dared to cover their lips to whisper comments. Hardly the celebratory reception she expected for a heroic knight coming home with his bride.

She tried to see Matthias's expression. Glimpsing the side of his face, she saw only the usual annoyance that plagued him since she'd first met him. Eyes dark. Jaw tense. Lips tight.

Wondering how he felt at that moment, she disregarded her own discomfort. Sure, he could be annoying at times, but she didn't see what the others found so repugnant about the man. She

89

supposed it was true he was usually a snob, but he didn't deserve such a hostile reception upon his return home.

Purposefully ignoring the stares, she placed her hand on her escort's arm and lifted her chin regally. Matthias didn't glance down at her but acknowledged her presence nonetheless, placing his hand over hers as they walked down the main aisle of the hall. His fingers squeezed hers lightly, causing warmth to spread across her cheeks. Carrie stole another look at his attractive face. She couldn't help it. Guided on his arm, she floated like royalty.

"Where do we sit?" she whispered.

Matthias nodded toward the raised dais at the head of the room where a table and chairs sat facing the crowd, like a pulpit to a church congregation. There had to be at least a hundred people in attendance watching them from other tables.

"Good grief," she murmured.

Matthias flashed a brief smile in return.

"Do you know most of these people?" From the rough state of their dress and fabric, she assumed most of them were the household staff or guards.

Matthias didn't answer her. His face drew into a sudden deep frown. She followed his gaze up to the table again, where three servants were seating the earl of Wyldnell.

He reclined amid a mountain of cushions. His silver mane had been combed back from his forehead in a severe manner, an attempt to appear dignified despite his frailty.

His dazed eyes looked first at Matthias and then at her, taking in every detail until she felt uncomfortable in her own skin.

The striking similarity to his brother's features and unwavering stare reminded her of the way Matthias appraised her just moments earlier. This time, however, Carrie didn't feel the attention was complimentary. If anything, the earl appeared agitated.

As they settled into their seats beside him, music hummed to life. Carrie turned her attention to the delightful sound of drums and trumpets. She discovered the musicians situated in a gallery in the wall above the floor of the dining hall. Their close proximity to the players made tickets to the symphony seem like a waste of money. The place was astonishing. New excitement coursed through her as the harmonious instruments chased the melancholy mood of the room away.

The earl leaned forward. "Jesu, she's rather plain, isn't she, Matthias?"

Carrie felt her stomach dip at Giles's rude remark.

"Do you really think so?" Matthias blocked her view of the earl, preventing her from reading his expression. She frowned at the back of his head.

She wasn't offended by the comment; she'd overheard it many times in her life. She was far from anyone's idea of homecoming queen, regardless of what Edwina thought. Yet, hearing the thought repeated by Matthias's brother made the blood drain from her face in humiliation. Matthias would lose the competition because of her. Did he think the same?

To her surprise, she was more concerned about Matthias's approval of her than she cared to admit.

Had she lost her mind when she'd traveled through time? Why should she care what he thought? She plucked at the sleeve of her dress angrily.

"I suppose you would've preferred me to wed some painted-up whore?"

"By the bones of St. David, nay!" Giles burst into laughter. "'Tis what I would've expected from you, though. Not to wed a woman of good breeding, as this one looks to be. You surprised me, that is all. How did you catch yourself a gentle lady, little brother? Wait. Do not tell me. Forsooth I know I would regret the hearing of it. She is fair enough. Aye."

Carrie leaned forward, catching the stare of the earl over Matthias's shoulder.

He relaxed and announced, "The woman will make a good son for you, Math. What she lacks in beauty, she makes up for in height and bones. Does she have a good backside, too?"

Carrie's face burned. What was she—cattle?

She leaned to Matthias's ear and whispered, "I've made my appearance. Are you satisfied? Can I go back to the tower now?"

Matthias turned to fix her with a piercing look. He spoke loud enough for the rest of the table to hear. "Carrie, this is my poor brother's way of paying you a compliment. Alas, he's not as worldly as I am, and he has no idea how to praise a woman for her attributes other than with brutish words. He's never been gifted with charm. Pay him no mind, for tonight you're so dazzling it has affected his wits, I believe."

A silent plea passed from him to her.

She needed no more than an instant of gazing into those compelling gray eyes. She would stay.

"True, true." Giles clapped his hands in amusement and graced Carrie with a wink. He laughed heartily until a cough seized him, shaking his bony frame.

A servant rushed forward with a cup of ale. He took a swallow and fell silent.

Another man unfurled a large white cloth that he placed in the earl's lap. Two more servants carried a heavy tray between them, presenting a plump, roasted boar to the earl and then to Matthias. A young man cut the bread trenchers and put them before the guests. There was only one for both her and Matthias. If she was expected to share her supper with him, it was going to be a long uncomfortable night.

Yet, if Matthias was in any way embarrassed by her or by Giles's behavior, he had the good grace not to show it.

The rest of the food arrived, platters of swan, feathered wings and all, and venison smelling strongly of saffron and pepper. After the assenting nod of the earl, everyone began to eat. Matthias cut the roasted boar meat for Carrie. His eyes crinkled in droll pleasure as she lifted a greasy bite to her mouth, trying to eat politely with no utensils.

The meal wasn't inedible, but the spices were overpowering. She couldn't identify some of the vegetables underneath all the herbs and seasonings. Surely, there were more garlic, onions, and mushrooms on their table alone than in any Italian restaurant she frequented. What did they do for indigestion? She had no doubt there would be many cases of heartburn that night. No wonder the poor earl was ill. Glancing at his trencher, she saw he'd already consumed half his serving. He looked peaked, worse than before they'd begun eating.

"Matthias, I'd like to talk to your cook," she told him in a low voice.

"What?" His eyebrows screwed together as he lifted a goblet of water to his lips.

"I'd like to have a look at your kitchen. Perhaps I could speak with your cook, too. I have an idea for him to make the meals more suitable for Lord Wyldnell."

Giles coughed again but managed to speak, "Math, has she taken leave of her senses? There's nothing wrong with the food."

Carrie felt her skin flush. She hadn't meant her words to be overheard.

"Carrie, this meal was prepared especially for you," Matthias hissed between his teeth. "We can send your ideas to Cook later."

For the earl, there may not be a better time, she decided grimly. Whatever his unidentified illness was, the food would only make it worse. As thin as a two-by-four, the man couldn't afford the wait.

Undeterred, she patted his shoulder and stood. She was eager to leave her domineering companions at any rate.

"Excuse me for just a few moments, Lord Wyldnell. I'll show you I have more than just height and a good backside. I don't mean to offend your kitchen staff, but I'm sure I can straighten them out. If not, this food may make you ill."

Before Matthias could argue with her, Carrie left the dais and found the man who'd served them. Inveigling his assistance, she was taken straight away from the hall to the kitchen.

****

Matthias stared at her exit in disbelief. Where had that come from? Maybe the woman was as batty as she was beautiful. He should follow her and drag her back before she caused any trouble.

He pushed his chair back from the table, intent on stopping her.

At his elbow, Giles mumbled, "No wonder it took you so long to return, little brother, if you've a headstrong wench to contend with."

Matthias eased back into his seat. He dragged his gaze from the door back to his brother. It was the first moment he'd had alone with Giles, which forced him into saying what he had to say. Despite their troubled past, he was still his brother, and Matthias couldn't ignore the weight on his heart.

"For what it's worth, Giles," Matthias began, taking an opportunity to broach the subject while Carrie was gone, "Rannulf told me about your loss.

You have my condolences, brother."

"'Twas an awful time. Isabelle—" his brother began, but was interrupted.

A trumpet sounded, interrupting Giles and announcing the end of the feast. Next would be the bardic tournament. Matthias sighed, thankful for its fortunate timing before his brother could say more.

The entertainment unfolded in front of the dais. A Welsh bard with a harp stepped forward to begin an ancient poem. Matthias had once loved the bardic sport himself, but it failed to engage him tonight. Feeling restless, his gaze searched the room for Carrie's return.

****

Carrie returned to the Great Hall no more than a half hour later, satisfied with her accomplishments in the kitchen. Wyldnell's cook, a Norman by birth, spoke only courtly French. Carrie had learned some French, first in high school and later in culinary school, before her interest in herbs drew her away from her goal to be a chef. Cook was pleased to converse with someone other than the Welsh and English servants of the kitchen. He took her constructive criticisms without any hostility, vowing to put some of her ideas to work for the earl's next meal.

People Skills 101. She ought to offer her services to Matthias's university and teach her own course. She smiled to herself as she crossed the room.

When she was finally able to leave this place and time, she could do so without a guilty conscience. She couldn't abandon Matthias's sickly brother, subsisting on gaseous peppers and onion of an unknowing cook. Perhaps her intervention in the earl's diet was what Fate had intended all along. If he were dying, at least it wouldn't be caused by the food.

Approaching the dais, she realized she'd been

left alone with Giles. Her escort was elsewhere. Someone had let the earl's hunting dogs in, and they roamed at will. Cautiously, she sidled past the circling beasts and slipped into her chair. She took a deep drink from her goblet. Hopefully the austere earl was too distracted by the entertainment to take much notice of her.

Unfortunately, she found she'd drawn his attention. She felt the weight of his stare as she strangled on a drink of her watered-down ale.

"And did my kitchen please you?"

"Yes...my lord." She smiled weakly, heat rising in her face for her presumptiveness.

"I have demanded a favor of my brother." He gestured across the room where Matthias stood with a group of cloaked men. "I have put him in the bardic tournament. Your husband weaves stories far better than anyone else here. Unless he has lost his touch, he'll make the rest of these fellows into fools. The others are competing to become the bard of Wyldnell for one year, of course. The winner will be my personal bard, though I shan't need one now that Matthias is home."

Carrie detected a note of pride in the older man's words. As she surveyed the entrants, her eyes were drawn to Matthias, who was looking back at her. The darkness of his gaze made her shiver. She had no doubt he was still angry with her for leaving the table.

She frowned as she picked at the cold food on her plate. She'd only been trying to help the earl, for Pete's sake and it wasn't as if she'd put herself in danger or as if she'd caused any trouble for him.

She darted a glance at Giles. Now that she was alone with him, she might as well try and find out exactly what had caused the rift between the two brothers. She summoned her courage to talk to him.

Taking a deep breath, she rushed out, "Matthias

told me he was banished from Wyldnell. May I ask what he did?"

Oh, God. Did she say really say that?

Her fingers squeezed her goblet as she waited for an answer. She made an inward prayer she hadn't gone too far with her directness this time.

The earl rubbed his whiskered chin, clearly considering the question. "Tonight isn't the time to speak of such things. This is a time for welcome and merriment." He glanced up and then shifted on his pillows for a better position. "Here now, listen. My brother begins his tale."

Carrie dug her fingernails into her palms beneath the table, bitterly disappointed by the earl's brush-off. Then, Matthias started speaking and all that mattered was the sound of his deep voice.

"My tale is from the *Mabinogion*," he told them, "and is about the beautiful Rhiannon and her heroic husband Pwyll." His masculine speaking voice purred the ancient tale, slowly bringing it to life.

He described the courting of Rhiannon. The lady was very self-confident and witty, and the valiant men of the tale were all that Carrie imagined Celtic heroes ought to be. She found herself quickly spirited away by the narrative of poor Rhiannon's plight. The woman Pwyll loved was the subject of false accusations, left to a Druid punishment of having to carry men on her back for seven years before being exonerated of the wrongful charges. Carrie hung on each word of the story as Matthias's resonant voice spoke and seemed to plumb her feminine core with its sensuality.

The still hall erupted with applause when Matthias's tale came to end. Members of the audience exchanged enthusiastic glances, murmuring with pleasure to each other. His tale probably hadn't made them forget their disdain for him, but it was a step in the right direction.

Sandra Jones

Carrie smiled when he glanced her way. His efforts were worthy of his brother's praise, and she wondered if Matthias noticed the new respect he'd earned from the audience. It was no wonder he'd been able to find work in modern times. She could just imagine the lecture hall of the university, crowded with students who preferred listening to his stories over boring history textbooks and dry dates.

Female students most likely outnumbered males.

The earl waved another bard out from the competing throng, and Carrie felt sorry for the young man who had to follow Matthias as the new entertainment. The next entrant rushed forward and in a swirl of his cloak, he withdrew a single, blood red rose. With his face upturned expectantly to Carrie, he lifted the flower in offering to her.

Giles chuckled, mumbling something about flattery and bribery that she couldn't quite hear. She took the offering with a smile.

Seemingly delighted with himself, the young man bounded back to the center floor. He began singing in what Carrie supposed was Welsh. She'd heard bits of the ancient Gaelic while in modern Cardiff. The words were foreign to her, but the honeyed voice of the singer made the lyrics almost comprehensible. He was singing of love, she realized, and the earl watched in pleased silence.

Carrie felt someone approaching them on the dais. As she glanced up, disappointment washed over her. It wasn't Matthias, but another tall knight with short, spiky red hair and dressed in an emerald tunic emblazoned with a tree. He plopped down into the vacant chair.

"Rannulf Fitz George, my lady," he introduced himself. "Captain of the earl's guards. Father of Ian, whom you've already met, and friend of your husband's, though I'm afraid there aren't many of us who aspire to that claim."

Carrie liked him immediately. "Which claim? Men who are friends of Matthias's or who claim Ian as their son?"

After a baleful look from Rannulf, both men began to laugh, and Carrie joined them.

"What ho! A saucy wench is she." Rannulf's smile grew by inches. "Poor Math. He doesn't stand a chance."

The earl passed barbs with his captain, burning Carrie's ears with the occasional vulgarity they shared. She began to relax in their company. Then the bard's rising tenor voice drew their attention back to the song.

"Do you know Welsh, my lady?" The guard leaned over the table toward her.

"No. Could you translate?"

Carrie watched Matthias as he moved around the tables in their direction. His eyes narrowed and locked on the captain. She dreaded his approach, figuring he was ready to rail her about her trip to the kitchen.

The captain began translating quietly, "The sun shines in the west, the sun shines in the east. The sun shines in Wyldnell. Flowers bloom in spring. Flowers bloom in summer. Flowers bloom in Wyldnell. Birds mate in the skies. Birds mate in the trees. Birds mate in Wyldnell. An angel sings in Heaven. An angel sings in the clouds. An angel sings in Wyldnell. A man kisses a woman. A woman kisses a man. A man and woman kiss in Wyldnell."

Finished, the bard bowed to Giles. Then he approached the dais.

"My lord," he intoned loudly for the whole audience to hear, as well as the earl, "in other courts I've played in, it's considered appropriate for a lady present to bestow a kiss to someone other than her husband. Is it so in your court?"

All talk in the room fell silent. Carrie glanced around to see every pair of eyes watching the earl. Beside her, Rannulf went tense. Under the table, she saw the discreet movement of his sausage-like fingers slowly curling around the pommel of his sword.

"My song says a man and woman kiss in Wyldnell," the young bard explained. "Would you not allow a lady's kiss in your Great Hall for your guests' entertainment?"

Who was this guy? Carrie wished Giles would set the dogs on him. Rannulf relaxed, but goosebumps rose on her arms, as she begrudgingly understood *she* was the lady the bard was speaking of.

Giles finally answered, "Aye, but let the *lady* decide who to favor, though." To Carrie, he said, "Bestow a kiss on the warrior or knight of your choice."

He waved his hand at the side tables, where presumably the visiting knights were seated. Beside her, she heard Rannulf's chair scrape the floor. As he stood, the ruddy captain grinned down at her expectantly.

Then more chairs moved across the room. Carrie looked around. Suddenly several men were on their feet, including the vile young Ian. Heat rushed to her face as her head swam from the attention focused on her now. More than a dozen knights and guards were on their feet. She wondered if she had the strength to stand. It was too horrible.

Must she kiss someone—a stranger—in front of everybody?

Bracing her hands on the table, she rose slowly. This was worse than the time she'd given a speech in the fifth grade dressed as Florence Nightingale in front of all her classmates and the boy she had a crush on. How could she do this without looking foolish?

Movement out of the corner of her eye drew her attention. Matthias stopped at the end of their table. The earl's giant hunting hounds were congregating about his feet. His arms were crossed over his chest, and he turned a malevolent glare on every man in the room.

The earl grumbled impatiently, "Hurry up about it. Just pick a man and be done with it. Lady Carrie, we want a kiss."

She made up her mind. What did she care what they did in other people's courts? There was only one man in the room she would kiss.

She swallowed hard. "Matthias is my husband but also a knight, my lord."

Giles nodded and released an exaggerated breath. "Aye. If that's your choice, then get on with it. We have a contest to finish."

Carrie walked around the table to find him already looking at her. One of the dogs had lain down at his feet, and listening to it growl over stolen table scraps, she didn't dare disturb it by coming too close.

Matthias stared down at her. His gray eyes watched her from under their fringe of soft black eyelashes. Carrie trembled, wondering if she'd disappointed or angered him again. His thoughts were inscrutable, as usual.

"My lady?" he prompted, his voice thick as molasses.

Carrie abandoned hope of returning to her seat or fleeing the room. She wouldn't shame Matthias. She wanted to make a good impression on the crowd for his homecoming. In her stomach, however, great Celtic knots were forming.

She stood on her toes, leaning precariously over the dog like a ballerina, and braced her trembling hands lightly on his chest. Matthias bent over her, casting her in shadow as his lips lowered to hers. His mouth was sensual, warm, and firm as she pressed her lips gently to his in a light kiss.

She started to pull back, but the dog between them gave a sudden lurch, yelping and growling. It moved so quickly against her leg that she toppled forward into Matthias's ready arms. Her groping hands caught his chest, finding the hard muscle beneath his soft tunic, and he held her firmly up against the steady wall of his body. Their mouths connected again, but this time his lips pressed harder on hers.

His hands moved against the small of her back, fingers curling to grip her closer. The action so small and reflexive made her stomach quiver. Carrie opened her mouth to him in heady anticipation, and his tongue plunged in to taste her. His mouth moved ever so gently, coaxingly on hers, as his tongue stroked her own. She breathed in the male scent of him, warm and spicy, eagerly allowing him to explore deeper and deeper. Heat spread through her like wildfire.

The crowd around them began to laugh, breaking through the web of desire that entangled her. They hooted and called for more, Rannulf's grating baritone above it all. Their enthusiasm echoed her own, as she reluctantly withdrew from his embrace.

Stepping back, Carrie avoided Matthias's expression. She'd instigated the second kiss, accidental though it was. She didn't want to see regret in his face.

He kept his hand under her elbow as she made her way through the undulating dogs toward her seat. She offered Rannulf a tremulous smile and practically dove into the safety of her chair. Rannulf quickly vacated Matthias's place at the table.

The crowd bubbled with merriment but

eventually settled down as the previous bard bowed to the earl. Another bard darted forward to replace him. The newest contestant had brought his harp, and he started to play. The conversation of the men at her table resumed, nearly drowning out the music as they spoke of King Edward's new castle building campaign in North Wales. The kiss was quickly forgotten.

Carrie traced the rim of her goblet with her fingertip, letting the sounds of the room fade to the back of her thoughts. Her skin began to cool from its riotous heat of embarrassment, and her heart rate slowly returned to normal. Feeling like a moon-eyed teenager, Carrie let her gaze float to Matthias next to her. She watched the back of his head, the way his long hair moved on his broad shoulders. He beckoned to a servant with the mere slant of his head, bidding him to adjust his brother's cushions. With the slightest motion of his fingers, the servants came scurrying to refill their goblets. Command came easily for him.

He had plenty of faults but she couldn't find any with his kiss. Her body still reverberated with the new yearning their public entanglement caused. She closed her eyes as the memory assaulted her once more. Though battle-scarred, cynical, and frustratingly cold, Matthias could give heavenly pleasure with a kiss.

Chapter Eight

This was intolerable.

Not a single woman in the castle knew Carrie's whereabouts. She wasn't with Edwina, she wasn't sewing, and she wasn't in bed.

"Where is she?" he barked.

"My lord?"

Matthias sighed impatiently. "My wife. Where is she?"

The spit boy's face brightened with a smile of understanding. "Right this way, my lord."

Matthias pulled on his surcoat as he hastened to keep up with the servant. He'd caught the young man coming out into the bailey from the kitchens. Now his leg ached with every step under the sword he'd hastily strapped at his side. These nights on the floor were going to be the death of him.

The man stopped at the kitchen door, waiting on him with another broad grin. "My lady has given the spit boys the morning off."

The young man opened the door and gestured inside where Matthias was supposed to find the cause of his worry. He'd spent a restless night in the loft of the tower, awaking early that morning to check on Carrie's sleep below, only to find the confounded woman missing.

In the kitchen, Cook carried a large pot of water. He saw Matthias coming and changed direction so fast water sloshed onto his clothes and the floor. He immediately disappeared into the cellar.

All the hanging pots had been pulled from the rafters, making the kitchen resemble a disaster area. As Matthias surveyed the room, a chicken darted across the floor with a man dogging its heels, followed by a nanny goat and another man, cursing heartily. Someone had untethered the animals. The rushes had been swept out, removed entirely. The hearth stood cold, an odd sight. Meat should be roasting for the morning meal.

Good God, Giles would be furious if he saw the chaos! Matthias raked his hands through his hair. Turning on his heel to chase down Cook and demand an explanation, he ran smack into a bramble of weeds. The moving wall of dry, yellow and white flowers blocked his way. Sputtering, he pushed the bramble aside, knocking handfuls of blooms to the floor.

"Hey. Watch it," the female voice drawled.

"I should've known." Matthias released a heavy breath. His drumming heart began to correct itself.

Carrie peered around the load of flowers in her arms. "Oh, it's you. Help me get these on the table since you've made me spill half of them."

Helping her was the last thing he intended to do. He crossed his arms over his chest. "Why did you leave the bedchamber?"

She crouched to pick up two handfuls of the herbs, spared him a glance, and grinned as she continued the task. Her smile sent heat rushing through him, making him feel angry, inept, and weak-kneed all at once.

"You introduced me to the household last night. You said I could come out today, so I did. I'm not a toddler, you know."

Nay, she was definitely a grown woman, and he'd been aware of that fact since the day he'd met her. Her feminine qualities were becoming more and more impressed upon him with each day he spent in her company.

"I didn't say you were. Only, it would've been

more practical for me to know you were going out. That way I wouldn't wake up feeling like a bloody fool, thinking someone had come in during the night and dragged you away."

She dumped a large bouquet of flowers on the table and offered him another dazzling smile. "Thank you for worrying about me. I just didn't want to wake you up. I heard you pacing and rumbling around upstairs all night. I figured you needed to sleep in."

"I wasn't worried about you," he lied feebly.

Of course, she was fine. He felt like a complete idiot. If either of them appeared wanting for brains, 'twas he, who'd strapped on a sword and bellowed at the servants like a madman.

"I didn't think you would roam the castle on your own. I thought you were frightened of Ian." He smoothed his hand over his hair, trying to look as though he wasn't a raving lunatic.

"Sir Rannulf's son?" She began snapping the tops of the flowers off, putting them in a large bowl. "I didn't think he would be a concern anymore. After all, I'm the earl's sister-in-law, right? Would anyone here dare, Matthias? You said yourself, your name was protection."

On that point, she silenced him. She was right. He'd done his bloody best to make sure every man in the hall last night knew how he stood. If there were those who would think to challenge him, he'd made it known that Carrie wasn't to be touched by another without repercussions. He'd branded her as his in front of everyone.

"That Rannulf is quite a character." Her fingers kneaded the flowers, combing them apart. She smiled. "He's funny. Everyone needs a friend like that. My assistant Allison tells the most vulgar jokes, but I love to be around her. She helps me blow off steam when I've had a stressful day. What about you? You have an assistant, right? And your caretaker, Nigel. Are you friends?"

She slanted a look up at him. Her purplish-blue eyes teased his blood.

"I've never thought about it."

"Well, I guess if they'd reminded you of Rannulf, you would've been better friends." She picked up a tiny flower and sniffed it.

"I get along with my employees. They have no complaints known to me." He rubbed the back of his neck. Her study into his character made him uncomfortable, forcing him to reflect on his treatment of the men. His assistant was well paid by the university. Nigel had a house, good pay. What more did she expect of him? To be boon companions with each person he encountered? Friendships were based on trust. No man should trust him. Temper frayed, he grumbled, "Would you mind telling me what it is that you're doing?"

She lifted the bowl and held it under his nose. "Smell. Isn't it wonderful? It's chamomile. The gardens outside are amazing!"

She was amazing. Her cheery smile disarmed him as surely as any Saracen warrior. He sniffed the flowers obediently before he realized what he was doing.

"Is that what all this is about? You're making fragrances?" He pushed the bowl aside, straining to keep his gaze from her mouth.

"No." She plucked a tiny flower off his surcoat and kept working. "It's for tea, for your brother."

"You're making tea—for *Giles*?" Matthias started to laugh and then smothered it under his fist when she looked up at him with a frown. "My brother won't even drink water. He won't drink that, for certes."

"It's better for him than ale or wine. Hey, at least it's worth a try. Why don't you take it up to him? Maybe he'll drink it if you give it to him. Then you can talk to him about his symptoms and how he's feeling." She put the bowl down. Facing him, she tucked a strand of wavy golden hair behind her ear. "I know neither of us has been to med school, but we both know more about medicine and diseases than anybody else here. Maybe we can figure out what is making him sick. Maybe it's something simple like his diet, or cleanliness. That's what I'm guessing."

She waved a hand at the room. "This place is a sty. Literally. Livestock live in here, Matthias. Right by the cooking area. Vermin, too. I've asked Cook to serve salad greens today while we work on getting the room sanitary. I've already been to the garden and made an inventory of what we have to work with. The monks deliver medicines and cooking herbs on Wednesday, so I'm waiting to see what they have. And later today, I hope to visit the healer, Maud. Cook says Maud has herbs that nobody else does, if I can convince her to part with them."

Matthias rubbed his hand over his face. Not Maud. Not yet.

"Carrie, I was planning on visiting with Giles later today, and I don't think it's a good idea to see Maud. She lives outside the castle's walls. It isn't safe. There are brigands. Wales isn't completely in English hands."

"Okay." She caught her bottom lip between her teeth and lowered her gaze as if in thought. Then she glanced up to continue, "But she might know something about the Druid ring and the moon plants. She could also give us some insight about your brother's illness. They say she doesn't live far from the henge. Maybe you could go with me. We could take some guards, or—"

"Wait." He held up his hand. "You just got here. One thing at a time. You won't be able to solve all our problems at once, you know. And as far as health, people here think differently than you do. They're seven hundred years behind your knowledge. It's a lot to deal with. I should know."

Carrie smiled, wiping her hands on the apron she wore. "Well, I guess that makes you living proof that people can change. Who would've ever believed that yesterday I saw you smile and just a moment ago you actually laughed at me?"

"That's from lack of sleep or mayhap the stress you're causing me." He frowned.

Carrie quit what she was doing and moved to stand just beneath his chin. Matthias realized he'd stopped breathing as she stared up at him. He battled his sudden urge to haul her against his chest. Half the night he'd spent either wishing he hadn't kissed her, or wishing he hadn't stopped. Maybe he'd been without a woman in his bed for too long. New levels of sexual frustration rose within him. He considered ripping her apron off and tossing her on the table, amid her flowers, to kiss her, and delve into her more intimately.

Mayhap the woman could read his mind. Although she stared at him with luminous eyes, she made no move to kiss him. Instead, her hand lifted to his face. She gently cupped her palm against his cheek and traced the circle under his eye with her thumb.

"You know, you could use some chamomile tea, too. I'll have some made for you tonight before bed. It might help you sleep."

He cursed his weakness. Fantasies were dangerous.

"I'd sleep better if I didn't have to wonder where you were," he said softly.

Matthias took a step back and bent to retrieve the dagger he'd stashed in his boot. He placed the hilt in her hands. "Here, keep this. I'll also rest easier knowing you're armed...I think."

"Thank you," she chuckled. "But don't you need it for your carving?"

"My creatures? Aye, I was thinking about starting again, but you need it more than I do. I'll get another."

Matthias lingered in the kitchen a few moments more. He told himself he was seeing to her safety, but he knew he was really just admiring her shapely waist as she twisted to secure the dagger in her girdle.

Once outside in the bailey, he kicked at imaginary obstacles on the ground. Something about this situation had to change. It took far too much effort for him to remain a gentleman around Carrie. If she kept touching him, he'd soon show her a better cure for his sleeplessness than her damned tea.

****

The abbot arrived at noon with an entourage of men. Matthias found himself stalled at his own brother's door, told to wait, until the earl made his regular confession. Then he was finally allowed admittance.

Watching from the doorway, Matthias remembered the last time he'd seen Abbot Sidney of Marsten for his own confession, just before the Cistercian clergyman made his recommendation to Giles that Matthias should leave Wales forever.

In modern times, Matthias had done his best to find out what had happened to his brother after he'd left. He wanted to know how long he'd lived and if there'd ever been another of Hugh Thorne's descendants born in Wyldnell, but the Cistercian record was missing. A church fire in 1716 claimed the only written accounts of Wyldnell's medieval history. Even if he tried to avoid changing history, it would be impossible to know what that history would be.

The current abbey was completed while Matthias had been away, from what he'd been told by the guards. Constructed of timber, the building fairly dominated the landscape to the north. It was an ambitious undertaking for the abbot, who'd been born the second son of an English earl just like Matthias. The Cistercian Order was growing in Wales and a few individuals, such as Marsten, enjoyed the power it afforded them. Now the abbot was trying to persuade his brother to part with land on the river.

"...agriculture is important to our order. We provide for the needs of the people. We feed them, clothe them, and we'll even house them. But if we're to have sheep, we must have more land."

The robed abbot sat at his brother's bedside, leaning over Giles in a way that somehow reminded Matthias of a carrion-eating bird.

Giles began to cough into a cloth already soiled from sickness. His frail body shuddered as he tried to quell it. Matthias could watch no more and stepped forward.

"Marsten, you've come at a bad time for a charity. My brother needs to take care of his own welfare right now. The land can wait." Matthias grabbed a drink from the bedside table and pushed it into Giles's outstretched hand.

The abbot, slightly older than Giles, rose to address him. "Sir Matthias. Lord Wyldnell told me you'd returned, but I've yet to hear why."

Matthias rested his hand on the hilt of his sword, the remnant of an old habit. "Do I need a reason to visit my family's home?"

The abbot's thick gray eyebrows rose. "For a man who committed a crime against his own brother? I'd say you have no possible reason to visit him."

"Marsten," Giles said hoarsely, "you and I will

deal later. Presently, I need to speak with Matthias."

A dark expression passed over the clergyman's face, but he bowed his tonsured head. "My lord. I will see that my men have settled their delivery in your kitchen." He placed a hand over his heart. "My sincerest wish is that it will please you, my lord. I will visit anon."

When the abbot and his entourage were gone, Matthias sat stiffly at his brother's side. In daylight, Giles looked worse than the night before. His lips were dry and cracked from dehydration. His sunken eyes would haunt Matthias long after he left.

"I'm not dead yet," Giles argued, reading the thoughts behind his brother's expression. "I've a strong will. You know that, Matthias. Marsten has been after our land ever since you left. Yours and mine. The king would've dispensed it, but I objected. I've sent word to Edward that you've returned and that you wish to renew your fealty."

Matthias's skin went cold.

"God's blood, why would you do that, Giles? He'll have me on a spit!" Perhaps that's what his brother intended. Matthias stood, blood thundering in his temples. "I don't give a damn if you turn me in for deserting the king, but I have Carrie to—"

Giles waved his hand and added with a cough, "Seat yourself. Calm down. King Edward needs you here. You've naught to fear. The barony—"

"Forget the barony!" Matthias yelled. Oh, what a mess. "I don't want it. I don't even know how long I'm staying. I haven't made up my mind yet, but I'm not planning on being your heir."

The word curdled on his tongue.

"Math, calm yourself." Giles's coughing intensified, rocking his body on the cushions. "I—don't—plan—on dying—just yet. It's your future son I want to have the—title!"

Matthias handed him the drink again. Red wine

dribbled down the earl's chin as he tried to swallow. He raked a shaking arm across his lips as he struggled for recovery.

Matthias felt his chest tighten. "My wife wants you to drink her tea. She—we both think it would be better for your stomach."

Giles sneered, shaking his head. "Since when did you start listening to what wenches say, little brother?" Then he leveled a serious look at him. "Your wife is amusing and rather odd, but that's your affair, I suppose. What I want to know is why you haven't told her about Isabelle."

Matthias froze. "There's no need for me to tell her anything."

There was nothing he could remember about that hellish night, even if he did choose to tell her. His memories were of naught but drink and fog in the Great Hall.

"She knows you were banished, Math, but you didn't tell her why. Did you not think she would ask?" His gray eyes rounded under raised eyebrows.

"I don't speak of it. I *never* speak of it." At least Giles hadn't told her yet. God had granted him that blessing. Matthias's hands fisted at his sides, impotent to threaten his bedridden brother but on the cusp of losing his self-control nonetheless. He shook like a leaf. "By God, you will not speak of it to her either, Giles. She's already been through a lot in our travels, and she's...fragile."

He imagined the terror on Carrie's face. He'd seen it before in the bailey when she ran from him. Never would he allow himself to be the cause of such fright. Not when she might have a seizure.

Giles sighed and lowered his eyes. "Matthias, I've spent nine years thinking on your punishment. So many times I've wanted to see you once more. I didn't want to die before I saw you one last time. Deceit isn't—"

Matthias growled, "Tell her, and I'll leave. I swear it!"

Giles frowned, affronted at Matthias's rare interruption. Then the scowl slowly fell away, a thin smile growing in its place.

"So if I don't tell her, you'll stay?"

"By the rood, Giles, I—"

He interrupted, continuing, "If I protect your reputation from your bride, you'll keep your son here?"

The threat should've been an expected one. Matthias cursed inwardly. He of all people should have seen it coming. Although bound to his bed, an invalid, and barely keeping his food down, his brother's conniving ways remained the same as ever.

Matthias's breath became shallow.

He couldn't leave the room quick enough. He wouldn't answer the question, but the thunder of his boots as he turned to vacate his brother's bedchamber did not drown out Giles's harsh laughter.

Chapter Nine

Nothing vanquished his anger and frustration like a good fight.

Concentration was the key element to victory in physical contests, he'd always told his medieval warfare students, and one must keep one's mind totally focused on your opponent at all times, lest you find your arm lying severed on the ground.

Modern-day shrinks had naught on him and his brand of catharsis.

Rannulf sat up in the dust, spitting out the mouthful of dirt he'd just eaten. They hadn't been at the fight long, but Matthias appreciated the time spent honing his sword skills at the university. The captain wasn't easy to best, even when they'd sparred a decade ago.

"Matthias! I've been looking for you." Hearing a voice across the yard, he looked up from Rannulf.

Ian made a determined approach toward him across the training yard. He wore full mail and surcoat, tugging on his gloves. Matthias narrowed his eyes. What was the boy up to?

"Math practices here daily. You should as well, Son." Rannulf rose with Matthias's help.

"Practice is no replacement for real action, Father." Ian returned in a clipped voice.

Father and son exchanged a dark look.

Between his own years spent in warfare and as the king's retainer, Matthias had applied nearly every day of his youth training in the lists, practicing swords, archery, or tilting at the quintain. The physical exertion had also kept his mind off earthly vices, as his conditioning had this afternoon, also.

"I thought you might wish to fight someone of less advanced years. Then mayhap we could talk, as well," Ian taunted him, his voice full of youthful bravado.

Rannulf growled, "Bite your tongue, whelp, before I—"

Matthias wiped a blistered hand across his sweaty brow, and his lips curved at the challenge. "Aye, young Fitz George. I'll fight you. In truth, I'm out of practice, as I think even your father will agree." He moved between father and son. "But mayhap you can refresh my skills. Rannulf must have trained you. As you can see, I've bested him before, but I know he is a fine trainer of men. I look forward to our sport."

Ian's boastful smile faded slightly. Then he shrugged and responded with a sneer, "'Twill be a shame to sully the great reputation of Sir Matthias of Wyldnell."

So, Ian remembered his past, as well. Another name to add to his list of admirers. And he had been so young.

Matthias waited as Ian collected his sword from his attending squire and sized up his opponent. Ian's movements were rife with energy and the enthusiasm of his age. The big brawny youth would be a challenge.

Beads of perspiration rolled down Matthias's back from his exercises against Rannulf. The boy would have an advantage, being fresh. Impudent fool. After a week of practice in the lists, he ought to be in perfect condition to soundly trounce the lad but sleeping on the stone floor had made him unusually achy and tired.

"What did you want to talk about, *whelp?*" Matthias used Rannulf's familiar taunt as the boy met him.

A few men gathered in a ring around the combatants, and curious workers put aside their toils to see their lord's wastrel brother defeated by a boy.

Matthias pushed them out of his mind. They meant nothing to him, these vassals of Giles's. He would find satisfaction in fighting Ian, even if he lost in front of the whole castle.

"There is a matter I would like your thoughts on. Lord Wyldnell won't make a move without your advice." Ian made his first lunge with such speed that Matthias was taken off guard. He barely moved quick enough to dodge the blade.

Ian jibed, "Don't wait on me, old man. I'm ready for what you have to give."

Matthias laughed and sent his sword toward Ian with a jab that skidded off the boy's mail with an ominous squeal. The crowd murmured in shock, and Ian paled. In spite of his better judgment, Matthias pulled his gaze to the growing collection of witnesses, vainly wanting to see respect on their faces. He found it in one pair of eyes. Lovely violet ones. His blood quickened.

Metal pinged against his blade. He looked back to see a smug smile on Ian's flushed, pimpled face. "Hasn't anyone taught you not to let a woman distract you from your opponent, Sir Matthias?"

Matthias spun his blade in a flashing arc in the high afternoon sun. "Obviously, you yourself were similarly disposed or else you wouldn't know who drew my eye. Isn't that so, Rannulf?" He lifted his voice to the crowd. "'Tis true, Math."

Ian's gaze jerked to his left where his father's copper head raised high above the others. Maybe Ian needed to keep his mind off the crowd, but Matthias earned his living in modern times conversing with his students while demonstrating slices and cutting blows. He took the opportunity of Rannulf's distraction to lunge at Ian. Knowing his offense was his weakness in the heavy mail, he took his strikes when he had time, as he had now. He brought his blade down hard on the boy's sword, nearly knocking it free. The hilt vibrated against his raw palms.

"Bastard," Ian said under his breath, using both hands to steady his heavy, wavering sword.

"Not quite," Matthias corrected, catching his breath. "Pray you, what advice does my brother need from me?"

Ian gnashed his teeth as he avoided another strike from Matthias. "The king has called all his Marcher lords for support against the uprising Welsh. Obviously, we should fortify the walls and send out knights to subdue the locals. Ooofff."

The youth ducked a lunge. He took a deep breath and sent Matthias a murderous look. "I say take their weapons and food stores now before they decide to lay siege to the castle and starve us inside it. But my lord awaits your say. He fears he'll anger our neighbors and cause distrust. I say, who can trust a bloody Welshman? If we wait, they'll kill us in our beds."

Ian's down stroke landed with a shuddering blow against Matthias's sword. Thinking of the Welsh wars instead of the battle at hand, Matthias faltered, losing a foot of ground. Forced with his back to the crowd, he swung his sword forward defensively and only made the boy move sideways rather than backward as he hoped.

"If the locals side with the Welsh, 'twould be ludicrous." Matthias grunted as he sidestepped a quick strike. "Prince Llywelyn is only waging war against the crown because his brother Dafyd has already stepped on Edward's toes. Dafyd ap Gruffyd is a dullard. He stole an English occupied castle and will have to pay the consequences. Llywelyn is stuck between family loyalty and the duty of a vassal."

"He's committed treason. Welsh scum."

Ignoring the barb, Matthias continued, "His chosen loyalty to Dafyd is misplaced and mark ye well, he'll die because of it. I would ask Giles to have more sympathy for our neighbors. Don't invoke their hatred. When their Welsh nobility are gone, they will be good vassals for England." He carefully chose his words, not wanting to have to explain why he knew so much about the outcome of the current struggles.

Ian defended one of Matthias's best strikes with enviable skill and speed. "For a man who is half Welsh, I'm surprised you don't join Prince Llywelyn and the rest of your kinsmen," he panted.

"I don't claim them as kin any more than the English." Sweat rolled down his chest under the mail and his thick, padded hauberk.

"I trow you don't claim kinship with anyone, do you? What are you doing here, if not trying to claim kin with your dying brother?"

Matthias felt rage fall like a black curtain in his skull as he countered a strike Ian aimed at his slower leg. The familiar ring of metal rode on the tide of a thousand ugly memories.

A stratagem quickly formed in his head. He would win in five strokes.

"You condemn my brother to the grave too soon, whelp. Perchance he makes a recovery? He has lasted this long."

This time, Ian tripped under Matthias's heavily descending blow and stumbled backward on the toe of his own boot. Unable to regain his balance and ward off Matthias's four lightning-fast sword strikes, the young man collapsed on his backside. Matthias's sword pointed at his Adam's apple.

Matthias hissed between his teeth as he stared down at his grimacing opponent, "My comings and goings are not your business. I don't give a damn what my brother plans to do with his keep, but I'm here to guarantee he doesn't leave it in the hands of anyone who wishes harm to come to him. Understand me, *whelp?*"

"You're not the man your brother is. You don't compare in the least to the kind of great man the earl is," Ian seethed, purpling in anger under the sharp tip of Matthias's sword.

His fingers hardened around the hilt of his weapon. He pictured himself running the blade through the lad's throat and the satisfaction it would give him. So what if the fool respected Giles? It meant nothing to Matthias. Giles would get over the loss—or not.

Giles would likely banish him again. And Rannulf would kill him for murdering the only child of his beloved dead wife, Ursula.

Ian's jaw tightened in defiance, though Matthias detected a trickle of fear in his eyes.

The youth had been spoiled by his parents, and he deserved punishment for inciting a man like Matthias to more violence.

"Matthias!"

He jerked out of his blood-lusting fantasy to find Carrie's face in the crowd. She had moved to Rannulf's side and now watched with wide eyes.

"Don't hurt him, Matthias." Her eyes pleaded with him, but she kept her voice composed. The crowd moved aside and watched her reaction in silence.

He looked back down at the youth at the end of his blade. Of course, he had no real intention of harming him. In truth, he didn't like him at all, and he loved having him at his mercy. Yet his chivalry remained intact.

An idea came to his mind that would put Ian in his place and mayhap reward himself for the victory.

"You want me to let this oaf go, my lady?" he called to her.

Carrie nodded fervently.

Bending deeply over his sword, Matthias whispered down at Ian for his hearing alone, "Never give me cause to fight you again, whelp, or I will show you what it feels like to have your throat carved like roasted meat...and *never, never look at my wife again.*"

Ian's eyes widened as his gaze went to Matthias's scarred throat.

Straightening, Matthias called back to Carrie, "What will you trade for this fool's neck?" A smile tugged at his lips, one he quickly tempered but not before he caught the answering twinkle in her eyes.

"He's not worth much," she teased, casually planting her hands on her slim hips. Several of the men murmured in agreement. "What would you take?"

Matthias smiled at her and shrugged. "Running him through would be a great pleasure."

"Aye. The boy needs a lesson in holding his tongue," Rannulf growled, casting an irritated look at his son.

"I would trade that pleasure for another." Matthias watched Carrie's expression closely. The crowd murmured, but posed no distraction. Carrie's eyes flashed with understanding. He announced for all to hear, "Another kiss from my bride for our audience."

The small male crowd broke into laughter and cheers.

Carrie's lips quivered, almost forming a smile, but Matthias chalked it up to relief. She probably didn't want to see the color of Ian's blood. She nodded her acceptance and crossed to him as Matthias lowered his sword, releasing the youth. The boy moodily yanked off his gloves as he strode away. When Carrie reached him, her cheeks were aflame with color. He sincerely hoped it wasn't from mortification. Her embarrassment hadn't been his intention.

Slowly, Matthias faced her. The crowd around him watched him revel in his small triumph. Knowing this, subtle warmth seeped into his chest. He'd shown his peers he wasn't completely evil, giving up the boy without a mark. Weary, unpracticed, and sore, he'd still managed to live up to his distinction as one of Edward's more skillful knights. In his time, he'd earned land, a title, and money while on campaign and in tourneys, but this small victory held more worth to him than the largest campaign.

Matthias ran his gaze over his prize. Carrie wore a pale yellow wimple and matching gown. Like walking sunshine, she was an elegant vision. Beautiful. Her half-smile remained as she looked up at him. He felt dirty, sweaty, and tired, not worthy of being in her sight, but this one brief prize was all-important.

Though she wasn't truly his, no one around them knew it. He could kiss her in front of everyone again. Dammit, he wanted to feel her satiny lips against his, to taste her warm sweet mouth, and feel the power of victory as he held his woman in his arms for one moment.

"My chivalrous hero," she murmured, lips curving enchantingly. "I guess I'll never have to fear any man as long as I have you around."

She played her part as a newlywed with the skill of an award-winning actress, but he shoved that unwanted thought to the back of his mind.

"'Tis true, you should not. Now for that kiss."

Matthias put his hand at the small of her back and drew her closer to him. He leaned over, breathing in the slight fragrance of lavender that clung to her. Her eyelashes swept down, hiding her eyes, but her cheekbones remained pink, and her luscious lips beckoned.

His lips touched hers, chastely at first, remembering their audience, but he couldn't restrain himself. The opportunity would be gone soon enough. He wouldn't deny himself his reward.

He pressed his mouth harder against hers, and a surge of desire like the one he'd felt the night of the feast shot through him. Carrie's arms moved around his shoulders, and she opened her mouth to him. He greedily found her tongue and suckled it. She moved her body to fit his, pressing against him. He cursed the metal barrier of his mail between them. Then one of her hands left the mail at his shoulder and tenderly cupped the back of his neck. Oh, would that she put her hands on the rest of his flesh!

There must be some narcotic in her kisses that he'd become addicted to. Let the world go to the devil. He ran his rough hands over the curving valley of her back. The pleasurable sensation of her body against his replaced the sting of his blisters. When had he wanted another woman as much as he wanted Carrie? His tongue swirled in, out and across the line of her lips to their corners, tasting her. As her body molded to his, he longed to insinuate his hands between them, to free her of her dress and grasp her—

Behind them, someone cleared his throat.

Matthias ignored the interruption. He pulled away from Carrie's mouth, only to return to lay several softer kisses on her swollen lips.

"Excuse me, whelp." Rannulf said from the farthest reaches of his consciousness.

Matthias slowly dragged his mouth away from Carrie's. Keeping her in his arms, he glanced up through narrowed eyes to see Rannulf smiling apologetically. "What?" he asked in a husky voice.

"As much as I think a new bairn would ease your brother's sufferings," he said, sotto voce, "I trow hearing about your coupling on his training field would give Giles an apoplexy."

Carrie broke their embrace, stepping back with her face turned from him. He couldn't see her reaction, but he thought her hand lifted to her lips. Her shoulders heaved with a ragged breath. Had he crossed the line? Had he gone too far? Seconds ago, he'd had the impression she was enjoying herself as much as he, but now...what if he'd misinterpreted her acting for ardor?

Matthias gave the captain a look that sent the guard turning on his heel. He heard him chuckling as he hastened to catch up with the rest of men to return to their exercises.

Carrie brushed her garment briskly with her hands, as if she was trying to get his sweat and grime off of her.

She murmured, "Nice work, Professor. There should be no doubt from the castle gossips now."

Was he the only one affected by the kiss? His gut twisted at his foolhardiness.

"Aye, 'twas very convincing acting."

He spared another look at her, catching her demure smile just as it shattered upon his words. A line appeared between her eyebrows. All too late, he knew she had only been teasing him.

Her back stiffened. A thread of anger ran through her voice as she returned, "Well, I guess we don't need any more public displays then. We don't have to touch each other at all now."

She planted her hands on her hips, facing him with her eyes flashing a challenge. He stared at her, mute. She'd stolen his wits.

She let out a long breath of air and turned. He watched the mesmerizing swish of her hips as she marched away from him. He fought the urge to run after her. His head swam with thoughts of grabbing her back to him, kissing her, and whispering apologies in her sweet ear. His skin still tingled from the electrifying contact between them. Living with Carrie and not being able to touch her was naught but torture. What had he done?

****

Alone in the pitch darkness of the tower, Carrie heard the door open. A yellow glow filled the room, blinding her, so she squeezed her eyes shut. Boots and spurs scraped the floor, mail grating in the movement. She kept her eyes closed, not wanting Matthias to see she was still awake as she lay in bed. She didn't want to talk to him.

The way he kissed her that day was the single sexiest thing that had ever happened to her. No twenty-first century boyfriend had ever made her feel so desired, so beautiful, with a single kiss.

Not even in bed.

She'd felt Matthias's kiss all the way to her toes, for Pete's sake. The way he'd fought Ian with a sword and with such skill and strength. Then he'd asked for another kiss from her, making it seem like she was the only woman on earth.

Usually the only guys who showed any interest for her were complete jerks like Ian—adolescents who made vulgar remarks, loitering outside the entrance of the shopping mall. Men, especially those as attractive as Matthias, never gave her a second glance. Yet today he'd not only looked at her as if her dress was invisible, but he made her feel like he was really attracted to her.

And it was all for the sake of her protection.

She bit her lip. That kind of protection she could do without. Especially when his kisses made her blood heat and her nipples harden. When she looked at him in his heavy suit of mail, knowing all the flesh and muscle that filled it out, she couldn't help but picture him naked. It sent a shiver of delight down her. When he wrapped her in his arms and held her against that glorious male body, she went weak in the knees. And experiencing those kisses...at any instant she expected herself to melt into a puddle at the man's feet.

If the barrier of mail hadn't been between them, she'd bet money she would've had proof at least one part of him wasn't "acting."

Thud. Carrie flinched, and her eyes flew open. Matthias sat in a chair and removed his other boot. His face set hard in the light of his candle. He'd already removed his scabbard and sword.

Carrie intended to close her eyes before he caught her awake, but then his movements changed her mind. He loosened the laces of his tunic and pulled it over his head. His skin glowed warm in the candlelight, flickering shadows over smooth muscles. He probably thought she was asleep. She experienced a twinge of guilt. Ignoring her conscience, she boldly allowed her gaze to take in every inch of his chest below the scar on his neck. A decadent pleasure but one she would gladly indulge in.

Dark hair lightly covered the front of his chest, tapering into a line that disappeared into his pants. Her fingers itched to run over his rippling chest, to skim his nipples, and trail that inviting line of hair into his pants.

Matthias winced as he leaned back in his chair. Stretching out his legs, he closed his eyes on a sigh. The sight provoked a dark desire to straddle his narrow hips and put her mouth to his.

How was it that he didn't have a wife? Or at least a woman who shared his bed back at his modern home in Cardiff?

A frown creased his brow under a tumble of

dark hair. The circles under his eyes were darker, making him look weary. Little wonder at the rate he'd been practicing that day. Keeping his eyes closed, he attempted to re-position his back in the wooden chair. The man looked pained, no longer defiant or angry. And despite her anger at him, she couldn't ignore his discomfort.

"You know," she sat up on one elbow to playfully complain, "any decent human being would come in quietly and put out their light if someone was trying to sleep."

He quickly sat up and reached for the candle. She immediately wished she hadn't spoken.

"Wait. It's okay. I wasn't asleep."

His expression closed, and he turned from her gaze. "One of your spit boys made me drink your tea before I came up." His voice dripped with contempt, but she wasn't sure why. Maybe he wasn't a tea drinker.

"That was Simon." Why they called them spit boys, she didn't understand. Simon had to be twenty-five if he was a day. Smoothing the blanket beside her, she told him, "I asked him to keep an eye out for you. I was going to remind you to drink the tea myself, but you stayed out too late."

"I rode out with some of the knights to survey the area." His gaze followed the movement of her hand on the bed. "I don't think the herbs will do any good, but thanks for the effort."

His gray gaze flicked up at her briefly, and then he looked away. The candle caught the brackets of weariness around his mouth.

"Matthias," Carrie braced herself for the rejection her offer would surely cause and then plunged ahead, "you don't have to sleep in the loft or the floor or the chair. You could sleep in the bed with me. It's big enough for us both."

An unreadable emotion crossed his face. "Aye,

but...you look comfortable when you're sleeping. I haven't wanted to bother you."

She'd be lying if she said it wouldn't bother her to sleep next to him, so she didn't say it. "You're making yourself miserable. I know you'll sleep better if we share the bed. It's okay, really."

He made a sketch of a nod of gratitude and blew out the candle. In the blackness, she heard him amble over to the bed, and he climbed in to take up the space she'd given him.

The ropes of the bed gave under his weight, and her body rolled toward him on the mattress. She quickly scooted away before their bodies touched. Though she couldn't see him, she could feel his presence beside her, warmth emanating beneath the cover from where he lay. His breath came in a steady rhythm, but the small movements he made told her he remained awake.

Oh, this wasn't a good idea, she thought dismally.

"Carrie?"

"Yes?"

She heard him swallow. "I think if you rubbed my hand again, it might relax me."

She almost laughed. So he wanted her to touch him again without anyone around to see?

Yet the tone of his voice told her what the request cost him.

Although she would rather avoid touching him and the powerful longings their contact caused her, she couldn't say no. Feelings of empathy outweighed her sense of self-preservation. "Okay. If you think it'll help."

She reached out toward him in the dark and caught his outstretched hand. Their fingers interlaced briefly, and then she took his big palm between hers. He rolled toward her on the bed, but moved no closer. Her fingers worked over the new blisters on his fingers and palm, the results of his practice earlier that day. She squelched the urge to kiss his rough hand, not wanting to give him more grief.

"Back at home, I always read a book before I went to sleep. It took my mind off the day," she told him. "We don't have any books here, but maybe you could tell me one of your bardic tales."

His hand relaxed under her ministrations. "Are you saying my stories would bore you to sleep?" She heard the smile in his voice.

"Oh, no. Definitely not. I loved the story you told about Rhiannon. Where did you learn to tell stories like that?"

"It's a tradition among Druids to have a bard in their clan. In the ancient days, bards would meet at the dolmen in the standing stones. Maud's husband Iago was the local bard until he died, while I was still fighting in Acre. I used to visit him as often as I could get away from the castle."

He sighed gently, making her wonder if it was from her massage or from the memories.

"It drove my father crazy, but I had more interest in learning the old Welsh legends than in my training. Iago taught me every story he knew, hoping I would replace him some day as a bard. But I was destined for knighthood instead," his voice grew wistful, filled with ironic humor. "I think as a young squire I longed to fashion myself as one of Arthur's knights from the bardic stories, as if all kings were bent on wars for noble causes and all knights for chivalric ones."

To look at him, Carrie would've never guessed he was capable of telling such wonderful stories. When she'd first laid eyes on him, he certainly hadn't appeared scholarly, either. Just a warrior, looking out of place in business attire.

Her fingertips grazed over the strong bones of

his hand. "You enjoy teaching at the university, don't you?"

"'Tis easier than war, and it was nice to be in charge of my own destiny. As a knight, my life and my body belong to King Edward."

Holding and caressing his hand, she imagined what that body looked like in the dark next to her. Although Matthias sounded as if he disliked his body belonging to anyone, she wished she could possess it.

Matthias switched hands, silently urging her to caress the other. Then he began another tale from the *Mabinogion* collection about Culhwch's quest to free Mabon, the Celtic god of youth. Matthias quietly breathed life into the old story. His Welsh heroes piqued her interest as he spoke. His story told of jealousy, King Arthur, ancient animals who talked, and a prisoner set free. The tale fascinated her more than she'd ever been entertained by a dumb action movie.

The rich characters came to life with his Gaelic-tinted purr, and Carrie dared not interrupt him to leave the tale unfinished, even as the hour grew late. She'd take his rousing voice any night over a book.

Eventually, his words tapered off. Carrie suppressed a complaint for him to finish the story. She heard his breath flowing evenly beside her in the dark.

Had he fallen asleep?

"Matthias?" she whispered. She didn't want to wake him. He'd earned the rest.

When he made no answer, she rolled onto her side, trying to make out some outline of him in the dark. Why hadn't she left the window open, at least a crack?

Her hand reached toward him and found his arm. She ran her palm up the warm, hard curves, and she whispered his name once more. Nothing.

Asleep, then.

Her stomach squeezed agreeably. There was something completely sexy about Matthias even in his sleep.

Carrie chewed her lip thoughtfully. She'd said they didn't have to touch anymore, but what would it hurt to kiss him when he wasn't awake to know about it?

Leaning over him, she followed the sound of his sleep—the even ebb of air directing her in the dark—until she located his mouth and his breath warmed her ear. She pressed a soft, lingering kiss to his lips. His mouth filled her head with intimate fantasies she would never experience.

Settling back on her pillow, she smiled, somewhat satisfied with her secret conquest.

"Goodnight," he murmured.

Chapter Ten

For the first time since their arrival, Matthias awoke from a night that held no nightmares. His brain registered a good deep rest, and he hadn't been disturbed in his slumber by the memory of Ian's clutch on Carrie's clothes, of Giles's emaciated face, or of Isabelle's crying. Warmth pressed against the flesh of his side, reminding him why the torturous memories had left him in peace. He opened his eyes to see soft, honey-colored hair lying against his upper arm and a slender arm lightly draped across his abdomen. Carrie wore only her chemise to bed the night before, and now the swells of her breasts lay exposed to his view in the unraveled laces of her garment. His loins tightened.

Villain that he was, Matthias considered turning her onto her back so he could get a better view of her in the flimsy gown. Better still, he could run his hands inside the gaping neckline and fondle her soft round breasts. Knowing she would likely wake up and catch him, provided the only reason he chose to keep his hands out of her clothing. Well, that and the fact that she'd invited him to the bed out of concern, not to be groped by his clumsy self.

Taking great pains not to disturb her, he shoved more of the pillow under his head, keeping his view of her luscious body. His fingers lifted of their own volition to her face, trembling with care as he smoothed a stray lock of silky hair away from her lips. With his view of her face unobstructed, he admired her features.

Giles's illness must've addled his mind for he'd

never seen anyone more beautiful than Caroline Greer. Her brown eyelashes fanned against youthful peach skin. Her cheekbones were high, noble, but he recalled how sweetly they colored each time he'd kissed her. His gaze drifted to her mouth, and a fantasy spun in his head of her waking and lifting that mouth to his, as if they were truly married.

The same way she'd kissed him goodnight.

He'd never had the pleasure of waking up with a woman beside him before. He'd visited women's beds of course, when invited, but he never stayed long enough to fall asleep with a woman. He dared not, fearing that the moment he awoke, the ugly memories of another morning would return.

Bruises darkening on alabaster skin...

Matthias shook away the thoughts. He mustn't think of that now. He'd dallied in dangerous fantasy and longings too long.

"*Carys.* Carrie," he roughened his tone, hiding away the vestiges of his weakness. In Welsh her name meant "to love." Its irony mocked him.

"Hmmmm," she moaned groggily.

In her sleep, her fingertips raked softly, provocatively, across his abdomen, coming to rest just above his groin.

Matthias covered himself to his waist. He needed to get her up and out of bed immediately, before she saw the state he'd gotten himself into.

"Time to wake up."

"Oh." Her eyes opened, and she sat up blinking.

Matthias cursed himself for being an idiot. Carrie's chemise slid down in the movement, offering him the glimpse he'd yearned for. A dusky pink nipple peaked out between the loosened white laces of her gown. His mouth watered with sudden hunger.

As her sleepy eyes focused on him, her face went pink. With a guilty smile, she babbled, "I didn't mean to crowd you. I guess the bed wasn't as big as I thought. Sorry. You could've just pushed me off, you know. I wouldn't have been offended."

Still a knight, no matter the tarnish of his armor, Matthias reached for the opening of her chemise and drew it across her beautiful breast, hiding her from his view. He crossed his arms and secured his hands firmly beneath them before he lost all leave of his senses and removed her clothing. "Yes, you would've."

The pink of her face went scarlet clear down her neck. "Oh." She caught her lower lip between her teeth.

His tongue felt thick, but he managed to speak. "Get dressed, and after breakfast I'll take you to Maud's."

Mercifully, she did as he asked, leaving the bed in a flash. She grabbed a tunic and surcoat, dashing upstairs to dress in the loft. Matthias gathered his own clothing and left the chamber for a much-needed cold bath.

Taking two armed guards as insurance against a Welsh attack, Matthias and Carrie rode the path toward Maud's cottage. Seeing the horses in the stables had reminded Matthias that Carrie couldn't drive a car due to her seizures. Horses could be another transportation hazard. She protested she could ride her own horse, but Matthias refused to allow it. He knew precious little about epileptic seizures, but he knew more than enough about falls from horses. As long as they were in the Middle Ages, she would have to ride with him or not ride at all. Keeping her settled in front of him, safe in the circle of his arms, Matthias enjoyed the fragrance of her hair and the sweet torture of her perfect buttocks situated between his thighs.

When the familiar wood of the forest came into view, looming so near the henge, it shook him from his lustful thoughts. For some reason, the idea of being anywhere in the vicinity of the standing stones again gave his heart an icy chill. He hated the stones. Always had, since he'd known their potential. They had the power to unite people and the power to separate them. He hated the portal more than ever.

They reached the cottage at the edge of the woods. Matthias heard Carrie gasp when the dwelling came into view.

To strangers, the place could've been a mirage. But it was real.

Pastel-colored flowers flanked the modest house as if in an enchanted fairy-tale. Aware of Carrie's interest in flora, he had little doubt the wattle and daub cottage surrounded with Maud's summer herbs in full bloom impressed her. Among her other talents, Maud had a green thumb.

The riders reined in their horses. Carrie tossed back a radiant smile at Matthias, causing his chest to constrict.

Damn. He stopped his horse just short of the path to the cottage. Instantly wary, he remembered why he hadn't wished to bring Carrie here. Maud was no witch—he'd known that even as a child—but the healer didn't live inside the castle walls. Although she was living on Giles's land as his tenant, Maud's position outside the castle walls ensured her freedom from following orders. If Giles had even thought to silence her about Isabelle, Maud wouldn't care. Cantankerous and unpredictable, she would do as she chose. If she wanted to tell Carrie about his past, then by God she would.

Suddenly, Carrie slid out of the saddle. Before he could think of a way to stop her, she swept up the stone path, winding her way through the tall, bright hollyhocks toward Maud's door. Panic held him. He was at the crone's mercy.

****

As if expected, Maud met Carrie at her doorway.
The grandmotherly old woman had gray hair tied in
a leather band behind her back and wore an equally
gray tunic. Her apron, once white, bore a variety of
green-tinged stains, evidence of her work. She
greeted Carrie with wide curious eyes. As soon as
Carrie introduced herself as Sir Matthias's bride, the
old woman threw the door open, gesturing warmly
for her to enter.

Carrie glanced over her shoulder.

Matthias remained several feet behind. What
was the matter with him?

The guards' troubles were transparent. They
dismounted yards away, keeping a suspicious eye on
Maud at the door. Likely, they expected her to turn
them all into toad frogs or worse. But Matthias?

A man of reason and intelligence, he wouldn't
believe the healer to be a witch, surely. Carrie
frowned as he finally followed her inside the house.
His face pulled into a deep scowl.

The old woman offered them a seat. Incredibly,
the little cottage seemed even smaller on the inside,
especially with Matthias's large frame crowding the
room, but the true lack of space had to be from the
amount of things crammed inside. Shafts of sunlight
spilled through holes in the straw roof illuminating
the collected work of the healer. There were pots,
pans, clay jars, and drying herbs from the ceiling to
the floor. The air smelled thick, almost
overpowering, with the aroma of so many potent
plants in one place. Mints, sage, savory, lemon balm,
basil, and so much more. Carrie breathed deeply.
For her, the cottage was heaven.

Maud's eyes twinkled as a smile creased her
face.

"At last you've come home, Math," the healer
spoke to him first. "You must tell me about your
travels."

The old woman leaned expectantly toward Matthias. Her eager expression still held beauty. She regarded them through wise brown eyes, and her appearance wasn't marred in the least by its deep lines of many years' knowledge. Crow's feet of a thousand smiles spanned over her taupe-colored cheeks, and Carrie fell instantly at ease with one who had taken such pleasure in her life.

"What do you know of my travels, Maud?"

Carrie sensed the caution in Matthias's deep voice.

Surely he didn't distrust the sweet old woman. Her husband Iago had once been a great teacher and friend to Matthias. If they were lucky, she might even have knowledge about the time portal and the henge's secret.

Maud chuckled and shrugged. "Last I saw you, you were riding a warhorse hell-bent toward the river. That was on Beltane. Then we heard of you no more."

Carrie and Matthias exchanged a look. Was she privy to the portal's power? Did they dare tell her? If she knew nothing about it, even the local witch would think they were crazy. There had to be some way to ask her.

The healer looked at Carrie with eyes that seemed to reach inside her. "So, Math brought you back with him. What think you of Wyldnell? What think you of us?"

Carrie twisted her hands nervously in her lap. "I think Wyldnell is very large, very magnificent. Who did you want my opinion of?"

"Anyone. Everyone."

Carrie looked at Matthias, who was no help. His dark brows furrowed, and his stare fixed on the old woman. At least he wasn't looking at *her*. After the kiss she'd stolen last night and since he'd seen her half-naked that morning, she'd barely been able to meet his eyes without flushing furiously. Even the short horseback ride to Maud's had almost been too uncomfortable to bear. The heat of his body excited her. His hard thighs around her as they'd sat in the saddle filled her head with wild fantasies. But he must not have liked what he'd seen earlier since he'd been so quick to cover her.

Carrie began to tell Maud about the individuals she'd met and gotten to know.

"There's Sir Rannulf. He tells some great off-color jokes. I mean, he tends to speak of things that aren't suitable for young ladies to hear." Carrie cast a look of apology at Matthias for her faux pas and then went on. "As big as he is, I think he could be useful as a friend rather than a foe."

Maud nodded, smiling. Then, growing serious, she informed her, "Rannulf ignores his ailments. I have to watch him like a hawk, lest he suffer in silence. The stubborn oaf."

Carrie filed that piece of information away. She rubbed her chin and continued, "I also met Edwina."

Maud folded her hands in her lap. "Aye. Now there's someone who knows more about the castle than the earl himself. She's lived there nearly as long as him."

"Yes." Carrie conceded with a grin, "And she's eager to share her knowledge."

"No secret is safe with Edwina, I fear."

Maud exchanged a knowing smile with Carrie. Then her brown eyes cut to Matthias and narrowed. When she glanced back at Carrie, the look was gone.

Carrie chewed the inside of her cheek. Was the old woman hiding something?

"And the earl? What do you make of Math's brother?" Maud gestured toward Matthias, who merely scowled back and directed his attention to the rafters.

"Matthias's brother is very decent to us,

allowing us to stay in Wyldnell. I'm told he admires your work with herbs, and he uses your medicine to appease his sickness."

The old woman laughed. "To say Lord Wyldnell 'admires' my work is being too generous. 'Tis more like he *fears* my work, I trow."

Carrie smiled. The new direction of the conversation reminded her of her main reason for visiting. "You've seen him, Maud. You know how sick he is. I came here today thinking perhaps you and I could work together to help him get well. Where I come from, I grow herbs and harvest them. I know some of their uses, too."

Maud smiled openly at Matthias, revealing a surprisingly healthy set of teeth. "You were always a clumsy boy, Math, despite all your experience in battle. It was very clever of you to wed a healer." She patted Carrie's hand briefly. "I am glad you are here, my lady. The earl's illness is very grave. It does not help that he takes my medicine without paying any heed to my advice. I have done everything I know to do, so he should have been cured by now. Mayhap you can persuade him to use my medicines properly."

"I'll try, but I don't think he'll listen to me either. He talks about me as if I'm not in the room." Carrie heaved a sigh.

She told Maud of her two disappointing encounters with the nobleman.

Maud nodded, a sad smile on her lips.

"Our world doesn't hold smart women in the highest regard. Men simply don't trust intelligence in females," she explained. "It reminds them that they're not as necessary to us as they think they are."

Maud's words were true sometimes even in the modern world.

The healer asked what herbs she needed to take

back, and Carrie recited the list she'd memorized. Finally, she asked if she had any moon plants.

Maud's gaze lifted to where Matthias sat brooding in unfriendly silence.

She asked Carrie quietly, "Do you have need of them, my lady?"

Halleluiah. She knew the plants. "Yes. Well, I'd hoped to try them, anyway. They're for me."

"The falling sickness." Maud placed a cool, withered hand on Carrie's cheek. "I do have some, my lady, and you may come back for more whenever you need."

The old woman began to collect the herb bundles. Carrie closed her eyes, filled with relief. When she opened them again, she shot Matthias a smile, but his dark eyes remained on the healer.

"Matthias," Carrie spoke, bringing his attention back, "would you fetch my sack from the horse?" She'd brought a cloth bag from the castle to carry back the herbs.

His narrowed eyes tracked Maud across the room. He didn't budge.

"Please, Matthias. We need to get these back to your brother as soon as possible."

After what appeared to be a great inner struggle, he finally rose and went outside.

He'd been out of the room for no more than a few seconds when Maud laid an ancient hand on Carrie's sleeve. There was a sense of urgency in her voice as she told her solemnly, "Watch yourself in the castle, my lady."

Her eyes peered up into Carrie's face, full of seriousness.

"W-what?" Carrie gasped, unable to account for the swift change in the kindly woman, but her heart quickened.

"There is danger in Wyldnell for you. Evil, lies, deceit. Math will try to protect you, but he's been away a long time. Even he doesn't know or recognize the true danger. Use caution. You're in danger, my lady. Math—"

"Math, what?"

Carrie gave a guilty start. Matthias's figure filled the doorway at the mention of his name, barring the daylight and casting a shadow over the women. There was an angry edge to his voice. It had once frightened her. She no longer feared him or his temper.

"Maud was telling me that she thought we were in some sort of danger in—"

"Maud can pack her things and find a new home," he interrupted bitterly. His chest rose and fell in heavy breaths. "I'll not tolerate a gossip and neither will Giles."

Her stomach plunged. "Matthias!"

Carrie's horrified censure fell on deaf ears. In jerky movements, he began to shove the chosen herbs into the bag.

As he continued to collect the medicines, Carrie protested to his back, "She's only trying to help us. She's already helped us so much, and she's Iago's wife. How could you be such a jerk?"

Angry tears filled her eyes, but she didn't care if he saw them. It wasn't right to evict an old woman from her own home.

He looked at Carrie, his face closed and impassive.

Then rounding on Maud, he told her, "One more word of gossip or warnings of evil to Carrie and you *will* find yourself a new home. Understood?"

With her mouth set in a hard line, Maud handed him another pouch of medicine. She returned quietly, "Banished like you, Math?"

Matthias snatched it, stuffed it in the bag, and reached for Carrie's wrist. Dragging her behind him, he told her outside, "You may never come back here.

141

Her gossip is like venom."

His hard grasp hurt. His fingers held like a vise.

"I don't see why you're so mad. What harm could that nice woman do? Let go."

He released her so quickly she almost fell backward. Carrie pushed past him and dashed for the horse. Her heartbeat thundered in her throat. By the time she reached the animal, her eyes dripped with tears. His anger made no sense, no sense at all.

Try as she might, she couldn't mount the giant horse as easily as she'd dismounted. Her foot in the stirrup, she strained to gain enough momentum to get her other foot over him, only to slide back down again. She hated being dependent on anyone, but especially Matthias at this moment. His boots crunched over the grass behind her, and she felt his hands grip her waist. With ease, he hoisted her up to ride sidesaddle and mounted behind her.

Carrie tried to will her tears of anger away as Matthias drew their horse alongside one of the mounted guards. In a low voice, he said something to the man Carrie couldn't hear. The guard whipped his horse back in the direction of Maud's house as they went ahead to the castle.

Worry seized her. Why had Matthias sent a guard back to Maud? What was he doing? Why was he so angry about the old woman's warnings? Maud probably meant no harm. Was he going to evict her, after all?

He hadn't even bothered to ask Maud about the standing stones. Did he no longer care that they might not be able to go back?

A sob escaped. She bit her lip to stifle more.

She gripped the saddle as they rode, taking care not to touch Matthias, but she couldn't avoid the contact with his legs and arms. His arms encircled her as they had before, strong and secure then, but now shaking.

"What is wrong with you?" she finally yelled.

Matthias pulled the beast under them to a hard stop. He put a shaking hand under her chin and gently turned her face to him. "Please. Dry your eyes, *Carys*."

He reached inside his tunic and withdrew a clean white handkerchief. Carrie took it, trying to avoid his searching gray eyes. She dabbed at her eyes and damp cheeks and then looked at the cloth. It was the one she'd brought with her through the portal and had left with him when he'd hurt his head. She frowned, astonished he'd thought to keep it after everything that had happened that day.

But his brief chivalry wasn't enough to make up for his ruthless actions.

Over her shoulder, she snapped, "Explain yourself, Matthias. What did you say to that guard? Did you decide to throw Maud out after all?"

She twisted the cloth in her hands. When she glanced back at him, she caught a red flush as it crept up his neck.

He grumbled, "I told him to fix the holes in her roof."

"Oh."

Tongue-tied, Carrie averted her face, wiping again her eyes and nose. Her frustration melted. His intentions were nobler than she had given him credit for. One of Matthias's hands fell on her shoulder, and his fingers tenderly caressed her. Her traitorous body gave a great shudder under his easing touch. She couldn't pretend she didn't welcome it. Leaning back against his sturdy chest, her body slowly righted itself. Above her head, he blew out a deep breath that stirred her hair. And warmed her heart.

They sat still for several minutes with him holding her that way until the horse shifted impatiently under them. The rest of their ride to the castle was made in blessed silence. The slow progress gave her time to collect herself. His behavior confused her more than any mystery she'd ever known.

Her own behavior was little better—crying like a child.

Yet, something in his quiet presence soothed her. In spite of Matthias's unpredictable foul moods and poor manners, she was beginning to adore him. Surely, she was doomed for disaster.

Chapter Eleven

Spending the afternoon in Edwina's company, Carrie sought the solace that only one thing brought her—work. First, they created a storeroom of medicines in an unused chamber of the keep, and she labeled each vessel of dried herbs with ink and a quill pen. Then she finished reorganizing the kitchen with Cook's help. Later Edwina brought more clothing for mending, and in spite of her dislike of the chore, Carrie felt pleased to be busy and have someone to talk to. Whenever she lingered too long in thought, her mind strayed to Matthias and his contradicting actions of kindness and displeasure.

Their public displays of affection meant nothing to him. For her, the passion was a chemical change. Her body went into spontaneous combustion, while he found her offensive. At least touching her *seemed* to be offensive to him. There was no telling what he thought about her tears that morning, but Carrie had no doubt her crying had been the cause of his quick departure from the castle.

She was sick of being dependent on him, wanting his approval, and then only earning his aversion. Matthias hadn't even seen her at her worst yet. How would he react when she had a seizure? If she repulsed him now, she couldn't bear to think of his rejection of her then.

There were only a few days of medication left. The moon plants might delay the seizures just as her prescription barbiturates had, but nothing would cause the spells to stop completely. She'd long ago accepted that fact. It was important to tell people around her what to do when the time came. There were many dangers for epileptics and for those who tried to interfere with the seizures, but she dreaded speaking of it to Matthias.

He would see it as a reminder of her inadequacy. Though she longed to be strong and independent, she only presented herself as weak and incapable in his eyes.

However, she couldn't ignore the butterflies when he showed concern for her. She enjoyed a momentary pleasure each time he performed some small act of gallantry. She guiltily reveled in sharing a horse, how he checked to be sure she was taking her medicine and saw to her comforts in their shared room.

Edwina sighed impatiently beside her, pausing in her stitching in the sunny chamber to purse her lips thoughtfully. "My lady, how would you like to go out for a while? 'Tis a shame to waste a beautiful afternoon."

Carrie shook her head, flushing at being caught woolgathering. "I've already been out today. Besides, we have two more pairs of braies to patch."

"At the rate you're sewing, my lady, 'twill be a fortnight before they're done."

Carrie cringed. It was true. She'd barely sewed an inch in the last twenty minutes.

"You were interested in the orchard, were you not?"

Her mood lifted instantly. "Oh, yes."

Giving no more argument, Carrie abandoned her stitchery for the outdoors.

Matthias's mother had designed the landscape of the orchard and outer flower garden. Seeing the life growing there, Carrie ached with longing for home, but the place was filled with such spiritual beauty and tranquility. She couldn't remain melancholy while surrounded by Eden.

Her own small garden in old Charleston's historic district was simply a courtyard space with a large magnolia tree stealing much of the sunlight and gardening area. Her plants were restricted to four flower beds. Wyldnell's plantings were vast in comparison, spreading across acres. Sculptured rose gardens were planted and tended at one end of the orchard and grape vines at the other. There were apple, pear, plum, and peach trees gently shading the field.

The medieval gardening methods intrigued her, so different from her own. She meandered past strange straw baskets turned upside down and scattered throughout the orchard. A bee whizzed past her head and disappeared inside one of the baskets. Not upside down at all. Hives, used for making the castle's wax candles and honey. Edwina found an apple tree full of ripe round fruit and started to fill her apron with them for Cook to put in a pie.

Laughter, coming from the other side of the grape vines, penetrated the serenity of their peaceful work. Curious, Carrie followed the sounds. Peeking between the broad leaves of evenly staked vines, she saw a meadow bordered with strewn bales of hay. An arrow whispered through the air, descending into a bale. Rannulf's hearty laugh of approval scared the birds back into the orchard. Three young boys armed with bows and arrows took aim into the air under the direction of Rannulf and Matthias.

Matthias stood behind one flaxen-haired boy about twelve years-old as he pulled his bow back, pointing the arrow high at the cloudless sky. Carrie strained to hear what he said to the boy, but she was too far away. His pupil released his arrow, and it sailed up before arcing down to spear the target. Ecstatic, the youth shared a big smile among the others. Matthias ruffled the boy's hair and patted him on the back.

Carrie's heart fluttered.

Fatherhood would do him good and make him take more pleasure from life. Inasmuch, a child of his would surely be lucky to have such a protector, who could tell exciting bedtime stories of heroes until the wee hours of the morning.

Some words exchanged between the red-headed captain and Matthias, and the two men picked up bows of their own. The boys moved aside as the men took their places in a friendly contest. Rannulf released an arrow into the same bale that his protégé had targeted and struck it to the left of the previous arrow. Matthias threw back his head in laughter, and Carrie's heart leapt. Handsome when he was smiling, Matthias was devastating when he laughed. She couldn't take her eyes off the sight.

Continuing the contest, Matthias sobered. His countenance altered completely as he took the same stance as Rannulf. He narrowed his eyes as he scanned treetops for wind changes. His arms rippled with sinewy strength as he drew his arrow, studied the target, aimed and fired. Matthias's arrow came to a stop at the dead center of the target.

"Hoorah, Math!" Edwina yelled beside Carrie.

Carrie jerked involuntarily at the interruption of her thoughts. She'd been so consumed in watching the men she forgot her friend.

Edwina turned to her and boasted, "Rarely does any solo archer hit a target with a longbow. The Welsh use the longbow in groups, firing on enemies by storm with no true accuracy. But not my Math. 'E always was the best with the arrows."

Carrie thought to duck behind the grape vines for cover, but it was too late. She would look like a complete moron if she tried to dodge their notice now. The group of archers slung their bows over their shoulders and came to address them. Matthias lagged behind the others, the last to join them.

"Did Dionysus lose two nymphs in his vineyard?" Rannulf winked at the ladies. Sweat made his bristling hair sparkle like copper wire.

Edwina blushed and launched an apple at his head, missing him. "Nay, there's no god of wine in Wyldnell, but mayhap an Apollo or two."

He shrugged a big shoulder. "We're just showing these young squires what capable teachers we are. I think they're ready to be done with us, though."

One of the boys took a bite of the apple Edwina had thrown.

"Do you lads want to help Cook gather the rest of the apples? He's baking apple pies tonight, and—"

The youths excused themselves and ran for the orchard gate before Edwina could finish her sentence.

"So what about you, ladies? Are either of you ready to play Artemis, goddess of the hunt?" Rannulf gestured toward his bow.

Carrie allowed herself a glimpse of Matthias. Leaning against a fence post by the lush vines with his arms crossed over his broad chest, he didn't seem interested in the conversation or entertaining women at archery. Sweat lined the sides of his face, and his dark hair seemed almost black where it clung to his moist brow. He wore only a tunic, and made damp with exercise, it amplified the contours of his muscles beneath the white fabric. The sight had an erotic effect on her. Intoxicating. She chewed her lower lip as her gaze devoured him. He was Eros, if he was any god of myth, and if she was his target, the arrow had found its mark.

His sleeves were rolled back to his elbows, exposing the capable tanned arms she'd been admiring during their practice. She would die if he helped her shoot the bow. Surely, the intimate proximity with his large, hot body would kill her.

"Nay, not me, but my lady would love the diversion," Edwina told Rannulf.

Carrie shot her a withering look.

"What luck then, for Math is an excellent tutor—as you've seen for yourselves. Come, Lady Carrie." Rannulf motioned toward the gate.

Matthias shifted on his feet, frowning slightly.

"Oh, no. I...I don't think I want to," Carrie demurred.

Edwina moved behind her and attempted to steer her by the shoulders. "You've got two good men to help you, milady. Go, go."

Carrie gave a slight smile, but her stomach felt queasy. Quailing from head to toe, she dug in her heels. "I really don't want to. I mean I'd like to, but just not today."

"'Tis easy," Rannulf beckoned. "We'll even move the targets closer, won't we, Math?"

"My lady-wife is not dressed for the sport. Her kirtle would be dirtied," he murmured with a shake of his head. His gaze slid from hers when she looked his way.

Edwina and Rannulf persisted, probably thinking her shy, but she held firm. There was no way she was going to encroach upon Matthias further today.

A shout interrupted their discourse. Ian ran across the meadow toward them. He could hardly breathe when he reached his father and Matthias.

Leaning deeply over his legs, he said, "It's Lord Wyldnell. He's having trouble breathing and he won't stop vomiting."

****

"He's asked for you. He won't see the physick anymore or even Maud," Ian told Matthias standing at the foot of Giles's bed. "He won't accept anyone's help."

Matthias looked down at his brother, feeling as

helpless as a babe as Giles coughed up nothing but
air. His skin had taken a pale green pallor with the
sickness. Jesu, what could he do to save him? If only
he could make the portal work. He'd take him to a
hospital emergency room. With tests and proper
care, Giles would probably be saved from his plight.

How unfair that he'd been the one to travel in
time while Giles remained here, dying. Had the
irony of Fate and the capricious portal forced him to
be a spectator at his own brother's death?

"What has he been eating today?" Carrie asked.

She spun from Giles's bedside to examine a
nearby tray on a table. Edwina opened a window,
letting in more air for his gasping brother.

Baldric, one of the earl's attendants answered,
"My lord has eaten all that Cook sent. To break his
fast, salmon and eggs."

"That wasn't what I told him to make," Carrie
complained, sniffing a dirty bowl.

Matthias and Ian helped Giles settle back on his
pillows. Weakened, his brother could hardly move on
his own. His entire body shuddered with cold.
Edwina shuffled to the bed, carrying an armload of
blankets. Matthias helped her draw covers over
Giles's skinny form.

"Did Cook leave out the spices, at least?"

"Nay, my lady. His lordship received a tray
without seasoning first. He took one bite, spit it out,
cursed Cook for a demon and sent the tray back for
spices. Garlic, peppers, and horseradish."

Ian nodded. "Cook wouldn't dare do aught
against his lordship's wishes."

Carrie moved to Giles's side and checked his
brow for fever. Concern flashed in her violet eyes as
she leaned over him and admonished him quietly,
"You're a fool, my lord. You're making yourself
worse. In the hospitals where I come from, sick
people eat bland food. No spices. Until you're better,

you can't keep eating that stuff."

Giles lifted his head long enough to gargle at Matthias, "G-get your wench out of here. I am suffering enough without hearing her nag!"

Matthias met Carrie's eyes over his head.

He didn't want her to go. He needed her composure, her strength, but he felt his heart ripping. "You'd better leave us."

"Don't side with him, Matthias. You know he's wrong."

"It doesn't matter. He needs peace."

A wall of pain fissured inside him. Dear God, not his brother. Giles trembled violently, huffing for air. Defeated, Matthias sat at his brother's side and dropped his face in his hands. He should stay there until the very end, even if it tore him to pieces.

He would gladly take all the pain upon himself if it were possible.

"Ian, can you read?" He heard Carrie ask.

Giles would've insisted on the young knight's education. With his generosity to the neighboring abbey, Giles provided all the young squires with monks as tutors. It was one of the few things Matthias and his brother agreed on.

"Aye, my lady. I can."

Carrie commanded quietly, "Good. Go to my storeroom. Edwina can't read, but she can show you where my medicines are. Find the jar labeled foxglove. If you don't see it, lily-of-the-valley will do, but try to find foxglove. Also, ask Cook for the earl's tea."

Matthias glanced up to see them depart. Carrie handled a bowl and a cloth at Giles's bedside.

She murmured, "Rest easy, my lord. You'll soon feel better and we can discuss your new diet."

Rubbing his pounding head, Matthias watched his brother's face contort with horror.

"I don't *want* a new diet. There's naught wrong

with my food."

Carrie gently applied a wet cloth to his perspiring brow. His distressed brother didn't realize how much she looked like an angel at his side. Her golden brown hair glowed in the candlelight as she administered her care. Matthias kept his eyes on her, desperately seeking the comfort of her beauty over the gut-wrenching sight of his brother in agony.

"Quiet, now," she soothed. "We'll argue later. The tea I've sent for has chamomile tea sweetened with honey and some medicine. If you're going to be ill, at least you'll have something in your stomach to come up. The herb is very smooth and mild."

He let out a wail, "Matthias!" His silver brows pinched together.

"Carrie." Matthias couldn't take it anymore. Something in him snapped. He grasped her forearm across the bed. "You're overstepping your bounds. My brother wants you gone."

"I'm trying to help him, Matthias. You've got to let me try."

"Nay." Could she not see it was too late? If Giles was dying, he needed to be left alone.

Her eyes pleaded with him. Glancing at his hold on her arm, he saw angry red and white marks where his fingers bit into her skin. Appalled, he released her as if he clutched fire.

He crossed his arms over his chest, hands restrained. Carrie went about her business as if nothing had happened.

When she turned her attention back to Giles, Matthias stood in his brother's chamber just as he had nine years ago, watching Isabelle as she tended to some care of her husband's. She had loved Giles and he had never doubted it. Giles had worshipped her as well.

Giles didn't deserve to die alone with him. He deserved to die with his wife at his side, although now that wasn't possible.

Matthias knew what he had to do. His brother would die in the arms of an angel attending him, not with a black-hearted demon like him looking down.

"Carrie," his voice came out as a rasp, "will you stay with him until it's over? Take care of him. I'll leave."

He backed away from the bed.

"I don't want you to do that, Matthias. Please stay. Stay here with us in case—"

"Nay!" He shouted. Her eyes were imploring, but his emotions were a maelstrom twisting out of control. He whispered roughly, "He needs you, not me. Dammit, I don't want to be the last face he sees."

Carrie reached out, making another protest, but he avoided her and stormed out the door. Matthias tore down the stairs, putting as much distance as he could between them. Carrie didn't understand the guilt he felt. She would probably hate him forever for abandoning her, but staying was impossible. Some sins were worse than leaving his brother's side.

****

Edwina and Ian stayed with her until late in the evening when the earl finally fell asleep. Carrie half-expected Matthias to return to check on his brother's condition. When he didn't, she believed he would be waiting anxiously for news of Giles's health, or perhaps he'd already anticipated the man's passing. The scene had been traumatic when he'd left them. Edwina told her later that Rannulf followed Matthias out, saying he didn't like sickbeds, but Carrie had a feeling he wanted to keep an eye on his friend. For that, she was thankful. With Rannulf in attendance, she needn't worry about where Matthias had gone or what he was doing in his agitated state.

Weariness saturated every inch of her as she mounted the stairs to their bedchamber, but she braced herself for a confrontation with Matthias. He'd abandoned his brother at an ungodly time when the ill man had needed him most. And, she balled her fists, when she'd needed him, too.

Unforgivable, and yet she harbored a hope no, a surefire *faith* that Matthias wasn't as self-centered as he appeared tonight.

At her chamber door, her theory about Rannulf proved correct. The big captain sat on a chair at the top of the stairs and stood when he saw her. "My lady."

His sorrowful eyes were downcast. To ease his suffering, she hastened to inform him that the earl had survived the worst.

"Praise God!" He closed his eyelids, relief easing lines from his big face.

His lips moved in prayer, and then he opened his eyes with a new look of severity.

"But Math is in his cups," he mumbled, casting a dark look over his shoulder for the occupant inside. "He bade me ask if 'twould be possible for my lady to, er, take her rest tonight in a guest chamber. Edwina will see to your bed, my lady." He shifted from foot to foot.

Carrie couldn't believe her ears. Her cheeks puffed with outrage. He was throwing *her* out? Of all the—!

"Let me in, Rannulf." She planted fists on her hips.

"My lady, he's been drinking for nigh—"

"I don't care. He needs to hear about his brother."

"You shouldn't go in while he's like this." He blocked her path to the door.

"Rannulf, do you think I can't handle a little drunken vomiting? After what I just went through with Giles?"

"'Tis not that—"

Sandra Jones

"Whatever Matthias is up to, I'm perfectly capable of enduring it. Do I seem like a weakling to you, too?" Anger fueled her courage and stamina. Lord, her heart was thumping with rage. How could he? "I'm not fainthearted. I can handle my husband just as well as you can. I'm going in there, so if you want to stop me, you'll have to use brute force."

He made an exasperated sound in his throat, but Carrie pushed past him. Luckily, her words must've reassured Matthias's trusted friend because he didn't try to further thwart her entrance into the bedchamber.

As the door closed behind her, the stygian darkness of the tower swallowed her. No one had lit any of the torches. Even though it was the middle of May, the room lacked warmth. The only light came from the waning moon outside the window where Matthias sat in luminous silhouette, half-dressed and shadowed. His bare back was to the door, but the sound caused him to slowly turn.

Carrie scanned the room. A tankard lay on its side on the table, dribbling its contents. Mead. She could smell the thick scent of the honey-sweetened wine in the air. Enveloped in the darkness with Matthias, she felt an odd tug of foreboding, which made no sense at all, because she didn't fear him. However, in the nocturnal lair, he emanated danger and unpredictability.

Matthias gave no immediate acknowledgement of her presence. He returned to his study of the night outside the window.

Carrie's tense back eased slightly. He wasn't as drunk as Rannulf made it seem. He was so very still. Was he mourning? Perhaps he thought Giles was dead.

"Your brother is going to be okay," Carrie rushed to tell him.

He made no reaction in the painful silence.

156

"I gave him a slight dose of digitalis from foxglove to aid his circulation. His pulse was very, very weak. It took several hours, but his body finally eased toward normalcy. He's breathing well."

To her dismay, he answered her with nothing. She studied the line of his silhouette, searching for any inkling of relief or emotion whatsoever. Did she imagine that a deep breath heaved his great shoulders?

She went on, hoping he was listening, "Giles spoke to me before he fell asleep. He said...he needs to talk to you. He begged me to bring you to him if he was dying."

"Then I'm glad he lives," he mumbled at last. "Now I won't have to talk to him."

Carrie bit her lip, trying to stifle a smarting retort for his attitude. He didn't mean it. He was baiting her, and she wouldn't take his bait. Her chest ached with sorrow and anger for his callousness.

After several moments, he finally turned to face her. "Thank you." The two words, barely audible.

Carrie remembered his haunted expression as he'd left his brother's side and was convinced his gratitude was sincere. She wrapped her arms around her body to keep out the window's chill, but she longed to wrap her arms around Matthias instead. She'd never had to deal with loss in her life, but she could imagine how difficult it would be to nearly lose her mother or her grandmother, her only family since her father had abandoned them before she was born. Perhaps she had already lost them if she was unable to return home. The pain cut deep as any knife wound.

He spoke quietly, "What folly took Rannulf that he should let you in against my wishes?"

At least he wasn't bellowing—an improvement—but his tone could be deceptive, his fury ready to explode.

She tilted her chin up, bracing for his anger. "You needed to know your brother's condition."

He snorted and cast a smile down at the window seat he still lounged on, his shaggy dark hair dangling around his face. Although his ill-placed humor perplexed her, Ranulf claimed he'd been drinking heavily. At least it seemed to calm his temper.

In her vast experience with hospitals, waiting rooms, and patients, she knew grief when she saw it and pain, too. People dealt with it so many different ways. He sought the comfort of the mead.

She approached him with caution.

Lightly easing onto the seat beside him, the moon afforded her enough light to see his face. His body relaxed, more than she'd ever seen it. His bent knee formed a rest for his draping right arm with his foot sitting casually on the casement. His unreadable eyes watched her as his head rested against the edge of the wall.

Carrie wet her lips. "I know what you're thinking, Matthias. I mean, I don't know the feud between you and Giles, but I understand one thing for certain. I'm positive he regrets the loss of your affection, and I'll bet you care a lot about him, too."

Matthias returned his gaze to the moon. His impassiveness shut her out again.

Carrie reached for the limp hand resting on his leg. He felt warmer than she'd expected. She grazed her thumbs across the back of his hand in a comforting gesture, and his eyes slid back to her, shimmering silver in the moonlight.

She continued, "You're feeling guilty about this feud because Giles is sick, so you're here with the mead instead of with your brother. You've hidden yourself away in your fortress tonight with Rannulf keeping others out, so you could block out your feelings. If you and Giles could just talk—"

"You think these walls are my fortress?" A cryptic smile spread across his lips, and his white teeth flashed in the darkness. The wolfish look returned. He shook his head slowly. "This room isn't my fortress. It's my *cage*."

"Your cage?" A slight tremor ran through her.

His smile was sensuous and bold. His fingers curled around one of her hands, drawing it closer to his warm chest.

"Aye, a cage for a beast." His smile disappeared, and he studied her hand, rubbing his thumb across the pulse point of her wrist.

"You're no beast, Matthias." She made herself smile in spite of his dark warning. "Grumpy, always, but no beast. You want your privacy, and I think that's understandable—"

"It's true." He shook his head again, a frown furrowing his forehead. "Rannulf may have let you in, but I guarantee he's just outside the door listening. He's listening for you to sound the alarm, for furniture to fly. I am...infamous."

"That's ridiculous. Rannulf's probably back in his own quarters by now. Why would I raise such a ruckus?"

His hand tightened on hers. "Care to test me?"

She figured he'd meant his notion about the eavesdropping knight, but for some reason the way he'd said it, voice all deep and gravelly, she conjured up intriguing images of her testing *him*. All of him.

The stone walls were thick. You had to be right by the door to hear raised voices within. She could sing at the top of her lungs and probably nobody would hear to come ask what the racket was.

"If I kissed you...would you scream?" he whispered.

"Of course I wouldn't." Oh, she hadn't meant to sound as if she welcomed another kiss. Which she just might. "I mean, kissing you isn't exactly frightening. Right now, you're paranoid and drunk, but you're not a beast. I'm not afraid of you, and nobody thinks you're going to hurt me. I certainly don't."

He pressed her palm to his lips for a warm kiss and then placed her hand just above his heart. Butterflies danced in her stomach at the sensation of his skin beneath hers. His chest rose and fell on deep breaths. He stroked his knuckles along the sensitive skin of her inner arm, outstretched toward him. Awareness spurred the blood in her veins to quicken under his motion.

Matthias rocked slightly and then leaned closer. His gaze settled on her lips and at this proximity, she could smell the sweet mead on his breath.

"You're courting the very devil coming in here."

Carrie shivered but forced herself to return his stare. "I'm not afraid of you. You have no reason to be angry with me."

"I never said I was angry. But you should be afraid, even so. What I'm feeling right now is far from anger."

His eyes drifted down her body meaningfully.

Carrie's stomach flittered, but she ignored it. Now wasn't the time to be indulging in fantasies involving Matthias. "Your mead is talking, because you have no interest in me when you're sober."

His eyes glittered with a strange new intensity. "Sober or drunk, I'm always a beast. The thoughts I have are the same—thoughts about you, Carrie. Only, the mead loosens my tongue and weakens my restraint. You'll soon wish you hadn't come here because I feel no compunction, only wants and needs."

His voice softened to almost a purr in his heavy Welsh accent. He leaned nearer so that her arm was the only barrier separating their bodies. At this angle he seemed very much like some predator, come to carry her off in his teeth. A mouse, however, had more defenses at the moment than she did. A mouse could run and hide from its hunter, while she felt glued to the spot, caught up in the trap. His words both excited and shocked her. She was glad he couldn't feel how hard her heart was pounding.

"You're driving me crazy, *Carys*." He'd called her that before. She meant to ask its meaning, but his next words came out as rasp, scattering her thoughts. "I want to make you feel just a fraction of what you're doing to me."

Carrie was startled by his frankness as his mesmerizing silver eyes searched hers. Then his gaze again found her lips, and he swooped down to press his mouth to hers.

With frightening intensity, his mouth ground against hers until she gave way. Her resolve not to allow his touch or kisses evaporated as she opened her mouth to him, allowing him to possess her from within. His kiss was hard, punishing, as if he was trying to drive her away or scare her.

Carrie couldn't flee if she wanted to. Like a moth to a flame, she drew up against him. His tongue tasted of the honey wine and moved impatiently along hers as he devoured her. The hold on her shoulders was tight and compelling, making her experience his sense of urgency.

He wanted her. And they had no audience this time.

Though it was madness, oh, how she had longed for this. She ran her free hand down his thick neck and through the rough hair on his chest. Her fingers skimmed his nipples, causing them to pebble, and he moaned in her mouth.

When Matthias finally broke his kiss, he stood, his breathing quick and shallow as he stared down at her. He drew her up with him, guiding her into the shadows. He moved her to a chair by the table. As soon as she sat down, he put his hands on her shoulders and leaned down to take her lips again. He thrust his tongue in her mouth, and she was aware of him moving to kneel in front of her. His fingers sank into her hair, kneading it lightly with the languorous motion of his kiss. All around, her senses were full of him—his breath on her, the taste of his mouth, and the warmth of his body.

His fingers trailed away from her hair to trace her throat and the curve of her chest. His large hand engulfed a breast, caressing her as his kiss deepened. She allowed her own hands the freedom to roam over his smooth, muscled skin from his shoulders to his back. Her fingers traced the hard long valley of his spine, feeling it bend slightly as he took his mouth from hers and leaned over her breast. He replaced his palm with his mouth, taking her nipple, and he nibbled it softly through the fabric of her tunic until it ached.

Yearning to feel his body against hers, Carrie opened her knees. Matthias ran his hands under the hem of her tunic, gathering it up as he slid his hot palms up her legs. He moved into the space between them, his naked torso wedged between her bare thighs.

Carrie whimpered in protest as he lifted his marvelous mouth from her breast, but she was soon placated by the touch of his fingers on the laces of her tunic as he slowly opened her garment. His hands trembled as he eased the fabric away from her shoulders and breasts. Exposed to his view, the cool night air encroached around her, but Matthias drew her close to him, warming her. His lips nibbled hers repeatedly, and the hot rush of feminine desire pooled between her legs. He trailed kisses from her mouth down her neck and laid his head against her collarbone, breathing heavily as he nuzzled her.

She cradled his head in her hand, willing all his pain away with her embrace.

"I want you so, Carrie," he murmured.

She wanted to tell him she wanted him, too, but she was too terrified to speak. Her fingers sank in his soft hair. She was afraid of doing something wrong. Afraid he would sober and want her no more.

His fingers found her nipples and stroked them into charged buds. He bent down over her breast and sucked her into his warm, wet mouth. Carrie couldn't control the groan that ripped from her when his tongue lavished her aroused nipple. Her fingers dug into his thick shoulders, holding him to her. His hands caressed her aching breasts as he loved her with his mouth, and his soft hair tickled her chin and neck.

"*Carys, Carys.*" He spoke between kisses.

His Welsh twist of her name made her feel closer to him.

"Matthias."

Carrie put her hands in his disheveled hair and urged him to look up at her. She wanted him to see how she yearned to have more of him.

Their eyes met briefly before her mouth met his for another kiss, and she ran her palms down his chest. His body rocked against her as she caressed his hard stomach. She boldly traced the rigid outline of his erection beneath his pants, longing to free him. He made a gurgling sound and suddenly broke their kiss.

Catching both her hands in his, he said roughly, "Nay! I'm about to lose the last fragment of decency I possess." With shaking hands, he grabbed her tunic and pulled it back up. Breathless, he told her, "I don't want to hurt you, but I know I would."

He climbed to his feet and pulled her up with him, being careful to keep her at arm's length.

Carrie's dress fell like a curtain wall between

163

them, and she felt her body grow cool without him near. Her eyes stung with tears.

"I know you won't hurt me. Why do you keep saying that? I'm a grown woman, not some inexperienced girl."

She stepped up to him and put her arms around his waist. His thick arousal brushed against her before he moved away.

Was it her epilepsy? Humiliation knifed through her. That was exactly the problem.

He wanted her but feared causing a seizure.

"You shouldn't have come in here." His eyes narrowed accusingly at her, shadows making his angular face seem more wolf-like than ever.

Carrie backed up against the table, seeking support for her weak body. Anyone else but Matthias. Not rejection from him. Inside she crumbled. A tear fell from her eye, and she quickly wiped at it with her fingers.

"Jesu," he swore and reached for her.

Carrie couldn't bear his pity now, knowing that was the only thing it could be and certainly not any true feelings for her. She sidestepped his hands, rounding the table. A mouse escaping the cat. He'd toyed with her more than enough for one night.

"Don't touch me, Matthias." Her hip bumped the table in her haste to distance herself from him, and the empty tankard of mead fell to the floor with a noisy metallic clatter that echoed across the room. Carrie bent to pick it up.

"Leave it," he ordered.

"Math?"

It was Rannulf, standing in a span of yellow light from the door. Carrie jumped to her feet, quickly replacing the fallen vessel.

"Take her out," Matthias ordered. He turned his back to them and retreated to the shadows.

Carrie shook her head. "Rannulf, it's okay. I'm

just clumsy."

She kept her face averted and hoped he couldn't hear the tears in her voice.

"Now. My lady." The guard put his large hand under her elbow, tolerating no protest or struggle as he steered her firmly toward the door.

Rannulf's expression was grim. Matthias had warned her. Now the captain appeared reluctant to look at her at all. There was no point in arguing to stay where she clearly wasn't wanted.

Chapter Twelve

Giles survived the night.

His greeting to Carrie was as crusty as ever. "There you are. I've been up for the past hour waiting."

With his voice hoarse and his throat probably sore from the sickness, he still managed the familiar supercilious speaking tone both brothers used.

She waited while he adjusted his covers, trying to maintain an air of dignity. Her heart went out to him in spite of his once offering her to Ian and then calling her "plain." No one should have to endure the night he had.

She couldn't believe her fortune—the earl actually allowed her into his room after yesterday. She'd almost expected him to have a guard at the door, demanding she pack her bags and leave.

She'd been very harsh with her orders about his diet and great medieval barons weren't to be gainsaid, she supposed. Being a middle class American and pretty much sheltered all her life, she had no experience with powerful people or nobility. She wasn't exactly sure how to deal with someone as stubborn as the earl. He could probably have her head for ignoring his complaints last night. Nevertheless, she'd treated him with the same directness she'd learned to apply to Matthias.

During his suffering, she'd disregarded his threats of having her horsewhipped and thrown out the gates. She'd ordered him to lie still, demanded he drink his draught, and forced him to swallow. Degrading for a nobleman or anyone else for that

166

matter. She'd done what she had to do.

He looked better. Dangerously thin, but better. The room had been freshly cleaned, and a giant bouquet of pale purple columbines sat in a metal vessel on the table.

"You were waiting for *me,* my lord?" She asked when his gaze returned to her.

He scowled.

Uh oh. She cast a fearful glance over each shoulder. Where were the armed guards hiding? Would it be shackles and chains for her or merely a quick trip to a chopping block?

"I should've sent one of my men to haul you out of my brother's bed but you deserved your rest. I knew you wouldn't dare leave me waiting long."

Carrie felt her face heat. The earl hadn't heard that she'd spent the night on a pallet with Edwina in the servants' quarters, and she wasn't about to tell him.

She took a step backward, prepared to make a run for the door as soon as he issued her punishment.

"I have the staff awaiting your orders, Lady Carrie, and the kitchen will not carry on without them."

Carrie's hand flew to her heart. Had the night transformed him so dramatically?

"My orders? Are you saying that you're going to allow a change in your diet?" She bent over his bedside and put one palm on his forehead and her fingers on his cool wrist. When he pushed her hands away, she admonished him with a slight smile. "My lord, I was checking to see if you were feverish or if your pulse was weak."

"I trow that!" he grumbled. Then he surprised her by grabbing her hand and pulling it to his dry lips for a brief kiss. "I've decided that you are a gift from God, Lady Carrie. Never again will I doubt your good sense. Last night you surely saved my life with that awful brew of yours. I kept thinking I wanted you to be wrong about my food, but as I recall, I do get worse after some meals. Mayhap you would tell Cook what you think I should eat today. Naught as awful as porridge, I hope."

"No, my lord." She made her voice serious, hiding her relief. "I'm very sorry to tell you, but you're going to have to drink tea or broth only for the rest of the day. Your stomach might not tolerate any solid food."

At his glum expression, Carrie laughed and withdrew her hand from his to cover her smile. Her lips were still sore and swollen from Matthias's kisses. The slight burn on her skin sent a jangled mixture of unrequited desire and humiliation coursing through her.

"Don't hide your smile, dear. It's your best quality," he ordered, although his gray eyes twinkled with humor. "Your smile is lovely, and you're endowed with wondrous healing talents. No doubt that's why Matthias wed you. So...will you or nil you?"

"Be in charge of your meals?"

"Aye. Convention be damned, why not? Matthias will likely be furious at me for putting his wife in the kitchen, but what do I care? Cook welcomes you so that is that."

"Thank you! That's super news. I promise I'll do a terrific job," she gushed, full of relief.

The earl frowned. "Where did you say you were from?"

Drat! Carrie's heart stilled. She'd made an error in her expressions. She bit her lip.

He shifted on the pillows. "And tell me, how *did* my barbarian brother win your heart?"

Needing to change the subject, she searched the room, spotted the bouquet, and created a distraction.

"What beautiful flowers!"

The lavender burst of color lightened the mood of the otherwise austere room. She left the earl's side to smell the arrangement. She buried her nose in the tickling petals, avoiding his shrewd gaze.

"Well, I guess you just answered my second question, Lady Carrie. I'm glad you like the flowers because they're yours." He sighed.

Carrie glanced up with a questioning look that he answered with a bemused smile. "Aye, they're yours. Matthias brought them up a while ago when he visited. He said I was to give them to you as a reward for your kindness to me last night. I wasn't to tell you all that, though. Rather, I was to say they were from me. He thinks I know naught of chivalry. Bah! I can bestow my own tokens without any help from that bounder." He rolled his eyes morosely under the silver wings of his brows.

Carrie touched her lips, recalling sweet, rough kisses. If the flowers were from Matthias, then he was pacifying his guilty conscience.

"Besides," he continued, "columbines are wildflowers, common in these Welsh hills. I would've chosen roses."

Carrie forced a smile for the earl, straining to push Matthias and his fiery kisses from her thoughts. "You're still very thoughtful, my lord. They're lovely, but I would prefer you to keep them here. This room could use some cheer."

"Are you sure? Mayhap you would like them in your chamber while your husband is gone, so they might remind you of him."

"Gone? What do you mean?" Carrie looked up sharply, feeling an uneasy quiver in her stomach.

Giles grimaced and coughed. "T-that b-bloody oaf didn't tell you he was going? Math was leaving for Chepstow when he brought the flowers to my room earlier. One of the king's retainers arrived early this morning. Edward and his men are staying at Chepstow, so Matthias and five other knights rode out to bid him news from Wyldnell."

Carrie battled to keep the shock from her face. She visualized the map of Wales she'd seen in her tour guide. Chepstow Castle was at the mouth of the Wye, to the south, near the famous Tintern Abbey. Wordsworth had written a poem about it—*if only I'd paid better attention in my high school World Lit class, I could remember something about the place.* Had she known what the future had in store for her, she wouldn't have wasted her time passing notes to Mimi Sanders. She would've been memorizing bits of history and reading the unabridged version of Chaucer's *The Canterbury Tales* instead of the Cliffs Notes.

Chepstow couldn't be more than fifteen miles away. Less than a day's ride for the knights, not far at all, but a bereft sensation sifted through her.

"Um, did he say when he would be back?" She extracted a flower from the bouquet and came back to the earl's side.

"'Twill be less than a sennight unless the king has some use for him. I told him King Edward would attend us here if he would only wait, but my brother is headstrong, as you well know."

Of course she knew. He was also doing what every other guy did when faced with an unwanted attraction to her—bolting.

What other explanation could there be?

None.

She stared at the flower, wishing she could will away her hopeless longing.

The earl sighed raggedly. "Math is afraid if the king comes here, he'll see my illness and strip Wyldnell from me. I'm not planning on dying yet!" His shouted exclamation aggravated his chest and he coughed.

Baldric entered the room with a draught Carrie had already ordered to be sent up. She squared her shoulders and put the flower aside.

"No, you're not, my lord," she announced and handed him the draught.

So there was hope. Maybe he didn't leave solely to be away from her.

****

Roger Bigod, fifth earl of Norfolk and Marshal of England, strode across his lower bailey to greet Matthias. Just nine years older than Matthias, they'd become acquainted when Math squired at the great castle as a youth. Roger's passion centered on the castle and evidence of his ambition for the great fortification lay throughout. Work had already begun on a stronger barbican. Stonemasons busily set masonry into place as Roger greeted him with a clap on the back. They turned to walk together.

"Look, Math. At the end of the season, work will be complete on an addition for the tower. The barbican will be impenetrable. Did you see anything of the like in Spain?"

"Nay." It was a castle that would stand the test of time, but Matthias couldn't share that information with his friend. "Chepstow only gets better with every passing year. You've done a fine job."

"Tintern Abbey grows, as well. You should visit it whilst you're here. The Cistercians are completing the great church. Your brother's abbot is here to supervise the work, although I trow he's eager for a similar undertaking at Wyldnell."

Matthias eyed the great hall with trepidation. Would Abbot Sidney of Marsten hold his confidence or tell the king why Matthias fled nine years ago?

"How are the locals at Wyldnell? Hostile? I'm adding catapults soon to defend against the Welsh uprising, if there is one."

171

"'Tis a good idea," he told Bigod, "but the Welsh princes will never get this far east. And the locals don't give us any trouble."

Roger's eyes widened, and he guffawed. "Ever the confident one, aren't you, Math? It does me good to see you again."

Roger invited his guest into the great hall to meet the king. Sidney of Marsten had beaten them there. Sitting at the hand of the king, the robed abbot followed Matthias with his eyes.

Matthias sank to one knee before the king.

As a half-Welsh knight, how would he ever explain marrying a Welsh woman when his countrymen were attempting an uprising against the English crown? King Edward still held a grudge against the once loyal Prince Llywelyn for marrying Eleanor, daughter of his enemy, Simon de Montfort.

At least, he'd had the foresight to ask both Giles and Rannulf to swear they would protect Carrie if the worst should happen. Before he'd taken leave from Wyldnell that morning, he'd received their oaths. In the castle's chapel, he'd even said a brief prayer for the king's mercy in case someone listened.

Instead of coming to Chepstow, he could've waited for the king to come to him, but it would serve him better to appear contrite. Seeking out the king in person to apologize and offer fealty seemed more appropriate.

And then there was Giles. King Edward would never leave himself dependent upon a dying man as one of his powerful Marcher lords at such time as this. Edward didn't tolerate weaklings any more than he tolerated usurpers of his power. He would surround himself with only the mightiest, most loyal men to serve as barons for the strategic strongholds of Wales.

Also, if Matthias stayed in Wyldnell to await the king, he would be drawing danger nearer to Carrie.

If Edward disapproved of the match, he could easily have Carrie dispensed.

"Matthias," the king spoke.

"My liege."

Two guards assumed stances a few yards behind, ready to detain him if called upon.

"Marsten told me you'd returned. Will you stand now and tell the crown why you abandoned us nine years ago?" There was no welcome in his voice.

The abbot's presence prevented Matthias from making any creative explanations, lies or half-truths.

Matthias spoke quietly and evenly, "I broke the code of chivalry. My brother, Giles, earl of Wyldnell, banished me from his lands, so I traveled far away in penitence for my transgressions." He kept his eyes downcast. "I trow I haven't paid my debt to you, my liege, and I meant naught by taking leave without your knowledge. I've come for your punishment willingly."

The king cleared his throat. "Giles hasn't told me about any crime you committed, nor of banishment, but if you say you broke the code, then I believe it, Matthias." Edward "Longshanks" stood, rising tall on the dais before him. "What exactly was your crime? You always conducted yourself as a chivalric knight among my retainers and in Acre. You were dedicated and moral before most others of your age."

"Out of respect for my brother, I do not speak of it, my liege." He swallowed hard, fighting bile in his throat. *God, let that be the end of it.*

Edward folded his hands in front of his robes, and his face hardened. "This is very distressing, Matthias. You're now boarding at Wyldnell again. How is that, if your crime was against Giles?"

He'd been asking himself that same question ever since he'd returned. It troubled him, not knowing for certain what his brother was thinking.

He shook his head. "I do not know. I only stopped at Wyldnell to pay my respect to Giles, and he asked me to stay. I know not why."

"Do you not?" Edward raised his voice, incredulous. "Marsten says Giles is quite ill."

"Aye." Matthias lifted his eyes to the seated abbot for a brief second, long enough to give the clergyman a measure of his anger. Marsten looked away. "He was, my liege, but he's getting better."

"Giles doesn't have issue, does he?"

Issue. Must everything always revolve around who will inherit?

"He may yet produce heirs, if 'tis God's will."

Edward laid a hand on Matthias's shoulder and turned him from the dais, drawing him to walk. "Aye. They're still young enough for heirs, but you're not being atavistic. You never were ambitious, were you? At Acre, while the other knights became wealthy looting and plundering, you were busy questioning the Saracens about their horses, architecture, and weaponry. I trow you were one of the most capable of warriors, but your only goals were the ones I gave you. You took what I offered you and nothing more. Have you naught that you want for yourself, Matthias?"

Though he answered his liege with a negative shake of his head, he had one thing he wanted for himself. The same as nine years ago, and it hit his stomach like a fist. He wanted a wife. Not just any wife. Carrie, in truth, to be his wife. The old dream of his youth came back with a vengeance. But now his dream had a face.

Carrie's. Although he could never have her in reality.

He couldn't help remembering the night before, when he'd watched the sky from his bedchamber. Deep into his cups, he'd mused on every constellation he could identify, trying to keep his mind off his brother's anguish. Then Carrie came, rescuing him from his grim thoughts.

Mayhap she was right and Fate had sent her to change their destiny. She'd saved Giles's life. Matthias had seen death too many times to not recognize its presence, yet she had somehow stopped the unstoppable. With her quick thinking and tender care, she'd broken Giles's illness and rescued Matthias from more grief.

Then, when he should've been pledging his undying gratitude to her, he cast her away.

It had been nine years since he'd last allowed himself to be drunk and in the same room with a woman. *Damn Rannulf for letting her in.*

The things he'd said! Then forcing his kisses on her, feasting his eyes on her body, touching and tasting her flesh—he never should've come near her. He never should've kissed her at all. How was he supposed to live in a platonic relationship with her now when he still wanted, *needed* more?

With his brain awash with mead, he'd intended to scare her away with his lust, but her responding body lit a stronger fire—one he was powerless to ignore. His mind had warred for control of his body and actions. He hung on a precipice, nearly falling for the urge to say everything he longed to say and do exactly as he pleased. To pretend he was another man, a man deserving Carrie's kisses.

If he'd been someone else, he would've led her to their bed and finished undressing her. On his knees before her, he would've slid his hands around her smooth, supple calves, boldly raked her body with his gaze, and kissed every square inch of her from her dainty toes to her petal-soft eyelids.

Was there naught that he wanted for himself? Aye, he wanted all right. He wanted.

Longshanks continued as they walked in a circle

around the hall, "You've returned at an opportune time. I'll need a new baron for Wyldnell if your brother dies."

"Giles isn't going to—"

The king lifted a hand to silence him. "Ambitions would benefit you, Matthias. I have several retainers who've earned their titles and lands, and they're eager to prove their mettle by protecting Wyldnell from the Welsh. I need a Marcher lord who's able to conquer the Welsh, not just defend strongholds against them. I need an army." He studied his fingernails as he spoke. "Llywelyn and Dafyd are thorns that must be removed from my mantle. In this your Welsh dam may be an asset instead of a curse. With your mother's blood, the Welsh will listen to you. I'd like to begin a new course, hiring paid native soldiers to fight in the Marches. What think you?"

The king leveled an expressionless look at him as they stopped near the dais again.

Matthias nodded. "Aye. It's a good idea. 'Twill work, my liege."

Edward chuckled. "Subservience and flattery from you, Math? That's unexpected. Nevertheless, here's what I intend to do. I will send you back to your brother. You will remain as my retainer in Wyldnell until Giles dies or is incapable of marshalling the border. Then you will step in, and your son will inherit the barony."

"I don't have a son, my liege."

"This I know, so I have a bride for you. The girl is from Scotland, the daughter of a baron. The connection will be a useful one."

"I cannot, my liege." Matthias felt his stomach drop.

"She's ten and three years of age. Very biddable, I'm told." The king turned to face Matthias. "Understand me; this is my will for you."

"I cannot. I've taken a bride already." Matthias set his jaw.

Marsten spoke up from his seat, "Sir Matthias has brought his bride to Wyldnell, so he can sire a bairn to appease his brother."

"Is this true, Matthias?"

He dropped his gaze. "Yes," he lied through gritted teeth.

"And she's Welsh, my liege."

Matthias's knuckles crackled in fists at his sides as he angled a warning look at the abbot. No, not a warning. A promise. *Say one more word...*

Abbot Sidney was too smart to engage him in private, but with the king and his guards, the bastard apparently thought he could prod him at will. Well, by the saints, he would not!

"Welsh?" the king roared, drawing Matthias's attention back.

If the stone floor under his feet suddenly broke in two and the earth swallowed him whole, he would've been better prepared. King Edward's normally stoic face went livid with the blasphemies that followed.

After a *royal* cursing for marrying without his permission or guidance, Edward poured out questions: *Did you not think the king would find a bride for you? Where did you meet her? Who is her sire? What is her dower? Why did you marry? If not Wyldnell, where did you intend to make your home? What did you have to offer for her hand in marriage? Why a Welsh woman?*

The great hall filled to the rafters with Matthias's adept lies.

The deceit sickened him. Not even his answers to the barrage of psychiatric interviews he'd endured at Newport Psychiatric Hospital equaled the breadth of the yarn he spun for his king. By the end of his interrogation by Edward, he'd fashioned their so-called marriage into a sweeping epic.

And his king bought every lie. Matthias's shoulders sagged with relief when the nobleman finally returned to his seat on the dais and addressed Roger with some new concern that had crossed his mind during the conversation.

"My liege, forgive me for interrupting. May I address Sir Matthias?"

Matthias's head whipped back to where Abbot Sidney sat. His question caused Matthias's blood pressure to rise. Damn the bloody vulture, he'd almost been done with the inquisition.

The king inclined his head with an airy wave.

Marsten leaned forward in his chair, and Matthias braced himself, feet planted a foot apart, hands clasped together behind his back. He gave the abbot a slight smile, imparting the pleasure he would enjoy when his fist finally met the man's face. But the abbot was more than arm's length away. He'd never reach him before the guards caught him.

The abbot gazed at him, unperturbed. "All these years your brother has longed for another Thorne to command the garrison at Wyldnell. Our order has been blessed by his beneficence, and so I am pleased his prayers have finally been answered with your return. But—" his lips flashed a wan smile, and he placed a thoughtful finger to his temple, "as a church leader, I'm compelled to ask about a point in your story that puzzles me. You said you married in Coventry on your return here?"

"Aye." Matthias made a mental backtrack. Nine years of what should've been his life in this century were missing. A gap in time. He had to be certain of his facts. He knew Peace Chapel, renamed as such, still stood in the twenty-first century. It was safe to include in the tale. What was the abbot insinuating?

"And you married when?"

"Seven months ago, as we traveled from her

home in Sutton, where her father was a fisherman," Matthias repeated the lie he'd fabricated. He and Carrie had memorized a collective tale of key events in their past, should either one be questioned.

The abbot's finger ran across his lips.

"And you said you were married by a priest outside...where was it...'Saint Thomas' Chapel?" A small frown line divided his forehead. "Though I search my memory, I do not recall this chapel in Coventry."

Peace Chapel, he was certain, was first called St. Thomas Chapel. Named for Thomas à Becket. "It stands by the new North Porch, where we exchanged vows. A grand building, Holy Trinity. Have you been there?" Matthias dug his fists into the base of his back, trying to keep his voice cool, his demeanor calm.

Marsten's gaze held his steadily. A smile played in the eyes of the cursed clergyman.

An answering chill ran down Matthias's spine. Wrong. But how? Sweet Jesu. He'd erred. Even Roger and the king were looking at him now as if he'd just fallen off a hay wagon.

"Aye. I have been to the ruins there. Not more than three months ago." He gave a slight shake of his head. "The Norman church burnt more than twenty years ago, but I recall work only just beginning on the new chapel at the North Porch when I visited. Was there a chapel already there four months prior to my visit? Surely I would've noted if the chapel had already been built." He tapped his finger on lips drawn into a tight, knowing smile.

Matthias felt his mouth open but no words left his tongue. The solution to his stupid mistake escaped him.

What a complete fool he was! He could claim he had the name wrong, but what other chapel could he

179

possibly confuse with Holy Trinity Church? And to mistake Coventry for another borough? Madness.

"I—we did not exchange vows at Coventry, my liege." Cornered, he had nothing else to do but admit that fact. He sank to one knee, bowing to the king. *Oaf, now fix it!* "I wanted to marry her there but was afraid to take the time. We made such haste, you see, that there wasn't a chance—"

"My liege." Abbot Sidney chortled, and Matthias glanced up to see his sidelong look passed to the king. "The knight continues to pursue his pleasures—"

"Enough, Marsten!" the king snapped.

Edward released a long breath. "Finally. The knight *finally* shows me his vice. 'Tis women. Bigod, would you believe this of our valiant Math, whose monkish ways turned many a Saracen whore aside?" He laughed, a happenstance Matthias rarely witnessed, as Roger simply shook his head.

"So you've brought a wench under Giles's roof? I assume you never wed the creature. 'Tis rich, Matthias. Does the idea of marriage not suit, or is it the wench?"

Edward pulled on his chin whiskers as he regarded Matthias with a lingering smile.

Matthias's skin went ice cold. "Truly, my liege, I meant to do the right thing—"

Marsten cleared his throat. "I dread to tell you, fornication isn't new to your Welsh knight, my liege."

Matthias rose to his full height. He gave the guards a checking look, gauging their threat to oppose him. Primitive instinct demanded he silence the abbot any way he could. His face burned with vehemence. He'd failed Carrie. A sword through his heart would be less torture than living with the knowledge he'd failed in his vow to keep their secret safe.

"Back down, Thorne!" The king raised his voice.

Edward lifted a quelling hand from his armrest. "You say you meant the right thing, but you didn't *do* the right thing, Matthias. Your intentions matter not. If you share a roof with an unmarried woman, then you're committing a sin in your brother's house, according to his beliefs." The king's lips pulled into a mordant expression, showing he didn't share Giles's viewpoint, but he continued with his own perspective of Matthias's situation, "And, pray, what if your 'intentions' are to marry her and sire a bairn, but you delay in fulfilling your intentions? Is that not another lie, Matthias? You were once a man of your word and virtues. Now your vice of women turns my stomach almost as much as it amuses me."

Roger coughed into his sleeve, but Matthias thought he saw a hint of a hidden smile. The wretch was laughing at his misfortune.

His hands began to perspire.

"The only cure for fornication is marriage," Edward informed all in attendance. Then to Matthias, he commanded, "Two days hence when we've done with our plans for my new Welsh soldiers, you will go back to your brother and tell him the truth. Then, when I am done with Bigod and Chepstow, the abbot and I will attend you at Wyldnell. While we're there, Marsten will marry you to your Welsh woman or any other bride you wish to make your bed with."

"I—but, my liege, it's sudden. There'll be no time for—"

"The time has passed already, Matthias. Nine years of it wasted. Now you must marry with your king as witness. And Marsten, you'll perform the wedding of your benefactor's brother to his bride, won't you?" The king glanced at the abbot.

"Aye, my liege," the abbot nodded dutifully.

No doubt the clergyman wanted to tell the king

more about Matthias's crime, but everyone in the room sensed the resolve of Edward's mind. Only a fool would try to argue with him.

With heart heavy, Matthias left the room. Apparently the king didn't care who he married, so long as he married.

The parapets offered the best night view of the dark, muddy Wye later that night. White splashes of moonlight and stars brightened the ripples on the river's surface. With the castle perched high on a cliff, the lookouts could see for miles downriver, even in the night. Matthias sought the solitude atop the walls, with only the birds and a passing sentry to disturb his thoughts. Leaving Marsten and Roger Bigod alone with the king was akin to leaving foxes in a hen house, free to bend his ear to their wishes, each wanting to improve their property. And Matthias wanted no part of that conversation.

Bigod pledged his undying fealty to Edward for the time and men to build the garrison of his dreams, while Abbot Sidney took great pains to plead for Wyldnell land for his monastery's sheep. As for Matthias, Longshanks requested more time of him, so he promised to spend the next day discussing plans for recruiting new Welsh soldiers.

Matthias picked up a loose rock along the parapet and hurled it far below into the moonlit river.

What if he wasn't able to take Carrie home on Beltane—this year, or the next, or the next? She deserved to choose her own destiny, whether it be with him or, more likely, with another man. Someone worthy.

He could still offer her a choice. Allow her the chance to remain under his protection without being made to be his bride. After all, the king had ordered *him* to wed, not her.

Then, if she chose him...perhaps he would tell her why she should not. Or...he could bury the darkness of his soul, hide it, for as long as he may to enjoy his only chance of fulfilling his dreams.

The latter was infinitely more palatable.

Chapter Thirteen

Carrie entered the barracks behind Rannulf, carrying a remote sense of unease in her chest. A male place, where the knights and guards resided, the area was devoid of any feminine influence. Grim, but practical for men's needs. The place smelled of dirt, sweat, and unwashed bodies. The armory was within spitting distance of the knights' apartments though many of the men simply slept beside their posts by the wall or at the gatehouse. Passing the heavily armed guards in such a place would've made Carrie much more uncomfortable, perhaps the act even impossible for her, if she hadn't been in the venerated company of their captain.

Rannulf had approached her earlier that afternoon in the storeroom. She stood sorting seeds into jars and jabbered merrily about Cook's plans for the meal that evening and the elderflower cheesecake they were baking. She could tell Rannulf's mind was diverted to other things more serious in nature than what he put in his stomach, and Carrie guessed from the looks of the beefy knight that placing anything above the condition of his appetite was a rarity.

At first, she imagined he wanted to speak of the last night she'd seen Matthias, two days ago when he'd been drinking. That night represented too many conflicting emotions for her. If she didn't stay busy, her mind replayed everything that happened in his bedchamber. Her heart still ached for the way she'd found him, so very alone. She could feel the same sensations coursing through her body that she'd felt when he'd crushed his body against hers, embracing her, kissing her, telling her of his needs.

Then, rejection.

The final hard look on his face left a cold knot in her stomach.

Keep busy. Don't dare think on that night.

Rannulf shuffled in awkward silence as he listened to her gabbing about food, and at any moment she anticipated he would offer her some sort of uncomfortable apology for letting her visit Matthias—or ask her what had happened behind the closed door. She kept talking, hoping he would lose the nerve to speak of it.

His large fingers played with a wooden spoon on the table between them. Then he surprised her. "Lady Carrie, you are a healer, are you not?"

Carrie's hands went still as she finished tying muslin loosely over a handful of fennel to catch the seeds. "I guess maybe I am. I try, at least."

"Would you...be persuaded to attend one of the men? One of the sick?"

His prior reservation in asking the question made her wonder if she'd done something to make him think she wouldn't help a man in need. "Of course I would."

She handed him the bunch of fennel and some twine, gesturing to the rack above his head.

As he obligingly hung the herbs, he said gruffly, "The earl has fared well in your care. We have a physick, though I don't always like his ways. It's probably wrong of me to ask such a favor from you, my lady," his voice softened, and he looked at her plaintively through his puppy-dog brown eyes, "but I don't know what other measure to take. The men don't appreciate Maud's presence in the barracks. They don't trust any of the locals."

"Don't be silly, Rannulf." She laid a hand on his arm. "I'll help if I can. What's this man suffering from?"

"Ague."

Before going to the barracks, he'd told her the man's symptoms. Ague, she gathered, was a high fever with shakes and head pain. She collected a selection of herbal medicines and followed the knight, ready to do her best.

She didn't expect what she found there.

Rows of pallets lined the barracks' floor. Only one makeshift bed was occupied. A few men and their squires gathered at the entrance, watching the spectacle of the patient's misery.

"Unless you're helping, get out," Rannulf barked at the soldiers' backs. "You all have duties or training. See to it."

Carrie avoided the men as they funneled through the door. One man remained. A shabby tunic covered his lithe frame. He kept his back to them as he bent over the motionless body on the floor. Beside him, a collection of rusty tools and instruments lay on the bare floor.

"The physick," Rannulf intoned. Deep lines bracketed his face at the corners of his down-turned lips.

Careful not to interrupt, Carrie sidled near the pallet to observe the physick's work. His hand selected a metal bowl from his side and placed it in front of him where Carrie couldn't see exactly what he was doing. Then the same hand reached for a small knife, moving it toward the patient's arm.

Bloodletting. Carrie shuddered and bit her lip to keep from yelling at the man to stop. This was the Middle Ages, she reminded herself, recalling Matthias's instructions that she couldn't invoke seven hundred years of medical progress in one day. In these times there would be the bloodletting and leeches and God only knew what other horrors.

If only she'd gotten there earlier. She dug her

nails into her palms, took a breath for courage, and moved two steps sideways to see the patient's face.

"Oh!" She sucked in an alarmed breath.

The physick whipped his head around. The knife in his hand dripped blood on the ground. The patient was just a kid!

Carrie fought the prick of tears in her eyes. He was the same squire she'd seen Rannulf teaching at the archery range.

"Leave him alone!" she cried.

The physick's long face puckered as he stared at her, and then he glanced at Rannulf behind her. "You should keep this woman out until she's needed later. She can bathe and dress the boy then."

"No, let me take care of him."

The physick narrowed his eyes. "Sir Rannulf, we don't even know if she's a healer. I've been the earl's physick for nigh four years."

"Oh, gee, that's something to brag about," Carrie remarked dryly as she pushed up her sleeves. "We can all tell you're doing a swell job."

Rannulf made a snort behind her.

Her disgust made her forget to censor her modern words until it was too late and even then she didn't care. The man was a monster.

Ignoring the outraged stammers of the physick, Carrie sank to her knees beside the boy. From the looks of him, he was about twelve or thirteen. His youthful skin was white and pasty. Stripped of his clothes, his bare ribcage quivered with short breaths. One thin arm lay across the physick's knees, a trickle of purplish-red blood pouring into the dirty bowl. The boy's eyes were closed, blissfully unaware of his sufferings.

Carrie looked at the dirty rags the physick had strewn beside him. She wouldn't find bandages there. She pushed the physick's grisly collection of tools aside and dropped her own bag of medicines in their place. A bleeding wound wasn't something she'd planned on treating this visit, so she improvised, tearing cloth from her clean gown to staunch the blood flow.

"But—he needs to bleed. His illness is the result of evil trapped within." The physick stammered his words, noting her intention.

Carrie grabbed the bowl and flung it aside. Temper climbing, she bit the inside of her mouth to keep from saying something she shouldn't. She wrapped the cloth around the boy's bleeding forearm.

The physick peered at the contents of her open bag. "Are you a witch? Is this woman you've brought a witch, Sir Rannulf? God help us."

"I'm not a witch." Satisfied the bandage was tight enough, she placed the boy's limp arm gently at his side.

"Then you are nothing but a woman. Sir Rannulf, how can she help? The boy is your squire, the son of a nobleman. If he dies and his father gets word that you let a female take the place of a physick—"

"Then we must be sure he doesn't get word of it." Rannulf bit out. Carrie glanced up from the boy in time to see the knight hauling the physick to his feet. "Get out of here. You've done enough."

"Rannulf. I need something else for the boy," Carrie called out. "Physick, would you bring some honey to aid him?"

"Honey?" Rannulf cried, paling. He kept the physick in his clutches.

"Yes, honey. Don't ask, just bring it. Also, I need some warm water and clean cloths. I'll do my best, Physick. If I fail, you can tell the whole castle how I caused the boy's death, if you like."

The physick's brow smoothed, and a wicked gleam lit his eyes. Rannulf released him, and he gave them both a curt nod before dashing out.

Aware of Rannulf's stern gaze as she covered the boy with a blanket, she knew she would have to restore the knight's confidence in her. She'd lost his faith with the mention of the honey. There was no way she could explain that the honey would prevent infection in the physick's knife cut, since he had no concept of germs to begin with.

"When did the fever start?"

"Yesterday."

"Is anyone else sick?"

"No. Just young Richard."

"Has your squire been injured recently? Fallen or...beaten?"

"I don't beat boys," he asserted, sinking heavily to the ground beside her. "He's not had any injuries that I know of. He was well the day before yesterday. I gave him the afternoon off after the archery lesson. After picking apples, he and some of the other lads even went swimming in the pond."

If Richard had contracted a disease, the pond would likely be infected and all the fish in it. Then she had another thought—

"Are there any mosquitoes by the pond?"

"God's wounds, yes. Terrible things. I wouldn't swim there myself even if I could swim."

Malaria. Although she couldn't be positive, the symptoms of the disease sounded the same as Richard's ague. Did they have malaria in this part of the world? Matthias had told her the climate now was very different from modern times. Medieval man hadn't yet recognized the dangers of mosquitoes.

If it was malaria, Vitex or agnus castus roots could be ground into a powder for tea, but the plant probably wouldn't be found this far west. There were other herbs used in Asia, native there, but what could she use against malaria in Wales?

"Rannulf, how do most people fare with the ague here?"

He shrugged. "Most live. Some don't."

Carrie shut her eyes. Bolstering her nerve, she withdrew a bag of wormwood flowers from her medicines. It wasn't much, but it was the best she could do. "Rannulf, I need you to take this to the kitchens. Boil the flowers in water to make a tea and bring it back."

He took the herbs, gave her a solemn nod and hurried off.

Rolling up her sleeves, Carrie prepared herself for the long work she knew lay ahead. She leaned over the boy and stroked his fevered brow.

He moaned slightly at her touch. Just a child, she thought miserably, and who was she to care for a child so ill? She was no doctor, but neither was the physick, she reminded herself. She could do no worse. The boy needed her, Rannulf needed her. She would do her best not to let them down.

****

Richard's fever broke shortly after midnight. Rannulf woke Carrie the next morning and escorted her back into the barracks to check on the boy's progress. Carrie had begged to stay with him, but Rannulf wouldn't allow her to remain in the men's quarters at night. The boy was too sick to be moved, so Rannulf had stayed at his young charge's bedside.

Richard's eyes were open when they greeted him at his pallet. His pallor remained pale, but not pasty. Carrie touched his brow and found it cool.

"Your draught worked, Lady Carrie," Rannulf murmured in awe.

Richard offered the captain a weak smile.

"You owe your life to Sir Matthias's wife." He gave him a soft pat on the head. Then to Carrie in a lower voice, he smiled and said, "Physick won't be pleased."

"Thank you, my lady," the boy murmured. "I'll be sure to tell my father our family owes its gratitude to you."

His voice sounded hoarse and dry. Carrie brought a cup of water to his lips and gave him a drink. "Richard, you're welcome, but I should give you a warning."

"What, my lady?"

"Tell your friends not to swim in the pond until the mosquitoes are gone. In fact, stay away from the pond completely until the cooler months."

"Aye, my lady."

She sighed with relief.

Later, when they'd left the boy to rest, Rannulf walked with Carrie across the bailey. The big captain ambled over the field with lightness in his step that had been missing the day before.

Unsure of malaria and her choice of treatment, Carrie had some lingering doubts. "Do you think he's over his illness already?"

"I pray he is, but you're right to wonder, my lady. Often the fevers return. He's made a good recovery this morning, though. It bodes well."

"Thank goodness. I knew you were worried about him, Rannulf."

"It hurts me to see a youth so ill. Besides, as squires go, he's very competent. A quicker young mind I've not seen in several years, not since Matthias went off to squire at Chepstow."

Carrie glanced at the gatehouse for the umpteenth time since Matthias left. The guards she saw there were at ease, no sign of Matthias's imminent return.

"May I ask, are you sure you're not a witch, my lady?"

Carrie looked up at the guard's unexpected question.

"If you're a witch, I wouldn't tell a soul, upon my

honor. If 'tis true you're a witch, I know you're a good one. You've saved the earl's life, now young Richard's. God knows you bedevil your poor husband."

"I'm not a witch," she laughed.

"But the honey and the mosquitoes..."

"I promise I'm no more witch than you, Rannulf. I can't explain how it works, but it does."

One of the men at the gatehouse gave a shout. A few guards hurried from the bailey to the gatehouse to see what caused the guard to cry out. Her heart stopped.

"That would either be Math or the de Harcourts," Rannulf told her, staring in the same direction.

"Who?" She didn't recognize the name.

"We received word yesterday evening while you were with Richard. Lord Wyldnell will be hosting some noble guests from the north."

Her spirits sank.

"The earl is far too ill for guests," Carrie complained, still tracking the movement of the guards. "He should've sent word back that they'd have to wait."

Rannulf dropped a hand on her shoulder and laughed. "Maybe *you* would tell a baron to wait, but here only the king would have such testicles of iron." Remembering himself, he withdrew his hand, shock gathering in his eyes. "Forgive me, my lady. I often forget you're a lady. You have a strength about you uncommon for a woman."

"Me?" Carrie gaped at him. "You've got to be joking, Rannulf. There's nothing strong about me. Believe me. You can ask Matthias, if you have any doubt about that."

The lines around his warm eyes crinkled. "You are as strong in spirit as many men I know. Math sees your strength too and respects your tenacity.

He's not blind. If he treats you like glass, 'tis only the knight in him. Let it not trouble you. Don't allow yourself to think that his chivalry toward you reflects your inner character or weaknesses. Chivalry is paid by knights to all women, but respect...well, now that is uncommonly given by a knight, especially to a woman."

Her epilepsy prevented her from earning Matthias's respect. She was certain of that. He'd made it clear from their meeting her condition made her weak in his eyes. If he thought her strong, he would've finished what he'd started in the bedchamber. Rannulf knew nothing about her seizures, but she ought to thank him for the nice compliment anyways.

Something in Rannulf's expression stopped her, though. She followed his eyes to the gatehouse where a guard was waving at the captain.

"'Tis Math." He patted her shoulder again with a smile. "I'll go tell his lordship."

Chapter Fourteen

Matthias's chilly reception from Carrie at the gatehouse was a deserved one. As soon as he rode in the gates, his eyes eagerly skimmed over the faces in the bailey. His gaze clapped on her as if magnetized. Wearing a simple green gown that hugged the curves of her body, she glanced at him briefly before redirecting her attention to a passing guard.

During his short time at Chepstow, he'd wondered how he would be welcomed home by her. He should've known. He'd left without telling her he was going, in spite of his reassurance he wouldn't leave her unnecessarily.

Yet, bloody hell, when had he needed to distance himself from their situation more than now? She didn't know what Pandora's box she'd opened when she'd come to him, after he'd been drinking for hours.

The only difference between his last night in Wyldnell and the fateful night nine years ago was that he couldn't remember what had happened with Isabelle. But he could recall every blissful second of his time with Carrie.

His mind had long accepted that he'd acted upon a youthful attraction to Isabelle. She'd been extraordinarily beautiful. Many times, he'd had to cool his appreciation for his sister-in-law and avoid looking at her pretty face. It only served to reason that drink had merely been a catalyst for baser needs buried deep within him. Savage instincts ingrained in him from war.

However, he'd never before burned with the

passion he'd experienced for Carrie. When she was near, he could *sense* her. And when parted from her, a mere memory of her hardened him. He'd told her the truth. His fantasies and desires for her ran rampant with or without alcohol. He'd wanted her from the moment she'd trespassed in his life. His desire had only grown more dangerous since then.

But the only time he'd possessed the courage to warn her about his true villainous character had been from the bottom of his drink.

Sometimes, he almost believed the allegations against him had been false. Through the years, he'd kept his sexual encounters with women at a minimum, giving them what they wanted and taking only what they offered. He'd never aggressively pursued a woman for favors—didn't think he had the right. He knew how to be brief, how to restrain himself and not let lust control him. In nine years, there'd never been another incident. Not once.

His crimes against Isabelle made no sense in light of his treatment of Carrie. For, wanting Carrie the way he did, far more than he could remember wanting to bed his brother's wife, why had he been able to stop himself with Carrie and not with Isabelle? Could Isabelle have been wrong about him?

Tormenting wishes! They were naught but denial and dreams.

He'd seen the bruises with his own eyes.

Now that he must make marriage a reality, he was only trying to deceive himself about who he was and what he'd done. He would never make a decent husband for any woman, but especially not for Carrie. She deserved a much better man.

The sight of Carrie's stiff back from across the yard flooded his thoughts with regret and pining. It was no wonder she couldn't tolerate the sight of him. He'd given her reasons not to trust him, sending her away from their room without a full explanation, then leaving her. There was far more he'd left unsaid.

After confessing their lack of nuptials to the king, it was likely she'd think even worse of him.

Could a woman be wooed after such a mess as he'd made?

Mayhap Rannulf would know what to do. He'd been married to Ursula, so he knew how to deal with women. Although, asking his friend would mean having to confide in him about his deception—that he wasn't married to Carrie yet—but sooner or later everyone at Wyldnell would know that.

Giles knew nothing about courting women. Before his marriage and his fervor for godliness, his brother had usually offered money to women he'd thought beautiful, and that method had always worked. His match with Isabelle had been arranged by King Henry before he'd even met her. Although they loved each other, Giles and Isabelle rarely shared a bed. No, he'd not find any good advice there.

But his feet were already headed in the direction of Giles's room.

He took the stairs two at a time, rehearsing his repentant confession in his head.

****

Arriving at Wyldnell less than an hour on the heels of Matthias and his men, John de Harcourt and his son, Sir Philip, tossed their reins to an awaiting groomsman with hardly a glance. Both men scrutinized the bailey in a hawkeyed stare, as if seeking some hidden treasure within Wyldnell's stone walls. Edwina told Carrie about the visitors as they watched the guests approach.

"Here he comes. The one man in the kingdom with more swagger than our Lord Wyldnell," Edwina jeered.

De Harcourt, one of King Edward's barons from

the northern strongholds, no doubt made comparisons between his concentric fortification and the one he was standing in. A well-fed, well-dressed nobleman, he walked with a saunter of confidence Carrie found arrogant. Sir Philip, closer to her age, followed his father at a distance.

The son, at least, hadn't put on a paunch yet. Quite the opposite, really. With shiny, golden locks and dimpled cheeks, Philip's bearing had a more appealing nature than the other knights she'd met. He could've been the poster boy for the Middle Ages. He was a few inches shorter than Matthias, but his athletic build was similar.

His power to charm became evident watching him tossing masculine smiles at Ian and Rannulf, who'd met them at the gatehouse. With his handsome face, Sir Philip should've been born in her century, where he could earn a living by his appearance alone and not by risking his neck for a king's whims. He belonged in the spotlight, as a popular politician or an actor.

Their guests brought an entourage of twenty men, one lady and her attendants. The lady, Edwina told her, was John de Harcourt's nineteen year-old daughter, Margaret.

Matthias ought to be here. Carrie frowned her displeasure as she and Edwina watched the procession from the kitchen garden, but Matthias had already gone to Giles's chamber.

Giles would be in better spirits today. He'd been awake and eating solid foods all morning. The earl couldn't get enough of her grandmother's Southern-style biscuits and gravy Carrie had learned to make in the kitchen hearth.

She could only hope the news from the king was good. At least Matthias finally wanted to speak with his brother. Maybe they were making further progress towards reconciliation in their rocky relationship.

Preparing to get back to work, she shoved her sleeves up. Was she jealous of Giles just because Matthias hadn't gone out of his way to come greet her? Well, maybe a little.

Pigs would fly before she'd let him know that she cared. He'd make them both miserable because of his doggone "protection."

Carrie helped Edwina fill a cart with leeks and cabbage. The earl would have rabbit stew tonight if he could tolerate it—with more stew than rabbit. The rest would eat partridge, venison, and roasted vegetables.

"Wina," Rannulf called, folding his barrel-like body to duck under a gooseberry branch as he ran into the garden. His face broke into an enormous grin. "Lady Carrie, Edwina, 'twill be a joust!"

"Are you certain, Rannulf?" Edwina dropped a handful of leeks into the cart.

"Aye. Sir Philip just told me of his wish to joust with our knights. Edwina, you know Lord Wyldnell will be pleased by the diversion and by my troth, so will the knights."

****

In the Great Hall that evening, the servants dutifully served the earl's guests. Matthias wasn't drinking much, Carrie noted, because each time a serving man moved to pour wine in his cup, he covered it with his hand. As for the others, they'd probably drink the buttery dry.

Giles had seated her between him and his brother, and the siblings weren't speaking beyond grunts. Although Matthias was courteous, assisting with her meat and keeping her supplied with food and drink, he'd spoken very little. Something was on his mind since he'd returned, and she'd bet money the something was *her*. No doubt thinking of ways to distance himself.

She imagined his contrition in the same manner as Danny Landers last year at a friend's party. She'd wanted Danny to ask her out for weeks. He'd cornered her alone on the terrace beside fragrant bougainvillea, told her how sexy she looked that night, and then they made out on the beach. It was all very romantic beneath the stars with the sound of the waves behind them. The next day, Danny was *"Oops, sorry. I didn't mean to get so carried away. Too many beers, I guess. You know how it is."* Yeah, she knew.

But if Matthias meant to have a serious conversation with her about his conduct, his company prevented it. John de Harcourt had Matthias's ear most of the evening, asking about King Edward's plans for Welsh soldiers, English control of the local boroughs, and how to conquer the two princes.

Carrie strained to keep her eyes from Matthias, not wanting him to see the lingering effects his passion created in her. She satisfied her wandering gaze with tantalizing glimpses of his profile and his gesturing hands. Flickering sensations stirred in her with each remembered touch of his fingers, each caress, each tease on her body. She pictured his shoulders as she'd last seen them, bare with rippling deltoids and biceps bathed in blue moonlight. Her flesh heated, she forced her attention to others at the table.

At Giles's left, Sir Philip regaled him on his tourneys and exploits in Normandy.

Carrie pegged Philip as an adrenalin junkie. Selling herbal energizers and stamina boosters, she'd known her fair share of the adventuring sports-type and had made the mistake of dating a couple of guys like that. Philip loved competitive sports more than even Matthias and Giles, from the sound of him. Nothing wrong in sports or competition, Carrie supposed, but Sir Philip was one of the guys who talked about nothing but himself and his skill in various adventures.

"...That was how I won my newest warhorse. Before that, I took two palfreys in tournament. I gave one to Margaret, though she doesn't ride." Sir Philip muttered, "Wasteful wench. Mayhap I'll keep the other palfrey for a wedding gift to my bride."

Carrie hid a yawn.

Beside her, Giles interrupted the subject of the young knight's conquests. "Are you betrothed, Sir Philip?"

"Nay, but I'll soon take a wife. Father wants to wed both of us off this year." Philip waved the cup bearer back to the table to more wine.

"I would've thought the king would have his own plans for you."

"We were hoping we would meet Edward here, but if not, mayhap we'll meet him at Chepstow. I think father wanted to give the king news of Margaret's betrothal."

"Oh," Giles asked politely, "was there a betrothal for Lady Margaret?"

Philip laughed, pausing as he raised his cup to his mouth. "When we met one of your men on the way here and learned of Sir Matthias's return, 'twas hoped that he would ask for Margaret's hand."

"You wanted Matthias to marry your sister?"

"Truly, my lord. Father wanted to petition the king for your holdings if Matthias wed our Margaret, and then the estate would remain within your family."

Carrie twisted her hands into fists beneath the table as she listened. At least Giles didn't know she and Matthias weren't really married. That would be awful. De Harcourt's plan sounded too tempting for Giles, who wanted Matthias to have children, and alluring for Matthias, as well. Margaret, seated on the other side of her father, had caught the eye of many of the men that evening with her shiny ebony hair and exotic brown eyes.

If Matthias had been able to choose his own bride, would he have chosen Margaret?

"But now we learn that Math has wed, and you're growing better, too, my lord?"

The earl's fingers drummed on the table, hesitating before answering the knight's question. "Aye. We've spoiled your plans." His voice trailed away. Maybe Giles would've chosen Margaret for his brother too, and now he could only regret the lost connection.

"'Tis no matter. Father will manage to find her a suitable match. Margaret and I must return home with broken hearts, though," Philip said, raising his voice for Carrie's hearing, as if she'd had any trouble hearing his loud swanker. "Margaret talks of seeing Matthias returning from Acre when she was a child, and I am half in love with his beautiful wife."

Carrie averted her face, trying to keep from rolling her eyes at his attempted flattery. She didn't think Matthias had overheard the remark. He still hung upon the elder de Harcourt's every word about the war.

"As am I," Giles intoned. "Lady Carrie is a marvelous healer, but I'm told she's a disastrous seamstress."

"What an ungrateful remark, my lord! My lady, should I allow him to say such a thing?" Philip's visage darkened as if he were truly affronted for her.

"Um—oh, yeah. You only need to examine Matthias's tunics from a distance to see the results of my sewing. Pitiful." Carrie laughed over the rim of her wine.

Philip dimpled. "Ah, but you have other charms, I'm sure, my lady. Tell me, what would you do with a palfrey if you were given one?" He rested his chin in his palm as he gazed attentively at her.

The earl's gaze swung between them, his expression unreadable.

"I guess I would probably take it riding as soon as I could. I like horses. They're beautiful animals."

"Verily? And what about jousts? Do you look forward to our contest tomorrow?"

Carrie shrugged. "There are lots of good knights here. It'll be fun to see who the best is, I guess. Lord Wyldnell certainly enjoys it."

"So do I and our king. 'Tis a pity Lord Wyldnell cannot compete. His reputation in the tourneys is well-known. As is your husband's."

As much as she hated to admit it to herself, she was looking forward to seeing Matthias compete.

Carrie reckoned her father had the same kind of charm as Sir Philip. Her mother had once told her he had a flirtatious nature. A smarmy smile with lots of compliments and good intentions. Then the Paris Island marine had abandoned her pregnant mother four weeks before she was due, never to return to Charleston.

Fully engaged now, Giles went into a diatribe about his prowess with a lance and his escapades in the rowdy melees of his youth. Swallowed by his robes, his bony body became animated as he recounted a few times he'd beaten famous names in the tourneys.

"Mayhap I could take up a lance for a bit and show—"

"My lord," Carrie interrupted, horrified by the notion of the frail man even thinking of sitting atop a horse, "I'm sure we would love to watch you, but if you joined in the fray, who would I have to sit with me?"

"The women." Giles shrugged.

"Of course, there are other women, but I know very little about all this. The ladies couldn't tell me as much as you could." She touched his scarlet sleeve in entreaty. "With you, I'd have an expert to explain the details of the sport. I'll bet you could help me predict who the winners are going to be, too."

"For certes, Lady Carrie, if you desire my company, I'd be more than happy to assist you." He twisted at the rings on his fingers.

Carrie rubbed her temples where a slight headache throbbed.

"My lady." Sir Philip angled his shoulders to face her fully. "Your enthusiasm for sport warms my heart. I wonder if I might ask for your favor tomorrow. 'Twould bring good luck, I'm sure."

"My 'favor?'"

Giles's eyes twinkled with amusement. "A token, of course. He's asking for your sleeve or your wimple. Your father has been much negligent in your upbringing, my girl."

Carrie's face heated. "Well, I'm not sure, Sir Philip. I—"

"My sister has already given hers to Sir Matthias, and you are the only lady here whom I would ask."

She swiveled a look back at Matthias, still deep in conversation with de Harcourt. In his hand, he held a dark green sleeve, matching the young girl's dress. Taking a glimpse at Margaret, she discovered the girl's wanton young eyes pinned on Matthias.

That biddy! Carrie's fingers played with her knife. Had she fallen from the Middle Ages into a seventies swingers' convention?

Carrie cast a smile back at Sir Philip.

"If you think it'll give you good luck, Sir Philip, then I'd be happy to give you my favor tomorrow."

"Wonderful." More masculine dimples.

Carrie fell out of their conversation about weaponry, as she solidified her plan not to share her comfortable bed with Matthias that night.

****

The de Harcourts' sudden arrival prevented the field from being properly dressed for a tournament. Matthias had thought Henri, the castle steward, would surely die of a heart attack when he'd learned he would have to arrange for the impromptu combat. Giles preferred a great spectacle with flags, tents, and seating. The arrangements ensuing from the last minute plans weren't remiss, however. The field looked as fine that morning as could be expected on short notice.

Truth be told, the de Harcourts ought to wait for the king. Matthias had warned them their liege wouldn't be pleased to hear that he'd missed the tourney by mere days. No one loved a good contest more than Edward, so he would find their impatience insulting. Yet Matthias was almost as eager to enter the lists as John and Philip.

He hadn't many things to offer in marriage in these times, but at least he had some skills to recommend himself. He'd seen Carrie give her scarf to that arrogant knave, Philip, but he hoped her eyes would be watching *him*.

After giving Carrie plenty of time to fall asleep before joining her the night before, he'd slept on the floor again. The bed looked appealing, and he could think of nothing more pleasant than waking up with her in his arms again. But he couldn't bring himself to lie next to her after the liberties he'd taken the last time they were alone.

Fantasies had become real. New desires awakened. He dared not trust himself with her.

First, they needed to talk.

Matthias allowed his squire to adjust his helm. Knights were gathering at opposite ends of the field. There wasn't time to tell Carrie about the king's order for them and of their impending wedding. He would have to explain the king's decree once the tournament was over that afternoon.

Giles seemed only slightly miffed by Matthias's lie about the marriage. He approved of Carrie, thanks to her knowledge of herbal medicine. However, his courting advice was a stunning disappointment.

"Put your seed in the girl. Offer her your estate in Powys, promise her you'll construct a great castle there once the Welsh are defeated. 'Twould be more than adequate trade for her offspring, would it not? After all, she has no lands or dower of her own to offer you."

Somehow, Matthias didn't think the offer would be enticing for Carrie. She owned and managed her own store in the States. Would she even want a castle in Wales?

If they were back in the twenty-first century, Matthias knew exactly how he'd woo her, with a romantic trip to Greece, expensive dinners, fine jewelry, and luxurious nights in his bed. He had naught of the tools for romance here.

His hand patted the leather bag hanging on his horse's flank. He felt the long, hard object inside, confirming he hadn't lost his gift in the preparations for the joust.

He'd intended to bestow his token to her before the first event. That idea had been trounced. The bastard Philip had blocked his way as he rode up to Carrie. Anticipating him, the bribing knave offered her a damned horse if he won.

His simple wood carving paled in comparison to a gift as expensive as a palfrey.

Giles ought to show the lot of the de Harcourts to the gates.

Matthias tied Lady Margaret's sleeve to his lance. The girl had fawned over him most of the night, trying to oust her father from their company. She obviously hoped to garner Matthias's attention with talk of the tournament. Unlike her brother, Philip, Matthias had more important things on his mind.

The herald announced the beginning of the tourney. Ian entered the field first from Matthias's end. One of de Harcourt's men took up a lance and met him as the others fell away. Ian unseated the knight on the third pass. Matthias eyed the throng of men at the other end as the two combatants squared off. He found Philip waiting on the edge of the fray.

In his previous experience in tourneys, Philip had apparently learned to save his strength for the end. Matthias recognized the man's plan, and he agreed with him. Fresh, they would be able to conserve their strength for each other.

****

Although the lances had been dulled and the hauberks the men wore to protect their bodies were well-padded, Carrie felt her heart thudding with the sound of each thundering pass of the horses. The shock of the lances connecting with shields or bodies made her gut twist into knots. The action looked much milder in the movies. She didn't think she could watch the entire spectacle without being sick.

Putting themselves in danger, the contestants rode headlong into the full force of speeding knights. The worst part of the contest had been seeing the men unseated from their horses. She could hear the groans from where she and the earl sat as the men hit the hard turf, dirt flinging into the spectators. It was a wonder no one broke their neck.

Philip unseated Matthias on the third pass, but Matthias defeated him in sword combat. The crowd evenly split in shouts of each knight's name. Carrie found herself on her feet, watching and praying Matthias wouldn't be injured.

She'd like to have that honor herself.

In the rush of the crowd after Matthias's victory, Carrie lost her place at his side to Margaret, who'd gone to retrieve her sleeve, no doubt.

Carrie scowled and lingered to help the earl's men lift him into his conveyance to return him to the hall. She felt almost as tired from the day's event as the earl looked. As she helped him get situated, she felt the presence of another behind her.

She turned to see Philip waiting behind her, helm tucked under one arm and sweat pouring down his golden locks.

He grinned winningly. "My lady!"

Carrie bid farewell to the earl who was yawning so often now, she figured he'd be asleep by the time his men got him inside the walls.

"Sir Philip, I enjoyed your fighting." It was lie. Philip was an awful coward, striking his opponents when they were down and unable to defend themselves. He repulsed her. "I suppose you've come to give me back my scarf. Sorry it didn't bring more luck."

He shrugged. "'Tis no matter. I'd like to keep it, if I could, in remembrance of a beautiful lady." He moved closer to her, the smell of his unwashed body invading her nostrils. "I actually wanted to be sure you'll still accept my gift of the horse."

Carrie took a step back. "I meant to tell you earlier, Sir Philip, but I think the gift is too great. You said yourself the horse would be for your bride, and I don't really need a horse. I couldn't use it."

He shook his head, sweat dripping on his shoulders. "Nay. 'Tis naught. I have many others in my father's stables. You must accept the palfrey. The horse is excellent, my lady, and easy for a woman to ride. And, I would only ask a small favor in return.

"After I bathe, I want to view the estate, especially the woods, but I'm not familiar with the way. Would you attend me? On a ride?"

"Oh, no. I couldn't. I don't ride by myself. I'm sure one of the guards would be happy to—"

Sir Philip grinned down at her and touched his heart, "My lady, 'twould be a small recompense for my loss at swords and a great boon for my day which has been a terrible disappointment so far. I'm an excellent horseman. I'll take good care of you and return you safely to your husband."

Glancing back, Carrie watched Margaret standing tiptoe as she sponged perspiration off Matthias's brow.

He continued, "Your palfrey hasn't been ridden in weeks, and the exercise would serve it well."

Philip's cajolery took second place in her decision. Distancing herself from Matthias and his doting young beauty took precedence.

"I'll meet you at the stables after I've changed."

"Excellent, my lady." Satisfied, he beamed.

Edwina helped Carrie choose a dress for riding. The surcoat was dark brown to hide any dirt from the ride, and the tunic underneath was pale blue of sturdy fabric. Carrie thought she heard her cluck her tongue in displeasure as she turned to leave.

Meeting Rannulf on her way to the stables, he suggested they ride east, hugging the pastures, not near the higher cliffs and thick woods by the river. The captain expressed his disapproval of the ride with a frown and offered to accompany them, but she saw that he was nursing a sore shoulder. He favored his arm, standing before her with his elbow cradled in his hand. A hard lance had glanced off his hauberk in the tournament.

"No, Rannulf. Go and ask Edwina to make a poultice of lavender and rosemary. Soak your wound in warm water and then ask Edwina to apply the poultice. I'll come check on you when I get back, okay?"

"Aye, as you wish, my lady. But there are other men who could accompany you."

Carrie shook her head and reassured him it would be all right. Despite his faults, Sir Philip was about as strong as Matthias and not a likely target for an attacker. Besides, she'd been told there hadn't been any assaults in years and the sentries made frequent rounds outside the castle walls.

She found Philip waiting with the horses ready. The palfrey he led was very gentle, but the mare seemed dauntingly high when she climbed atop it.

Carrie ignored Matthias's voice in her head, telling her she couldn't ride without him. The promise had been elicited before he kicked her out of their bedchamber and before he took favors from flirty young women.

Philip mounted his own tall, gray horse and led her to the gates at a slow, easy pace. Outside the curtain walls, Philip encouraged Carrie to take advantage of the open meadow and urge her horse into a canter.

She couldn't believe how exhilarating riding could be. She kept the reins tightly twisted in her grasp, afraid to lose them, but she gave the horse freedom to run. The palfrey bounded across the meadow. With the spirited horse beneath her and the wind in her hair, she could almost forget her obnoxious escort as he closed the distance behind them. If only she could make him stop talking. He chattered incessantly to her about which of his horses was the best.

"By God, what a dense forest!" he suddenly exclaimed.

They were near Maud's house.

"Oh, we've come the wrong way," Carrie told him, slowing her horse.

"Nay, I'm told there's a wondrous old henge. Do you know the place?"

"Yes," Carrie turned the horse's head. Her temples began to ache. "We shouldn't go there, Sir Philip."

"Why not? We have plenty of time."

He kicked his animal into a trot toward the woods. Carrie wheeled her palfrey around and called out to the knight, but he kept going deeper into the choking bramble and rock-strewn earth. She followed against her wishes.

Their horses were barely able to navigate the overgrown path, stumbling over rocks and running under low limbs that left the riders dodging. Once they'd long passed Maud's, Carrie felt dread of the stones creeping into her heart. She didn't want to be anywhere near them without Matthias.

"Philip, come back. I want to go home now." At the sound of her voice, the horse vaulted forward as if she'd spurred her.

"Are the stones this way?" He slowed, allowing Carrie time to catch up.

Before she reached him, nausea ran through her, squeezing out all thought. Her eyes clouded, and her vision of Philip vanished in fog and intense pain in her head.

Chapter Fifteen

After rising from his bath and donning a new tunic and braies, Matthias went in search of Carrie. She should've been in their chamber, but finding her gone, he checked her storeroom and then with his brother.

Matthias stood in the doorway as Giles stroked his whiskers absently, contemplating the view from his open window with a lazy yawn.

"She's your bride, Math," Giles grouched, still waking from his nap. "You ought to be capable of keeping track of her yourself. If not now, what will you do once you've actually wed her?"

Matthias reined his temper and struggled for patience. "When I saw her last, she was taking care of your sorry ass." His current mood caused him to blurt the modern expression before he could stop himself.

The corner of Giles's cracked lips lifted in a half-smile. "Bothers you, doesn't it, brother?"

Matthias squeezed the door he was leaning on, but didn't deign to answer the jibe. He was actually relieved to have Carrie watching after Giles. Whatever she was doing for him was working, and the responsibility kept her out of harm's way.

Giles sighed and dropped his grooming hand. "I haven't seen her since the tourney. The last person I saw her with was Philip de Harcourt."

Damn. The thought of Carrie with that arrogant bastard didn't sit well with him at all. The knight's flirtation with his woman grated on Matthias's nerves as he strode out to continue searching for her.

His woman? Well, she wasn't his woman yet. Unless he made her so, Carrie had every right to flirt with whomever she wished in either time. Flirting, touching, bedding any man she wanted. With the sexual freedom of the future, she would've known other men before him. To imagine anyone but himself between her legs filled his soul with a howling demon.

But he meant to make her his. If he could only find her.

Winding through each room of the castle and its towers, he looked everywhere he thought she might be. Belatedly, he checked Edwina's chamber.

He scanned the room for Carrie, but found Edwina and Rannulf instead. Edwina diligently wrapped a binding around Rannulf's shoulder.

"Don't tell me you broke your bloody arm in that minor skirmish," Matthias chided.

Rannulf laughed. "Nay! 'Tis naught but a bruised muscle and wounded pride. But your wife bade me truss it with a poultice. While you were gone, she saved young Richard from the ague, you know."

Matthias smiled as pride crept into his chest. "That sounds like her. Do you know where she is?"

"Aye," Rannulf's smile faded. "It seems you should've lost the sword match today, whelp. She took pity on the loser, and they went riding together."

"Went riding?"

"Aye." Edwina clucked her tongue with disapproval as she tied off Rannulf's bandage. "He wanted her to try the new palfrey."

"Sir Philip is an arrogant dog," Rannulf grumbled. Scowling, he pulled his tunic back on. "He's probably out scouting the estate for his father. Those two don't recognize defeat."

"I cannot believe it. I cannot believe she went

riding." Matthias's stomach clenched. "Dammit, I told her not to ride. It's not safe for her." He shoved an impatient hand in his hair.

"Math?" Rannulf frowned.

Matthias had no time to stay and explain. "This is folly. I'm going to bring her back."

Tearing out of Edwina's chamber, he heard Rannulf's boots behind him. "I'm coming, too, whelp."

The men rode in the direction Rannulf had recommended her to take. When they saw no sign of recent horses having passed there, Matthias had a sudden horrendous thought. Surely, Carrie wouldn't have taken her escort to Maud's—or worse yet, to the standing stones.

He drew his horse up shortly, tossing the idea to Rannulf. Then he kicked the horse into full speed toward the woods. His mind raced with what he might find. He didn't know what Carrie had been thinking. She didn't know the man and didn't know his intentions. Though Matthias was no saint himself, he would *never* consciously treat her with indignity. But if she thought every knight she met was chivalric and honorable, she had much left to learn. Didn't Ian teach her the lesson not to trust strange men in this age? A powerful, landed knight like Sir Philip could easily rape her, and no one would believe her, being half-Welsh as they assumed she was.

In the farthest reaches of his mind, a dark prospect loomed. What would he do if he found her and her young knight engaged in a tryst? De Harcourt had been flirting with her, giving her gifts, and wearing her scarf in the tourney. Carrie might've been smitten by the bastard and hidden away with her swain for an afternoon of lovemaking.

He would kill him.

Rannulf yelled, shaking him from his disturbing

thoughts. "Math, 'tis Philip."

Coming from deep in the woods past Maud's, they heard limbs crashing and the heavy breathing of a horse. Soon Philip burst from the bramble.

"Oh, praise God! Now I know I'm on the way out of here." He slowed his horse as he approached them, panting. His eyes were wild as he threw a glance over his shoulder at the woods.

Matthias saw nothing but trees behind the man. "Where is she?"

"Matthias, Rannulf," he gasped for a breath of air. "Don't go in there. I beg of you, do not. The lady, your wife, she's possessed of a demon."

Matthias launched his horse at the man and caught his reigns. Through gritted teeth, he raged, "Where is she? What have you done?" He felt his skin tighten with fury.

Philip shook his head, eyes rounding. "It's not me, Matthias. The woman...she's spooked her horse. The damned thing ran out from under her, terrified to death. It's a demon inside her, I tell you. Stay away from her."

With a curse, Matthias released the man's horse. Philip spurred his beast and raced away, leaving Matthias to follow the broken path through the wood. Rannulf followed, but the brambles were thick. Matthias scanned the area for signs of Carrie. Philip's path proved obvious with shattered branches and limbs laid to waste. He tracked their way easily. Then in a small clearing littered with rocks, he saw her, lying haphazard atop the stony earth, her body writhing.

****

Pain splintered like rockets in Carrie's head. A thousand firecrackers exploded at once. Her eyelids felt heavy. She was unable to open them even if she wanted to. There were garbled voices above her head. Something told her they were talking about her, but the words made no sense. Then, as if an out-of-focus motion picture projector slowly winding up to speed, the sounds gained meaning, no longer foreign.

"...falling sickness. Move the rocks. Move them away."

Her body was lying on knife points spearing into her back. Then warm hands moved in, replacing the pain.

She tried to speak, but her tongue felt too thick to move. She suddenly knew why she felt so odd—she'd had a seizure.

Each movement resulted in inexplicable pain. She moaned. Her head ached unbearably.

"Carys."

"M...Matthias," she heard herself finally utter.

She forced her heavy eyelids open. Matthias was looking down at her. His gray eyes shifted over her face searchingly.

"Grand mal," her voice crackled.

God she hurt. Headaches and muscle aches were normal, but this pain searing through her was not. Matthias was attempting to move her gently, but everything hurt. Tears burned her eyes and spilled down her cheeks.

"Rannulf, the castle's too far. We're closer to Maud's."

"Aye."

Matthias's voice sounded strange to her ears, but she had little mind to consider it. He settled her deep against his chest and stood, cradling her in his arms. Through bleary eyes, she saw the horse and knew he intended to put her on it. She groaned again and pressed her face to his chest.

He murmured something in Welsh against her ear and placed her in Rannulf's arms. Rannulf passed her up once he was mounted. His arms pulled her close against him, and then he set the horse in motion. She managed to wrap one arm around his waist, but the other arm felt cold and heavy. What was wrong with her?

She was vaguely aware of Rannulf riding ahead of them and heard him shout out to Maud as they drew near her cottage. The old woman opened her door and came outside as soon as she recognized them.

The pain throbbed in her arm as Matthias handed her down to Rannulf. When he leapt from his horse, there was an enormous crimson stain on his tunic. She gasped.

Matthias gingerly drew her back in his arms and told her softly, "'Tis yours, not mine, Carrie."

Entering the house, he explained to Maud that she had fallen in a spell. The old woman listed herbs aloud as she set into motion, and Carrie knew it was meant for her hearing.

Matthias found Maud's bed in the corner behind a curtain. He laid her out upon it and sat beside her. Maud moved back into her vision with a handful of cloth bandages.

"We've got to staunch the blood." Matthias took the cloth.

She caught the flash of a dagger blade out of the corner of her eye. Matthias slid the blade into the sleeve of her dress and ripped a line up the fabric, severing the sleeve in two. She tried to see the wound that was making her miserable, but he quickly covered it. She winced as her own arm touched her side.

"The ribs," Rannulf told him. "You need to see if she's broken any."

"I...I don't think I have."

"Let him check you to be sure, my lady." Rannulf told her. "You fell on a great pile of rock from a running horse. 'Twas like dropping an egg on an anvil."

"Rannulf! Fetch some water," Matthias ordered.

Once the captain was out of sight, Maud held the cloth to Carrie's bleeding arm, and Matthias took hold of the laces of her surcoat. He managed to get the side open without her feeling his touch, and he eased the outer garment over her head with care. Then he tugged at the strings of her tunic, pulling the edges loose.

Carrie couldn't help but wonder if he remembered the last time he'd unfastened her laces and her cheeks warmed. The backs of his knuckles grazed across her breasts with each tug. The soft brush of his fingertips against the curves of her skin distracted her from the pain.

As soon as he'd created a wide enough opening, he slid his hand inside to touch her lowest rib. Perspiration glistened on his brow. His fingers delicately traced the length of the bone before moving up to the next. Once his fingers met the sensitive swell of her breast, his dark, smoky eyes slid to hers, and the corner of his lips twitched. Carrie felt too weak to swing out at him and too embarrassed to admonish him in front of Maud. She smiled beneath her tears. Some color came back into Matthias's taut face.

Then a disturbing thought alarmed her.

"Did you see me—y...you know?" she asked, fearing the answer.

His fingers glided past the flesh of her breast and nipple and examined the bones beneath her arm.

"In the seizure? Yes."

"I'm sorry," her voice broke.

"No broken bones. Just bruises." Matthias declared. He removed his hand and took the cloth from Maud, allowing her to return to gather medicine. He then bent down to kiss one of the tears on her cheek. Resting his forehead against hers, he teased, "You managed to frighten Philip more than I did, and verily I meant to."

Carrie closed her eyes tightly, willing away tears.

Matthias drew back. "I'm sorry, *Carys*. He should not have left you."

"Oh." Carrie opened her eyes. Did he think she cared what Philip thought? Quickly, she explained, "Very few people have ever seen me like that, in a grand mal. The way Sir Philip reacted wasn't any different than what I would've expected him to do. Guys hate my spells. I'm used to it."

A line appeared between his brows. "You shouldn't be treated that way. De Harcourt needs to be hung by his spurs."

"It's okay. If it had been *you* who had abandoned me, then I would've been upset."

"I wish you'd told me what to expect, what to do. I felt completely helpless." He stroked her hair idly.

"You did everything right. It's my fault. I know you're going to remind me that you warned me not to ride and believe me, I feel really stupid."

Rannulf returned to the bedside with a bowl of clean water. Maud brought freshly crushed herbs and a jar of oil to set on the table.

"The wound needs stitching," Rannulf announced.

Carrie shuddered. She hated the feel of needles, having endured the sting of them most of her life.

Maud nodded. "I'll sew. I've plenty of experience with it. Will you hold your lady, Math?"

Matthias swallowed. "Aye."

He moved behind her, cradling her head against his thigh as he held both her hands. The pain of the gash on her outstretched arm was nearly enough to make her vomit. Maud took out a bone needle, the same kind Carrie had used sewing with Edwina and some thread. Carrie's teeth began to chatter.

"How will we clean the wound?" Matthias asked.

It was a question Carrie knew she would've thought to ask herself if she wasn't so rattled from the fall.

"Lavender, chamomile, and juniper." Maud nodded toward a jar she'd placed on a nearby table.

"Have you any h-hyssop leaf?" Carrie gasped and squeezed Matthias's hands in a wave of pain.

"Nay, my lady." Maud looked up pointedly at Matthias. "But the monks do. I often trade herbs with them."

"Let's stitch her up and then I'll go fetch what you need."

Maud poured the oily mixture she'd made over the open wound and rinsed it with water. She talked as she worked. "I should go, Math. The monks know me and are more willing to trade with me. Besides, I know the plant she's asking for."

"All right, but take Rannulf with you for protection. Go first to the castle and tell them Lady Carrie had an accident, so no one will think we've been attacked or that there's any truth to Philip's dim-witted claims of demons." Matthias flashed Carrie an apologetic glance. "Then ride north as fast as you can travel to avoid enemy assault. 'Tis nearly dark now. I know we shouldn't expect you until morning."

Maud stitched quickly, but the end couldn't come soon enough for Carrie. Tears trailed down her cheeks as she felt the needle's sting. She wished she wouldn't cry because she knew Matthias disliked her tears. A muscle in his jaw worked as he held her. Pushing the pain from her mind, she imagined how many times he must've seen battle wounds closed in a similar fashion.

Leaning back, Maud announced, "'Tis finished."

Matthias handled Carrie's arm lightly, studying the stitches. "Your work is good."

He eased Carrie's wounded arm down to relax at her side.

Maud told him, "There's a stew on the fire for dinner and bread on the table. I've already eaten." The old woman then gathered a few items to exchange for the hyssop. "Your lady is welcome to borrow my clothes when she feels able to change. I still have some of Iago's tunics for you, as well, Math."

As they were leaving, Matthias murmured, "Thank you, Maud."

The healer nodded. He asked Rannulf to keep her safe and return quickly.

As soon as they were gone, Matthias pulled a cover over Carrie. His face was grim as he wrapped her wound with the cloth bandages.

Carrie sniffled. "It's not that bad. The worst is over. Thank you for staying with me."

Matthias's eyes widened. "Did you think I would leave?"

"Well..."

"I don't think I could leave now if I wanted to," he said softly.

When he finished with the binding, he placed a kiss on her forehead. Carrie watched his worried gray eyes travel the trails of her tears. He bent over to press a light kiss to a teardrop near the outer corner of her eye. His lips moved to another tear on her cheek and another. Her body started to tingle pleasantly. When all the tears were gone, he softly kissed her mouth.

"I should let you rest," he told her as his face hovered near hers.

Regretfully, Carrie knew she needed to sleep. Instead of leaving her, Matthias stretched out on the mattress beside her. His fingers gingerly stroked her hair, coaxing her to relax. Her headache subsided, and she soon drifted off.

Sometime in the middle of the night, Carrie awoke. The fire in the hearth was still burning, warming the cottage, but not making it too uncomfortable for a woman used to the muggy nights of low country summers in South Carolina. Maybe it wasn't as comfortable to Matthias, who was lying with his face turned to her. His eyes were closed. The golden skin of his shoulders glowed with the sheen of perspiration.

A million or more disposable cameras sat in drugstores back home in the twenty-first century at this moment, and she'd trade anything for one of those cameras to take just one picture. To capture an image of the beautiful man beside her. *As if she'd ever forget.*

Taking precaution against waking him, she lifted her side of the blanket and threw it off. She sat up slowly, assessing her aches and pains. Though her side was sore, it wasn't unbearably so. Most of her pain had been from her wound and from sheer mortification. The bandage on her arm was secured well, a comfortable fit with only a small amount of blood having soaked through. Matthias's bloodstained tunic laid discarded on the floor.

She tried to stand, but lightheaded, the room spun. Her hand flew to her forehead as a wave of nausea hit her.

"God's sakes, woman!"

Matthias reached for her and drew her back against him.

"You lost too much blood to be up and about," he scolded tenderly in her ear. "What do you need? I'll get it."

"You can't."

"Oh." He thought for a brief moment. "Well, then I'll take you."

Before she could protest she didn't want him to go, he picked her up in his arms and carried her outside. When she was finished taking care of her needs, he carried her back inside and settled her back on the bed.

"I'm not that ill," she complained. "I could've walked outside myself."

"Of course you could've," he smiled, and his expression mocked her. "How's your side?"

"Not bad. Probably turning a pretty shade of purple, but it doesn't hurt much." Carrie grinned wryly.

"You hit your back on the rocks, too."

"Did I? I don't remember. I never remember anything that happens during a seizure."

"I could check it. See if we missed any cuts or scrapes that need tending." His gaze darted from hers.

"Thank you."

She sat up and finished unfastening the tunic. Turning, she slid the shoulders of the garment off and exposed her bare back to him.

She heard him take a deep breath behind her.

"Is it that bad?"

"Just a few small bruises." The tips of his fingers fell upon her shoulder blades, causing her to tremble at the softness of his touch. "I should feel your backbones, as well."

She smiled to herself. He wouldn't find anything wrong. Her back felt okay, but she wouldn't dare interrupt his search.

He moved her hair over her shoulder, giving him a better view. His fingers glided ever-so-softly across the skin of her lower back and then higher until they came to rest at the top of her spine. He planted a warm kiss there, his breath trailing across her skin as he lifted his head.

"Nothing broken?" she murmured.

"'Tis hard to tell. I should examine more, I think. Am I hurting you?"

"I'll let you know."

He dropped more kisses up her shoulder to the nape of her neck. His mouth was hot against her cool skin, stirring sensations inside her. She rippled with arousal and tilted her head to the side, allowing him better access to her neck. Large, warm hands slid around her chest to cover her breasts. His mouth moved up her neck, his breath quickening, as he fondled her. He made taut kernels of her nipples as his teeth gently grazed the back of her neck, creating a primal desire in her to mate. She leaned into his chest, closing her eyes to soak in the full vibrations he created with his mouth and hands.

As she reclined into his ministrations, she laid her hands on his thighs. The muscles beneath his braies were thick and hard. She wondered how they would look naked. His breath against her ear grew deeper as he touched her. His hands moved down her ribs and over the valley of her stomach, stopping at her hips where her fallen gown barred the way.

"You should lie down," he whispered hoarsely in her ear and kissed her earlobe. "I should let you rest."

He moved from behind her and rose.

Carrie caught his hand. "Don't you dare, Matthias. Don't push me away again."

He tenderly cupped her cheek. "I don't want to hurt you. Your arm—"

"You won't hurt me. I'm not made of glass." She smiled up at him.

"Nay, you're not."

His thumb rubbed across her cheek and then slipped to trace the edge of her lower lip. Sliding his thumb gently between her lips, he bent down to replace the fingertip with his mouth against hers. His tongue slid between her opened lips as he lowered his body to the bed. He cradled her head in his hand as he kissed her deeper, easing her onto the pillow. His kiss was gentle and seductive, his tongue exploring her mouth in ways that made her think of other bodily explorations. When he finally lifted his head, he sat back, his eyes dark and sensual.

"Now it's *my* turn to make you forget *your* pain," he told her.

Before she could ask how, he ran his hands down her legs, and she instantly knew she would like this much better than the headache cure she'd given him.

Moving over her, he took hold of her ankles and gently but firmly opened her legs. His hands smoothed upward over her bare calves and knees, easing her gown up to her middle. When his warm fingers touched her sensitive inner thighs, she gasped and bent her knees.

The gray of Matthias's eyes brightened to silver in the firelight as he looked into her face. "You're so beautiful, *Carys.*"

Then he held himself over her as he covered one of her breasts with his mouth. His tongue lavished her nipple, and Carrie felt his warm palm slipping up her thigh. His fingers splayed against her, and he began to make a slow circle with his palm. Her entire body felt tethered to the spot where he caressed her. When his mouth moved to her other nipple, he eased a finger between her folds, stroking and teasing the sensitive part of her center. Sweet, rhythmic torture, he played with her until she clutched at his shoulders, needing more.

He moved down to the juncture of her thighs and kissed her. His hands slid under her buttocks as he filled her with the warmth of his mouth. His tongue, hot, wet velvet, taunted her. All her nerves tightened until she went frantic, hands shaking, opening and clutching his shoulders convulsively.

As Matthias kissed her, waves of pleasure washed over her. Arching her hips, Carrie cried out his name. Her fingers sank into the shiny dark locks of his hair as her body gave in to sweet release.

Matthias lifted his head and dropped kisses along her stomach as she fought to catch her breath.

"Forgive me, Carrie. I cannot help wanting you," he murmured over her body in a voice fraught with desperation. "I'd like to make you mine. Will you let me?"

Oh, God, would she! Whatever *that* meant, she liked the sound of it.

"Yes," she breathed.

Matthias sat back on his heels as he untied the lace on his pants. Carrie leaned up on her good elbow to help him, but he gently nudged her back to the bed. His powerful body rose above her, naked now for her view. He was large, swollen, and so very ready.

His body quaked as he eased over her. She grasped the steely muscles of his arms as he held himself above her, and she could feel trembling deep at their core. The expression on his face was one of determination. Restraint. It was the first time her powerful warrior had ever appeared vulnerable.

Just when she thought she couldn't possibly care more for the man, her heart swelled, nearly bursting with love.

"Please, Matthias..." She entwined her fingers behind his neck and drew him down to her. She rained kisses across his throat and up his chin, her erect nipples brushing his chest.

Matthias groaned, and she leaned back, catching the moment he relinquished his willpower to need.

Uttering her name, he closed his eyes and took a deep centering breath. She felt his arousal brush against her, tentative and hot. Then he entered her, surging with power into her wet sheath. She felt a twinge of momentary pain as her body adjusted to his thickness, but the sensation quickly turned to molten desire and fulfillment. When Matthias opened his eyes again, ecstasy burned there, consuming her in its heat.

His mouth pressed to her neck again and he nibbled hungrily. He pushed further into her, running one large hand underneath her to cup her bottom. His rhythm increased along with their breathing, deep and frenzied, as he pulled her against his hips. She met his thrusts, longing to share her pleasure.

"Yes, Matthias!" she moaned.

Her gaze riveted on his face. Rapture filled his expression as he drove into her and withdrew again and again.

A frown drew his brow, and an anguished sound of unwanted surrender ripped from his throat. He laid his forehead on her collarbone, muffling his rough cry against her flesh as he filled her twice more. His body shuddered as his seed pumped deep inside her, and then he went still, his breath coming in ragged gasps.

Lying beside her, he pulled her into his arms and kissed her hair. She wanted more, *much* more of him, but she knew he feared he would hurt her. There would be a better time to have her fill of him, and she was buoyed by the joyful knowledge he was far from being done with her, too.

As they lay together, he broke the silence.

"Carrie?"

She cringed inwardly at his hesitant tone and made herself answer. "Yes?"

Here it comes. She stiffened as the heady scents of their lovemaking and Maud's drying lavender hanging above became the acrid memory of bougainvillea, the ocean, and the sound of Danny Landers's remorse.

"When I heard you'd gone riding with de

Harcourt's son, I thought you might've decided...well, I...I wondered if you'd taken an interest in him."

She blinked, surprised and deliriously pleased he might be jealous. "And *I* figured you'd taken an interest in Lady Margaret."

She ran her fingertip in a pattern through the dark hairs over his heart.

He smiled. "I have no other interests—only you."

Chapter Sixteen

After rising to the sounds of a man in the kitchen and then later being fed by him, Carrie decided all her agony the day before was worth it. She stretched to work out the kinks of the night before. Her arm throbbed, stitches stinging from the motion, but she could handle the pain. A slew of pleasant memories, kisses and caresses softened even the worst of her injuries.

Although she would have preferred staying in bed with Matthias all morning, she acquiesced to follow his lead. After all, they were guests in the healer's house and didn't have the luxuries of time and privacy.

Rannulf and Maud returned to the cottage shortly after she and Matthias had finished eating and dressing. They'd brought the hyssop she'd requested. A Greek herb, she knew it was an extravagance in the Welsh Marches.

"I'm sorry to be so much trouble, Maud." Wearing one of Maud's borrowed garments and sitting on the edge of the bed, Carrie thanked the healer for getting the costly plant. "The bruised hyssop leaves should help the cut heal faster. What did you have to trade for it?"

"Nothing, my lady. When Sir Rannulf told the monks it was for Sir Matthias's wife, they insisted you have it without trade. I even have enough to keep some for myself. The Cistercians did ask if you would deliver some things to the earl's cook."

Carrie nodded. It was the least she could do.

Maud checked the stitches on Carrie's arm.

Satisfied the blood had stopped flowing, she put some fresh medicine on it and an oily layer of hyssop leaves before dressing her arm with a new bandage. Carrie tested her arm, bending it back and forth, and discovered she was feeling stronger. She felt the weight of Matthias's stare as he stood over her.

His serious gaze searched her face. "Do you feel well enough to go to the castle?"

Maud spoke before she could answer. "Stay as long as you need, my lady."

Carrie watched an unspoken message pass between Maud and Matthias as the healer ignored Matthias's censuring look. She was aware of his new frostiness since Maud returned. She chewed her lip. She didn't need to stay, but she didn't know why Matthias wanted her to go back with him so expeditiously. He made it obvious he aimed to get her out of the cottage as soon as possible. But why?

"I think I'll be all right now, Maud. Thank you for all your help." Carrie cast a stern glare at him, which seemed to roll right off his shoulders.

He was being ornery again, but she doubted he would endanger her health if he didn't think she was able to travel. After his compassion for her following her seizure, she trusted him implicitly. As long as she didn't have to lift anything major, there wouldn't be a problem. After all, her arm was the main injury.

Carrie helped Maud fill a leather bag with herbs while Rannulf went outside to ready the horses. Matthias hovered nearby.

"I know you don't want to hear this, but," Maud spoke to her as she fastened the sack, "Lord Wyldnell may be in danger."

"In danger?"

Matthias grumbled, "Giles is doing better."

The healer continued to ignore him. "I've long been wary of his health. The pains and his sickness come and go. His illness follows no path known to me. His symptoms make no sense."

"What do you *think* might've caused Giles's ailment?" Carrie asked. Maud probably knew the local illnesses better than anyone.

"That's the true problem, my lady. I don't know the cause."

Matthias took Carrie's good arm. "We've already found the answer. Obviously Carrie's changes to his diet have helped because the old cur is almost back to normal now."

"She's only lessened the symptoms," Maud argued.

He steered Carrie toward the door, but she stopped him, planting a hand on his chest as she paused to think. "Wait a minute. She's right, Matthias. I've only helped his digestion, but we still don't know what was causing his illness."

She hated the thought, but cancer crossed her mind. When she was in the hospital once having one of her countless tests done, she'd shared a semi-private room with an elderly woman who had stomach cancer. Spasms racked the poor woman constantly. The patient had been released from the hospital weeks earlier only to return. The earl's symptoms seemed similar.

Carrie laced her arm through his, seeking to share his strength.

Behind them, the healer spoke. "Perhaps the illness does not lie in his food. Mayhap it lies in the company he keeps."

They both turned to look at Maud.

She picked up a blanket and began to fold it as if she'd said nothing at all.

"What do you mean?" Carrie asked.

Maud looked back and forth between them. "'Tis probably only the fancy of an old woman, but if you're concerned for the earl, you'll keep a close watch on him."

"You think somebody wants to *poison* him?"

Matthias muttered something unintelligible beside her. Then, patience at an end, he threw the door open. "No one wants to hurt my brother."

Carrie had to agree. Giles was well-respected, if not feared, by everyone she knew at Wyldnell. "Surely you're wrong. His sickness must be caused by something rather than someone, but we'll keep a close watch over him, just in case."

****

That afternoon, the castle swarmed with life as if under siege from those within its walls. Every building turned inside out, preparing for the visit of the king and his entourage. Carrie found herself a virtual prisoner in her own chamber. Matthias insisted she stay in the safety of their solar until her body became used to the medicine of the moon plants.

The prescription barbiturates ran out the day before yesterday, and she supposed the lack of medication had been the catalyst for her grand mal seizure—along with the fatigue from watching the tourney and her long vigil over the sickly boy. There was no guarantee the herbs would work, but she didn't feel apprehensive about its possible failure to prevent seizures. Strangely enough, she wasn't worried about the next spell at all.

She'd tried to convince everyone who came to check on her condition that she felt better. Apparently, fearing Matthias, Sir Philip hadn't told a soul about Carrie's seizure. Aside from Rannulf, the rest of the castle thought her injury was from a simple fall from her horse. Her arm was wrapped up and healing. Her side was sore, but she had perfect flexibility. It was more like those muscle aches from workouts in the gym, certainly nothing insurmountable.

No, her injuries weren't fatal, but staying inside

when there was work to be done was killing her.

She could imagine the state of kitchen. Edwina had told her that the earl had demanded venison, suckling pigs, and twenty pasture cattle served up for the night of the king's arrival. Unless King Edward had a hearty appetite and an army with him, she knew there would be far too much waste.

Edwina also related the facts that new tapestries hung in the Great Hall, the rushes were being swept and replaced, and the garderobes cleaned.

Abbot Sidney of Marsten would be attending, as well. His presence would call for a resplendent place of worship. Matthias was taking great care with the steward in seeing to the upkeep of the chapel. Maybe abbots were nearly as important in this age as the king. Fifty beeswax candles were ordered for the chapel alone.

She reluctantly accepted she must be content watching the work from the tower window.

At least Matthias cared about her health.

His words spoken in passion replayed over and over in her mind. Just what exactly did he mean by "making her his?" Was it something from the heat of the moment, or something more?

He'd made no move to touch her or kiss her that day, and she wondered if they were having one of those awkward "day after" moments. Maybe she was wrong about how he felt about making love to her, and like Ian had put it, he'd plowed her until he got his fill.

The de Harcourts exited the castle gates as she looked on from above. This time, Sir Philip led the party. Margaret turned pitiful glances over her shoulder at Wyldnell as they rode, but Carrie didn't feel the least bit sympathetic toward her. Good riddance. According to Edwina, they were leaving before the king's arrival, due to business in the north, but she felt their departure was simply because of her seizure.

She bubbled with laughter. This was probably the first time her condition brought her good luck instead of misery!

Later that evening her thoughts turned to her empty stomach. Was Matthias going to let her come out for dinner? Maybe he'd forgotten her in all the preparations for the castle's royal guests. Word had reached Wyldnell that King Edward would be there the next afternoon, a servant had told her during a visit, so the grand feast would wait another day.

Just when she'd started contemplating, in droll humor, how hard it would be to catch a bird on her windowsill and pluck it for dinner, she heard Matthias return.

She sighed as he closed the door behind him. "I hope you brought a five course meal with you."

She eyed the skinny leather bag in his hand as she left the window.

"Are you hungry?" He gave her a lopsided grin.

Would she ever get enough of the sight of Matthias's smiles?

"Duh!"

She tried to reach for the bag, but he sidestepped her. "Mind your stitches," he scolded lightly. "I didn't bring any food, Carrie."

"You're kidding me." She planted her hands on her hips. "I've been stuck here all day."

"Cook was supposed to send your lunch."

"Yeah, he did, but I got hungry again an hour ago. How can you expect me to stay here? It's ridiculous. I'm not planning on doing any weight lifting, so my arm will be just fine."

He offered her an outstretched palm. "Come outside with me. Let me make it up to you."

The depths of Matthias's eyes twinkled with mischief.

She lifted an eyebrow at him. "Is there a pizza restaurant around the corner? If not, I'd rather go see what we can scare up in the kitchen."

"No pizza parlors here, but if you'll come outside, I promise you won't regret it."

She was skeptical, but he was being too friendly to continue the argument. By all appearances, he was in a cheerful mood, and she should enjoy it while it lasted. She put her hand in his, and he led her out to the bailey.

The sun set as they walked the grounds. The sky dazzled with pinks and purples stretching out over the wall. He led her directly to the garden his mother had taken great pride in. Holding her hand, he navigated through the winding rows of lush, leafy rose bushes to the heart of the flower garden where a table had been set for dinner. Torches illuminated the site for the imminent fall of night.

Carrie's first impulse on seeing the arrangement was to check to see if he had a fever. She could hardly believe Matthias arranged such a thing. Her stomach somersaulted at the romantic gesture.

"Is this for me?"

"Aye, unless you'd like to give it to some other hungry person."

"Not a chance."

He'd laid out a trencher of chicken breast cooked in garlic butter, vegetables, bread, and a slice of pie. A cup of watered-down mead had already been poured for her. The meal smelled better than anything she'd eaten in a month.

There was only one setting.

"Aren't you eating?" She glanced up from the table at him.

"Nay, I grabbed a few pieces of bread earlier when I was too busy to stop." He pulled out a chair for her, watching her expression. "Do you like my surprise, then?" A lock of hair fell over his forehead in the movement.

How could he doubt it? She smiled, floating into her chair. "This is wonderful, Matthias."

He sat across from her, and she hungrily wolfed down her food without care or concern for how she looked. She offered no apology for her appetite since it was his fault for keeping her inside all day. His lips twisted in amusement when she managed to clean her plate and stuffed the last bite of her bread trencher in her mouth.

"You know," he murmured, "most modern women of my acquaintance would only order a salad for dinner and pick at it. 'Tis good to know you're a woman who'll never waste away from lack of eating."

Carrie rolled her eyes and smiled. "Don't forget, I'm from the American South, and I was raised to love good food. We have a big kitchen at my mom's house. It's where we entertain. No one leaves our home hungry, believe me. When we get back, I'll have to cook you some of our family recipes. Frogmore stew. Hoppin' John. Sweet potato pie."

He cocked an eyebrow at the names of her favorite dishes. She laughed. "You'll love it. Hey, they don't sound any worse than clotted cream and spotted dick."

The wistful recollection left her thinking of her family until she realized Matthias hadn't refused the invitation. He'd inclined his head with a smile. She accepted his nod as a good sign. She'd love to see him sitting at her mother's dinner table, talking and laughing over breakfast with her whole family.

Full and content, she sighed. "Thank you. This almost makes up for having to put up with your grouchiness. The only thing missing from this meal was the fork, and I'm getting used to that."

His attentive gaze suddenly left her and a slight frown creased his brow. Had she insulted him accidentally by her joke about his grouchiness?

"I'm sorry. I was just kidding." The last thing she wanted to do was send him back into one of his darker, melancholy moods. "How are the preparations going for the king's arrival? I hope you and Rannulf aren't overworking the men."

He didn't offer much to say in the way of conversation. His eyes remained on the ground, and a muscle worked in his jaw. When she could think of nothing else to talk about, she decided to throw in the towel.

She pushed back from the table, weary and defeated by his moodiness. "Well, are you ready to—"

Matthias suddenly tossed the leather bag he'd been holding onto the table, interrupting her with the thump it made. When she looked up from the bag, he told her, "'Tis for you."

He watched her intensely in the torchlight.

She opened it and withdrew its contents slowly, certain there must be a venomous snake inside for all his dark demeanor. But instead, she held a long wooden spoon. Wetting her lips, she looked up at Matthias again, expecting him to say something, but he didn't.

She turned the spoon over in her hand. Carved of dark wood with a rich grain, the handle led to the form of a fearsome, rearing dragon with a large heart at its clawed feet. Intricate in every detail— sharp eyes, teeth, and even scales. The meticulous craftsmanship made her heart skip a beat. A single wooden chain link adorned the top, making it ready for attachment on her girdle. Her fingers rubbed the smooth dragon's wings involuntarily.

"You made this." Her voice came out as an awed whisper.

He shrugged one shoulder. "Carving is a good way to pass the time when one's not sleeping."

"It's amazing, Matthias."

She searched his face again. He cleared his

throat and looked away.

"What's it for?"

He frowned. "'What's it for?'"

"Yes, it's beautiful, really. But what's its purpose?" Carrie gave him her most innocent smile, a giddy lightness in her chest.

"It's...it's just for you. I made it for you."

"You don't want me to eat out of this spoon, surely."

"Nay. It's just...I made it for you to have. That's all." His voice grew rougher. He rose and ran a hand through his hair. "It's getting bloody hot out here. Let's go inside."

Without waiting for her agreement, he stalked toward the garden, leaving her to follow. She clutched her gift at her side, grinning to herself. She knew exactly what it was for, having seen replicas for sale in gift shops during her sightseeing day in Cardiff. Lovespoons were a traditional Welsh gift from a man to the girl he was courting. So, *was Matthias courting her?*

****

Matthias ignored the scratches of rose thorns as he brushed past. Walking in the garden at night had once been one of his pleasures at Wyldnell. His mother had orchestrated the positions of each shrub to be observed from all sides, so the moon lit the petals of the roses like a silver mantle. The rows spanned over acres creating a formidable maze. Tonight however, the moonlight was too dim for navigating.

Giles's new bard was performing, and he had meant to bring Carrie to the Great Hall to listen since she seemed to enjoy the entertainment so much. And, not the smallest of his consideration, he also hoped there would be another demand for a kiss from her.

That was before he'd opened his mouth and

inserted his foot.

He could hear Carrie's soft tread behind him. It was dark, and he was being a clod for leaving so abruptly. When he stopped and turned to let her catch up, she nearly ran into him. Her fingers brushed his chest lightly as she stopped and took a step back. She laughed merrily.

"Sorry. Look, I put the spoon on my belt. That's right, isn't it? That's where it goes?"

Matthias planted his hands on his hips and wished he could be angry with her for not understanding his gift. But how could he be mad at her when it was his own fault for not explaining the common rituals of his time? He had explained lovespoons eloquently to his classroom full of dewy-eyed, first-year pupils. Yet he remained inarticulate before her. Had she taken his tongue along with his heart?

Only Carrie made him that way, turning him into a stammering idiot. If telling her what a stupid lovespoon was meant for was so difficult, how the hell was he going to ask her to wed him tomorrow?

"Carrie, I can barely see you, let alone your girdle. You can do with it whatever you wish. I care not."

"Well, give me your hand and feel it then."

Her hands caught his in the dark, and she drew one to her waist. She moved closer to him, putting her palms on his chest. His pulse quickened.

"Carrie, we need to talk."

She swayed closer to him, and he could feel the heat of her body, her warm breath across his neck.

"Is that why you brought me out here? To give me dinner and talk?"

Her hands slid up until she had her arms around his neck. Sweet Jesu, one more brush of her breasts against his chest, and he knew he would be lost to reason. He allowed his hands to rest on her lovely hips.

He swallowed hard. "Aye, but nay. But...well, aye. I wanted to talk to you about tomorrow and what's expected."

Her fingers moved into the thick of his hair, becoming entangled. The sensation of her holding him thusly was simply exhilarating.

"You mean with the king. I suppose you want me to stay out of sight or something." She sighed. "It's not every day a girl from Charleston gets to meet a king, but if you think I can't fool him as your wife, then—"

"Nay, I don't want you to stay out of sight, and I do think you can fool him. There's no problem with that. It's just that I—"

"If it's about my deportment or some sort of royal etiquette-thing, I'll ask Edwina to help me tomorrow."

Standing on her toes, she pressed her lips to the hollow of his neck.

Aye, he was lost.

His hands had somehow fallen to her comely buttocks.

He spoke softly into her ear, breathing in the fragrance of her hair, "It's not about you. There's something the king expects to see. I—"

She gently pulled his head to hers and stifled his mouth with her kiss. Soft and giving, her whole body melded against him, and he realized he'd already begun to shift her body closer to the part that longed to feel her most. He felt his body turn traitor, blood surging to his nether region. Her tongue moved against his invitingly, and he accepted her invitation.

But when her body came in full contact with his erection, he fought for control, breaking the kiss.

He panted, "Carrie, I must speak..."

"Since when do you ever want to talk,

Matthias?" She cupped his face in her hands, bringing his head down for another intoxicating kiss.

She tasted of apples and honey mead, and he'd never savored anything more appealing or addictive. God's teeth, she made it so hard for him to speak. He had to tell her, had to ask. But if her answer was no, as he knew it should be, he wouldn't have this night with her.

One night to love her, to show her how much he needed her. To relish her trust and innocence, her passion, before it was taken from him. In the morning, he could ask her to be his bride for real and at least he'd have this last night in her arms. *Would that be so wrong?*

With his cheek cradled in her tender palm, he sensed her other hand running down his chest, stopping when she found his braies. He rippled with anticipation as her hand moved across his stomach, inside his pants, and down, wrapping around his straining flesh.

He released a moan into her mouth.

He flexed his hands against her firm bottom. When she made a sound in her throat like a purr of pleasure, he decided his talk could definitely wait. He ended their kiss and scooped her up in his arms and carried her to his tower.

Chapter Seventeen

Carrie didn't care who saw them. As Matthias placed her on the canopied bed, servants passed in and out the door, filling a tub with steaming water. The water was too hot for a bath, so she knew he'd meant for them to use it later. Perhaps this was yet another part of his plan for their evening. Whatever he'd intended, she liked it.

With his hands on his hips, he gave the attendants a sour look, and they scampered out immediately.

"Matthias," she crooned softly, "you know you'll catch more flies with honey than with vinegar."

"And what's that supposed to mean, *Miss Scarlett?*" he drawled mockingly.

She grabbed his hand and pulled him down to the bed, grinning. "It means, if you're nice to people, they'll be nice to you."

He lifted a brow. "And how many men have *you* commanded?"

His hands closed around her waist as he lowered a kiss to her neck.

Dying to touch him, she loosened his tunic and ran her fingers underneath the fabric, skimming across his skin. "One."

"Do you intend to command me tonight?" He pulled his tunic over his head.

"Aye, Sir Matthias," she mocked. She tilted her head and curled her lip in a charade of arrogant nobility. "Since you've sent a bath up, I order you to help me bathe. It's terribly hard to keep the bandages on my arm from getting wet, you know."

He kissed her full on the lips. "We'll have to wait until the water cools."

"I like hot water. How about a sponge bath? You could use one, too." She bit her lower lip, allowing her brazen gaze to descend his length.

He suddenly went very still over her, his eyes almost mercury. "You would do that?"

She put her arms around his bare shoulders and brought her mouth to his, her body promising him anything he asked. He plucked her from the bed and stood her on her feet.

Matthias helped her remove her clothes down to the bandage underneath. As he flung her chemise away, his eyes licked over her nude flesh like flames, ridding her of any shame she might have felt over her nakedness.

"You're exquisite, Carrie," he murmured as he expelled a breath. Taking her hand, he led her to the tub.

She perched on a stool at the edge of the bath and watched as he knelt beside her. The water smelled of heavenly lavender, and she felt the rising steam curling tendrils of hair against her neck. The servants had left a cake of soap and cloths for washing and drying.

Had she died and gone to Heaven?

Matthias dampened a cloth, frowning at the heat. "'Tis very hot. Are you sure?"

"Yes, but not if it's too hot for you." She turned her back for him.

He made a manly grunt, and she felt the cautious touch of the wet cloth on her skin. She smiled at his show of effort and leaned into his care.

The hot water drizzled from the cloth in his hand, down her back, to the cleft of her buttocks. He lathered her back with soap and sponged it. She felt his fingers gathering her hair, drawing it aside, and he put his mouth against the curve of her neck. As he kissed her, tingles ran up and down her body. His slippery hands glided from her back to cup her breasts, the heat of the bathwater warming her inside and out.

He washed her front, being careful not to touch her bandaged arm while keeping her back pressed against him. Both their bodies became lathered, with his chest sliding against her shoulders erotically as he washed her. His hands explored her body freely, roving her breasts, her stomach, and her hips. His straining erection nudged her backside like a rock. The combination of the mead she'd drank, the temperature of the bath, and the languid heat of Matthias's expert hands made her dizzy. She wanted him badly.

As if he'd read her mind, he began to sponge her off. When he was done, she turned around and took the cloth from him. They traded places. Kneeling in front of him, she began to sponge the soap lather off his chest. She was aware of the power of his gaze as he watched her.

His chest rose and fell hypnotically with labored breathing as she smoothed away the traces lingering around his nipples. The steam caused a sheen of perspiration on his neck. She washed it off and placed a row of light kisses along his scar. His eyes fell closed as she moved to lay kisses down his chest and suckled his nipples.

Her hands unfastened the damp braies, and she helped him remove the clothing. His lips parted in surprise as she fanned her fingers over his naked hips and found the heavy organ in the cradle of his thighs. His muscles clenched at her touch, arms drawing up to grip her sides. She washed him slowly, rubbing her hand rhythmically along him until the lather rinsed away.

"Carys!"

She ignored the plea and lowered her mouth to

deliver kisses down the hard wet plane of his abdomen. Intending to give him the pleasure he'd given her the night before, she kissed the velvety length of him and stroked him with her tongue. He made a low noise in his throat, leaning back for her.

His hands curled gently around her wrists, stilling her. "Please, Carrie," he said raggedly. "I'm dying for you."

He drew her to stand along with him and they dried each other. Then his powerful arms swept her up, and he took her to the bed.

Matthias lay beside her, his aroused shaft teasing her thigh. As he kissed the sensitive skin below her breasts, she thought she would die from the taunting caress his member gave her below. Her body arched as fingers smoothed over her stomach and down her hip. A muscular thigh slid over her and parted her legs. He entered her with a predator's grace, moving in slowly, building her pleasure. One deft hand slid between their bodies and found her sensitive nub. He manipulated her with expertise, teasing her. Like a surf nearing high tide, the urge to bring him deeper swelled within. Glorious torture, she writhed under his touch.

"Matthias!"

When she could take no more sweet torment, she lifted her knees, bringing her hips up to meet his thrusts. He sprinkled tiny kisses her under her chin and on her neck. His hand moved underneath her body to cup her buttocks, driving ever deeper. Her body quaked with pleasure, and her fingers dug into him as she rode the spasms of release.

Matthias pressed his forehead against hers. "Carrie," he rasped and shuddered against her, going over the edge.

His body sank heavily against the bed beside her. Carrie made a move to get up, but Matthias drew her back, pulling her against his naked body to wrap her in a warm cocoon of male. The drumming beat of his pulse matched her own, and she allowed it to lull her. Nothing had ever felt so complete, so perfect.

She lingered in the comfort of his arms a few moments more, before she felt a hard pressure against her buttocks. He didn't need to say a word.

She rolled over and straddled his gorgeous body. His eyes flashed with wicked satisfaction as he smiled up at her. She slanted her lips across his and gave him a kiss that commanded him to give her more.

****

Carrie awoke to the sounds of servants in the room the next morning. Matthias's side of the bed was empty. She smiled, a little amazed he had the strength to leave so early, knowing what she'd put him through the night before. He was probably in the Great Hall ordering more work to be done. Or perhaps he was practicing in the lists.

A laundress entered as Carrie sat up in bed, carrying a glistening blue gown of silk.

"Where did that come from?" Carrie marveled at its beauty.

"A gift from the king, my lady."

The king? For her? That was unexpected. She'd thought it was yet another of Matthias's surprises. She gasped in alarm. Had she slept through the king's arrival?

When the woman was gone, she threw back the covers and hopped out of bed. The new gown would be best used for dining with the king later that evening, the time when she'd seen the most finery being worn. For now, she needed something to wear that could take the abuse of the day's work. She dressed quickly in an old surcoat and tunic and dashed down to the kitchens.

She found Cook muttering in French when she

arrived. Smiling, she greeted the cantankerous Frenchman. Nothing could ruin her mood. She grabbed his elbow in passing and gave him a buss on the cheek. His chubby face turned a pink tint, and he favored her with a brief smile.

"Mon Dieu! My lady, I apologize for my temper. If I'd known you were present, I would not have—"

"Hush. That's okay," she cooed, still grinning at his flustered face. "What's got you so upset?"

"Just take a look, my lady. My kitchen is being overrun!"

With a harried glance over both of his meaty shoulders, he left her and paced the room in circles, waving his fists like a lunatic. Surveying the room, Carrie couldn't see what had flustered the Frenchman. There were only the usual kitchen staff present and the visiting lay-brothers of the monastery. The kitchen help were minding their own business, avoiding the churning arms and wild eyes of the cook. The monks were carting in basket loads of herbs, and she supposed that was the invasion he spoke of. One of the monks waved her over.

As she approached him, she saw he was a lay-brother. As Edwina had told her, the lay-brothers wore the Cistercian robes, but didn't wear their hair shaven in tonsure. Some wore beards like this one.

He spoke in English. "Please, my lady, would you inform the cook? We don't speak his language, and the abbot has sent the spices the earl has requested."

The monk's voice wavered, and seeing the reddening face of Cook, she could understand his reaction. She allowed him to show her all the spices and herbs he carried. He named more than a dozen items, unaware she easily recognized them. He spoke of other herbs that would be blooming later in the summer.

246

"My lady, the earl has requested some spices that we do not grow. As Cistercians, we espouse the belief our foods should be more banal, more plain. Therefore, we don't always have what Lord Wyldnell requires."

Carrie grimaced. In spite of her warnings, the earl still had a taste for strong herbs and spices. Perhaps he was getting better and could tolerate them. Even so, she decided she would stow away the garlic for much, much later in his recuperation. It could be very healthy in a diet, but not when his stomach was so weak.

"I'll tell Lord Wyldnell. I'm sure he appreciates what you're able to supply."

"Thank you, my lady." The monks gathered their baskets and drifted out.

Cook threw his hands in the air at the next invasion of the kitchen, vocalizing his displeasure, but the castle steward didn't pause to speak to him as he passed. Henri made a straight line for Carrie.

"My lady, we've been looking for you. Your presence is demanded." Henri gestured toward the door with a slight bow.

"Who needs to see me?"

"Sir Matthias sent Edwina to your chamber to find you, and Lord Wyldnell bade me look for you here."

Carrie sucked in her breath. "The earl, is he—"

"He is well, my lady. He asked me to bring you to him."

Carrie wondered what Matthias wanted, but at the urgency of the steward's request, Carrie half expected the earl to be ill in spite of Henri's reassurances. She allowed herself to be whisked to his room, telling herself she would find Matthias next.

Contrary to her fears, the earl never looked better. When she approached him in his chamber, he

247

stood, wearing a green robe trimmed in fur. His silver hair had been combed to a regal mane, and his skin took on a more normal, fleshy shade. To match, his eyes were bright and alert. His hands, still withered, bore many rings and drummed impatiently on the arm rest of his chair.

He took one look at her, and his eyes rounded. "Good God, you're not wearing *that*!"

Carrie frowned. "My lord?"

"Where is the fine gown the king brought for you?"

"I...I was going to wear it tonight."

"Tonight? Who cares what you wear tonight! This is the only time that matters."

Carrie's frown deepened in her puzzlement. What on earth—?

Giles's eyes narrowed. "My brother hasn't yet told you, has he?" He eased into his chair.

"What, my lord?"

The earl touched his chin in thought. "I thought...Matthias hasn't told you?" he repeated, clearly stunned. His bejeweled fingers tugged on his silver whiskers as he studied her, and his eyes formed narrow slits as they made their assessment. "The king discovered that you and my brother weren't married. I understand, as Math tells me, there is no binding between you."

Carrie mistrusted her ears. She clasped her hands together. It couldn't be possible. Her mind reeled.

He blew out an impatient breath. "I'm not a young man anymore, and I have no wife, no children. This fortification is the entire legacy I possess. The king will bequeath it to the man of his choice when I die, and we both want that man to be Matthias." His shrewd gaze passed over her. "I rejoiced in your union, that Matthias could continue my plans for the castle with his son, but you weren't ever wedded.

That being so, while he was at Chepstow, the king ordered Math to take a bride to marry on the day of his arrival here. Today."

The earl leaned on his elbow, watching her closely. She couldn't keep the shock off her face. What had gone wrong? What was Matthias thinking to share their secret? Reason escaped her, and her heart thudded painfully. Did he *want* to be rid of her?

She had hoped...

Oh, what foolish nonsense! She had hoped he loved her.

The earl continued to explain, "I'd wished Math would choose Margaret de Harcourt, which would've made the most advantageous union. However, she left, and today is the day the king wants Math wedded. This garrison is built for war, not a court of love. I keep no wards or eligible ladies in my castle. You're the only woman he can possibly marry, and he must marry now."

Her mouth went dry as cotton. How could Matthias treat her so? There must be a good reason why he'd told the king about them and why he'd neglected to inform her of what was happening.

"I tell you these circumstances so you'll know how important it is that you marry Math, but Carrie, I also want you to know if it weren't for the king, I would wed you myself."

Blood thundered in her ears. Only half-hearing his words, it took several seconds for his declaration to reach her thoughts.

"I—I thank you, my lord."

"You are a good woman, and much better than my brother deserves." He sighed.

"When—when is this wedding supposed to take place?"

"This hour, my girl," he snapped impatiently. "Matthias has sent Edwina to fetch you. He and the

249

king wait with the abbot in the chapel."

Carrie returned to her chamber in a daze. She opened the door to find the new gown where the laundress left it on her bed. Woodenly, she removed her work clothes and dressed for her wedding day.

The past few days flickered in Carrie's thoughts. The tourney and young Margaret. As soon as the girl left, Matthias had become more attentive to her.

The dinner, the garden, the bath, the smiles and jokes.

The lovespoon, of course, symbolizing his courtship.

Then last night, their lovemaking.

He'd tried to talk to her, she remembered, but she hadn't let him. If only he was a fraction as open and truthful as Giles was blunt!

Had Matthias told the truth to the king in an attempt to remove her, the albatross, from around his neck, only to be forced to marry her anyway? Was that what he thought of her? Were none of his attentions heartfelt? She believed the time at Maud's had been magical for them both. He'd been so caring. But even that tender moment had happened after he'd been to Chepstow and received his orders from his king.

Asking someone to marry you was probably hard enough for a man, but to have to say the words to someone you didn't *want* to marry...

Tears blurred her vision.

No!

Livid with herself, she rubbed her eyes ruthlessly. No, she wouldn't feel self-pity. There'd been more than enough of that in her life, and she vowed she wouldn't bear any more.

Heck, in one week she'd attracted the attention of three different men. Matthias, Philip, Giles...

Things like that just didn't happen to her. Giles was right. She did deserve better treatment. If she had to marry Matthias by the order of some king, then fine, there was no way out of that. The king was too powerful. She'd seen medieval kings in movies, and she didn't want to wind up with her insides carved out like a fish fillet or with her head in a basket.

But there was no way she'd let Matthias bully her into anything else after the ceremony. Just because they were living in medieval times for God-only-knew how long, that didn't mean she was his property. She had a right to know what was going on when it concerned her. Matthias may be a professor, but he still had a lot to learn about people, as far as she was concerned.

****

Attention to detail. Matthias paid heed to the twenty-first century mantra when planning the ceremony. He'd tried to personally see to everything from the bouquet she would carry to the candles on the altar. Though he was no wedding planner, he wanted to create the best possible event for his bride. It was the least he could do, since he'd never actually asked her if she *wanted* to marry him.

If she trusted him enough to wed him now— though he'd offered her no promises or pretty words—was there a chance she would still trust him later when the truth about his past came out?

His glance took in the chapel, closed to all but his brother, the king, the abbot, and his bride. Candles and flowers, new cushions on the altar, and a rug on the floor, he'd tried not to let any detail, no matter how miniscule, escape unattended. Rose petals strewed the ground. For himself, he wore a surcoat emblazoned with the family crest, his own mother's fingers had embroidered, and tried his best to look presentable with a freshly polished sword.

The king probably found his ceremony odd with all its modern traditions. Couples of his time usually married outside the chapel, but Matthias knew what Carrie expected.

What he hadn't expected—or rather tried not to expect—was her reaction when she entered the chapel. Her eyes shot daggers at him. Then she looked away. No wedding procession since there was no pipe organ. She moved stiffly in her exquisite blue dress and came to stand at his side as if a maiden of ethereal beauty sent to be sacrificed to a bloodthirsty dragon.

Once the vow exchange was over, Matthias turned to face his bride. The abbot asked for their hands. Carrie wouldn't meet his eyes. She extended her hand, her lips pressed together in a tight line. For the first time since she'd entered the chapel, Matthias now dared look longer at her, and he instantly recognized the redness of her eyes. It wrenched him inside. He tore his stare away from her and put his hand atop Carrie's, clenching his jaw. The abbot loosely bound their hands in a length of pale blue ribbon.

She didn't want to be bound to him.

'Twas wise. What woman would?

The abbot asked them to kneel at the altar for the blessing. Matthias clasped his hand around Carrie's and went forward with her. She kept her distance, being careful not to let their clothes touch as they knelt beside each other. Matthias closed his eyes and prayed. If ever a couple needed prayer to begin a marriage, it was he and his bride.

****

The best night of her life was followed by the worst day of her life. As much as possible, the earl had kept the castle unaware of the wedding taking place that day. No one knew about their perfidy except the earl, the abbot, and the king. The ensuing feast that night was thought to be on account of the king's presence, just as Carrie had believed earlier.

In an inauspicious beginning, her so-called marriage began with toasts to King Edward and England and war, not to the bride and groom. Though honestly, she didn't miss the white wedding cake and brightly wrapped presents bearing toasters and electric can openers. She didn't even regret not having the Wedding March played on an organ or a singer crooning some cheesy love song from the seventies. All she really missed for her wedding ceremony were her mother and grandmother.

What would they think about her wedding? Her mother distrusted all men period, and probably would've argued against marriage until she got to know him. She would've raked Matthias over the coals about his intentions and his provisions for her only child. No doubt, her mom would've insisted on a prenuptial agreement, too—if they'd had those in the medieval ages—to protect the store, before finally allowing her only child to wed him.

But her grandmother loved weddings and anything dealing with romance in general. She'd been married twice already and had a new boyfriend when Carrie had left the States. He managed a golf course in Myrtle Beach. They'd met at a Scottish ceilidh, and she'd found his knees a turn-on in his flying kilt. Yeah, Grandmother would've approved of her medieval wedding.

She missed them like crazy. Emotions clogged her throat, and she tried to wash them down with a swig of her drink.

The earl summoned the musicians, drawing Carrie out of her reverie. Some of the servants began to dance, but she wasn't in a festive mood. Rannulf tried to persuade her onto the floor, but Carrie flatly turned him down. His face crumpled in a sullen frown, but he soon found a willing partner in Edwina.

In spite of her anger, she wondered if Matthias

had ever liked to dance. His lame leg gave him little trouble, but Carrie imagined his not dancing had more to do with his mood than his dexterity.

Something nudged Carrie's chair, and she looked in time to see a passing hound, foraging for pheasant bones on the floor. She couldn't see the earl's dogs without thinking about her first night in the Great Hall and the first kiss she'd shared with Matthias.

Enough!

King or no king, she'd borne their entertainment long enough. Matthias hadn't spoken to his company much at all that evening, spending most of the night staring darkly at the table. Even the hound passing the table gave him a wide berth, sensing the man's mood. It was past time to put an end to his secrecy and her misery. She doubted the noble guests would miss them if they left.

"Matthias," she said in hushed tones, keeping her eyes firmly off his handsome face, "I'm going to our tower. You can come there now and talk to me, or you can find another place to sleep tonight."

Chapter Eighteen

Matthias excused himself from the king's table, mumbling an awkward attempt at an apology. Edward merely flicked his wrist at him. Domestic relations of the knights were of little concern to the monarch. Nonetheless, Matthias breathed a sigh of relief that he and Carrie hadn't inadvertently offended the king.

Giles, the soulless spawn of a devil, remarked on his exit, laughing as he passed his seat, "I'm pleased to see you're so eager to do your duty for King Edward, Math."

Matthias's jaw clenched as he shouldered his way past the serving men. The laughter of the Great Hall rang in his ears as he stormed off.

Mounting the stairs of the tower, nausea rolled in his stomach. What would he find when he reached his rooms? At least Carrie was willing to still speak to him. That was a blessing in itself. Yet doubt niggled at his mind, making him wary. She could be at the end of her patience. After today, she had every right to be through with him.

He found her waiting inside the door, arms crossed under her bosom, eyes blazing.

He pushed the door closed behind him and rubbed the back of his neck. Silence swelled between them until she broke it.

"The ceremony today—was it real? I mean was it a true wedding or a hand-fasting—like that 'one year and a day' thing I've seen in movies?" Her cool tone crushed his heart.

"The vows were spoken. 'Twas real."

Sandra Jones

A hand-fasting? Her reaction was worse than he'd expected. Did she think she could get out of it? After all he'd done to attempt to make the ceremony perfect, she thought it was for show? *Before God, we made the vows.*

Matthias gave his attention to the floor, anywhere rather than see her disappointment. He tried to sound detached. "For as long as we're in this time, we're married."

"What happened at Chepstow? Why did you tell the king about us?" Her voice went very tight, making him cringe.

Matthias glanced up at her, and she looked away. He'd wounded her—just as he feared after he'd told the king the truth. He'd lay down his life for her, without hesitation, but he'd never told her so. Of course she was confused. Hurt. He hastened to explain.

"I made a mistake. The chapel I claimed we were married at—it's not been built yet. Abbot Sidney knew I'd made up that part of our story. I didn't know how to fix the mess, so I confessed to my king. You weren't in danger. I would never put you in harm's way. If the king decided to part us, I knew my brother wouldn't let aught happen to you. The dotard is too attached." More attached than necessary at times. His hands closed in fists.

When he'd first told Giles they weren't married, he'd half thought his brother was going to leap from the bed to strike him. Defending the honor of women had always been Matthias's business in his youth, striving to be the perfect young courtly knight, but now the tables had turned. Giles stood on the side of virtue, Giles had committed no sin, and Giles was the righteous one.

His brother would happily marry Carrie to keep her safe and at his beck and call for the rest of his days.

Matthias would've let him take his swing, if he'd tried, but he would never let his brother have Carrie. The thought brought his blood to the boiling point. She was fast becoming as vital to his being as the air he breathed.

He dragged a hand through his hair, collecting his feelings to answer her. "Edward is my king. I've never lied to him, and I was tired of fabricating truths to everyone. Both he and Giles expected us to have a son. It just grew worse and worse. Lies on top of lies."

He saw her small nod. So she felt the same. He sighed, slightly relieved.

"I didn't mean to cause you suffering. I'm not a tyrant. I would've given you a choice in the matter, had I the freedom to give it."

Carrie laughed bitterly. "Hey, King Edward isn't *my* king! I come from a country that's had no monarch for over two hundred years. Back there, I have equality on my side." She paced the floor, hands opening and closing at her sides. "Don't think I wouldn't have left you waiting at the altar if I chose to, buddy! I have some marketable skills for this century, too. I could've run out the castle gate and found another place to stay. I could be a healer like Maud, if I wanted."

Matthias's skin chilled at the thought. "'Twouldn't be prudent. Women don't run businesses here. Likely as not, you'd starve before you'd earn enough money, and then you'd become either a nun or some man's whore."

Carrie halted. Her eyes flashed blue lightning at him. "At least it would be my choice. Joining the church or selling the use of my body, I still wouldn't be a man's property."

Matthias could stand no more of this line of reason. Her words cut him to the quick. He gritted his teeth. "You're not my property, Carrie. I respect you more than that."

"'Respect?'" She marched up to look into his eyes, her chest heaving with angry breaths, her indignation palpable. "How can you stand there and tell me you respect me? If you respected me, you would've *asked* me to marry you. You would've allowed me to make a choice—whether it was the one you wanted or not. If you'd thought of my feelings at all, you would've at least told me what had happened. I had to be told by Giles, who practically ordered me to wed you!"

His throat closed. Ordered? Then she wouldn't have chosen to marry him—past sins or no. Desperation for her understanding and contempt for himself warred within him.

"I tried to speak to you last night." He groped for the right words. They both knew what had prevented him from telling her about the wedding, and after making love, Carrie had fallen asleep in his arms. He waited to ask, not wanting to wake her. But he had no excuse for not telling her that morning, just his own cowardice. "Giles shouldn't have told you. Damn him, always meddling in my affairs! Why couldn't he, just this once...I sent Edwina to find you, so I could explain first."

"Why didn't you just explain to me this morning?" Staring up at him, her eyes glistened with unshed tears.

Matthias preferred her anger. He resisted the urge to pull her into an embrace he knew she didn't want.

Air. He stalked to the window and threw it open. He needed fresh air badly, so he braced his fists on the casement and sucked in a breath. "The king's demand meant nothing to me. I already wanted to make you mine, but I didn't think you'd have me."

She made a small noise of incredulity. "Why not?"

The cool night breeze filled his burning lungs, but didn't ease his sense of foreboding. "We've discussed it, Carrie," he ground out. Did she want him to admit his worthlessness yet again? "You know what I am."

But nay, she didn't know. *You haven't told her.*

The words were on the edge of his consciousness, ready to fill the air between them. Three words—the confession that would make her realize exactly why he wasn't the sort of man she would want to marry. With those words he would earn her hate and fear.

Her light footsteps came up behind him. He stiffened.

"What are you, Matthias? A beast? Are we back to that?"

Back? As if he could ever cast the mantle of sin off.

"I don't expect you to understand." He yearned for reprieve, something to make him more acceptable to her. But what could possibly compel such a miracle?

"I don't understand, because you won't *tell* me. Why? I want to understand."

He shook his head. He couldn't tell her.

"Would a beast tend me when I lay wounded in the woods?"

It only proved he had more decency than that damned upstart, De Harcourt.

"Would a beast bind my wound, guard me? Shelter me, here at Wyldnell, the last place he wanted to step foot in again? Would he protect the woman who caused him to leave everything he cared about seven centuries away?"

She thought he cared for his modern life? Thank God she stood behind him. Otherwise, she would've seen the look of incredulity on his face. Beyond his career at the university, he had nothing at all there.

Just an empty flat, a useless estate, no true friends to speak of, no woman. Everything for him was here. Now.

After a long silence, he felt her hand on his back. "You didn't think I'd have you? Are you kidding me?" Her voice filled with soft humor.

He turned to see what had brought on the change and found warmth in her eyes. Her expression gave him hope.

"I believe even my mother would eventually approve of me marrying you, Matthias, and she doesn't trust most men. You take better care of me than my own family, and I thought *they* were worry-warts. If you would've asked me, I would've said yes."

"You would've agreed? Even if you had a choice?" Once the question slipped out, Matthias wished he could take it back. He didn't want to know if she preferred not to have to marry. He prayed his voice didn't betray just how crucial her answer was for him.

"A girl could do worse." A coy smile played at the corners of her lips.

She was teasing him. He knew her too well. If she hadn't wanted to wed him, she wouldn't have.

Carrie touched his cheek tenderly. Matthias turned to kiss her palm and then wrapped his arms around her, drawing her tightly to him. He breathed in the scent of her hair and closed his eyes, thanking God this wasn't to be the last time he'd hold her this way.

He was doing her a great injustice by marrying her. If she ever realized how poor her choice was, she would take back everything she'd said. There was no way in hell she would marry him if she knew the truth.

By God, he would do aught to keep her!

He kissed her cheek and then her lips, cupping

her face in his hands. She was his, bless the saints, she was his.

Carrie's body responded to his kisses, moving sensuously against him. When his hands cupped her breasts, he felt her nipples harden beneath the layer of the silk gown. He teased her lips with his tongue, marveling at the rapture he felt for her.

His wife.

Matthias scooped her up in his arms and laid her out on the bed, the blue silk of her gown rustling in the movement. He undressed, feeling her eyes upon him. Desire burned like a bonfire. Every muscle tensed as he held himself back. But he didn't think she was ready to experience that. He must keep himself in check to keep from tearing the stitches in her arm.

With trembling hands, his fingers fumbled with the delicate laces. Then her hands fell on his, stilling him.

He saw in her eyes an intensity that equaled his own.

Her fingers replaced his, tugging away at the laces with an impatience that aroused him even more. Once the garment was loose, he curled his hands in her skirt and carefully pulled it over her head. Her hair tumbled free, caramel waves that cascaded over her supple shoulders, rippling down to dangle over her breasts. Her sultry eyes never wavered from his. A fairy goddess, her confidence in her dominion over him showed in her wanton gaze.

Pressing his hungry mouth to hers, fervor urged him to bury himself in Carrie, but he held back. Lying beside her, he ran his hand along her soft, naked skin as he assaulted her mouth, barely managing his burgeoning passion. Her hands clasped his shoulders, suddenly pushing at him.

He drew back in alarm. His heart hammered. Had he hurt her, been too rough?

Her hands still on him, she sat up and urged him down, guiding him to take her place on the bed. Matthias stared up at her, scarcely able to breathe. She rose up, her hair whispering over his chest. Her fingertips replaced her teasing hair, softly raking his skin, shoulders, chest, stomach, and thighs. When he thought she could give no keener sense of expectancy and excitement, she slid her slender calf across his hips. The juncture of her legs brushed against him intimately. She took his mouth in a wild kiss, his head and shoulders half off the bed to meet her.

Carrie took him inside her, her movements savage and eager. She was warm, wet, tightening around him. It took every fiber of his strength not to lose himself, to shatter with ecstasy under her wondrous assault. She dug her fingers in his shoulders as she built a tempo. The rhythm increased to a crescendo that threatened to either drive him mad or to fuse his soul to her forever. His hands cradled her bottom, loving the fit of her curves against his palms as she slid over his slick length. He watched her face, delighted at the bliss in her expression, her playful gemstone eyes.

She leaned in to capture his mouth again, her tongue darting inside between the motions of her hips. Her fingers winnowed through the hair on his chest as she impaled herself again and again. Small sounds of passion vibrated from her throat into his mouth, sealed inside their lips. His blood beat with the rhythm of their bodies and then surged lower and lower.

Matthias slid his hand into her hair, cradling the back of her head as he leaned forward. Without breaking their kiss, he rolled her into the sheets beneath him, careful not to crush her under the burden of his weight and ardor. When he lifted his lips to gaze down at her, he saw the rosy flush of her skin and watched her mouth curl into a seductive grin.

"Don't hold back, Matthias."

Of its own volition, his body responded. He pushed himself inside her, thrusting in primitive stabs, which she met, lifting her hips beneath him.

Their release was immediate, crying out together.

They made love for hours, a union of body and soul. Man and woman. Matthias channeled every ounce of his being into pleasing her because God knew she gave him more pleasure than he could repay.

Sometime late in the night, during a moment they shared cuddling, she uttered the words he'd never thought to hear.

"I love you." Her small fingers traced a pattern over his chest.

He pulled her close, allowing her to rest over his heart. His fingers smoothed over her silky hair. 'Twas all he could manage in return.

One day, she would only hate him.

Sandra Jones

Chapter Nineteen

She was probably changing history.

Carrie looked at the roast beef slices piled high between two pieces of bread. Cook never served sandwiches and probably hadn't ever heard of them. She wrapped her creation in a cloth napkin and took it up to the earl's chamber.

He looked surprised to see her but even more surprised when he unwrapped the sandwich she'd brought for his lunch. She sat at his bedside.

"Meat and bread! 'Tis peasant food. Do I look like a meat and bread man to you?"

Carrie smiled. Nothing could spoil her mood. She'd had two days of the best sex of her life—her honeymoon. Giles's opinions of how food should be eaten were suspect most of the time anyway. "Mr. Skinnybones, let me tell you, this is the ultimate dish where I come from. Everyone eats them. It's called a sandwich, and it's famous for being ordered by an earl."

"What's this earl's name? Do I know him? He cannot be a very powerful man if he eats his meat in bread."

She ignored his comments and continued, "I made a sauce especially for you of a small amount of mustard seed powder and cream. The meat is layered with cheese. You'll like it."

Giles peered under the top slice of bread with renewed interest. "Mustard seed, did you say?"He sniffed it. "Roast beef needs horseradish powder."

Carrie rose to go get some, but the earl motioned for her to sit. He reached under his pillow and pulled

264

out a small cloth pouch tied with a string. As she watched in astonishment, the man withdrew a pinch of the powdery substance inside and scattered it on the sandwich.

"You keep horseradish under your pillow?" Carrie balked.

"Ian just brought it up from Cook this morning. Don't look at me so, wench! I've not grown horns on my head! It's been hard these past days with naught on my food."

Carrie fought her laughter as she stared at him. If the guy didn't have such a hard time with his illness, he'd probably weigh a ton. At least there were no fast food restaurants around for him to be frequenting and no snack cakes to be stuffed under his bed covers.

"Well," she sighed, still smiling, "thank goodness it's horseradish and not onion. Horseradish is probably good for your digestion."

He took a bite and fell back into his pillow with a moan. "I should throw Cook out the gates. I wonder why he's never made this."

Carrie grinned, glad to have found something the earl actually enjoyed eating. She'd kept her word to Maud, watching over him. She still agreed with Matthias, though. The crusty baron had no enemies aside from the Welsh, and Rannulf had told them there'd been little adverse activity from the locals over the past six or seven years. His illness was surely food borne, maybe salmonella or botulism from unsanitary conditions. With close monitoring of his food, he might just be good as new in a few short months.

"Where's my brother?" Giles took another bite and rolled his eyes appreciatively. "What keeps him from your bed sheets today?"

Carrie felt her cheeks heating. They'd spent a lot of time in bed the past two days, but hearing it from his brother was embarrassing.

"He's with King Edward. They're addressing the other knights about what sort of Welsh men would make good soldiers. They're gathering an army to hunt down Prince Llywelyn."

"Hmmm. My men won't care for rubbing elbows with the Welsh. There'll be dissention."

"Not if they value their liege and Matthias's wisdom."

He eyed her closely. "You put a lot of trust in my brother."

"When it comes to matters of politics and war, my lord, I think you should put all your trust in him." Matthias had spent nine years studying the outcome of the Welsh wars which relieved one worry from her mind. At least she wouldn't have to wonder about impending battles and whose side to root for. She poured Giles a cup of wine. "I'll bet you'll be feeling like your old self soon. You pride yourself on the upkeep of Wyldnell. Do you miss being in charge?"

"Aye," he murmured and took a sip of wine.

Then he frowned and snapped, "Who said I wasn't in charge? Math must bear in mind he's only maintaining the castle temporarily. As I told you before, I'm not dead yet."

This time, Carrie knew he meant it. The earl loved his power, and it would do him good to have something to live for. She only hoped his recovery wouldn't be the cause of more friction between the brothers—so much so that the earl would renew his former orders and have them both thrown out of Wyldnell this time. If only she knew the reason for Matthias's banishment, perhaps she could smooth things over with Giles.

But since he didn't consider Matthias's leadership permanent, she wouldn't drudge up the past today. Matthias was right. His brother was impatient.

****

When the king left for London two weeks later, Carrie was relieved, thinking she would have Matthias to herself and no longer have to worry about doing anything foolish to raise the ire or suspicions of the powerful monarch.

She soon learned she had Giles to compete with. Matthias's brother, on the fast-track to good health, had taken it upon himself to oversee the training of Matthias's new Welsh recruits. The two men were now at odds constantly. The disagreements began with Matthias's choice of men. Then Giles disapproved of Matthias's selection of weapon training. Giles preferred cavalry, and Matthias wanted to concentrate on archery. The brothers were near to blows when Carrie came upon them the day before at the quintain, snarling at each other like wolves. Had it not been for her intervention, they would've forgotten their shared blood. She'd had to literally step between them, cutting them off from throwing any punches.

She looked around the bailey in the afternoon sun. The heat was intolerable for most of the men, who'd moved into the shade or the cooler areas of the castle, but not her husband. Matthias, she was fast learning, could be a workaholic if she let him.

She adjusted the leather bracer on her arm, preparing for a much-needed distraction. She'd make certain she was the last archer Matthias would see that day. If she didn't succeed in seducing him from the field, at least she might incur his anger enough so that he'd drag her from the archery range. She smiled to herself and checked her tunic, braies, and belt. Luckily there weren't any other people about.

To medieval men, she probably looked ridiculous, but for her own time, she looked pretty sexy.

It was time she got to the bottom of their troubles, whether Matthias wanted her to know what had happened or not. She'd admitted her love for him, but he hadn't returned the sentiment. Perhaps he didn't love her. It didn't matter. She knew he cared deeply for her, and maybe his affection would become more someday.

Nevertheless, there was an undercurrent of secrecy that still stood between them.

Since their wedding night, she'd known that whatever had happened in Matthias's past, he believed his actions were truly evil. Whatever he'd done, it was something so horrible that he wouldn't even allow himself to speak of it. Proud to the point of obstinacy, sharing his difficulties with her seemed out of the question.

She'd started to think on it, imaging what dark secret a young knight might have. Each time she pictured him in the Crusades, she cringed inwardly. He'd told her how he'd gotten the battle wound on his neck. How he'd fallen from his horse to be captured by a Saracen with a wicked crescent blade. The disfigurement was meant to be a reminder for him that his enemy had held his fate in his hands that day. To listen to Matthias, though, she knew Acre wasn't the object of his self-loathing. His talk of war was nonchalant. Blood-spilling and battles were commonplace experiences for a medieval knight. Something else must have happened.

Locating Matthias on the archery range with his Welsh sergeant, she marched up behind them, bolstering her courage.

He swung around, a frown forming as she approached. "What the...Carrie?"

"I was wondering if I could practice for a little while. Maybe you could show me a few pointers when you have time." Spotting a discarded bow and arrows leaning on a stool nearby, she went to pick the bow up.

The weapon was enormous, about six feet long, but it was surprisingly light. The archery range had been redesigned for the soldiers. Replacing the hay, six mounds of earth had been formed and wooden stakes protruded from four of the mounds.

"Carrie, in case you haven't noticed we're training for battle." He rubbed a thumb across his forehead.

She gave him her most brilliant smile. "Oh, I've noticed. You go on and work. Don't let me get in your way. I guess I'm aiming for the hills until I get really good. Then I aim at the stakes, right?"

"Carrie, we'll practice together later. I'm busy now." His brows pinched together as he exhaled a breath.

"That's okay, Matthias. You do what you need to, and I'll just keep launching arrows at that pile of dirt. Go on!" She bent over to pick up an arrow, smiling sweetly over her shoulder at him.

Behind her, Matthias paced to his sergeant, his stare on the ground. She knew by the set of his shoulders he was furious.

The string of the bow was tighter than she'd expected. Struggling, she pulled it back to her chest and released the arrow. It landed a mere four feet away, diagonal from the course she'd intended. The targets sat at least fifty feet away.

Carrie overheard the sergeant saying, "Sir Matthias, I would teach the young lady to shoot the longbow, if it pleases you."

"Nay, it would not please me. Now, as I said, I've ordered aged yew, along with sapwood and heartwood brought from Italy. How many arrows would we need to make for, say, a hundred Welsh longbow archers for one battle against Llywelyn's men?"

Carrie released another arrow, which hit a

target—three rows to the right.

"Sir?" The sergeant asked.

Out of the corner of her vision, Matthias waved his hand, giving the archer permission to approach.

Although the sergeant hadn't been her intentional focus, Carrie appreciated his helpfulness as he moved to aid her. The man took the longbow and demonstrated how to draw the weapon to her ear. He then handed it back to her. Carrie tried to pull it back as he'd shown her, but her muscles weren't as strong as the seasoned warrior's. She should've spent more time at the gym because she'd already depleted all her strength. She frowned. If she couldn't draw the arrow, she wouldn't have an excuse to stay and disturb Matthias.

The sergeant laughed and shook his head.

Taking pity on her, he stepped behind her and guided her to draw the arrow again. This time he took hold of her hands and helped her complete the pull.

When the arrow was level with her ear and its point high in the air, he told her, "Now release."

The arrow whistled into the ground just in front of the target.

Carrie tossed him a grin. "I can't believe we got it that close. That's amazing!"

The man reached down to retrieve another arrow, but Matthias caught his arm.

"That's good for today, Owain. We'll work with the archers tomorrow," he said, his tone brisk.

"Aye, thank you, Sir Matthias."

With a nod to them both, he left.

Carrie looked up at Matthias from under her lashes. His expression undeniably dark.

She waved an arrow under his nose and lifted her chin in challenge. "Wanna try?"

"Draw it."

He took the sergeant's place behind her as she

tried to pull the bow back again. Her arms were getting wobbly. Then Matthias's arms encircled hers, his hands covered hers, and her body became instantly charged by his touch. He pulled her arm and the string back with ease. His mouth pressed close to her ear as he murmured directions. In her thin braies, she felt his burgeoning erection behind her.

"Ready? Release it."

The arrow lifted high on the air and fell, to sink directly into the mound of earth.

She turned to him and smiled. "That's harder than it looks."

"You don't know the half of it," he mumbled. "What are you doing in my clothes?"

"Archery."

He lifted a brow. "Wanton wench. You meant to end our work."

Carrie denied it, shaking her head emphatically, but Matthias appeared unconvinced. Smiling, he drew her into his arms and ran his hands down her backside.

"Let's save these clothes for my eyes only from now on," he told her. "At least until the portal works again and takes us past Women's Lib."

"Are you a male chauvinist, Sir Matthias?" She smiled.

"No, just selfish about what's mine." He kissed her mouth hard, and she opened for him, allowing his tongue to swirl around hers.

Her feminine magic worked its spell. By the time they pulled apart, Matthias was ready to leave. He took her hand to return to the tower.

The rest of Matthias's day belonged to her alone. Later, much later when he was in a more relaxed mood, she would open the subject of his troubles again.

****

271

Later that night their sleep was interrupted by a pounding on the door.

"Math!"

Matthias pulled on his braies and opened the door. It was Edwina.

"We need Lady Carrie. It's the earl again."

Carrie donned a gown and ran to her storeroom. She gathered a collection of dry medicines in the skirt of her gown and followed Matthias and Edwina to Giles's chamber.

The sound of retching filled the stairwell. Several men moved aside as she and Matthias passed, their faces downcast and bleak.

The earl hung halfway out of the bed, writhing in spasms. Matthias pulled him back to the mattress, just in time to keep Giles from falling on his head. Carrie spread the medicines on the table, knocking aside his dinner tray and spilling its contents on the floor. Giles's seasoning pouch hit the stone at her feet puffing out a cloud of horseradish powder.

"Is he feverish?" she asked Matthias.

"Not yet."

"What did you eat, my lord?" she asked over her shoulder.

The earl didn't answer. His breathing was heavy, his skin sallow.

She went to his side and got very close to his face. Pressing her hand to his cheek, she repeated, "What did you eat tonight, Giles, please?"

The man began coughing too violently to answer. Thick perspiration soaked his tunic. Carrie checked his heart and found it beating irregularly.

Foxglove again, she decided. Matthias kept him still as Carrie made a tonic with Edwina's help. Ian, Rannulf, Marsten, and the earl's concerned retainers began to fill the room.

"No! They've got to go." Carrie worried for the

over-excitement of the earl.

"You heard her." Matthias jerked his head at the door.

When everyone except Matthias, Carrie and Edwina were gone, Carrie asked Matthias to help her get the medicine into the earl. This spell so much worse than the last.

Together, they held him still. After four attempts and messy spills, they were able to force the brew down his gullet. Carrie held his head and stroked his hair, murmuring soothing words. When the earl's body began to relax, Carrie spared a look at Matthias. Though normally stalwart, her husband looked as though his heart was breaking. His face and neck had faded to the same color as his white tunic.

Edwina moved to clean up the mess on the floor, but Carrie stopped her.

"Leave it, Edwina. I want to check it out later."

Matthias's eyes riveted to hers. Although she couldn't disclose her suspicions in front of the earl, she had no doubt this time. He'd been poisoned.

When Giles finally rested about an hour later, Carrie cautiously picked up the pouch of horseradish and touched a tiny bit of the powder to her little finger and applied it to her tongue. It tasted like horseradish. She then went back to the earl's bedside and shrugged at Matthias. Maybe she was wrong.

Then her tongue began to tingle.

****

Matthias stayed at his brother's bedside until dawn. He would've stayed longer, but Carrie refused to let him. Only when Rannulf came, offering to sit with the earl, did he agree to leave him. On their way from the earl's chamber, Carrie approached one of the earl's men and asked him to bring Maud the healer to the castle. Matthias was too weary to argue. Besides, if the crone's presence could help his brother, he would gladly fetch her himself.

Back in their bedchamber, his blood boiled as he considered Carrie's reaction at his brother's bedside.

He grilled her as soon as the door was shut, barring all eavesdropping ears. "You think someone is trying to kill Giles, don't you?" His suspicions were confirmed by the trembling of her body.

"It's in his spice pouch. That's why his sickness is so erratic. It comes and goes. It's the horseradish. He doesn't use the seasoning all the time and so far he hasn't consumed a fatal amount."

"Are you sure? How can you tell?"

"I wish I could tell you from my knowledge of herbs, but I'm afraid I recognized it from a novel I read years ago. I don't even remember the name of it, but it was a murder mystery."

"What about it?"

"Someone in the story was poisoned by the herb monkshood. The only natural antidote is foxglove, though it isn't very reliable. Well, I know that foxglove has digitalis, and it restores the circulation. Giles's body seems to be restored by drinking a tincture of digitalis."

Matthias frowned his skepticism.

"Hey, several people in my century have died from monkshood poisoning by accident. It's not uncommon. The roots look like horseradish, and the leaves look like parsley, so sometimes people get it mixed up."

He ran a hand through his hair. "So mayhap someone accidentally mixed up the horseradish with the monkshood?"

Carrie bit her lip and nodded.

Matthias doubted anyone of his acquaintance would be stupid enough to mistake a toxic plant for a kitchen seasoning destined for an earl's dinner, but it wasn't out of the question.

Yet no one else in the castle suffered Giles's malady.

"Are you absolutely certain the horseradish was tainted with the plant?"

"My tongue went warm and then numb when I tasted it. It's still numb. That's not horseradish."

Matthias's heart stilled as he recalled watching her sample the lethal powder.

"You shouldn't have tasted it, Carrie! 'Twas dangerous."

"I had to know. Oh, God, your poor brother, Matthias! Think of what his poor body has been through. No wonder he's so frail."

A wall of rage fell within him. He would kill whoever was responsible.

"Hey, we don't know that Giles wasn't given the monkshood on accident," Carrie told him, obviously reading his thoughts.

He made a mental list of people who came in contact with the earl's food. It was a nightmare. Sundry servants helped Cook prepare and deliver the food. The Cistercian monks sent herbs and seasonings. So did Maud.

"Who gave him that bag of powder?" he demanded.

Her eyes rounded, but she didn't say the name.

"Carrie!" He clutched her shoulders and gave her a light shake. "You know who?"

"Sir Ian, but it couldn't be him."

Matthias flew at the door, but Carrie followed. She moved in front of him, blocking his way.

"It can't be him. You've seen how he reacts when your brother is threatened."

"Carrie, how can you protect Ian? He would have—"

"I despise him. He's a reckless teenager, but I still think he has nothing to do with this. He wouldn't gain anything by Giles's death. You know that. And he's Rannulf's son."

"A son who's spoiled and violent."

"He's only eighteen."

Matthias stiffened. "You don't think a young man of eighteen can be capable of evil?" He'd spoken without thinking.

Something in his tone caused her to pause. Mayhap he'd said too much. He'd been near that age when he'd committed his own crime. But luckily Carrie didn't question him further.

She was right. Ian wasn't a likely suspect. If Ian had wanted to kill Giles, he would've done it openly, recklessly. The boy had no notion of methodical planning. He was too impulsive. Whoever wanted Giles dead—if it had been intentional—possessed enough cunning to cover his tracks.

He paced the floor for hours. His mind tumbled over theories and possible would-be murderers. Carrie sat on the bed watching him. After awhile, Matthias took note of her yawns and weary-looking eyes. She wouldn't sleep until he lay down also. She wanted to keep him in check, preventing him from doing anything rash, which was exactly what he felt like doing.

Reluctantly, he gave in, joining her on the bed. He gathered her close to him and allowed his mind to take rest for her sake.

****

A couple of hours passed before a servant knocked at the door and announced Maud's arrival. Carrie wanted to speak with the healer and try to assess the damage the poison had done to Giles.

"Matthias, get some more sleep," Carrie told him when he tried to leave the bed, putting a gentle hand on his shoulder. "Maud and I'll see to Giles for now."

She'd misunderstood his intentions.

"The nap was enough. I must speak with Cook." He gave her hand a squeeze before leaving the bed.

"I wish you'd wait. You're tired, and I—"

"No. If there's someone within these walls who wants to harm my brother, I want him found now."

As he strapped his sword around his waist, he caught her look of worry.

"It's okay, Carrie. I'm only looking for information."

"With your sword?"

"It's a habit." He wrapped an arm around her waist and pressed a kiss to the line on her pretty forehead.

She stammered, "Just don't...you know...get upset at anyone before we know for sure what's happened."

He forced a smile to placate her and tilted her chin on his fingertips for another kiss. "If you'd like, you can send Rannulf to the kitchens to make sure I keep my sword in its sheath, okay? I remember what you told me. I'll try to catch flies with honey."

She finally smiled. "Thank you."

Matthias walked her downstairs and watched her disappear in the direction of his brother's chambers. A niggling feeling bothered him as he made his way to the kitchens. Although Maud had been the one to first think Giles was being poisoned, she could've been trying to cast suspicion elsewhere. What if Ian had been right to suspect her in Giles's illness? If she was the attempted assassin, he'd just allowed his wife to attend her alone, thus putting both of the people he cared for most in danger.

However the idea held little merit. Even though Maud disliked the English, she'd helped Giles in the past. Lady Isabelle had been very fond of her, visiting often during her earliest attempts at pregnancy. Maud was happy with her lot in life and didn't possess an ounce of regret or vengeance. She wasn't a likely murderess for Giles.

Matthias forced himself to forget Maud as a

suspect and think ahead to Cook. He needed to have a plan. He couldn't just go up to the Frenchman and demand to know whether or not he'd been putting poison in his horseradish. Carrie was right. He needed to coax the information from the man, not try to tear it from him at sword-point.

****

Maud showed no trace of surprise when Carrie gave her the news about the poison from outside the earl's bedchamber door.

"I knew you'd summoned me because of Giles," she told her. "If it had been *your* arm and *your* wound, 'twould have been your husband asking for me."

Carrie touched her bandaged arm briefly, having forgotten all about her own injury in the chaos since last night. "No, my arm is getting better. The wound is healing. Please, Maud, tell me what you think about Giles. Matthias is questioning Cook. We don't know who would want to do this, but I do know it's poison. Monkshood. Do you know who has access to the deadly herb?"

Maud smiled sadly. "Ah, so it's monkshood. I have the herb, and the Cistercian monks do, too. I'm afraid it grows in the wild here, as well. I've seen horses die when their owners mistakenly allow them to eat it."

"So anyone who has access to the kitchen could've done it." Carrie groaned. She was no detective. Her only brush with a criminal was a teenager she caught shoplifting a bottle of energy capsules in her store.

"Aye."

"Oh, Maud," she sighed wearily. "Discovering who is responsible is beyond me. I was hoping you could help with Giles. I don't know what to do for someone who's been poisoned. What if I do something wrong? He needs to be purged of the poison. If the toxin stays in his system, he could still die. Who knows what damage it's done already."

Maud put her hands over Carrie's and gave them a bolstering squeeze. "My lady, you've saved his life before. If anyone can help him, 'tis you. Of course I'll help you, but you must have faith in your own abilities. If he doesn't live, at least you'll know you did as much as you could for him. The earl needs you."

Chapter Twenty

Matthias found Cook slicing eels in the kitchens. The French master of cookery had worked in the Wyldnell kitchens since Hugh Thorne's time as baron. Cook was a gift to his father for supporting King Henry III against Simon de Montfort, in whose court Cook last worked. Could there be some hard feelings hidden below the surface of Cook's well-meaning façade? Was he waiting for a day to take revenge for the death of de Montfort?

Cook shook his head when he saw him. "She's not here, Sir Matthias. I've not seen Lady Carrie all morn—"

"I'm not looking for my wife," he conversed in rusty French.

The Frenchman waved a piece of eel at him. "Well, then, if you please, I'm very busy. The abbot has ordered a meal fit for a king."

The abbot? He'd come to Giles's room the night before to perform last rites if they'd been needed—which they nearly had been. The abbot should've taken his leave when King Edward had left them. Were the amenities of the monastic life running low? Did Mass no longer entertain him? Giles was too liberal with the man, allowing him to linger past his welcome and eat all the food stores empty before winter.

Matthias dropped a heavy hand on Cook's cutting board and was relieved when the chef's knife froze in the air.

"It's you I've come to see."

"*Moi?*"

"I need another special meal prepared." Matthias remembered Carrie's advice and reined in his temper. Flattery was the key to persuading Cook, a man who adored his work and took pride in his reputation. "My wife loved the chicken you made her, and I loved that she loved it."

Cook laughed quietly. "But it was not the food alone. The roses, the wine, and the candle lights..."

"Aye, but she cannot stop talking about your chicken. I must have more of that dish served tonight."

"*Bien sur*. You need only send word with one of the maids, and I'll happily serve you, Sir Matthias."

"I know you would, but I also have another request." Matthias casually picked up a bowl of saffron and sniffed it. "Roast beef."

"For the lady or yourself?"

"For the lady, of course. I would eat it as well, but I want to please her first. She has a special sauce she likes with beef. She tells me it's made of mustard seed, wine vinegar, ginger, onion, horseradish, and pepper. Is this sauce familiar to you?" He placed the bowl aside.

"It is easy, to be sure. Is there anything else?"

"No." Matthias rubbed his chin thoughtfully. "My wife has a keen sense for spices, does she not? I've never cared for more than salt, myself."

Laughing wryly, Cook shook his head. "Forgive me for saying this, Sir Matthias, but I think Lady Carrie should've been born a man. She would've made an interesting rival for me. Yes, she knows how to create fantastic sauces. If she likes this sauce, I'll wager there are hundreds more who would eat it."

"Hundreds more, you say? Now there is an idea. Would you be able to make this sauce for dinner today—for the rest of the castle? Do you have enough ingredients?"

Sandra Jones

Cook huffed. "*Bien sur*! We never run out of onions. The monks have brought ginger and pepper. The crone fills our stores with mustard seed. Wine vinegar we have aplenty. The horseradish is your brother's favorite, so we're running low, but the monks will deliver more in less than a fortnight. They always do. We will eat Lady Carrie's meal for dinner this very day."

"Who prepares the spices for you?"

He puffed out his chest. "I prepare all the spices in Lord Wyldnell's kitchens. Do you think I would give them to a scullion? The valuable spices? *Non*!"

"Lady Carrie likes her spices finely ground."

"*Oui*. I'm not an amateur. I grind them all."

"You grind them from leaf, seed, and root?"

"Aye, that way I can throw away any plants that aren't edible. If the monks ground the herbs, they would foist rotten weeds on us. I'm not a simpleton, Sir Matthias! I know they would put trash in our goods."

Matthias scanned the kitchen. Sanitary. Spotless. Orderly. A far cry from the shambles it was before his wife put her brand on it. But meals in Wyldnell's Great Hall had always been renowned throughout the kingdom. The Frenchman deserved his accolades, whether Matthias found the cuisine to his liking or not.

"This is interesting, Cook. I never knew you did all this. Do the monks tell you what they've brought each visit?"

"Some do, but some speak only Welsh. It's difficult to communicate, but the earl gives them a list of spices for each visit. They bring only what's been requested."

"Nothing more? They never surprise the earl with new herbs?"

"No, they are practical men, who deliver only what they are paid for."

"Do you...I would think it would be hard to remember what each herb was. Have you ever mistaken one herb for another?"

Cook looked up at Matthias from under his serious gray eyebrows, the corners of his mouth registering affront. "Does your wife? I'll wager not! I prepare what I'm given. Does my work not please you?"

Matthias didn't answer. "On second thought," he sighed, "your eels look very edible today. Carrie would probably like eels cooked on the fire with butter and carrots. We'll have the beef another day."

Rannulf joined them in time to see the look of bewilderment on Cook's face. The cook wasn't poisoning his brother. At least not on purpose. He hadn't shown any reservations about serving food with horseradish, and if he'd been guilty, he would've shown some flash of wariness. Cook's expression was full of pride and self-importance, not evil.

Matthias drew Rannulf outside and informed him of their suspicions. His visage darkened as the news sank in.

Rannulf ran a hand over his beet-red face. "I wish I would've seen it earlier. I never thought...who could do such a thing? I know of no enemies in Wyldnell. Had the Welsh soldiers been here months ago, I would've believed the murderer to be one of them, but they weren't, Math. Did you ask Cook who he thought was guilty of tampering with the food?"

"No, I don't want the murderer to know we've discovered his treachery yet. If he's alerted, he may hide his deed, and we may never know who he is. If we're careful, we might still be able to discover him in the act. Carrie is telling Maud now."

"Why? What if the crone is the one trying to kill him?"

"Right now my brother can use all the help he

Sandra Jones

can get to recover. I don't think Maud is guilty, and Giles needs her knowledge. You've seen how he is."

"It's worse than before. The poison is damned deadly."

"I need to go to the monastery. I think the answer is there. Some of the monks are Welsh, Rannulf."

"Aye, but 'tis dangerous. I'll go with you."

"Thank you." Matthias glanced back at the kitchen door, trepidation tightening his gut. "We'll stay here tonight and go in the morning. I want to make sure Giles and my wife have adequate protection before we leave."

Uncertainty of the attacker's identity bothered Matthias above anything else. Who could he trust?

****

Carrie retired to her bedchamber early that evening at Matthias's request. They were both bone-weary from spending most of the day trying to trace the source of the deadly monkshood and striving to bring Giles's strength back. Carrie had done her best with the latter. The earl rested most of the day, having wasted all his strength the night before.

Matthias insisted they both watch as their food was prepared. Carrie knew if Cook hadn't been suspicious before, he was now.

Before bed, Matthias reminded Carrie to take her medicine.

"Are the herbs helping?"

She'd all but forgotten her own health trials. He meant the moon plants. How strange, the tiny flowers once consumed her thoughts so thoroughly that she'd crossed the ocean for them. Now they were the least of her worries.

"They seem to be."

His hands cupped her face as he stood in front of her. "Is it possible to know when you're about to have a seizure?"

Carrie shrugged. "I usually feel more exhausted than normal. That's my only warning."

He kissed her forehead. His own eyes looked tired. "You've been working too hard. Sleep late tomorrow. I'll try not to wake you."

"I wish you'd wait until I could leave Giles. I'd like to go with you."

Matthias smiled slightly. "I'd rather bring you than Rannulf, but I need to get to the bottom of this before it happens again."

Carrie nodded and leaned into his embrace.

"I'll be back as soon as possible. The monastery is less than a day's ride." He drew back and tipped her face up to his. "Don't eat or drink anything you haven't seen prepared yourself. Promise me that, Carrie."

She couldn't help but smile at his concern. "I promise."

Blocking out all her worries, Matthias led her to bed. Lingering over her, he made love to her slowly and gently, mindful of her weariness. Carrie abandoned all concerns of her own and gave him the same measure of desire.

Each day they'd been together was a small miracle, and she didn't want to be parted from him for a single night. She knew tomorrow they might not be so lucky. Giles's would-be-murderer was on the loose, and until he or she was stopped, their own lives were in danger.

They fell asleep in each other's arms, drifting into dreams.

Sometime in the middle of the night, Carrie felt the covers jerk from her. She sleepily drew them back to cover her nakedness and settled anew alongside Matthias. In a dream, his long legs bumped hers, and he made low, unintelligible sounds.

Sleeping with a man was something she had yet

to get used to. She smiled to herself as she tried to go back to sleep. She ran her hands down his smooth, muscled side, trying to soothe him to a more peaceful rest.

He fretted in his sleep, his mumbling deep and ominous. His head suddenly thrashed upon his pillow. A nightmare had him in its grip.

One hoarse word passed his lips in slumber and shattered the placid mood she bore from the night's sweet lovemaking.

"Isabelle!"

Chapter Twenty-One

Isabelle? Why on earth was Matthias dreaming about his late sister-in-law?

Sleep eluded Carrie until nearly dawn when she finally nodded off. The shock of Matthias's nightmare kept her awake with worry for him, for her, and what it might possibly mean. When she awoke later than she'd intended, Matthias had left just as he'd said, without rousing her. His side of the bed felt cool to her touch.

Her stomach twisted. If she'd only awakened him, she could've gotten an explanation.

Anyone can have bad dreams, she rationalized, and gave her pillow a hearty whack as she rolled over in bed. Matthias had more reason than most for nightmares. The combination of his experiences in war, traveling through time, and now with his brother being in danger could plague him with enough stress for a lifetime. Perhaps post-traumatic shock caused his restless night.

There was only one "Isabelle" that Carrie had heard Matthias mention and that was Giles's deceased wife. Edwina had explained that Lady Isabelle died of a fever shortly after Matthias left Wyldnell nine years ago. Why was she in his thoughts now?

Probably, Carrie speculated as she lingered in bed, Matthias had been thinking of his brother's wife while Giles was ill. Her husband was sympathizing with Giles, demonstrating more evidence that brotherly love existed between them. Their cool animosity had been fading away for weeks now, leaving only the kind of sibling rivalry that bonded most brothers.

Maybe someone mentioned Isabelle's name to Matthias, making him think of her and how much Giles needed her now.

Or, was there another reason?

Goosebumps ran up her forearms. Could the brothers' feud be over Lady Isabelle?

Sitting up in bed, Carrie contemplated Matthias's stormy moods whenever his brother was mentioned. Would an argument over Isabelle explain the resentment they bore each other? Maybe it was all conjecture on her part, but did it somehow fit in with Matthias's belief that he was the epitome of wickedness? Was Isabelle the cross Matthias bore?

She recalled the tortured sound of Matthias's voice when he'd uttered the woman's name.

Had he once cared for Isabelle? Or—she wrapped her arms around her body and imagined a worse scenario—had Matthias slept with her?

Carrie refused to think of the latter. She threw the covers off and dressed. There was an explanation that would make her feel like an idiot for worrying. Hadn't she dreamt of French-kissing Coach Brock, her crater-faced biology teacher in the ninth grade? She'd woken *herself* up from that disgusting nightmare!

Ask the right person and she'd find the answer.

Giles was still resting. Besides, he had already refused to talk to her about the feud. Edwina was far too loyal to Matthias to tell her anything without a bias toward "her Math." She'd sugar-coat his every deed.

Carrie ran her fingers through her mangled hair, snarls unyielding in the twisted locks. To heck with it!

As for Maud, staying to help care for the earl, Carrie doubted the old woman was apprised about matters inside the castle's walls. There were others, surely, who knew the reason why Giles banished Matthias from Wyldnell all those years ago. Someone would remember the details. Maybe she could persuade them to share with her.

Honesty...honesty...honesty. Who was honest? Or, more precisely, who would be the most willing person to share her husband's past?

****

Over one hundred forty monks and even more lay-brothers devoted themselves to the care and keeping of the timber monastery. Matthias begrudgingly acknowledged a respect for the Cistercian order, in spite of his dislike of their abbot.

On the whole, Marsten's monks were self-sufficient, unassuming, and like himself, appreciative of their privacy. They kept large herds of cattle and sheep on thousands of acres of land donated by the crown and Matthias's late father. Their farming methods were far superior to those of the local society. Matthias had long espoused in lectures to his students that the Cistercians' development of agricultural techniques led them to continue to prosper in the Wye valley until Henry VIII's dissolution in the 1500's.

All the monks wanted was to be left alone in prayer and to their modest living wrought from working the land. Matthias believed the only resident wanting expansion and increased prosperity was the power-hungry abbot himself.

After meeting the porter, he and Rannulf were taken to Prior Godfrey, a man neither of them recognized, but who appeared to be both hospitable and pleasant. His tonsured head was ringed with white, wiry hair, and his forehead was lined with the marks of puzzlement. Curiosity lines, not wrinkles of anger or disappointment. Matthias instinctively took the prior into his confidence and shared the reason for their visit.

"Poison?" he whispered, eyes round. "I don't understand why anyone here would be involved, Sir Matthias. Our abbey has been blessed with Lord Wyldnell's patronage for many years, and I know of no one who would wish him to come to any harm."

"Do your monks grow the herb monkshood?" Rannulf asked.

"Aye. To inquire about herbs, you should see Brother Rhys. You'll find him in the garden. He gathers and delivers plants for the castle. If the poison came from our abbey, Brother Rhys will know of it." Hailing a passing monk, the prior asked him to guide Matthias and Rannulf to the garden.

Brother Rhys was a lay-brother, bearded with a head full of brown hair, but he wore the robe of a monk. Matthias had seen him before in the castle. When the lay-brother looked up from the ground he was hoeing, his gaze lighted on Matthias. He abruptly dropped his attention to the loosened ground beneath his tool blade.

The men patiently waited for the gardener to acknowledge them. A singular occurrence for Matthias in either time period. In his presence, most men snapped to attention. Was the fellow rude on purpose? Or did it portend something else—guilt? Matthias cleared his throat.

The lay-brother reluctantly stopped his work and leaned on the tool, looking both men over. He spoke to them warily in Welsh, "Aye?"

Matthias answered, "Are you the one responsible for delivering the herbs to the castle?"

Brother Rhys looked as if he had something to say, but no words left his mouth.

"Speak, man!" Matthias ordered, struggling to keep his anger in check.

The man quailed and tossed his hoe to the ground. In a flurry of robes, he took off running through the carefully turned soil, sending dirt clods flying off his sandaled feet. Matthias and Rannulf chased him from the garden to the cloisters. Rannulf went left and Matthias went right, trying to corner the fleeing monk. Brother Rhys held the advantage, knowing the grounds better than the knights. He kept a good distance ahead of his pursuers, ducking to avoid monks in reflection among the wooden posts supporting the roof.

Brother Rhys startled one monk, however, causing the poor soul to toss the book he was reading into the air. Standing helplessly in the way, the monk couldn't avoid Rannulf. The beefy captain barreled into him and landed beside the collapsed monk on the ground.

As Rhys paused momentarily to see what had befallen the monk in his wake, Matthias took advantage of his hesitation, skirting a wooden post to capture him at sword-point.

"Enough, Rhys!" Matthias ordered.

"I yield. I yield, sir," he panted, his back pressed against the post.

Winded from the chase, they both stood gasping for air. Rannulf helped the fallen monk to his feet.

"Why are you trying to kill the earl?"

Brother Rhys shook his head and spoke in English, "I'm not. On my oath, I swear I'm not trying to kill anyone!"

Matthias grabbed Rhys's hood and pressed his steel against the man's throat. "Innocent men don't run. Answer me! Why?"

Rhys turned pale, shaking like a leaf. "I knew it was wrong. I knew the horseradish and monkshood shouldn't be mixed. I warned the abbot it would be a mistake. The earl...is he...?"

"Alive! And far better off than you'll be." Rannulf pointed his own blade at the man's back, pinning him between the two larger men.

"Please, Sir Knights!"

Matthias ignored the brother's pleas. Instead his thoughts centered on one thought, "The abbot—? Do you mean Abbot Sidney knows about your poison?"

Brother Rhys's face crumpled to tears. "He knows. Of course he knows! He's the one who ordered me to send it." He sobbed, "He said to send monkshood and horseradish together. The roots would be separated in the castle's kitchens. I told him the two herbs couldn't be mixed. It's hard enough for me to tell them apart, but for anyone n-not expecting the poison, it would be nigh impossible to know it was t-there! I knew your cook wouldn't be able to tell the difference."

Rannulf caught Matthias's eyes, scowling. "Abbot Sidney wanted the poison to be used."

"Abbot Sidney wanted Giles dead," Matthias concluded. "Giles wouldn't grant him the land he wanted, and the king wouldn't either."

Rannulf swore. "The bloody abbot himself. And I'll wager you would've been his next victim, Matthias."

Matthias lowered his sword to the ground and put a hand to his head. The captain was right. Marsten knew the king was counting on Matthias to run the garrison and estate in his brother's stead. The greedy abbot would've sent him to the grave, as well. Now he'd left the villainous wretch unattended with his weakened brother and his wife. A knot of dread formed in his throat.

"Jesu! Rannulf! Truss this cur. We must bring him back to the castle with us."

****

The clang of steel led Carrie to the exercise yard. It seemed odd to wander upon the scene and not find her husband working with the men. He labored over the king's army each day since he'd received his orders. Matthias was nothing if not

292

diligent.

Even odder was the sight of Sir Ian training alongside the Welsh soldiers. Ian usually busied himself with the outriders, looking for trouble outside the castle walls. Carrie believed the earl's interest in the preparations had changed the young man's attitude toward his duties.

She no longer feared him. With the protection of both Matthias and Giles, she didn't think Ian would ever look upon her in the same way he had when she'd first arrived at Wyldnell. But just in case, she took comfort in the feel of the hard steel of Matthias's dagger strapped in her girdle.

"Lady Caroline," a squire announced for the rest as she approached.

The men stopped their exercises, dropping weapons and straightening from their stances. Carrie nodded to them, biting her lip. She hadn't meant to interrupt.

"Sir Ian, may I have a word with you?"

The youth cast a nervous eye at the other men. "Me, my lady?"

Carrie nodded.

Ian's brow furrowed, and indecision clouded his face. At last, he blew out a breath of air and joined her, leaving the other men to their work.

"I'm glad I found you. I have a problem I'm trying to figure out, and I didn't know who else to ask." She chewed her lip as she regarded him.

As they walked across the bailey, the young knight kept his body turned half away from her, as if she had a disease or something. "And you thought to ask *me*?"

"Well, yeah." *Carrie, you moron! Even Ian thinks it's a bad idea.*

Why did she suddenly feel like she was batting for the wrong team? All she was doing was trying to help Matthias. To find out why he thought himself to be evil, and why he said that woman's name in his sleep. Ian was simply a means to an end. That's all.

She had to gain Ian's trust first. "I also wanted to tell you that I've made a poultice for you."

He halted and stared with rounded brown eyes as if she'd gone mad. "A poultice? I'm not injured!"

Carrie gestured toward her face. "The bumps, I've made something that ought to get rid of them."

Ian's face reddened under the acne and freckles. He frowned angrily.

"You'll surely be looking for a bride of your own soon, so you'll want to look your best, won't you?"

Ian eyed her dubiously and then almost imperceptibly nodded.

"What did you want to ask, my lady?" He rested his hands on his waist and lowered his eyes.

Guilt sunk its claws deep. She should be asking her husband, not Ian. Of all the people in the castle, most of all not Ian. The young knight had only been a child when Matthias left nine years ago. Perhaps he wouldn't know the particulars.

But whom else could she turn to? Matthias refused, absolutely refused, to talk to her about his feud with Giles. The secret kept him from truly loving her. She felt it in her soul.

Ian was the one person in all of Wyldnell who wouldn't varnish the truth about Matthias, a man he so apparently hated.

Keep your friends close and your enemies closer.

"I've often wondered...well," Carrie stumbled over her words, trying to decide the best way to pry into Matthias's business, "why you always seem so distrusting of my husband. I know he's been away for nine years, but that's not the only reason, is it?"

Unwavering, Ian crossed his arms over his chest and jutted his chin out. "Sir Matthias will be lord of this garrison—"

"Please, Sir Ian," Carrie flapped her hands,

protesting, "I need to know what's happened between them. For the earl's sake as well as for mine."

"My lady, I beg you not to ask me. Your husband—" He retreated with the shake of his head, stomping away before finishing.

"You know something about it, don't you?" Carrie cried desperately, dogging his heels. No one was within earshot this far from the men, but she didn't care if anyone overheard. Her stomach clenched, dreading the answer, but she couldn't stand wondering anymore. "He won't tell me. I know he loves his brother, but he—"

Ian snorted. "Like Cain loved Abel."

He offered nothing more, walking on.

Carrie pulled the dagger from her hip and barred his way, turning the steel to his Adam's apple. "Tell me. What makes you hate him so much?"

The small blade seemed little more than a glorified envelope-opener before the strapping young knight, but she wielded it nonetheless. Maybe he'd get the point that she would find out one way or another.

Ian's face contorted with rage. Glaring down at her with scarcely concealed abhorrence, he told her, "*Somebody* ought to hate him for *raping the earl's wife!*"

She stared at him. She must have misheard.

Ian continued, seething, "Aye, the great bard of Wyldnell. The revered crusader. The chivalrous knight. The hero from the war. The earl's chosen successor." He spat in the grass. "Matthias drank himself into a stupor and forced himself upon Lady Isabelle in her own bed."

Carrie pushed the knife against his neck. "You're making that up. Matthias wouldn't do that."

"My lord ordered his household to never speak of

Sandra Jones

it, but it *should* be known. Matthias should never have been allowed through the gates unless he was dead."

"You're lying!"

Ian pushed her weapon away, sneering. "The earl didn't want you to know, Lady Caroline. He demanded our secrecy, because he thought if you knew, you wouldn't stay with his bastard brother to bear his children."

Carrie let the knife fall from her trembling hand. That sounded like Giles.

Tears sprang to her eyes. "Matthias wouldn't have raped anyone."

Ian nodded. "A laundress found Lady Isabelle in flagrante with the villain. When the laundress returned to the chamber with a guard, Lady Isabelle threw herself at them, begging for help. It was said she bore marks on her arms and legs, proof of the bastard's savagery and torture."

"It was a mistake," Carrie said as a hot tear fell on her cheek. "It couldn't be true."

"If it was a mistake, then why didn't the scoundrel defend himself?"

Ian picked up her dagger and slowly handed it to her, hilt first. Carrie took it from him, scarcely feeling the hilt in hands gone numb.

"My lady, I begged you not to make me tell it. I don't savor telling the tale."

He walked away from her, leaving Carrie to the full crush of his words.

And Matthias's.

I am a beast.

She walked away aimlessly. Faces blurred past her vision as she left the field in a daze. Not caring who they were. A woman's lips moved, speaking to her. A servant? A scullion? What was she saying? The agrimony was in bloom? It didn't matter. Nothing did.

Without knowing how she got there, Carrie collapsed in her bedchamber, burying her face in the pillows on her bed. Sobs racked her body as she heard the whole ugly truth in Ian's voice again and again in her head.

She didn't want to believe it and certainly didn't trust Ian as much as Matthias. But the truth had always been under her nose. The sneers of the servants and their whispers. The way people always changed the subject when Isabelle was mentioned.

Had she married a man who would sleep with his own brother's wife...even raping her? How could he take a woman against her will? How could he hurt a woman like that?

She'd seen Matthias fly into a rage, witnessed his stormy temper. He'd always managed to control it. If drink affected him so, why had he allowed himself to get so drunk that he would ravish Isabelle? How could it be true?

Although he'd told her nothing about it, he'd practically admitted his guilt to her.

How could she have love a man so very, very twisted?

I am...infamous.

Chapter Twenty-Two

Carrie cried until her eyes swelled and the pillows swam, and then she found she could cry no longer. She picked up Matthias's wooden carvings one by one and sat them on the bed with her. Her fingers ran over the smooth edges where the all traces of the knife's gouging had been painstakingly smoothed away.

She picked up the lovespoon last, choking back a sob. She remembered when she'd thought Matthias had only courted her because of the king's order. That was dumb. Matthias would've been carving the lovespoon on those sleepless nights he'd spent in the loft—long before he'd gone to Chepstow to meet with Edward.

Sleepless nights. She put the lovespoon aside and hugged a sodden pillow. He'd been unable to sleep then because he had no bed, and he had no bed because he didn't want to share one with her.

Of course, she knew full well, now, that he *had* wanted to share a bed with her, but he didn't want to force his attentions on her. He'd tried very hard not to. He'd kissed her only in full view of everyone and kept away from her like the plague when they were alone. He'd even placed Rannulf as a guard on his door the only time he'd allowed himself to drink.

These acts weren't those of a man prone to violence.

Unless...Matthias truly believed he was guilty.

The thought of his crime ought to kill any love she had for him. But it hadn't. Something was wrong with the idea of him committing the crime.

Matthias had been nothing but chivalrous since the moment she'd fallen into his century. Lancelot couldn't hold a candle to him. Everything he did was for her protection or for his brother's or for someone else. He'd never lost control of his anger in her presence, even when drinking, and Lordy, she was certainly capable of rousing the man's temper!

She couldn't love a man who committed the crime Ian described. Not a rapist.

Carrie took a deep, affirming breath. Matthias was innocent, and she had to get off her duff and find a way to prove it.

Edwina caught her as she descended the stairs.

"My lady, what's wrong? You poor dear. You look awful."

Carrie ran a hand through her tangled hair again. Her appearance was the last thing on her mind.

"I'm fine. I-I'll be all right. It's Matthias." Standing on the stair above Edwina, she put her hands on the older woman's shoulders and looked her directly in the eye. She strained to keep her voice from cracking as she asked, *"Why didn't you tell me?"*

Edwina stared at her with widening eyes.

"Someone has told you about Lady Isabelle." She lifted a hand to her mouth, backing up against the wall.

"Then it's true? Matthias...raped her?" Carrie swallowed.

Edwina shook her head, her eyes brightening with tears. Behind her hand, she said, "I never believed it. Not my boy!"

"Then how do you explain it, Edwina? Ian told me Matthias never denied it." Her heart hung in her throat as she prayed Edwina would give her a reason to hope.

She spat, "Rannulf's son! Ian is a great lout. He

wasn't old enough to know. Lady Isabelle must've lured Matthias to her bed somehow. I never trusted her," Edwina fumed through her tears. "After the war, Matthias had matured. He was no longer a boy dreaming of chivalry, but he still had some of the ideals of his youth. He yearned for independence from his duties. He wanted a wife and a family of his own. He couldn't wait to leave Wyldnell and begin building his own castle on the land he'd earned. Giles kept him as a retainer here when he should've been allowed to go."

"Did Matthias ever tell his side of what happened that night?" Carrie's voice broke this time as her chest constricted.

"Just that he was too drunk to remember. He was angry at his brother. They'd quarreled. Math told Giles it wasn't fair that he had Isabelle while *he* could have no one. He stayed up drinking long after the other knights were abed. Drinking in the Great Hall was the last thing he remembered doing."

Her hopes shattered. It was worse than she'd expected.

Edwina grabbed her arm. "My lady, when Math returns, what will you do?"

Carrie didn't know what she would do. Right now, anger was the only thing keeping her from crying anymore. If Matthias had been more honest with her, her heart wouldn't be in pieces. His silence was the worst kind of betrayal. Maybe the rest of Matthias's friends and family could ignore the past, but she couldn't.

"I-I don't want to see him yet. I have too many questions I need answered first."

She passed Edwina and headed down the winding stairs.

"Where can I tell Math you've gone?"

"Don't tell him!" she tossed over her shoulder flippantly. No, that wasn't fair. She paused on the stairs. With all that had happened, Matthias would worry about her. She sighed. "Tell him I've gone to sit with Giles."

****

Baldric greeted Carrie outside the earl's chamber as he left his room from delivering his drink. The man was on his way to watch Cook prepare his lord's broth in the kitchens. Matthias had left strict orders to keep someone trustworthy at Giles's side and that no food or drink should pass his lips that hadn't been inspected by at least one other person. Baldric said Maud was sitting with Giles presently.

Carrie found the old woman in a chair at the corner of the earl's chamber while Giles was resting. The room had already been prepared for night with cressets and candles lit. Despite the hot tallow lights, Maud's eyes were closed, and her face was gaunt. She'd probably been with the man for hours. Shame heated Carrie's cheeks when she imagined she'd been too wrapped up in her own troubles to do as she'd promised. She should've been attending Giles hours ago.

"Maud," she spoke softly, touching the old woman's shoulder.

She stirred, blinking her eyes.

"My lady," she glanced at the bed and sleeping earl, "Lord Wyldnell was asking for you."

"I'm sorry. I should've come sooner."

Maud smiled serenely. "You were with him for many, many hours yesterday. A break is understandable, for certes." She covered a yawn.

"As it is for you, too. Tell me what you've given him, and then go rest yourself."

Maud described what the earl had drunk and how much he'd been sleeping. There'd been no need for any medicines, since his stomach was probably too weak for anything to stay down.

Sandra Jones

"He's been begging for wine," Maud told her as she rose. "I asked Baldric to bring some up along with some water. The guard was supposed to watch him draw it. I think if we weaken it, he should be able to keep it down. It's better than him not drinking anything."

Seeing the pitchers on the bedside table, Carrie nodded. "You're right." This once she would allow Giles his favorite drink.

"Send Baldric to fetch me if you need aught."

When the old woman was gone, Carrie went to the earl's side and sat in the cushioned chair near the bed. His skin color looked slightly better in the firelight, but he was rail-thin under the cover. His breathing came in regular, normal breaths of sleep.

How he could breathe in the stuffy, hot air of the chamber? She opened the window, letting the lofty breeze of the river valley below flow in and returned to his side.

As she settled back in her chair, Giles's eyes cracked open.

"Hello, my lord." She smiled gently.

He grimaced.

"Are you all right?" Carrie put a checking hand to his forehead, but he batted it away.

"I'm fine as ever. 'Tis you who looks to be ill."

Carrie cringed with embarrassment. "I didn't brush my hair or wash my face before coming. I—"

"My servants attend me with better decorum, Lady Carrie," he told her, rearranging the cover over his chest. "Where is your husband? Doesn't he get tired of you always groveling over my carcass?"

"I'm sure he appreciates my attendance to his brother, which is more than I can say for you at the moment," she teased.

She had no intention of telling him that someone was trying to kill him yet. The plot would only serve to frighten him and make him more anxious than his heart was ready for.

"Why?" he scoffed at her remark. "Because I expect you to look presentable in my presence? God's wounds, of course I appreciate you. Not that you've *been here* today. You've left me alone with that witch in your stead. Surely you know having beauty at my side does more for my well-being than being attended by ancient crones or unkempt young wenches."

Carrie relaxed a little. His insults were delivered in his own dear way of showing care.

Feigning exasperation, she exhaled a short breath of air and put her hands on her hips. "I'm surprised you still have the strength to admire women today, my lord." She scolded him lightly, "We should be the least of your concerns."

His gray eyes narrowed on her. "It was the food I ate, wasn't it?" His voice went grave, and Carrie prayed he wasn't putting two and two together yet about the poisoning.

"Yes, probably."

His gaze took in her appearance, gray eyes tracking her clothes, face, and hair once more. "Where's Math?"

Carrie swallowed a lump in her throat. She couldn't tell him Matthias went in search of his attacker. Just thinking about Matthias in his brother's presence made her feel as if the tears would come again. Giles could be kind and caring in his own way, but she couldn't pour out her soul to him. She glanced away.

"He went north with Rannulf."

"You fought?"

Carrie looked back at him. She could see the sharpness in his eyes, so intelligent like his brother's. "No. We parted well, my lord. He's merely visiting the monastery."

"The monastery?" Confusion darkened his face.

A knock at the door saved Carrie from further explanations. Before going to answer it, she bent low over the earl's ear and said, "I need to talk to you later if you feel up to it." Somehow she had to get to more answers about what had happened that night with Isabelle.

It was Abbot Sidney of Marsten. He let himself in before Carrie left Giles's side.

The robed abbot stared at her as he approached the earl. His gaze was cool and reproachful, but Carrie didn't know why. Her only meeting with the man was for her wedding. Still, he sent chills up her spine.

"I see you're awake, my lord. Good."

"Aye, and I'm not alone, as you can see. I have no need for last rites today, so mayhap you'll take yourself out and leave me to my recuperation."

The abbot formed an unfriendly smile, his eyes firmly on Carrie. "Recuperation with your brother's wife? Is this a family custom for you both?"

Giles threw his cover away from his arms and seethed, "Now you've gone too far, Marsten! You'll not speak to me in that tone. Take your sanctimonious self out of my room."

Marsten bowed his head abjectly. "My apologies. As usual, I need to remind myself that I'm no longer a worldly man, but a man of the cloth. It was an ill joke, my lord."

Giles grumbled, "A joke I trow I wouldn't let another man walk away from. Lady Caroline is here to see to my health. I nearly died two nights ago, and once again she's saved my life. You owe her an apology, as well."

Carrie felt an urge to turn her head away from the abbot's dark gaze when he directed it at her. But instead she met his stare with all the placidity she could muster. No wonder the earl was outraged.

The abbot's "joke" only served to confirm the

truth—Matthias had slept with Isabelle.

But she had yet to learn if Isabelle had allowed him in her bed willingly or not.

"So, Lady Caroline," Marsten spoke smoothly, pausing as he wet his lips, "you are a healer, too?"

"I know a few remedies, yes."

"What do you think ails our Lord Wyldnell, here?"

Carrie sat down at Giles's side again. "Probably something he's eating. When I changed his diet and became strict with his foods, he became almost well again. Now he's returned to some of his old eating habits, and well, he's ill once more, as you see."

She pulled the covers back over Giles's chest and gave him a reassuring smile.

"How fortunate you are, my lord," Marsten replied. "And where is your brother hiding this day? I've not seen him in the lists or with the new recruits."

"Gone to visit your monastery, which is where you ought to be."

Carrie chastised the earl with a private frown.

Marsten moved closer to the bed. "And what, pray tell, is Sir Matthias doing there?"

When Giles didn't have an answer, they both looked at her. Carrie was suddenly struck by the notion that she didn't trust Marsten with the truth about the poisoning. In fact, if someone from the monastery was trying to kill Giles, Marsten would be in a position to know about it.

Or to be the instigator.

Carrie eased out of the chair. Perhaps she ought to bring the guard back while Marsten was visiting.

Mildly, she explained, "He wanted to see about some of the deliveries the monks have been making to the kitchens."

"Are the deliveries not satisfactory, my lord?"

Abbot Sidney stood so close to Carrie now that

she felt the sleeve of his robe brushing her arm.

"I-I don't know. Carrie?"

Her gaze left the abbot momentarily, as she thought to say something pacifying to the earl, but fleeting movement out of the corner of her eye caught her attention. When she turned to the abbot, he moved quickly behind her, barring her around her shoulders with one arm and around the waist with the other. A sharp dagger blade lay across her chest.

"Marsten!" Giles gasped.

"So you've learned the truth of my sport?" Marsten snarled in her ear.

Carrie tried to pull away, but the abbot's arms held her like taut ratchet straps with the knife's tip angled toward her heart menacingly. His age deceptive, he was stronger than her.

"The abbot's been poisoning you, Giles!" Of course, the abbot. He had clear motive to kill the baron of Wyldnell. Why had they not suspected the abbot? It wasn't the monks who sought to poison Giles. They'd been wrong to look in the monastery.

The earl's eyes blazed as he stirred on the bed.

"Nay, Wyldnell! You stay back or I'll kill the woman, and then I'll finish you off."

Carrie demanded, "Why would you want to kill the earl? Isn't he your benefactor?" She wasn't completely clear on how the Church and monarchy coexisted in medieval Wales, but she knew Giles heavily supported the monastery.

"'Benefactor?' Aye, of wealth but not the land we need. The Cistercians are an agrarian society. We've nowhere near the amount of land we need for sheep farming. Tintern Abbey has land aplenty. I'll not have an abbey to rival Tintern without my land."

"Good God, is that what this is about?"

Marsten squeezed Carrie's ribs so hard that she gasped, and then he yelled at Giles, "Aye, of course!

I've been telling you for years that we would need more land. Have you not been listening?" Ears ringing, Carrie craned her head as far away from his raging voice as she could while he continued to rant, "King Edward bears no compassion for the Church. He cares not what will become of my monastery. If I don't get Wyldnell land, we'll never grow to be as great as Tintern. We'll not grow at all!"

"You're insane!" Giles raged. "If you kill me, you'll accomplish nothing. My brother will take possession, and Edward won't grant you any land."

Marsten's fingers dug into her like claws. If only she'd brought her dagger. She'd left it in her chamber, her protection forgotten amidst her tears and laments about Matthias.

"I trow that. His reappearance has put a new spin on my plans, but it makes everything even better. I kill you, Wyldnell, then Matthias's wench, and then—"

"Then Matthias will kill you," Giles rasped and began to cough, his face reddening like a beet.

"Nay," Marsten purred in Carrie's ear, "I'll get him first. When he returns, he'll find the two of you here...in this bed. In his rage, 'twill be thought, he killed you both and then turned the sword upon himself. 'Tis not a hard thing to imagine. Anyone who wanders upon the scene will think Matthias had gone mad. It wouldn't be the first time."

****

Matthias dismounted his horse in the bailey and threw the reins at a squire.

"Rannulf, put the lay-brother in chains and help me look for Marsten."

"Aye, where do you want me to start?"

"Check his bedchamber, the kitchens, and the Great Hall. Take some men with you. He may put up a fight. Remember, he once trained to be a knight in his youth, so be prepared for him not to give up

Sandra Jones

easily. I'll check on Carrie and Giles."

Matthias ran to his tower as fast as he could. His heart was thundering when he reached his bedchamber. It was empty. Of course, Carrie would be with Giles. God bless her! She'd keep his brother safe. Damn, he should've checked there first.

Running back down the stairs, he nearly ran into Edwina. He tried to pass her, but she held fast to his arms.

"Math! Oh, Math! Thank God you're back!"

"What is it?"

Was he too late? Her eyes were red and round with anxiety.

"Lady Carrie. She knows! She's been told about Isabelle."

An icy chill filled his soul.

"Are you sure?" He could hardly breathe.

"Oh, aye. It wasn't me, though. I swear it, Math."

"Where is she?" He knew she'd find out eventually, but Jesu, this was the worst time.

Edwina's eyes filled with tears. "She said she doesn't want to see you."

Of course. She wouldn't.

Matthias broke free of her hold.

"Where are you going, Math?"

"Send some men to Giles's chambers. The abbot's trying to kill him. I'll explain later, but first I've got to see Giles."

"But Math—"

Her voice trailed him, but he couldn't stay to hear what she had to say.

Wish for the Moon

Chapter Twenty-Three

"For a man of the church, you sure don't act like one," Carrie complained beneath the knife's blade.

All Carrie's other attempts to sway Abbot Sidney from his deadly plan failed miserably. Her last desperate idea—make the man so pissed off he'd let go to shout at her.

In hindsight, probably not the wisest action she could've made, eyeing the silver gleam of the dagger just under her chin, but she had nothing to lose.

Beyond reason, the man wouldn't accept any alternative to killing the three of them to get what he desired in his unstable mind.

Marsten dragged her bodily away from the chair, kicking it out of the way with his foot.

"I told you, I was once a worldly man. Some desires are hard to relinquish."

He'd told them he planned to kill Giles that day, since the poison wasn't doing the trick. He'd waited until the door wasn't guarded and Maud had left for bed, but Carrie's presence was unexpected. Still, he went through with his preparations. Making Matthias his scapegoat was an afterthought, though a smart one.

"Hard to relinquish, like power," Giles said weakly.

The earl's face grew paler, marked by splotches of red on his cheeks and lips from his hacking coughs. If they lived through the encounter with Marsten, Giles's weakened heart might fail.

Keeping his knife and a heavy arm across her, Marsten dug in the folds of his robe and withdrew

309

his belt, a length of rope at least two yards long, which he dangled beneath Carrie's nose.

"Here. Bind Wyldnell."

Carrie could tell the abbot had no intention of releasing her from his hold, so with the dagger at her throat, she bent over Giles and took his hand.

"I'm sorry, my lord," she whispered.

The earl turned his head, a cough rumbling through him as she fastened first one hand and then the other to the bed post. When she was done, she tried to adjust his pillow to give him some comfort under his straining body, but Marsten pulled her away.

"That's good enough."

Marsten drew the chair to face the door. Then he sat in it, pulling Carrie down to sit on his lap. Forced to endure his touch, her throat closed in revulsion.

She worked over the possibilities of escape. If she pulled from him, he'd only slit her throat. He was more powerful than she and could certainly overpower her in a struggle. Some simple self-defense classes could've solved this problem, she was certain, if she'd only thought she'd needed them. Both her health food store and her house in Historic Charlestown were in patrolled, well-lit neighborhoods so she'd never anticipated an attacker there. She was a sitting duck! The tables would have to turn in her favor if she had any chance at all.

"What are we doing now?" She kept her back rigid, trying to avoid touching his body any more than necessary.

"Waiting for your husband."

"What if someone else comes first? Matthias is hours away. He might even be staying the night at the abbey."

Marsten's hand climbed up her surcoat from her

waist, groping the curve of her breast. Bile rose in her throat.

His voice softened in her ear, "I'm not a lackwit. I know he'll be back before long. If he found what he was looking for at the abbey, he'll already be on his way here. As for the others, the earl's guard is occupied in the kitchen for at least an hour. The herb witch is sleeping, as well. There'll be no interruptions." His lips grazed the edge of her ear as she strained further out of reach.

Carrie knew he was right about the guard. Cook was painstakingly slow when he made broth. No one else would disturb them for hours.

"Giles!" Matthias shouted outside the door. "Jesu, where's the guard?"

The door burst open. Carrie's heart stopped at the sight of him, both relieved and alarmed at once. He entered, clasping an unsheathed sword, but he was alone. Looking like an avenging angel, his dark hair fluttered wildly as he drew to a sudden stop. His steely eyes caught the abbot, and his body tensed visibly.

He deftly wielded the sword in a threatening sweep. Aggression radiated from his stance, attesting he was ready to deal a deadly blow if needed.

She wished he hadn't come.

Although she'd shed no tears for her helpless situation before, they brimmed in her eyes now.

"Shut the door and throw down your weapon," Marsten ordered.

Matthias's eyes darkened as his gaze dropped to the dagger Carrie felt against her chest. He closed the door behind him, surveyed the room, and reluctantly laid the weapon at his feet.

"Welcome, Sir Matthias. How do you like our little drama?"

Marsten's voice dripped with vile pleasure. To

make things worse, he ran his free hand across Carrie's breasts.

"Bastard!" Matthias said through his teeth. "She's not a part of this. Let her go and deal with me like a man."

The abbot laughed. "It's been a long time since I've bedded a woman. After I kill the two of you, I just might find some satisfaction with your Welsh whore here."

A tear rolled down Carrie's cheek. She angled her face toward a loose wave of her hair, trying to dab away the evidence of her suffering. She'd rather die than let her captor enjoy the pain he was causing her. Or for Matthias to witness.

"So what is your plan, Sidney?" Matthias asked, his hands resting at his waist, just above his dagger.

Marsten stopped his groping, angling the blade at Carrie's neck.

"These two will die at your hands in a crazed attack. Then you'll kill yourself. Fair enough punishment for your crimes. 'Tis a shame Lady Isabelle isn't here to watch, though I shall take her place." In Carrie's ear, he directed her to stand.

This was it. She rose on wobbly legs. There was nothing else for him to do except kill them.

"I wouldn't touch that!" Marsten snapped. Carrie caught the same movement of Matthias's hand above his knife. "If you touch your weapon, I'll let you watch your Lady Caroline bleed to death."

"You do that..." Matthias's voice became lethally quiet, "and you will die before your body hits the floor."

Carrie met his gaze and held it. She didn't want to be the one keeping Matthias from protecting his brother and himself. *I'm sorry,* she mouthed.

"You don't want to engage him, Sidney," Giles told him from the bed. "Matthias is very d-deadly with a blade."

Marsten's hot damp breath ruffled strands of her hair, and she could hear the smile in his voice, "I think the only person in the room with any potential to threaten death is me, at the moment."

"Who are you killing f-first, Marsten?" Giles asked. "'Tis a hard decision, because then you'll have two others left who'll try to stop you."

"Shut your maw! You will be the easiest, since you're halfway in the grave as it is. I'll save you for last."

Giles hacked again, hard and deep.

Carrie could feel the tension growing in the abbot, smell the sick, sweet scent of perspiration on his skin. He was uncertain of his next move, or perhaps just agitated under the threatening presence of Matthias and the constant cacophony of the earl's sickness. How could she use that?

There had to be a way. Fate wouldn't bring them here only to die like this.

"Abbot," she relaxed against him, "the earl has been begging for his wine. I was just about to pour him some before you came upon us. He's so parched. You hear him coughing. Could I please give him a drink before you kill us?"

"Nay!" he barked. The earl's cough crescendoed, and Carrie could feel the abbot's head pivot on his shoulders, looking between the two men, gauging his odds. After a moment, the abbot relented. "Oh, for God's sake! Aye, pour the dog his wine."

Her husband watched, and she knew his intelligent mind would be computing the possibilities for leverage. Carrie caught Matthias's eye and then moved the short distance to the table with her captor clinging to her. She poured a deep cup of wine, finding inspiration in the trickle of the rich, fruity burgundy.

"My lord, do you know, is this the wine from Bordeaux?" she said loudly enough for the earl to hear.

Giles nodded, unable to speak between his air-robbing coughs.

She glanced pointedly at the heavy candle beside the pitcher and continued talking conversationally, "I remember my first taste of the stuff. The sediment isn't pleasant, but it's harmless enough. So long as you toss it down and don't sip it."

But it's highly flammable.

Taking the cup in her hand, she made a half turn toward the bed and then tossed the wine behind her into her captor's face. Marsten took a step backward, lowering his arm for the half-second Carrie needed to purchase freedom. She lurched toward the candle just as Marsten swung his blade in arc at her midsection, but Matthias blocked his way, shielding Carrie with his body. The dagger's edge sliced against his side. Carrie grasped the candle and flung the flame at the neck of the abbot's cowl, igniting his clothing in a burst of flames.

Carrie stumbled away, feeling a quick push to safety from Matthias who'd retrieved his sword and angled it at the abbot.

As the hungry flames licked up his robes to his face, the abbot screeched in horrible pain and spun in circles, unable to see. Blindly he bumped the bed, the chair, and the table, before breaking into a run for the center of the room. Carrie grabbed the pitcher of water, but as she moved to douse the abbot, Marsten was at the window. Then he fell.

His cry descended along with him and then ceased abruptly. Matthias went to the window casement and looked down. Carrie followed him to do the same, but Matthias stopped her. Barring her way with his body, he caught her arms and held her back, though she strained to see.

"He's dead, Carrie."

She could scarcely believe she had caused the

death of a person, but looking into Matthias's serious face, she knew he wasn't lying. Her stomach turned with self-revulsion.

"I-I didn't mean to! I didn't mean to kill him!"

Her body began to tremble uncontrollably. Matthias put his strong arms around her and let her cry against his chest. She slumped against him.

"It was an accident," he murmured soothingly. His warm breath feathered over the crown of her head.

"I only meant to break his hold on me," she explained between sniffles.

His hands soothed, running up and down her spine. His body felt strong and safe, molded against her. He whispered against her temple, "I thought you were brilliant. He brought his end upon himself, *Carys*."

She felt him kiss the top of her head. "You're the bravest woman I've ever known."

Returning his embrace, her fingers brushed his side and felt the dampness where his tunic was cut.

"Matthias, you're injured!" she gasped and eased back to look at his side.

Beneath his arm, the fabric of his tunic parted, revealing a long crimson gash. Carrie felt her stomach sink.

"It's only flesh. Not muscle." He backed out of her arms just as she sought to examine the cut better. His expression was closed.

"Let me—"

Giles groaned.

"His ropes!"

Carrie left Matthias to help the earl. He'd twisted sideways on the bed, trying to fight his restraint. Carrie picked up the abbot's discarded dagger, so recently the cause of her misery, and cut through the rope binding Giles's hands. He wilted against the bed, his chest rattling on a breath.

"Here, Giles, you really do need a drink." She gave him a swig of water from the pitcher.

The earl closed his eyes briefly as he allowed the liquid to soothe him. Carrie was relieved to hear the end of his coughing as she stroked his clammy forehead.

"Matthias is gone," he rasped.

Carrie looked over her shoulder. They were alone. She wished he'd stayed long enough for her to look at his wound. She helped Giles take another drink, her hand at the nape of his neck. "He's probably getting help for the...body."

She blocked out a mental picture of the hateful abbot and his awful end. Matthias was right. She was glad the misguided clergyman was dead.

"Mayhap, but I would have you bring him back." Fresh perspiration beaded on his brow, and his breathing labored.

"He'll be back, my lord. I can't leave you."

"I'll be all right. Please. I saw the look on his face before he left just now. He's leaving. You must stop him and bring him back."

"I will, my lord. Rest easy."

In an instant, she was down the stairs and in the bailey. Her feet moved as though they had wings on them.

She spotted Matthias leading his horse from the stables.

Rannulf stood looking on as they paused to allow a squire to saddle the horse. Then seeing her, the captain strode out to meet her midway.

Matthias kept walking, his back to her, and she wondered if he knew she'd approached.

"My lady, Math told me you saved his life and the earl's. We're all of us—the whole castle—very grateful to you."

Carrie peered around Rannulf's bulk, keeping an eye on Matthias. He looked as though he was giving some instructions to the squire.

She gave his arm a squeeze. "The earl is going to be okay, I think. Excuse me, Rannulf. I need to speak to my husband."

"My lady," he stepped in her path. Eyes downcast, he told her, "Math says he's riding to the abbey for help with Marsten's body and also for someone from the abbey to come take his henchman off our hands. He bade me take you inside."

The captain's gloved hand reached for her, but she backed up, missing his grasp.

"Oh, really?" she snapped. He thought he could dismiss her like that? She lowered her brows and gave the man her fiercest look. "Move it, Rannulf! I'm not in the mood to watch you play bodyguard again!"

"I am sorry, my lady. Sometimes my friend is need of a swift kick," Rannulf grumbled. He gave her a conspirator's wink and bowed, allowing her past.

She caught up with Matthias as he was moving to plant a foot in the stirrup.

"Don't I rate a simple good-bye?" she demanded. But when he turned from his destrier to face her, her temper evaporated. His expression looked stark, his eyes cold and his jaw gone tight. Her insides twisted. "Oh, Matthias, please let me see your wound."

He stared at her, frowning, as if he would refuse her. He really *was* leaving. Carrie held her breath. Was the wound bad?

Matthias sent the squire off with a jerk of his head.

When they were alone, he crossed his arms over his chest and scanned the barbican. The horse lingered behind him, lazily sniffing at the ground.

Tersely, he told her, "Edwina said you didn't want to see me. I'll manage the scratch on my own."

He was so remote, building his walls within himself.

She forced emotion from her voice, "When? When you've ridden miles from here and gotten it completely infected or bled to death along the way?"

Avoiding his stormy eyes, she took hold of his arm and swiveled him forcibly for a better look.

Air hissed through his clenched teeth from the pain of the motion, but he said nothing, allowing her to look her fill.

The cut wasn't deep, and Carrie made an inward prayer for that blessing.

"We should clean it right away. You're lucky. You won't need stitches, and I have some hyssop left."

"Does it matter?" His voice resounded with wounded pride. "Would it not have been better if I died?"

Carrie dropped her hands from him. He was questioning her love for him? Did he think she'd be better off without him? When she'd said she didn't want to see him, it was only because she'd wanted time to sort through her feelings and find the truth. Her faith in him had been unwavering from the beginning, but she still had no answers. Just hope.

To mask the pain she felt, she made her voice brusque, "The earl sent me to bring you back. He wants to talk to you."

She could tell from her husband's widening eyes that he thought the worst about his brother's condition.

"Oh, no. He's not bad off. I think he's going to be okay. He just wants to get something off his chest."

Matthias made a half turn, a muscle in his jaw clenching. "Mayhap I don't want to hear what he has to say. I know what you've been discussing. Edwina told me that you know about...*Isabelle*," he uttered her name as though it had been ripped from somewhere deep within him. Even saying her name seemed to take a toll on him.

"Last night I heard you say her name in your sleep. I asked...someone about her, and they finally told me what happened." She didn't dare tell him who her informant was. It wasn't Ian's fault, and she didn't want to bring her husband's anger upon him.

Matthias's eyes shut briefly, and then he looked at her through eyes gone the color of the Welsh fog, breaking her heart. "Whatever Giles has to tell me— if it's about her, I don't want to hear it."

A dark wave of hair slid over his brow unchecked. His gaze challenged her to argue. Carrie said nothing, sensing he had more to say without her interference.

"My brother told me all he needed to say nine years ago. Cursed me to hell and back. I cannot change that night. I'd give my life to change it, but I cannot. You have every right to hate me. Now that you know the sort of man I am and how I kept it from you, I'm sure you want me gone—" He broke off with a sob in his throat and stalked away.

Carrie hurried beside him and put her hand on his arm, stopping him. "I'm not letting you go anywhere but to talk to your brother." She couldn't cry now. Though her eyes burned, she didn't want him to see how he'd hurt her. She bit her lip.

"I told you, I don't want to hear it!" His rough voice cut through her like a hot knife through butter. "Mayhap I don't want *you* to hear what he has to say, either!"

Tears of frustration emerged in her eyes. "Matthias—"

"You already know what I did. What good would it do to know more? Do you have to know the details?" He swallowed visibly. "Aye, I'm a depraved monster, and I kept the truth from you. I didn't want you to know, because I didn't want you to look upon me with hate or disgust in your eyes. I'll leave you alone. I don't blame you. I've never deserved you, and certainly I haven't deserved your love. *Carys,* I would give anything..."

Matthias's hand flew to the back of his neck where he rubbed ruthlessly. "I'll give you anything you want. But I don't know what evils I'm capable of. I don't wish to find out. And if I ever hurt you...Jesu, I'd rather die!"

"How can you believe it, Matthias? You don't remember what happened. There could be another explanation. Attacking Isabelle isn't something you would do." She heard the plea in her voice, willing him to listen to reason.

"You don't know that." He crossed his arms tightly across chest.

"Yes, I do know that about you." Carrie moved in front of him and smiled through her tears. "I know I love you and trust you completely. I also know I wouldn't still love you if you weren't that same man."

"You continue to trust me?" He shook his head, disbelieving, and turned from her. His voice became bitter, "Your faith in me is naive for an intelligent woman of modern day. I'm not fit to touch you."

He was going to close her out again. Carrie's mind searched frantically for the words to stop him. "Did you ever suspect that *I* was the one poisoning your brother?"

This earned her a look from him. His dark eyes shot her a stormy glance of absurdity.

She argued, "But I was the one closest to him with knowledge of deadly toxins. I ordered his meals and even cooked for him on occasions. Are you telling me you never suspected me for even an instant?"

"What? Carrie, that's ludicrous. He was ill before you ever came here. Of course you were capable of poisoning him. But any fool could see how you fought to keep him alive. It's not in your nature to harm anything," he groused with an impatient toss of his head.

"Not even if he made me mad for being so conceited, so bossy..."

Matthias snorted. "He makes me furious for that same reason, but I would never..."

"Never what?"

"Neither of us would..."

Hurt Giles. The unspoken words hung in the air.

Carrie watched as he assimilated what she was willing him to realize.

Matthias scowled and hung his head.

Carrie touched his folded arms, silently urging him to listen. She had to get him to talk to Giles. "Go with me. Hear what your brother has to say."

Forcing herself to be stern, she told him, "You owe me that, Matthias!"

His gaze, full of desperation and uncertainty, flicked back to her. After several seconds, he dropped his gaze and went back toward the horse.

Chapter Twenty-Four

Matthias rode across the Wye Valley, terrain he
knew like the back of his hand. As if a predator
roaming his territory, he couldn't allow himself to sit
or pause too long in one spot. Better to keep moving.
His mind craved action, his body demanded it. To sit
still was torture. Each time he rested, he endured
the dull ache in his chest until it drained the will to
live from his soul. How long could he stay in these
woods when every tree, weed, and wildflower
reminded him of Carrie?

The abbey offered no such reminders, so he
quickly went there in search of the prior. Riding
posthaste, he found Prior Godfrey and told him what
had happened to the abbot and lay-brother Rhys.
The prior lifted a shaking hand to his forehead, and
Matthias feared the man would soon crumble. He
guided him to a wooden bench in the cloisters.

The prior's eyelids closed, perhaps in prayer. As
they sat, Matthias felt conspicuously out-of-place
with the holy man in the sanctuary. He half-
expected someone to grab him by the tunic and
throw him out for bedeviling the poor soul. He
wouldn't stop them. He even cast a wary eye around,
but the cloisters were empty that night. The monks
had gone inside for their evening meal.

The timber-framed church nearby drew his
attention. The small building presented a silent
reminder of the ephemeral nature of the holy place.
Seven centuries later nothing of the monastery
would remain.

"The abbot had ambitions the rest of his flock

didn't share," the fatherly prior said quietly, breaking the silence between them.

"How long has he been coveting Wyldnell land?"

The prior stared at the folded hands in his lap. "He talked of the need for more land earlier this year. Ambition must've consumed him. I wish I'd paid more attention—"

"I doubt you could've guessed his illness. He hid his depravity. I only wish I'd been here sooner. Maybe I could've recognized it, ended the poisonings earlier."

The prior looked into his face, holding Matthias with clear blue eyes. "And you say your wife discovered the poison?"

"Aye."

"Well, the earl is fortunate to have a brother with such a wife. I will include her in my prayers today, along with you, Sir Matthias. Your presence has been a blessing to us all." He smiled gently. "Lord Wyldnell is a beloved benefactor to the abbey, as well as a righteous man. We would've been lost without his kindness and favors, despite what the abbot might've believed."

Matthias opened his mouth and closed it. What could he say? Though he didn't feel his existence could ever be fortunate for Giles, Carrie's was, for certes.

"Are you a man of faith, Sir Matthias?"

Again, the steady blue eyes studied him. 'Twas worse than talking to his king. The prior's gaze could bore a hole through his heart in search of the truth. It reminded him of Carrie and the promise of honesty he'd given her and broken. He'd seen his word go unfulfilled.

"Not of much faith. No."

The corners of the prior's lips fell and a line of worry deepened on his forehead. "Faith would serve you well. It has me and others. Mayhap it's saved your brother's life?"

Carrie saved Giles's wretched life. "Mayhap."

Matthias dropped his gaze to ground, unable to look into the holy man's soul-digging eyes any longer.

"The abbot will be excommunicated unless it's ruled that he had lack of full reason. If so, he won't be interred in our consecrated grounds."

"He died before receiving last rites. For that I pity him, but my brother was in danger. It was the abbot's life or ours." Matthias tilted his chin, defying the clergyman to challenge him.

Prior Godfrey's face softened. "Oh, Sir Matthias, I do not hold you and your wife accountable. I find no fault of yours or your lady's. What has been done is the will of God, clearly." The prior rose. "Will you walk with me, my son?"

Matthias rubbed the perspiration of his palms on his knees. A sense of self-preservation made his gaze swing to the cloister's exit. He should go. He could claim he had other matters to attend to.

A coward's way out. "Aye," he sighed.

They followed the square, stone walkway around the cloisters.

The prior walked very deliberately, forcing Matthias into an even slower pace than he was used to with his bad leg. "I feel led to talk with you about your lack of faith."

Bloody hell. He should've run when he had the chance.

"I've said prayers. I've seen some answered. That's faith, isn't it?" What more did he want?

Matthias kept his stare on the uneven stones under his feet.

"Your lady-wife, does she have faith?"

Matthias couldn't help but smile at the thought of Carrie's blind faith, even though it hurt to think of her. "The woman abounds with it. She should have taken holy orders."

Well, perhaps not. She could be as lascivious as him in the private confines of their bedchamber.

"A good woman." The prior nodded favorably. "But you said you don't have much faith. Has something caused you to lose it?"

"I was a knight." He shrugged.

"And you were in the Middle East, so I have been told. Seeing death made you lose faith?"

"No."

"The wars?"

"No." God help him, he couldn't tell this holy man of his sins.

"You lost faith because of the king, your country?"

"No. I was a knight, but I did as I was told. There's no shame in loyalty. I was true to my heart, and I think even to God."

"Then if being a knight wasn't the cause of your lost faith, may I ask what was?"

Matthias took a deep breath of air. He was a drowning man. "I've seen things that have defied reason. Things that could not be the work of God or holy. That's all I'll say of it."

As he spoke, his hands began to shake. He shoved them under his crossed arms.

The prior walked without speaking for a long time. Then, he replied gravely, "And what makes you think these things weren't the doing of God? He can make all things happen if 'tis his will."

"If that's the case, then God doesn't favor Matthias Thorne with his will." He shot him a look of disdain, bracing for a rebuke.

The prior merely folded his hands in front of him, regarding the wooden columns with his peaceful gaze. "You've had naught but suffering, I suppose, in your life."

He'd spoken in statement, not question, but

Matthias was compelled to answer.

Nay. He'd had heaven briefly and lost it. He'd had a treasure and felt it torn from his fingers.

"I've received what suffering I've deserved. Faith is for better men than me. Faith is for men like you and my brother who are without sin."

The prior surprised him by chuckling softly. "If that was the case, Sir Matthias, then all the apostles would be mere men and not saints. The earl and I aren't without faults, either. Do you really think Lord Wyldnell is ready for sainthood?"

Matthias smirked. "No. He does have his faults. I'll give you that."

"Lord Wyldnell always spoke of you with warm regard when we conversed about his family."

Matthias stopped, reaching the churchyard. "Then he was lying either to you or to himself."

The prior's white eyebrows drew together to form a perplexed line. "I am astonished you think so differently of him. Verily, I am."

The abbot's confused gaze circled the churchyard. Matthias looked over the small collection of tombstones scattered over the grounds. A sad collection, gray and decaying relics of times when these people were still remembered...and missed.

"Your brother's wife rests over there."

Matthias's stomach clenched. He followed the prior's outstretched arm to a large stone on the skirts of the consecrated grounds. His blood raced, demanding immediate flight from the area.

"Lady Isabelle made her final confession to the abbot and then to her husband. She was given last rites, and now she is with God. The earl has requested to be buried beside her. So you see, even suffering the loss of a beloved wife, your brother still makes room for faith."

The prior's all-knowing eyes sought Matthias's.

But he wrenched his gaze from the tombstones and stared, defiant, at the church.

The clergyman sighed beside him.

"The bairn is on her other side. Lost shortly before her passing."

Matthias's gaze riveted back to the prior's. "Bairn? She was pregnant?"

"Her marriage, pregnancy, and death all occurred years before I came to the abbey, but aye, Lord Wyldnell has told me the baby was stillborn—arrived too early. The mother died of fever shortly after."

Matthias surged toward the tombstone automatically. He stopped himself before he drew too close. The gray rock marked the place where Isabelle was buried. And very likely where his own son or daughter was buried, also.

****

The guard wouldn't allow her passage through the gate that night. Fingers wrapped around the iron bars of the portcullis, Carrie cursed the men in the dark, high above her head in the gatehouse. She demanded to be heeded. She was the earl's sister-in-law, Lady Caroline. Had they forgotten?

So much for chivalry. The noble knight idea ended with the order of Sir Rannulf, captain of the freaking guard.

He'd met her at the stables.

"Nay," he denied her flatly. "You know I cannot allow you to take a horse."

"Well, would you at least send a guard with me?" she'd begged, turning her best doleful gaze up at him.

"Nay, Math wishes to be alone. I'm sorry, my lady, very, very sorry." He shook his copper head sadly. "No armed escorts, either. Besides, no one would dare take you riding under any circumstances, barring Math himself. They remember Sir Philip's quick flight from here and fear Math's temper."

Where are you, Matthias? I can't stay trapped in this castle forever.

Carrie pressed her forehead to the cold metal of the gate and stared into the distance beyond the castle. He was out there, somewhere. His side was cut, bleeding. He'd made up his mind he was too evil for her. Too evil to be in the presence of his brother. He was out there punishing himself, but he didn't seem to care he was hurting all the people who loved him.

What was he planning on doing? Would he make his way back to Chepstow Castle? She knew he was friends with the baron who lived there.

Hopefully, he'd just gone to the abbey to bring back some of the men he had dispensed earlier. Rannulf had already arrested the abbot's entourage and had bound them in the cellar to await the earl's judgment. They may or may not have been participants in the abbot's crazy scheme, but Giles would need to question them personally and find out.

If Matthias wasn't at the monastery, then where else would he go?

Anywhere, God, anywhere but the stones.

All she wanted was to see her husband riding back to her.

She felt a light touch on her shoulder, snapping her out of her reverie.

Maud's wrinkled face smiled as she stood in the yellow light of the gatehouse. "Won't let you out?"

"No, the *jerks!*"

Carrie narrowed her eyes at one soldier peering down at her from above, but it was too dark for him to see her ire.

"Lord Wyldnell is doing better. The coughs are coming less frequently." Maud glanced up at the sky and the stars reflected in her eyes.

"Is he alone?" Carrie looked at Giles's tower. Dark now, she knew he must be sleeping, or at least trying to. She hadn't had the nerve to see Giles since she'd let Matthias get away. On a glance, she could tell by Maud's shoulders the old woman was weary. "I'll take your place."

"Baldric is with him. All will be well."

Carrie's pain breached her defenses. Putting her hand to her face, she felt the tears slide down her cheeks, hot and burning.

Maud enveloped her in an embrace. Her rough clothing smelled of the comforts of wild mints, smoke, and trees. Carrie laid her head on the old woman's shoulder.

"Why cry now, milady? Marsten is dead. There's no one wanting to harm the earl now. Math will soon be back," she crooned.

Carrie's tears dripped on Maud's shoulder, but she couldn't control them. "What if he doesn't come back?" she whispered.

Maud didn't answer.

Carrie would rather die than live without him. No one made her come alive as he had. She would be better off dead than to return to life without the man she loved.

Maud set herself back from the embrace with a last pat to Carrie's shoulder. "I need to get back to my little house. The earl will need more medicine, I trow. I'd best get busy."

Carrie nodded grimly.

"These fools will let *me* pass," she told her and then lifted her voice to the breeze above, "or I'll make their shafts run dry."

The gears of the portcullis grinded to life. The gate lifted for Maud.

Carrie gave a fleeting thought to making a run for it, but what would that accomplish? Matthias would return when he wanted. *If* he wanted.

"I'll keep watch for Math, my lady."

Carrie gave her a shaky smile. "Please. Thank you, Maud."

Chapter Twenty-Five

Matthias slowed to a stop at the henge, holding the reins of the horse he led in a tight grip. The stones stood quiet in the gray morning light. Summer was at an end. Though the time of day was the same, this moment was nothing like the day he'd awoken in the stone ring with Carrie. That first day of May promised a season of sunshine and hope.

The overcast sky above his head now filled him with a sense of bleakness. If he entered the circle, what would come of it? Would he travel ahead or back to some other time? Once he was gone, would Carrie still be safe? Would she be able to return to her time?

She had Rannulf. She had Giles. Wyldnell was secure now that Giles would recover. The people respected her. She wouldn't be mistreated.

He took a step closer. *But will she be happy being left in the Middle Ages? She wanted to see her family again.*

It wasn't fair for him to abandon her in a place not her own.

Matthias felt the horse's muzzle bump his shoulder. The beast nodded, its breath quickening slightly, nervous. He patted its nose and ran a reassuring hand down its glossy neck.

"I don't like it here any more than you," he murmured.

"Then why bother?"

Matthias whipped his head around. He felt heat climb his neck as he faced the crone. Appearing as if from out of nowhere, she walked up to him outside the ring. Her arms were crossed over her ample bosom. Her brown eyes stared darkly at him beneath pinched brows.

"Maud."

"Why on earth are you here, Math? Where have you been?"

Matthias stroked the horse. "I camped by the river. Don't you know everything that goes on in these parts?"

"Everything that I care to know." A breeze picked up a few strands of gray hair which had escaped her tight ponytail. They darted around her head in a serpentine rhythm. Tartly, she demanded, "Answer my question, why are you here?"

Matthias lifted an eyebrow at her stern tone. "You have not spoken to me that way since I was a boy."

"It has been many years since I have seen you act like one."

Her words angered him, along with those steady brown eyes that could see straight through to his black soul, but she produced the result she surely desired. Guilt. The same as the prior had, only his was unintentional.

He broke his gaze away from her. "I think you know why I'm here."

"It will not work."

His breath caught. Had she been the stranger who watched him disappear into the mists all those years ago? A hysterical urge to laugh seized him, but he held it back. He could've asked Maud about the portal long ago and saved himself—both of them—a lot of heartache.

His stomach felt like jelly as he regarded the stone spires. She was right, though. It didn't feel the same today.

Would he be here if he thought the portal would work? Probably not.

Nevertheless, he pried his fingers loose from the horse's reins, allowing the beast the freedom to walk away. Left alone beside the circle, he rebelliously turned to face Maud. Her lips compressed tightly.

"The magic doesn't work like you think, Matthias."

He lifted his arms, gesturing his defeat, and then ground out in frustration, "Well, how the hell does it work? Tell me. Must I wait until Beltane?"

A small smile crept over her lips. God, he couldn't wait that long. He needed to leave now. His will wouldn't hold out much longer. If he remained near Wyldnell, the need to be with Carrie would consume him. He could easily picture himself returning to her, to his brother, begging them to forgive him for his crime. To take him back.

If they did have pity on him, the day would come when Carrie would shrink in fear of him...or look at him with hatred for who he was.

"You stupid boy. 'Tis not the day that transports you there."

He threw his head back to toss an impatient curse at the sky. "Then what does?"

"'Tis the mist that takes you." Her eyes flashed with a twinkle of humor.

He wheeled around and eyed the stones. Not a chance of fog on this dry, gray summer morning. He'd come at the wrong hour of day.

He sighed. "I'll come again tonight—"

She made a short laugh. "Will not work then either."

What was she, a bloody meteorologist? Mayhap she was. Being a Druid, she had more insight to the weather and nature. "Then I'll keep coming back until the mist is here," he bit out, staring her down in a challenge for her to deny him the hope.

"Still will not work." She sighed and moved to greet his horse. Her withered hands ran over the

Sandra Jones

beast's muscular back.

He raked his hands through his hair. He couldn't stay. But he couldn't go either. 'Twould be better to find the answer and send Carrie back without him. She belonged there. He had yet to find a place where he belonged.

"Why won't it work?" he cried. "For mercy's sake, Maud. If you know the way, tell me."

As if reciting from memory, she spoke, "The mist knows best. The fog takes a traveler to his soulmate. Once united, you must never part. The mist takes you where your soul *wants* to be. You cannot decide a destination for yourself alone. The two soulmates must choose where to go together. That is the only way the portal works." She lifted her gaze from the horse long enough to grin at him. "Iago did not share all his legends with you, did he?"

Matthias sank to his knees in the dirt. It was as if the wind had been knocked from him. The henge wouldn't take her or him anywhere. Not alone.

Of course she was his soulmate. There wouldn't be another for him.

When they'd come through the portal together, Carrie had wanted to be where the moon plants were, to find the supposed cure for her seizures. He had been thinking of Giles, wishing he could somehow make amends for the past.

But the last time they'd visited the stones, tried to find the way to go back...he'd desperately wanted to be elsewhere, the future, anywhere but near Giles. Hadn't wanted to face his crime. Carrie had been with him that day. Why hadn't the stones worked then?

Could it be that she'd wanted to stay? To help Giles and work things out between them? Leave it to Carrie to put others' needs ahead of her own.

Mayhap neither of them had wanted to be separated from the other.

He stared hopelessly at the ground. There'd be no going anywhere in time for her without him.

His heart ached. He loved Carrie more than life itself. No place on the face of the earth or time in existence would be far enough away to ignore her pull on him. The anguish of losing her would be relentless.

Matthias heard a voice nearby. They were not alone. How had he missed the sound of the approaching horse? He lifted his gaze slowly to see the rider.

Rannulf rode unarmed, without armor. The captain met Maud and leaned down from his horse to speak to the crone briefly. Matthias couldn't hear what they said. It couldn't be good. Maud's brows pinched together. Rannulf looked up from the healer and spotted Matthias beside the monoliths.

Matthias rose. The heat of shame washed over his features. Disgraced, he could not hide the defeat revealed in his face and posture.

"What is it, Rannulf?" he called. His friend should not have left the castle. Something was wrong.

His heart hammered against his ribs. Sudden worry swept in.

The captain shook his head grimly. "Your wife," he said, drawing closer on the horse, "has had another falling spell."

"Is she all right? What in the hell are you doing here? Why did you leave her?" He battled the panic that filled him. "Is she—"

Rannulf lifted a hand to stop his demands. He leaned over the horse's neck. "She's not hurt. She was with the earl when it happened. Math, your brother thinks she's possessed of a demon. He has locked Carrie in her bedchamber, and he refuses to let her out."

Matthias thundered, "For God's sake, the cur

has finally lost his mind!" Carrie saved Giles's life, thrice, to be treated like this?

Unthinkable. He clenched his fists. His brother, one of the men he'd trusted with the responsibility of his wife's happiness, had imprisoned her in her own room.

"I know, Math. I know. I tried to tell him he was being unreasonable." Rannulf sighed and shook his head again. "But he's the earl. Who can tell him aught?"

"I bloody well can!" he roared.

****

For once, Giles didn't greet Carrie with his familiar grouching. Settled on his pillows, his eyes tracked her approach with weariness. His usually animated expression stilled. Carrie sensed the seriousness in his somber thoughts.

"My lord? Baldric said you sent for me."

She prepared herself for his disappointment. Time to tell him the truth. She had failed to stop Matthias, and now he was gone.

"Aye. Sit."

She lowered herself in the empty chair and faced Giles. He looked as weary as she felt. She'd spent most of the night outside the earl's door the night before after checking on him and finding him asleep. Rannulf had taken her place that morning for a few hours before Baldric came and told her that the earl requested her attendance.

"Where's Rannulf? He's supposed to be with you still."

"I've sent him on an errand. It won't be much longer now, I suspect."

His gaze went to the open window. She heard the approach of horses outside.

"Is something wrong?" she frowned.

The tone of her voice must've drawn the earl's attention, because he swung his gaze to her face. His

336

survey of her appearance resulted in a grimace. Carrie lifted her hands to her hair and swept it back from her face.

"I know I look awful, again. But I was sleeping when you sent for me. I haven't had much sleep at all this week."

"Little wonder, that. Wyldnell's been in a state of chaos since you've arrived here." He straightened the covers over his legs. "Not that you're to blame, my girl. 'Tis just that it's usually a much quieter, peaceful place—for a Marcher stronghold."

"W-what are we waiting for, my lord?"

"For Rannulf's return." His lips formed a half-smile.

Carrie narrowed her eyes. Giles never waited for anything.

"My lord," she chided, suspicious, "what troubles are you conspiring for Rannulf...no, for me? You've got that cat-who-ate-the-pigeon look on your face."

He cocked his head toward the door, listening for something.

"You'll soon see."

Carrie crossed her arms over her chest. She was in no mood for his enigmatic schemes. "Well, you're not acting sick anymore, so I guess I should feel relieved. Maybe the poison's left your system. Or maybe it's gone to your *head*. Tell me why you've sent for me, or I'm going back to b—"

The door crashed open, causing Carrie to break her sentence off. She jumped to her feet, knocking her chair over with a crash.

Matthias strode in, eyes blazing. He took one look at her, and her heart lurched at the sight. His hair was tousled and untamed, more unkempt than she'd ever seen it. Stubble darkened his jaw. His tunic fared little better, stained, open, and loose. Enraged and tensed, he'd never looked sexier.

His eyes widened at finding her there. Then he

directed his wild gaze at the earl.

"What's the meaning of this, Giles?" he bellowed.

Carrie dragged her stare away from her husband's crazed expression to see Giles casually fingering a lock of his hair.

"My ruse worked, I see," he replied coolly.

"Jesu!" Matthias's hand clenched shut above the pommel of his sword. "I should've known Rannulf's tale to be a lie. You would never treat her so. She has you wrapped around her finger."

Carrie looked back and forth between them. This was about her?

"'Twas the captain's idea, not mine. I didn't even know the woman had the falling sickness." He gave a short laugh. "You managed to keep her spells a secret, but I would've found out eventually. Not even Caesar's loyal men could hide his affliction. Although...it wouldn't have mattered to me in the least, so long as it didn't interfere with my diet."

Matthias averted his face, hiding his expression, but Carrie could see the rage boiling underneath his taut muscles. He'd been tricked into coming back. Her heart sank. He hadn't come back of his own accord. Of course not.

Numbly, she picked up the chair and righted it. She should leave before she started to cry. Already a pang pressed against the backs of her eyes.

"Math, I need to speak to you," Giles told him.

"My lord, I'll wait outside," she murmured, thinking the brothers needed some privacy for a conversation.

"Nay. Stay, please, Lady Carrie."

Carrie frowned, surprised the earl wanted to include her, but she nodded her acquiescence. She hoped Matthias would be able to talk freely with Giles without her being a deterrent in their conversation. She closed the door to keep the impending talk private, and then she fell back to a shadowed part of the room. The brothers might be able to forget she was there if she stayed out of the way.

"I've had many brushes with death lately, Math."

"Aye, and you're going to live long enough to have others, if I don't kill you first," Matthias seethed and paced the floor slowly beside the bed like a caged animal.

"A man starts thinking when he is close to death." Giles cleared his throat and pushed himself up higher on his pillows. "For some time now, I've been trying to speak with you. Well, I guess I've not tried over-hard. To give you the truth of the matter, I've been avoiding our talk. I've passed up several opportunities." He appeared contrite, fiddling with imaginary wrinkles on this bedcover.

Carrie's mouth dropped in astonishment. All this time, she'd thought Matthias had been the one avoiding Giles.

"Our father, as you know, raised me to be a selfish man, always charged with looking out for my interests, the title, the king, and Wyldnell. When you came back, I continued to be selfish. I used you in my plans for the future without consulting your feelings or ambitions." Giles cleared his throat again. "I even used your guilt to manipulate you. I knew you would do whatever I asked to appease me and assuage the guilt you felt for your crime against Isabelle. Your need for a roof gave me the plan."

"I never asked to stay," Matthias grumbled in argument.

"I trow you didn't, little brother, but I also thought you would stay if I asked...because of Isabelle."

Matthias suddenly froze and turned a lethal glare on him. "Did you ask me here to threaten me again? Because if you did, I'll have you know that you have nothing to hold over me anymore."

"Nay, but I have plenty to return to you, Math, starting with your innocence and your honor."

From her vantage point, Carrie caught the dulling glint of anger in her husband's narrowed eyes.

Giles continued, "I know now that my selfishness got out of hand beginning with Isabelle. In our last two years together, I rarely spent a moment with her that I wasn't insisting she bear a child. I got frustrated with her inability to conceive and finally forced her from our chambers. We shared a bed rarely, and then only on the occasions when she thought she might conceive."

Matthias watched his brother intensely, frowning. Carrie shared his discomfort, hearing the anguish in his brother's hoarse voice.

"When she didn't fall pregnant, she turned to Maud, who told her it was because English blood is weaker than Welsh." Giles chortled. "The witch wasn't serious, of course, but Isabelle, in her ignorance, believed her. She got a concoction from the witch to drug me, so I would bed her willingly. It was nothing new. She'd purchased the drug before and used it on me. 'Tis wondrous powerful. But instead of drugging me, she decided to drug you, brother, because you're half-Welsh."

What Giles didn't tell Matthias seemed obvious to Carrie. She had to stop herself from speaking out. Surely they realized it, too. Matthias looked just like Giles, only younger. Any baby Isabelle conceived with Matthias would pass easily for Giles's.

"When Isabelle was dying of fever, she confessed everything to me, Math. She told me that she'd watched and waited until you'd had too much to drink already during the celebrations in the Great Hall. Late in the night, she slipped a dram of the potion in the ale she served you. When you were nigh senseless, she convinced you to escort her to her room."

Matthias lifted a shaking hand to rub his temples.

"'Twas not part of her plan to cry foul against you. But fear of discovery plagued Isabelle. She was never very artful or good at deception of any kind." Giles made a sad smile at some memory before continuing. His words became slower, somber, as he recalled the events aloud. "She made a mistake. The next morning, she overslept. When a laundress came to her room and found you there, Isabelle insisted she'd been attacked and you had kept her there against her will. While the servant went to enlist help, she inflicted wounds on herself and then used them as proof to blame you for the crime. All this she did while you were still drugged and sleeping."

Carrie's hands clenched into fists. Did Matthias feel half as outraged as she did at hearing his brother's confession? If he did, his stance didn't show it.

"Isabelle did conceive, but lost the child, Math. Her fevers followed. She never recovered. I lost you, then her. You are innocent of the crimes she accused you of. This is what I've been trying to tell you."

Silence swelled between them.

Carrie eyed the door, feeling like an intruder. She should've left the room long ago. The conversation was so private, so personal and painful. Her heart ached for them both, but especially for Matthias, who'd been allowed to think the worst of himself for so long. His shattered expression tore her heart to pieces.

"I'm sorry I didn't tell you sooner—as soon as you arrived. But like I told you, I'm still self—"

Matthias lifted a quelling hand. "I know, Giles. You don't have to apologize or make excuses."

Carrie felt a surge of protectiveness. So what if

he was an earl? She charged forward from the shadows to stand by Matthias. "Yes he does." Hot tears ran down her cheeks. Full of vehemence, she contested, "How could you keep such a thing to yourself, Giles? Could you not see how cruel you've been to make Matthias think he—"

"Carrie!" Matthias pulled her aside. He ran his hands up and down her arms until she released the breath she'd been holding and went lax. For her ears only, he told her softly, "He loved his wife. I know why he kept her betrayal to himself. He loved her."

Matthias caught her hands in his and lifted them. His thumbs ran across her knuckles, and he peered steadily down into her tear-filled eyes through his own glistening gray ones.

His eyelashes swept down, and he pressed his lips to her knuckles, caressing them with a warm kiss. "I've been without faith for nine years, maybe more." He looked back into her eyes again, and whispered, "Forgive me for leaving and trying to desert you. You knew me better than I knew myself, Carrie. Say you'll forgive me, please, and give faith back to me. I've been miserable without you. I'll never leave you again." A mixture of hope and fear filled his expression.

"I'll try." She sniffed, though her heart danced wildly. She whispered, "But you're going to have a heck of a lot of groveling to do."

Matthias's hands lifted to cup her face, and he lowered his lips to hers for a kiss. When he pulled his mouth from hers, she opened her eyes to see the unfamiliar light of joy in his smile. Profound relief sparkled in his gaze. He pressed a quick, hopeful kiss to her lips again and released her to address Giles.

His brother made a pitiful form on the bed, beaten, weary, and desolately sad. He'd worn the mantle of self-importance to hide his pain and sorrow just as surely as Matthias had worn his own unapproachable gruffness. Both defenses kept out those who would've made each of them face their past.

"Okay, you old cur," Matthias announced forcefully. "I'm giving you time with my wife and Maud. Get better, get back to your old self, and then I want you to plan on meeting me in a tourney."

"A tourney?" Carrie echoed along with Giles.

"Aye, 'tis time for me to defend my honor. You choose the contest." Matthias led Carrie toward the door. Then he wheeled back, "On second thought, you'll probably choose lances. Wretch! We'll face each other in *all* the contests."

"A-all of them?" Giles stammered.

Another competition.

Carrie sighed and playfully informed Giles, "My lord, it sounds like you'll need to start a training diet. I'll speak with Cook."

Giles's mouth gaped in shock, a priceless expression to Carrie. She hid a smile behind her hair as she followed Matthias out.

****

Matthias brought her to the parapets later that evening.

Over the breathtaking view of the river valley, he said, "This has always been my place, where I could breathe the fresh air high above the castle and clear my mind of aught that ailed me." He lifted Carrie to sit on the stone wall and braced his hands on either side of her.

The breeze lifted her hair, and she was his beautiful Rhiannon with a violet sunset matching her eyes at her back. She smiled shyly at him.

He sighed with contentment and grinned himself. "Nothing ails me this day."

Carrie had patched his side with a fresh healing poultice and new bandages. He loved her concern and the way she took better care of him than he did. All his life, he'd had to protect himself. He'd learned to depend on no one else. He'd eked out a humble and lonely existence, barely surviving. But with his wife, he was suddenly a force to be reckoned with. Invincible. *Safe.*

"Matthias, I can't believe you're not angry with Giles. I mean I know he was hurt and insulted by what Isabelle did, but none of the tragedy was your fault. He's had plenty of time to tell you." Her perfect eyebrows met in a crease above her nose.

Matthias shook his head and lifted his thumb to softly caress the worry line away. "I cannot be angry with him. I disagree with how he handled himself, but I understand his motives."

She closed her eyes on a sigh and smiled.

Sliding his arms around her shoulders, he brought his lips to hers. She kissed him between smiles until he felt light-headed.

After kissing her, he told her, "I cannot believe I would've let you slip through my fingers. Because I hated myself so much, I would've run from you to another century. If I get angry at Giles about anything, it'll be that. Jesu, *Carys.*"

"I don't know how to feel about Lady Isabelle," Carrie told him, tilting her head thoughtfully. "I mean, I didn't know her, but I kind of understand what she was going through to do what she did. If she really did love her husband, the only way she thought she could make him happy was to have a baby. And she didn't think pregnancy would ever happen with Giles. She must've been so desperate."

"Aye. We should've noticed the change in her. When I look back, I think I should've seen her sadness. Depressed and quiet. Maud didn't know what Isabelle was contemplating. Not one of us did."

Matthias stared at the darkening purple of the sky, wondering if his unborn baby had been a boy or a girl, and what the child would've looked like had it lived.

Then he felt Carrie's hands smoothing across his chest. He allowed himself to be pulled back into the happiness and sanity he saw in her eyes. Soon there would be another child, he hoped. A child mothered by the only woman he'd ever loved.

His thighs leaned against her knees as he kissed her, and her arms wrapped around him, pulling him closer. Her kisses beckoned, making him want to take her directly downstairs for more. Before he did, though, he had to tell her. There had been enough deception. He wanted no more secrets to hide.

"I love you, Carrie Thorne. Here or there. It doesn't matter. I just want to be where you are and love you always. You and no other woman."

Carrie eased back in the circle of his arms. Her luminous eyes widened.

He traced her noble cheekbone with a tender finger. "It's your strength, I think, that I love the most."

"My strength?" she gasped, gesturing to the tears in her eyes with a self-deprecating smile.

"Aye. Nothing scares my Southern belle. You've been standing up to me since I met you, and 'tis something I'm not used to. My anger and threats never scared you." He paused to listen to the pleasant sound of the peals of laughter his remark elicited.

Sharing a smile, he finished, "Your illness didn't stop you from leaving home to cross the Atlantic alone. You faced me and my displeasure the way no one else has ever dared. You chased after your dreams at the standing stones without a care for my wrath or aught else, and I remember thinking you just might have enough courage for us both."

Carrie slid off the stone wall to land in his arms. "Don't tell me I've tamed the beast in you."

"Nay." He kissed her full, pouting lips. Then his face grew serious. "But I'll try to be a better man now...for you."

"I don't want you to be any different, better or worse. You're the man I love. You were always a good man in your heart. You've hidden the man you are for so long, you've just forgotten."

He groaned. "You may have to remind me how good I am from time to time."

Carrie pressed her lips to his neck in a soft, warm kiss. Her nose nuzzled against him. "Every day if I have to."

His fingers threaded through her silky hair, and he laid a kiss on the top of her head. "I like the sound of that. Spending every day with you..." he pressed lips to her tender earlobe and teased it lightly with his teeth, "and every night."

Chapter Twenty-Six

Matthias strode from the stables leading a handsome black horse. His brother followed him, fit and more troublesome than ever. Dressed in blue velvet with all the commanding grandeur allowed by his birthright, the earl stroked his ringed fingers over his silver beard and watched Matthias make the horse ready.

He saddled the stallion quickly, too impatient to be on his way to linger for a squire's assistance. He needed to collect Carrie. She left on a long walk with Maud earlier to wait for him at her cottage. Allowing her to leave his side for even a moment proved difficult in the best of circumstances.

"You could stay through Michaelmas, you know," Giles told him.

"I know. This time I'm leaving by choice. Now is when I want to go. When *we* want to go."

How much had changed in his and Carrie's former lives, he wondered. For Carrie's sake, he hoped that little had altered. He might've been replaced at the university and given up for dead, but apart from Wyldnell, his former life had little bearing on his heart. His wife, on the other hand, had her mother, her grandmother, and her business to return to.

The choice would've been hard for them to make—her family or his—but for one tiny addition to their lives.

Carrie would soon deliver his baby. Although she'd never complained, Matthias knew she would appreciate the medical resources of the twenty-first

347

century: obstetricians, pediatricians, sterile hospitals, prenatal vitamins, refills of her barbiturates, and though Carrie—avowed believer in natural birth—preferred not to admit it...prescription pain relievers. He also wouldn't deny her the opportunity to share the baby with her family.

"You know you do not have to wait so long to visit again." Giles's usually haughty voice turned melancholy.

"Well, this is a much nicer good-bye from you. We may do just that."

"If you do not, I'll understand, little brother. You will find a new lord to serve anon and lands of your own to settle. You've your own family now, and I trow that will keep you occupied."

Matthias laughed lightly. "Aye. And you'll be busy, too. Edwina told us we may have a new female addition to Wyldnell. Is that true?"

A wry smile spread under Giles's beard. "Now that Llywelyn is dead and his brother is hiding in the hills, no longer a threat, King Edward is relaxing his initiatives. I may have more time for sports of all kinds. I think I may take Maud's advice. She knows of a young woman descended from Welsh nobility— probably some distant cousin of yours, Math."

"Probably."

"By the by, Maud has sent for her to visit Wyldnell with her attendants. We're to have another tourney. I'm competing in the joust, of course."

"Of course."

"It wouldn't hurt for me to take a Welsh bride, especially with King Edward favoring the idea in your case."

"I think it's a splendid idea, Giles." Matthias made a broad grin, and he meant it. In his tearful goodbye to Carrie, his brother had shown more emotion than Matthias had ever witnessed in him.

Giles deserved to find his happiness, too.

"Maud seems to think we would be able to sire a child, but if not, I would still like the company. I've gotten used to someone nagging me to keep me on my best behavior." Giles's expression held a lifetime of hope.

"Jesu." Matthias waved a hand. "Don't make me pity the poor girl before she even meets you. Do you even know what your best behavior is?"

Giles frowned.

"God's sakes, get Edwina's advice or Rannulf's before you try to woo the girl."

Matthias laughed. The look of outrage on his brother's face told him he was laughing at his expense, but Giles's expression only made him laugh harder. Then his brother joined in.

****

Rain refreshed the warm countryside, brightening the verdant pasture and cooling the leafy forest. Even the unfeeling stones of the cliff above the river responded to the life-giving showers of the morning with glistening, green, velvet moss and lichen. Fall came heralded by a summer that didn't wish to end.

Carrie touched the slight swell of her stomach beneath her linen dress. In six months, she would welcome new life of her own. Matthias gave the horse a pat on the rump, sending him back to the castle in a trot.

"The moon plants are back. I suppose I could pocket a few for the trip, just in case," she told him.

Matthias nodded, though they both knew the plants weren't part of the process for returning to the future.

Weeks ago, Matthias had told her the secret of the stones. They should've asked Maud months before, but they'd both been afraid to leave. She feared becoming separated from him somewhere in time, and Matthias said he'd believed she would've returned to the States just as soon as they went back.

They still hadn't decided where they would settle. Matthias said he would gladly work wherever she was. He had skills as a history writer, as well as a professor, and he earned enough from his books for them both to live on comfortably. But Carrie loved Wyldnell as much as Charleston.

From outside the henge, Maud stood watching them, smiling encouragement. The air inside the henge went still and quiet. A thick carpet of cool fog rose under their feet.

"Are you ready, *Carys?*"

She gasped in amazement to see the ring actually worked like a charm when used correctly. "Just like a taxi for soulmates." She smiled, warming to the idea.

Matthias laced his fingers with hers. Carrie checked her belt to make sure she still had the lovespoon he'd made for her. It was the only possession she couldn't part with.

"Yes. I'm ready this time." Carrie and Matthias bid Maud goodbye and walked along beside each other into the chasm of time.

Epilogue

"Did you see it? Did you see it? It got off the ground!"

A jet airplane lifted as it taxied down the runway outside the plate glass window. A little blond-headed boy about six years old pressed his face against the glass, straining to watch the roaring plane until it completely left his view. Matthias returned his enthusiastic smile when the boy looked over his shoulder to share the joy. Then the boy darted off toward his family waiting in the chairs on the opposite side of the room.

Matthias supposed it was a little miracle each time a plane took off, though he'd not taken the time to think about it in years. Everything about the twenty-first century seemed miraculous to his eyes after the Middle Ages. The smallest devices amazed him: can openers, cans, plastic containers, toilet tissue, flushing toilets. It felt good to be home.

Even better to have Carrie in his home now.

Matthias strolled past the baby pram for the fourth time since he'd started taking count. He clasped his hands behind his back and tried to think about something that would take his mind off the impending meeting.

Was his tie straight? He lifted a hand to check the silk burgundy necktie and kept on pacing. After another pass of the pram, he ran a hand through his hair, smoothing down any untidiness. He didn't want to appear unkempt when Carrie brought her family over to meet him.

Some knight. He was a nervous wreck.

Sandra Jones

The three women stood in the arrivals hall, yards away, exchanging hugs and talking animatedly. Barbara Greer, Carrie's mother, had spoken to him on the phone several times. He recognized her first on sight as she'd greeted Carrie, coming straight off the plane. An accountant, Barbara looked a lot like her daughter but hid her beauty in a no-nonsense navy suit and wore her light brown hair cropped in a neat bob. Behind red-framed glasses, her gaze kept swinging to where he stood, making an appraisal of him from afar. He swallowed a lump in his throat.

The older woman could only be Nona, Carrie's grandmother, presently enveloping Carrie in her arms. To be such a renowned cook, Nona made a svelte figure in a red pantsuit. Only her platinum hair bespoke her true age. She threw back her head in a gale of laughter at something Carrie said to her.

Both women were slowly coming to terms with Carrie's disappearance and reappearance. Carrie hadn't explained it all to them, and he couldn't blame her. In time she would, but for now their acceptance of him was all-important. After all, Carrie had gone missing for four months only to turn up again, married and pregnant with the child of the man she'd flown to Wales to confront.

As soon as he could, Matthias had called his caretaker to tell him they were back and okay. They both had to bend the truth a little about where they'd been. Nigel reacted to their return with the most shock of anyone they knew. He recalled seeing them disappearing into the mist of the stones, and then they'd simply vanished. Everyone had presumed they'd fallen off the cliff into the river. A search & rescue team had combed the Wye looking for them. Upon seeing them alive, Nigel cried like a baby.

A soft sound beside Matthias intruded on his

thoughts, taking his attention from the reunion of Carrie's family to their newest family member. Genevieve. Or, Evie, as they affectionately called her.

The pram shook gently as a tiny foot in a pink sock emerged from the blanket as if to wave at him. Two bright blue eyes blinked inside the pink and white receiving blanket.

"Good morning, Miss Evie," Matthias murmured, heart melting as his baby daughter's lips curved.

She gurgled and blew a big, glassy bubble.

Close enough. He took it as an invitation. Sliding his hands under the soft folds of the blanket, he retrieved his daughter and drew her from the pram.

She settled in the crook of his arm as if she belonged there. Her hands flayed out from her teddy bear shirt, hands in fists, but her eyes were transfixed on her father.

Matthias painted a dopey smile on his face, and he felt certain the expression she gave in return held a smile.

He lifted Evie's head to his lips and kissed her downy tuft of black hair. Lingering over her head, he breathed in her baby scent and sighed. Then he kissed the soft, warm crown again.

Evie cooed. Her hands uncurled and caught his tie, restraining him. Face to face with her, he stared into her bright blue eyes and wondered what she thought. She was definitely thinking something. Her brow rumpled slightly as her gaze held him steadily.

"Now there's a girl who knows how to handle men."

Matthias managed to look up, still held captive by Evie's clutch. He smiled, feeling heat rising on his neck as he faced the violet-eyed matriarch of Carrie's family.

"Matthias, honey," Carrie moved to her grandmother's side, grinning at his predicament, "this is my grandmother, Nona."

Matthias nodded in greeting. At least Evie's clutch granted him one boon—he'd not have to choose whether to shake hands with Carrie's family or hug them. He'd pondered that decision most of the morning.

"I wonder what she's gonna do with him now that she's got him." Barbara joined them, adding a third pair of blue-violet eyes to his audience. A slight smile curled under her glasses, erasing some of her seriousness. She drawled in the same Southern accent he'd become so used to, "Seems as good a use for a necktie as any, I guess."

Evie tugged harder on the tie, and Matthias tried to balance her in one arm as he gently pulled the burgundy silk with his free hand. The tie didn't budge.

"I think she's testing your strength," Carrie said.

"You'd best wager on Evie, then." Matthias grinned, and then his face pulled in a grimace as he watched the burgundy go into Evie's gaping mouth.

"Oh, honey, your tie! She'll ruin it." Carrie flew to his aid. She frowned as her fingers worked gently on the infant's grasp. "Let me take her."

"It's okay. I have another just like it." His chest tightened at her concern for him. He'd never get enough of that. Or of the lavender fragrance of his wife's hair as she stood so near him. He glanced over her head as she worked on Evie. "I imagine Nona or Barbara would like to hold her, though."

Barbara chuckled. "You imagined right. Hand that pretty girl over to me!"

Matthias transferred Evie to Carrie's mother's arms. Evie relinquished the tie, and her wide eyes swung to the new face holding her. Barbara smiled a thank you at him, and then peered down at Evie.

Nona swept past Carrie to stand opposite him. "Now, let's have a look at you." Her lips pursed as she looked him over. Her eyes crinkled, and she folded her hands under her chin. "Oh, Caroline—"

Matthias ran his hand down the tie, which felt a bit damp now at the end.

"I always pictured him looking like Tom Jones, being Welsh and all, but this is even better. He's bigger than I expected." Nona winked at him and then said to Carrie, "I bet it makes kissing difficult."

His wife's gaze bore into his, a sly smile on her lips.

"The first time I had to stand on my toes." Carrie explained, adding that there was a dog in the way. "When the dumb animal finally decided to move, it tripped me. It chose the worst possible moment."

A bubble of humor rose in Matthias's chest. He couldn't hold back the pressure of the amusement building inside, so he gave in. He threw back his head and laughed.

"What's so funny?" Barbara asked, looking up from Evie as she rocked the infant in her arms.

Matthias wiped a tear from his eye with the back of his hand. Carrie's smiling eyes searched his face for an explanation.

"*Carys*, I think I should be grateful you didn't know. I'd hate to have you thinking the worst of me. I've never been cruel to animals in my life, I swear." He paused to draw Carrie closer, wrapping his arm around her waist. "But when that bloody dog wouldn't move out of my way when you tried to kiss me, I think...I stepped on its tail."

Carrie gasped. "You creep. All this time I thought I'd caused that kiss."

All three ladies shared in his laughter.

"I thought you'd told us everything about Matthias, Caroline." Her mother gazed at her sternly from under her eyeglasses. "What else haven't you told us?"

Feeling a chill of apprehension running down his spine, Matthias crossed his arms over his mangled tie. He watched Carrie, wondering how his wife would handle the question.

"Well, let's see...I told you guys about Matthias's cooking, and the book he's working on about Medieval bards, about our wedding..." she flicked her fingers as she listed the many things they'd discussed over the phone for the past nine months. "Did I tell you about our first meeting?"

Matthias heard his groan before he could contain it.

"Don't look at me with those sheepish eyes, Matthias," Carrie chided. Then, to her mother, she said sweetly, "I thought he was a little stubborn, but he warmed up."

He raised an eyebrow at her, and Carrie's eyes twinkled knowingly. They both recalled how rude he could be.

"Well, I didn't fly all the way here to stand around in an airport. I want to see that nursery we've been hearing about," Barbara told them, handing off Evie to a grateful Nona.

"Which one?"

"Both."

Carrie had told them about the baby nursery he'd added at Wyldnell while construction began on the manor house joining the medieval tower. The other nursery was Carrie's project, an herb nursery she would soon open to the public. Her own business to run, doing what she did best—helping people.

Nona and the baby turned toward the exit. Carrie, her mother, and Matthias followed, pushing the empty pram.

Barbara's eyes caught and briefly held his gaze as they walked. "Caroline seems content, but I hope you know she's giving up a lot of things she loves to be with you."

Although her tone hadn't been harsh and was meant with good intentions, Matthias felt as though he'd been kicked in the chest. Before he could form a response, Carrie slid her arm in his.

She stared up at him, her gaze sparkling with admiration and concern that he could happily sink into for all eternity. "He's given up more than you'll ever know."

Barbara shared a smile with him. When she moved ahead in the airport crowd to walk with Nona and the baby to the exit, Matthias stopped the pram, ignoring the flow of people around them and drew Carrie into the circle of his arms.

Her eyes widened with surprise. Recognition of his intentions crossed her expression, a rosy flush rising on her cheekbones. She started to object, but Matthias wouldn't hear it. His mouth slashed across hers, savoring the opportunity for a kiss without Evie—now safely ensconced with her great-grandmother. Carrie yielded. She slid her arms around his back, pulling him closer.

"I miss Giles and I miss our friends, but this is worth it. You're worth it. And Evie, too." He rested his forehead against hers, wanting her to look into his eyes and see how seriously he meant it.

Tears glistened as she smiled. "So are you."

He kissed her again, freshly yearning for her.

Carrie pushed his shoulder half-heartedly. "We're in public, Matthias!"

"Mmmm. Aye," he said, forgetting himself and allowing the word to slip. He took a long breath and ran his fingertip along her velvety lips. Keeping his passion under tight rein, he murmured against her ear, "Let's go home, *Carys*. Tonight we have Nona and Barbara—babysitters!"

A word about the author...

Sandra was born and raised in Arkansas. For as long as she can remember, she's been reading romance novels. Her passion for page-turners often led to books being confiscated at school. To appease her love of reading, she worked as a bookseller until she earned a master's degree in library science. She is married with two teenage sons and three pampered cats. When not reading or writing, she loves to travel, go shopping, and attend the occasional Renaissance faire. Huzzah!

Visit Sandra at www.sandrajonesromance.com

LaVergne, TN USA
06 July 2010
188476LV00004B/20/P